ALL I SEE IS YOU

SHELBY STORME

Content Warnings:

All I See Is You is intended for an adult audience and contains mature themes including explicit language, explicit sexual content, and the following triggers listed below:

- Toxic family relationships

- Age gap in certain relationships (10+ years)

- Alcoholism

- Attempted sexual assault to the Male MC (on page—very brief

- Talk of depression and anxiety

- Talk of therapy

- Talk of suicide

- Talk of Death and grief

- Talk of miscarriage and difficult conceiving (not graphic)

- The Male MC is visually impaired (blind) and has suffered from a TBI (traumatic brain injury). Because of this and his personality, he deals with his trauma through dark humor and, oftentimes tries to make light of his visual impairment by joking about it.

- Bodily injury (bull riding accident 2 times)

Reader's Guide

As this book heavily focuses on rodeos, there may a few terms that you might not be familiar with.

PBR: The **Professional Bull Riders**, Inc. is an international bull riding organization and the largest bull riding league in the world, and sanctions events throughout the United States, Australia, Canada, and Brazil.

NFR: The **National Finals Rodeo** is championship rodeo of the PRCA (Professional Rodeo Cowboys Association), which showcases the talents of the PRCA's top 15 money winners in the season of each event.

Rodeo Events:

Rough Stock Events

-Bareback bronc riding, saddle bronc riding, and bull riding

Timed Events

-Team roping, tie down roping, steer wrestling, barrel racing, breakaway roping

To all the diamonds in the rough out there.

I hope you find something that helps you shine.

Remember, you are beautiful. You are strong. You are resilient.

Contents

Chapter One

Rodeo

Hux

*E*IGHT SECONDS.

A whole hell of a lot could happen in eight seconds. It's crazy how fast things change. One breath, and the course of your life as you know it is forever altered. One blink, and things could never go back to the way they were again.

"Huxson Lane, you're up next! Chute three."

I glanced at the rodeo coordinator and nodded, my adrenaline ramping up. Blowing out a deep breath, I rolled my neck and made my way to the chute. A massive behemoth of a bull, Lights Out, had already been loaded in…and he was raring to go.

"Come on, Hux. You got this!" Reid Wilson—a good friend and my biggest competition—clapped me on the back as I climbed up the pipe-stall siding. We'd been neck and neck this entire PBR season for the top spot.

I pegged him with an easy grin. "Drinks after my win tonight?"

He scoffed, but his gaze sparked with amusement. "You mean *my* win?"

There was no way in hell I'd be losing tonight. Something big was gonna happen. I could feel it. Feel it in my bones, my nerves, my blood, even. Tonight was different from the rest. It was a winning night.

"Alright," I laughed even as I shook my head. "How 'bout loser buys the first round?"

"Deal," Reid replied with a smirk, clapping me on the back once more.

My grin fell away, a wave of stone-cold focus settling over me like a blanket as I slapped my thighs a few times to warm them up, climbed over the pipe-stall, and settled myself onto the bull's back. It was a process getting the bull rope situated, all the while my nerves rising higher and higher, like a storm building.

Getting on a bull was like that.

That moment before the storm. Where you could feel it surging, coming for you on the air. It was like a pause...like the very air itself was holding its breath.

The music, the crowd's shouts, the announcer's words muted and danced away on a phantom wind as my other senses took over. I felt every twitch, every breath from the bull beneath me. Its angry, eager snorts were as loud as damn fireworks. My muscles flexed and tightened as I wrapped my right hand in the bull rope.

One more win.

One more win was all I needed and I'd be right on track to compete at NFR for not one, not two, but *three* consecutive World Titles under my belt.

You got this. It's just eight seconds. You got this.

I closed my eyes, sending up a silent prayer, before opening them once more.

And then I nodded.

Lights Out tensed and leapt from the chute as the gate opened with a deafening clang. My thighs tensed, legs clenching to the sides of the massive bull. He leapt and twisted and bucked, each movement reminding me of punishing waves crashing into a cliff. But I clung to his back, going with his movements instead of fighting against them. The rush of awe, elation, and adrenaline thrummed in my veins.

This feeling. I'd never tire of it. There'd never be a day I didn't long for the thrill of bull riding.

It was the scariest, most enthralling eight seconds of my life. Eight seconds that might as well last an eternity. It felt like it, at least. Time seemed to slow down and stop altogether during my rides.

Lights Out bucked and spun, and I felt my center of gravity shift, but still I clung on. *So close.* I was so damn close.

But each movement felt like a losing battle. A trickle of fear shot through me, followed by an answering one of pure, stubborn, hardheaded determination. But that determination didn't mean shit up against a two thousand pound bull. My fingers began to slip from the bull rope.

Just. A. Little. Longer.

And then Lights Out did what he was known for. Every ride, he whipped out a particularly nasty buck. There was a reason he was undefeated still. I managed to keep my grip as he rocked back—the sheer power in the movement terrifying. But I was fucked when he surged forward with more force than a category five hurricane slamming into the coast.

I ragdolled as I crashed face first toward his head, pain roaring to life as I came into contact with his skull. But the pain was short lived as a wave of numbness, so cold and terrifying, spread through my veins like ice.

And then the darkness descended, swallowing me up whole until I knew nothing at all.

Chapter Two

Had Me At Heads Carolina

QUINN

H OLY GOD, TEXAS WAS hot. And humid.

I thought California was hot...but it was nothing like this. At least they believed in AC here. It blasted me in the face as I pulled up the navigation on my phone to get to my dad's place.

It still didn't make much sense to me why dad would move back here. My dad—the surf's up, sunshine, and suntans epitome of a Southern California dude decided on moving to basically the cowboy capital of the world?

It didn't make sense. Then again, nothing my dad ever did really made sense to me. Like this move. Or this engagement. Or this wedding. But it wasn't my place to judge him or tell him what to do. He always did what he wanted anyways, regardless of how much or how little it made sense.

"Okay, so I found this little kiosk on my way back from the bathroom that had all of these little pamphlets on things to do in Thousand Trees. Did you know they have one of those safari wineries?" My best friend, Whit, said as she slid into the passenger's seat of the rental.

I bit back a snort. "I didn't know that, but that sounds fun." I glanced over at her as I finished adjusting the mirrors to my liking. "You got everything?"

She nodded, smacking her backpack twice, a satisfied smirk on her nude lips. Leave it to Whit to look like a damn supermodel for a plane ride. She'd gotten her inspiration from some Tiktok influencer, and decided to call this her *lazy girl travel fit*… Only I'd hardly call having to spend close to an hour getting ready being lazy at all. "Yep. I'm telling you, you have to watch this Tiktok on how to pack a week's worth of clothes into a carryon. It's so convenient."

I huffed a laugh as I pulled out of my parking spot and followed the navigation's directions. "I mean, it's a cool idea if you *need* to, but…you get a free checked bag with a plane ticket, might as well take advantage."

Besides, I didn't have the willpower or the patience to be the level of extra that Whit was. I loved her, and she was the most amazing, kind, and helpful person ever, but there was no doubt about it, she was extra AF.

"Do you know how many suitcases get lost every day in travel?" She scoffed, tossing her perfect, long bronde hair over her shoulders. And yes, *bronde* was a hair color. She would know, she was a hairdresser.

"And that's what luggage tags are for," I offered back with a conspiratory grin.

She rolled her eyes. "One day you're going to need to pack a week's worth of clothes into a backpack—"

"And when I do, I'll make sure to come to you," I laughed.

Another eye roll, but she grinned, settling herself more into the passenger's seat. "So, how far is Thousand Trees from San Antonio?"

"Navigation says a bit over an hour."

She nodded and started pressing buttons on the car's screen, trying to find a music station, no doubt. "So, remind me again why your dad decided to rent in Texas of all places?"

I shrugged, my anxiety ramping up as I tried to get us onto the right freeway. "You know about as much as me, honestly. He tried to explain, but you know how he is. He talks like a mile a minute and never can finish a sentence, even if his life depended on it. He—"

"It's all that espresso," Whit cut in, pulling her sunglasses down to look at me.

I scoffed, a disbelieving laugh bubbling out of me. "What are you talking about?"

"It's true! He's gonna, like, overdose or something one day."

I just laughed, not about to argue with Whit.

The truth was, my dad didn't listen to anyone—least of all me. Besides, he was fifty-one years old. He could take care of himself. He had for years now since Mom died. I mean, most of that time he'd been a hot mess express, but weren't we all...sort of?

"*Anyways*," I said, pegging her with a pointed sunglasses stare. "From what I could make out of the situation, he and his fiancé are, like, renting the property for the next month leading up to the wedding..." My words tapered off in the end

.

None of this really made any sense—his relationship with Georgette, the proposal, the ridiculously short engagement—but then again, trying to figure out what Dad was up to was impossible. He was a live-in-the-moment, fly-by-the-seat-of-his-pants kinda guy. What he wanted today might change in a day from now. Mom had helped temper him a bit. Helped even out his intensity and impulsivity. With her gone...

"Isn't his fiancé, like, two years older than me?" Whit asked.

"Than you? yes. She's eight years older than me."

But I tried not to think about that too much. My mom had been younger than my dad by a couple years, but nothing like this. There was a...twenty-one year age gap between the two of them. I mean, who was I to judge, but it *was* a little weird thinking that my future step mom could basically be my sister.

"You think he'll have a kid with her?"

I gasped. "Oh my God, Whit! Stop!" My words held laughter in them, but it did little to hide the trickle of worry that sprung to life anytime I thought of this engagement. Was that why they were getting married so quickly? Oh God, please no. I couldn't have a sibling that was young enough to be my kid. No. I just... *Ew*.

I hoped, *prayed*, that my dad was smart enough not to have a kid with her.

Whit gave me one of her sorry-not-sorry looks. "What, it could happen?"

"Next subject," I demanded, even while urging a smile to my lips. "Like, I saw you flirting with that cowboy at the baggage claim."

"Girl, don't even get me started. I don't know what it is about a cowboy hat and boots, but that guy looked so delicious I could eat him up."

"Oh my God." I laughed. "You're too much."

She shrugged, a devious little smirk lighting up her face. "No, what's *too much* is how long you've gone not sleeping with someone. You and Devin broke up, what...like, five months ago?"

I bit back a groan, keeping my eyes forward instead of facing the weight of her scrutinizing stare. "It's actually been six."

Just the thought of Devin made me wither up and die a bit more inside. I'd been with him through most of college. Things had always been a bit of a struggle. He had no sense of responsibility and was quick to anger, but I could be indecisive and hated making waves or causing problems. It took two to have a relationship. I wouldn't—couldn't blame him fully for our breakup. Then add in the lack of intimacy, and, well, it was a miracle we'd lasted three years.

What made absolutely no sense, though, was that he had a new girlfriend in a week, after telling me that he needed to, quote un-quote, work on himself and his intimacy issues. Turned out that working on himself was just code for working on getting under someone else. They were engaged now, by the way. Yeah...I'd been convinced he was going to propose to me this past Christmas, but nope. I was probably—no, definitely better off for it, but he'd been my first adult relationship, and I'd be lying if I said I wasn't still dealing with the emotional scars his relationship left.

"Six months? Quinnie, you give him too much power over you."

I nodded, loosing a deep sigh. She was just preaching to the choir at this point. But I couldn't help it. I hadn't had any luck finding anyone worthwhile yet. And I didn't like the idea of just casual dating. If I was gonna date someone, spend time with them, I wanted the potential for a future. That only seemed to scare guys off.

"That's it!" She clapped her hands together, her words dripping with determination.

"Oh no," I huffed. "Whatever you have planned, just...no."

Her devilish grin was enough to make my nerves wind tighter. "We're going to find you someone. A distraction. A rebound. A way to get your toes wet and back in the game."

"I don't need anyone. I've got that job starting next month at the new wedding venue. It's all the distraction I need."

"I'm not saying you should settle down, but testing the waters wouldn't be so bad. Besides, these cowboys sure are yummy to look at. Bet they taste just as sweet."

I rolled my eyes, even as a traitorous smile threatened to spread across my face.

T HE ENTIRE DRIVE TO Thousand Trees, Whit tried to wear me down, bit by bit. She was tenacious, relentless, I'd give her that.

"Hey, mind stopping at this grocery store called H-E-B really quick?" she asked as we came into town. "I saw on—"

"Let me guess, Tiktok?" I grinned when she playfully smacked my shoulder.

"Actually, it was on my Reels!" She shot back, sticking her tongue out at me before continuing. "Apparently they have this peach tea that is, like, to die for!"

I shrugged. I didn't mind stopping. I probably should pick up a bottle of wine or something as a congratulatory present for my dad's engagement after all. Following the new navigation, we stopped in a spot and made our way toward the entrance to the grocery store.

I noticed a chocolate brown dog just outside the front of the store.

"Aw, I wonder if it's lost," Whit said as we passed by.

"I don't think so." It didn't look lost. Its coat was shiny and it wore a collar—not that those necessarily determined if it was lost or not, but it was like the dog was waiting. No matter how many people walked by, it just sat there obediently. Someone had spent either a lot of time or a lot of money on training it—probably both.

The glacial blast of air that greeted me as I walked into the grocery store was a godsend. I swear, I'd only been out of the car for thirty seconds and I was already sweating. Whit had grabbed a cart and ambled up the first aisle. It would be a hot minute until she was ready—she never could go in for just one thing. Shopping with her was at least a half hour ordeal. And talking to her would only be another source of distraction, prolonging us even more.

Better to just leave her be.

I set out for the wine section, which was jutted up to the beer aisle. "Had Me At Heads Carolina" played over the speakers in the store and I couldn't help but sing along. I was about as cowgirl as the white cowboy boots in my suitcase, which was basically not much at all. I didn't know the first thing about horses or riding or anything cowboy at all, but I sure loved Country music. And this song was catchy.

Swaying and singing softly, I moseyed my way up and down the aisle, trying to look for a wine my dad would like. He'd always been more of a beer guy, but during one of our phone calls a few weeks ago, he'd told me Georgette turned him onto wine—it was better for his heart and less calories than beer. Georgette's words.

I managed to find a wine that would do. He probably wouldn't know the difference between this and some two buck chuck, but whatever.

Now for a card.

I turned...and my heart stopped.

Ho-ly. God.

The guy standing before me in the middle of the aisle looked like he'd stepped off the set of Yellowstone or a modern day western—from the boots, to the dark wash Wranglers, a plain black t-shirt sheathing a cut, muscular build, and a light straw cowboy hat. He had wavy brown hair that brushed against his shoulders, and a good amount of scruff. I wasn't normally into guys with longer hair, but, damn, he wore it well.

Whit was right. There was something about a cowboy hat and boots that just transformed a man into the ultimate version of sexy. The guy had a handsome face, though I wished I could see his eyes, which were covered by the Raybans he wore.

The words to the song died on my lips, a wave of pure, undiluted humiliation washing over me. Oh my God. How long had he been there? How much had he heard of my singing? Shit. Well, this was embarrassing. I opened my mouth to...to what?

I wanted to go hide under a rock.

A nervous laugh made its way up my throat. "H-hi," I squeaked out, forcing an embarrassed smile on my lips.

But he didn't smile. Didn't even react at all. It's almost like he was looking right through me.

Oh my God. Oh my God. Oh my God.

I did the only thing that made sense. Tucking a piece of hair behind my ear, I kept my gaze down and murmured out, "Sorry about that. Have a nice day."

And then I walked away.

And not just walked, but like olympic power walked away. I was in such a frenzy, I almost forgot to pay for the stupid bottle of wine. It wasn't until I'd gotten myself into the car that I really thought about the situation.

Maybe it wasn't that bad? Maybe I was overreacting?

You ran away from him, Quinn.

Yeah...I hoped I didn't bump into him again, or else I might just die of humiliation.

Chapter Three
Blue Clear Sky

Hux

There was some shit—well, okay, a lotta shit—that sucked about losing your vision. There was the obvious, like, not being able to see, or do shit I normally could do with ease, but every now and then, something interesting came out of going blind.

My other senses became stronger, heightened in a way. Food had the chance to taste like fuckin' heaven or complete ass. I could smell now like a damn bloodhound. My sense of touch and sound were heightened as well.

Maybe that's why I heard her singing.

If I hadn't gotten hurt, if I hadn't spent the past three years navigating blindly through my shitty excuse of a life, I'd probably not even have picked up on her hushed singing. It's not like she was the next Faith Hill or Martina McBride—not that she was a bad singer—no, there was something soft and warm about her voice. Something that drew me in, clutched at my heart and squeezed gently. Nothing had gotten to me on such a deep level in a long, *long* damn time.

She was an aisle over, by the sound of it. Which meant...she was in the beer and wine section. She continued her soft singing. I wondered if she knew others were listening and simply didn't care? Or would she clam up and shut down if I said something?

Like a moth to a flame, I found myself slowly making my way over there. It'd taken me a long time to figure out the layout of this store. It didn't help that I refused to use a cane, but my spacial awareness had gotten better. It was weird, but I could sense where the shelves were without even reaching out to touch them if I focused hard enough.

She was still singing as I rounded the corner and slowly made my way down the next aisle. I wondered what she looked like. She sounded young, but voices could be deceiving—I'd learned. Thinking of her voice filled me with a sense of warmth. A warmth that grew and spread the closer I got to her, until I was close enough that I felt her presence. The heat of her body radiated out toward me.

I was so close I could reach out and touch her. Then what? She'd probably think I was a crazy person for being so close. And I didn't want her to stop singing just yet.

But what I wanted didn't matter in the end.

The air shifted before me, a wave of her perfume drifting to my nose—something citrusy, maybe lemongrass mixed with some softer notes, like vanilla. She smelled nice. Really nice.

Fuck, there was no doubt about it, I seemed crazy.

I heard her sharp inhale of breath, before she squeaked out. "H-hi…"

My words lodged in my throat. What the hell did I say to her? *"Hi, miss. I heard you singin' so I followed the sound of your voice just to tell you that."*

Yeah, right. She'd definitely think I was crazy.

Her panicked, high pitched words hit me before I could respond, "Sorry about that. Have a nice day."

The air moved once more, sending more of her perfume my way as the sound of her scuffling feet retreated down the aisle.

Well, what do you know, dickhead…you scared her away.

And I'd likely never see her—well, run into her again. I wouldn't know what she looked like even if I did miraculously get my vision back right now.

Something panged in my chest. Regret.

It'd been a while since I'd felt so drawn to something. Most days were all about routine. Same shit. Different day. Wake up. Work. Eat. Sleep. Then start the whole monotonous process all over again. It was a fucking drag. All the days just bleeding into one.

But that was life now.

Then this mystery girl—woman—showed up and sparked something where there'd been nothing.

My feet began moving before I fully knew what I was doing, this sense of urgency, of desperation, rising in my chest.

Was it pathetic that I wanted to find her? That I had this crazy longing, this *need* to know who she was? I didn't know my mystery girl from Eve. Didn't know if she was married, or single, or nice, or anything like that. But I liked that, for one moment, in her presence, my life didn't seem so dark.

I managed to get myself to the main aisleway, but with each step, my heart sank further and further. I was familiar with loss, and this sure as hell felt like a loss.

With a huff of disappointment, I made my way to my usual checkout stand. It was Saturday, so that meant... "Hi there, Miss Laura," I said, feeling around for the conveyor belt to put my basket on.

The older woman's voice was raspy. "Well, if it isn't my favorite, handsome cowboy. How are ya doin', sweetie?"

I shrugged. "You know, same ol' same ol'—"A thought came to mind, my words falling away for a moment. "Actually, have you seen someone runnin' through the store? A woman... She sounded younger. Had a pretty voice. She smelled like lemongrass and vanilla."

Frustration surged in me. How pathetic did I sound? Fuck, I hated this. I hated that I couldn't see what she looked like. Or at least gotten her name. Why had she run away?

"Hmm... I'm sorry, sweetie. I didn't. Did you need somethin' from her?"

I blew out a sigh, reaching a hand into my back pocket to grab my wallet. "Nah, it's not important. How much do I owe ya, today?"

For a minute, the only sound between us was that of her ringing up my few things. A six pack of beer off the third shelf, exactly fifteen steps into the beer aisle. A loaf of potato bread—hopefully. They'd gotten a new stocker, and sometimes they switched around the bread on me. And more peanut butter. About twenty steps down from the bread and on the second shelf down.

"That'll be fifteen dollars and seventy-five cents—you sure you're okay, sweetie?"

I forced a smile to my lips, wondering if it came off as more of a grimace than anything else. "All good, Miss Laura," I replied, handing her my debit card.

Remnants of the girl's warm, buttery voice echoed through my mind, my goddamn soul as the old woman bagged up my things and sent me on my way. I worked my way toward the left exit, closest to the grocery section, going slow enough to hear and gauge where others were at around me as I walked. I'd gotten pretty good at avoiding running into people. Either that, or something in my demeanor, or the expression on my face, kept people away.

Heat blasted into me and the darkness turned warmer as I was greeted by the scorching heat of the Texas sun. I whistled, and felt something brush against my right leg a moment later. Toenails clicked on the ground beside me. "Good boy, Rusty. See anythin' interestin'?"

My Kelpie didn't respond, but I didn't expect him to. He set his pace to match mine as we walked the fifty three paces I'd counted out when I'd gotten out of my friend and fellow coworker, Travis' truck. I reached out and found the corner of his tailgate and skirted around to the passenger side, feeling my way for the door. I blew out an annoyed groan when I found it locked. Damn, I should have waited inside.

"I'm here! I'm here!" Travis' familiar voice cut through the parking lot over the sound of cars and trucks. "Sorry, man! I was talkin' to this girl. Goddamn, was she hot."

Something tightened in my chest. "What did she sound like? Did she have a nice voice?"

"Um...I—" Travis stammered over his words as he unlocked the truck, the sound of the locks shifting. I opened the door and whistled for Rusty to hop in before I followed behind. Travis' voice sounded far away for a moment before rising in volume as the truck shifted and he settled in the driver's seat. "I don't know. I mean, I guess she had a nice voice. It was kinda...smoky. She definitely ain't from here. I didn't recognize the area code at all when she gave me her number."

Even as excitement sparked, an answering wave of disappointment washed over me. If Travis had gotten her number then it didn't matter. I didn't know what Travis looked like, but he didn't seem to have any problems picking up girls. "Did she smell like vanilla and lemongrass?"

"I don't fuckin' know, man. I wasn't smellin' her. Why all the questions?" A defensiveness lingered in his words.

"I ran into a girl in there and, uh, was wonderin' if it was the same one you were talkin' to."

"Oh." Travis' voice softened, interest replacing the defensive edge. "Well, what did she look like?"

I rolled my eyes, a huff of laughter escaping me. Travis and I had worked together for going on almost a year now, and the kid still forgot I was blind most days. I mean, in the end I couldn't really blame him. He wasn't the only one to forget. I preferred that though than people going out of their way to coddle me. I didn't need coddling. Didn't need handouts. I could work, and ride a horse, and hold my own fine enough.

"I don't even know what you look like, dumbass. How the fuck am I sup-posed to tell you about her?"

Travis chuckled one of those goofy, low-pitched laughs I'd come to expect from him. "Oh, shit. I forgot, man. I'm sorry."

I snorted, rolling my eyes. "It's fine. So, this girl you met... Did she seem like she was in a rush? I don't know, maybe embarrassed?"

I hoped that it wasn't the same girl I'd met. I didn't want to smell her perfume or hear her soft, warm voice again and know that she wasn't around because of me, but for Travis.

"Nah, this girl wasn't goin' anywhere fast, that's for damn sure."

A trickle of relief settled over me. Not that I'd probably ever see my mystery girl again. But still. "So, you said the girl you were talkin' to is from out of town?"

"Out of state, actually. She's here with her friend, visiting the girl's family, I guess." Travis' words floated over the sound of the engine rumbling to life. I felt the vibrations as the truck shifted into reverse. I clutched my bag in my lap, while petting Rusty with my free hand. His warm breath fanned against my leg as he panted at my feet.

"Nice. You gonna see her again?"

"I think so," he replied. "She told me to text her later, see what they were up to. Hey—" Something—correction—Travis' hand smacked against my shoulder. Not hard enough to hurt, but enough to startle me a bit. His words took on an excited edge. "Maybe her friend's the girl you were talkin' to!"

I nodded. "Yeah, maybe."

But I wasn't holding my breath. The world was small, but it wasn't that small.

Chapter Four
That's Texas

QUINN

MY NERVES DANCED THROUGH my entire body as I followed the navigation's instructions, turning into a gorgeous drive lined with weeping willows and green pastures on either side. I hadn't seen Dad since my graduation almost a month ago. It's when I'd first met Georgette. She'd been...well, let's be honest, she was a lot, but Dad seemed to be happy, so that's all that mattered.

"Holy shit. This is the place they're renting?" Whit's voice was full of awe as she gaped out the window. Not gonna lie, I was a bit in awe myself.

We came to a small fork in the road, where one lane branched off toward a fancy barn, a sign by it reading *Broken Creek Ranch* on it. I followed the main road to the house, all the while, my nerves winding tighter and tighter. Why would Dad rent this place? I mean, I knew they were planning on having the wedding here, but still. I guess you could get away with irresponsible things like this when you were ridiculously wealthy, though. At least, knowing Dad, he'd probably found this place for a steal because of his high profile realtor job.

But something still didn't sit well with me. Something wasn't right. There were missing pieces. And whatever this gut feeling meant, I doubted I would like it.

I scrolled through my phone and pressed my dad's contact, the ringing sound all but deafening as it connected to the car's speakers.

"Queenie! You almost here?" he asked, excitement in his words. I bit back a groan at my little nickname. It was cute when I was, like, ten, but I'd long since outgrown it. I put up with it though, because, well, it was Dad, and Dad got to do things like that.

"We're actually pulling up now."

"Great! Just park in the driveway. We'll be right down."

I hung up and continued up the path. My breath left me in a whoosh as the tree-covered drive opened up and a massive, I mean *massive* plantation style house with white wood siding and black accents loomed up before us. The nicely paved dirt path gave way to a flagstone circular driveway with a gargantuan fountain in the middle. A bronze statue of a cowboy and his horse rested in the center of it. A large, at least, six car garage stood off to the right.

"Holy. God," I whispered.

"Fucks sakes. I mean I know your dad's loaded...but damn."

Damn, was right. I mean, I guess he was just renting it for the month, but still, this place had to cost a fortune. I could only imagine how much it would be in California. Definitely a hell of a lot more than what my event planner salary could afford.

This had to be Georgette's idea. Sure we'd always been wealthy, but my dad was never this flashy. Renting a ranch for a month? How the hell did that even make any sense?

I put the car in park and got out.

"Howdy, y'all!" Georgette's fake twang drew my gaze and I nearly burst out laughing.

Oh, dear God. She looked like cowgirl Barbie in her baby pink corset crop top, a pair of light washed cutoffs that even I would feel self-conscious wearing, and a pair of sparkly pink cowboy boots. Her wide brimmed hat was the same color as her top. I mean, she looked great in it all. She had a hell of a body—tall, willowy build, legs that went on for days, and—I pulled my sunglasses down just a bit—were those abs? Yep…those were abs. Damn. Maybe she and I should start working out together. You know, some step mom daughter bonding. I bit back a snort.

Absolutely not.

I still didn't really know how to feel about him dating—I mean, marrying, I guess, someone just a few years older than me. But it wasn't my life.

Speaking of Dad…

I let out a muffled groan at his outfit. "Well, aren't you just a bonafide cowboy?" I said, urging a horrible attempt at a southern accent into my tone.

He'd traded in his board shorts and flip-flops for Levis and cowboy boots. A light-colored straw cowboy hat and—*oh God, is that a bolo tie?*

Whit and I exchanged a familiar look. The one that silently asked, *Do you see what I see?*

I bit back a chuckle as I walked toward the large porch he and Georgette made their way down.

"Hi, Dad," I said, coming to the bottom step. "Georgette."

My dad drew me into a tight hug. "Y'all made it!"

I stifled an eye roll. Since when did he say *y'all*? It didn't stop me from hugging him back though as I said, "Thanks for having us."

He pulled out of my grip just as Georgette slammed into me for a hug. "How many times do I have to tell you, Queenie? Call me Georgie." She squeezed me tight. "We have been dying to have you here! I can't wait to go over wedding details with you. It's gonna be so much fun!"

I drew back and offered her what I hoped passed as an enthusiastic smile. "Yeah."

It'll be interesting, to say the least.

I didn't miss the snort from Whit at my side. She hid it well, though, by saying hi to my dad and then introducing herself to Georgette.

Anxiety battled its way through my veins, rising and gaining in intensity as small talk was made and pleasantries were passed around. It's not that anything bad was happening. Everything was fine...for the moment. But it just felt fake. Everything about this seemed like it was a dream. Like it wasn't real.

My dad always had been larger than life, and was a bit of a schmoozer, a charmer, but right now I felt like he was a snake oil salesman about to sell me the *next greatest thing*. I just...I didn't like the unease coiling tighter in my chest.

"Well, what're we waiting for?" my dad asked. "Let's give you the grand tour!"

Georgette—Georgie—squealed and clapped her hands, more like an excited teenager than a thirty-year-old woman."Yay! Tour time!"

And this is supposed to be my step mom?

As my dad and Georgie led us up the porch steps, I glanced at Whit, sharing another pointed look with her as I mouthed, "What the fuck?"

She didn't seem anywhere near as concerned as me, more like highly amused. She just shrugged and snaked my arm through the crook of her elbow. "Come on, *Queenie*," she said cheerily, "Don't wanna miss the tour!"

Forty-five minutes later and my dad was still showing us around the property. We'd gone through each and every single room of the five bedroom, six bathroom main house, complete with a home movie theater and a gorgeous natural pool and spa—you know, one of those that looks like a pond, but it's fully functional as a swimming pool—and the *eight* car garage with a man cave built into it. We'd all gotten into the Gator to drive the ninety-five acre property after that, where Dad and Georgette drove us by two of the three guest houses—not including the third which was used as a bunkhouse for the ranch hands—and finally the main barn.

"The pretty one. Not the one the ranch hands use." Georgette's words.

She'd been right about the pretty part, at least. The barn was massive and beautiful. Flagstone floors, wood and wrought iron accented stalls, there were even chandeliers hanging in even intervals from the ceiling.

"How come there aren't any horses in here?" Whit asked, speaking up for the first time. She'd been surprisingly quiet since the tour started. Completely unlike her normal, loud opinionated self. But then again, it was hard for anyone to get a word in with Georgette around. Girl loved to talk. Not to mention, even I was a bit overwhelmed by the grandeur of this place.

"Well, once things settle down, Carl and I are gonna get ourselves a couple," Georgette replied with a grin.

I'd given up calling her Georgie, I just couldn't.

I pursed my lips, a hint of confusion flickering to life in me. Why would they get horses for this place if they were only renting it for the wedding? Before I could open my mouth and ask though, Georgette leaned into my dad, pressing a hand to his chest. It was an innocent enough gesture, but I hated the unsettling feeling constricting and wrestling in my stomach because of it.

Even though we were technically outside, I had to get some air—or, at the very least, I had to get away from them. I knew I was being dramatic, and probably a bit petty, but I couldn't help it. I don't think I'd ever seen Dad hold my mom like that. Touch my mom like that. Joke and laugh and act like a love-drunk fool. Granted, Mom had been sick the last four years before she died.

Every couple was different, though, I guess.

I couldn't even fathom acting like that in public when I'd been with Devin. He was super against PDA. Said that touching and kissing and holding each other was for us—a special moment for our eyes only. It seemed just as stupid now as it had then, but I'd been afraid to say anything for fear of causing a fight.

Story of my life.

Maybe one day I'd learn to say what I actually felt. What was on my mind. Like how Georgette stroking my dad's arm up and down the way she was made me want to throw up.

But then that meant potentially disappointing my dad, and I hated that idea even more.

Taking a deep breath, I tried to blow out all of my worries and frustrations. My gaze fixed on the other barn across the way, along with a guest house right beside it. It was close to a big sandy arena.

"Hey, you okay, Quinn?" Whit's voice rang with concern.

I turned back to find her, my dad, and Georgette making their way out of the barn.

"Is that the barn and bunkhouse for the ranch hands?" I asked, glancing that way once more. I couldn't look at her and my dad being all lovey-dovey. Maybe this could serve as a distraction.

I didn't know anything about horses, or ranch hands, or if they were the same as cowboys or different, but all of it sounded intriguing. And if all cowboys were as hot as the one I'd run into...well, maybe spending a month here wouldn't be absolutely terrible.

"Yeah. There's what, honey, four of them? Oh no, wait, five with Hux," Dad said, his gaze following mine to the barn.

Georgette groaned, drawing our attention. "Let's be honest, we might as well have only four. Hux, well, he's not much of an asset to this ranch." She placed a hand around her mouth like she was telling Whit and I a secret. "He's nice to look at though."

I frowned. Okay, ew. Was she really talking about how attractive one of their employees was in front of her fiancé? Also what was she talking about—he wasn't much of an asset? As if sensing the question in my gaze she huffed and went on. "He's blind, and with that equal rights employment thing, or whatever it's called, the previous owners felt bad and gave him a job. There's basically no use for him, but firing him would cause problems."

I scoffed, literally scoffed at the audacity, the ignorance, and the hatred falling from this woman's lips. Mom had always advocated for people with special needs and disabilities. We'd spent most of my middle school years volunteering at different events for them. If she heard this woman talking right now...

I glared at her before shifting my withering stare at my dad. "Do *you* think this about him?"

"Wh–what? No..." Dad's expression turned apologetic as he fumbled for words. "No, Queenie. You know I don't think that."

I huffed. Yet he was going to marry a woman who did.

"Quinn." My dad's tone held a desperate note to it. "She didn't mean it." He wrapped an arm around Georgette's waist. "Did you, sweetheart?"

Georgette looked confused, an expression she wore way too well, as she met my dad's stare. Something silent passed between them, and Georgette nodded slowly. "Right, I'm sorry, Quinn. Sometimes I just put my foot in my mouth, is all. He's a...good person."

"Right." I nodded, the lingering anger in my chest burning like hot coals. I needed to get away from her before I snapped. Up until now, I thought she was a bit obnoxious, but for the most part harmless. But being capable of saying something so awful, and mean... No. I didn't like those poisonous words. Didn't like even more how quickly my dad came to her aid.

I didn't want to start a fight, so I needed to get away.

"Well, uh, should we continue on the tour?" my dad asked, a forced lightness in his voice.

I found myself shaking my head. "Actually, you guys go ahead, I want to walk a bit, explore the grounds. You know, be out in nature."

A complete lie—this weather was miserable, and I felt like I was wading through a bowl of soup, but I couldn't be around them right now.

My dad frowned, his dark brows furrowing beneath his cowboy hat. "You sure, Queenie?"

"I'm sure, Dad."

"I'll stay with her," Whit replied, coming to my side and squeezing my shoulders reassuringly. I knew she sensed my anger. The squeeze was nothing more than a silent, *I got you.*

Dad's frown deepened a moment longer before erasing from his face entirely, an easy grin replacing it. "Alright. Dinner's in an hour."

"Don't be late!" Georgette said with a wide grin. "Else you might just miss out on Isidor's ceviche! It's to *die* for!" She flicked her wrist, that stupid ever-present smile bright on her face.

I wanted to punch that smile right off her. But I'd never been a fighter, so I offered her my brightest, fakest smile right back. I'd just kill her with kindness.

I waited until her and my dad retreated to the Gator and drove out of sight before turning to Whit.

"You okay?" she asked, her pretty face a mask of concern.

I nodded.

"Are we really going to explore in this god awful heat?" she groaned.

I chuckled. "No." Even I couldn't stoop to that level of petty just to avoid Georgette.

"Then what are we gonna do?"

Maybe it was the way Georgette seemed to talk down about the blind ranch hand, but something made me want to go introduce myself. "I want to go meet the ranch hands."

And before Whit could offer up a question or protest, I started marching for the house beside the barn.

WHIT CAME TO A stop a step or so behind me as I rapped my knuckles against the door to the bunkhouse in quick succession. "I wonder if any of them are hot," she mused.

The door swung inward and my heart stopped.

The cowboy from the grocery store.

"Hello?" he said, leaning a tan, tattooed, muscular arm against the door frame while holding onto the knob with the other hand. His hat was off, but it didn't take away from how drop-dead gorgeous he was.

I opened my mouth, but for the second time today, I struggled to find words.

"Look, I know you're there, what'dya want?"

My eyes widened, a gasp escaping me. I realized he wasn't looking directly at Whit and I, but between us. I just didn't notice at first because his glasses hid his eyes.

"Oh—oh my God. You're him...the um, well, you're the blind cowboy." I couldn't stop the words that bubbled up my throat and fell from my lips. *Oh my God. Talk about word vomit.*

This was the guy Dad and Georgette had been talking about.

Something hardened on his face, a muscle in his jaw clenching. "Jesus fucking Christ," he huffed, moving to close the door.

Oh my God. No. Why had I just blurted that out? "No. Wait!"

And even though it was completely indecent of me, I reached out and placed a hand on his holding the door. "Wait. Please. I'm sorry. That was completely horrible of me. I just… I was taken aback. I ran into you in the grocery store earlier."

The harsh look on his face softened, and his head cocked to the side. He inhaled deeply, and a look of…surprise washed over him. "You're the girl who was singin'."

Chapter Five
Ranch Hand

Hux

Fuck, I didn't know if people were getting more and more fucking rude nowadays, or if I was just getting offended too easily. It seemed I got more attention being the blind guy than I ever did as a professional bull rider. I hated it though. White-hot anger spread through my veins as if it'd been administered to me through an IV.

"*...I saw you in the grocery store earlier.*"

I paused at that. And just as the question popped in my head, an answering whisper of wind blew the scent of lemongrass and vanilla my way. Another sweet smell was mingled in there, but there was no denying *her* scent. I inhaled deeply, and all the anger pent up and growing inside me washed away—there and gone as quick as it came.

"You're the girl who was singin'," I blurted out, cocking my head to the side.

How the hell was she here? *Why* was she here? My heart danced rapidly in my chest. What a small, damn world.

She let out a little huff of nervous laughter, and I imagined she probably did something like tuck a piece of hair behind her ear or bite her bottom lip. "Oh God, did I leave that lasting of an impression? How embarrassing."

"Don't be," I replied, wishing like hell I could see her face. "I thought you sang nice."

Another trickle of laughter, this one filled with disbelief. "Thank you, but you don't need to lie. I'm terrible."

"Miss, I'm a lot of things, but I ain't no liar."

She made this soft, little noise in the back of her throat. Not quite a laugh but not necessarily a gasp either. It was soft and feminine and made me all the more frustrated I couldn't see her. I wondered if she was as pretty as she sounded. Not like it mattered anymore really.

"California girl! What're you doin' here?" Travis' booming voice startled me as his presence appeared at my side. Had I been so distracted I hadn't noticed him approach? I was usually pretty aware of my surroundings.

Another feminine voice joined the fray. "Shut up? This is so crazy! This is my friend I was telling you about. We're visiting her family!"

So the girl who was singing was Mr. Decker's daughter? I'm sure he and the missus would have something to say about the two of us talking. I got the impression Mrs. Decker didn't think all too highly of me. Not that I particularly thought all too highly of her either.

"Well, come on in!" Travis said, gently pushing me out of the doorframe to let everyone through.

The sweeter scent I'd smelled earlier filled my nose and the air shifted as she walked by me. Her footfalls were heavy as they scuffed against the wood floors. But then the other girl, the one I'd been talking to, moved past me so I could shut the door. She remained close by, I could feel the heat of her, the weight of her stare.

It's weird. Having my vision for so long and then losing it at least gave me a basis for what things generally looked like. After memorizing the layout of the bunkhouse, I'd come up with a mental blueprint of sorts. Behind her was the hallway to Travis's room, and off to her right and my left was the common area. From the quiet roar of voices, Travis was introducing the other girl to Wyatt, Dylan, and Brooks.

Something shifted in my chest that this girl stayed by me.

"So, you're Mr. and Mrs. Decker's daughter?" I asked.

An indignant huff. "She's not Mrs. Decker yet, and no, Georgette is *definitely* not my mom. That would be, like, biologically impossible actually with how close we are in age."

I fought the grin pulling on my lips. Apparently she didn't think too highly of Mrs. Decker either. "Do I sense some hostility?"

The girl—I still didn't know her name—huffed. "No, sorry. Georgette is just...not what I expected for my dad." A pause and then, "Sorry, I'm Quinn, by the way. I just now realized I never introduced myself."

"Hux." I held out a hand between us. "Huxson Lane."

I was more than a bit surprised at her firm grip as she shook it back. "It's nice to officially meet you, Hux. I–I really am sorry about earlier. I was so embarrassed, and when I said hi and smiled at you and you just looked right at me—which completely makes sense now, by the way—I just got the hell out of there because I was embarrassed." Her words held a slightly erratic, excited edge to them. From the way the air shifted frequently, I think she used her hands a lot to talk.

"It's all good. So, you came to visit your dad?"

"Well, I actually came here to help him plan his wedding at the end of this month."

I scoffed, rocking back on my heels. Wasn't there only a couple weeks left? "Ain't that a little shitty to ask that of you?"

"It's okay, honestly. My mom passed away when I was seventeen, so I've had plenty of time to come to terms with it. I'm just happy my dad found someone. And I'm an event planner, so it makes sense he'd ask me."

Her voice didn't hold any anger or resentment in it. It was soft, light, warm. Like a midsummer night. Not like this shitty, humid weather we were having, but the ones where the sun burnt low on the horizon, casting everything in a warm glow. The type of night that was meant for stargazing in the back of a pickup truck or going on a night ride.

God, I missed that.

"Ah, well, then my apologies for jumpin' to conclusions then, Miss. Quinn."

"No worries," she replied. "So, what exactly does a ranch hand do? Are you like a legit cowboy?"

It amazed me that she hadn't made her way over to the others yet, and it amazed me more that she sounded genuinely interested in talking to me.

I chuckled, my lips curving up into a smirk. "What do you mean a legit cowboy?"

"Like...you know, do you break and train horses? Do you, like, lasso cows and ride bulls?"

The last question hit me like a ton of bricks, straight to the chest. If only she knew what all I'd done. How close I'd been to being a three time consecutive World Champion.

"You rope a cow, not lasso it," I said, hoping my words didn't come out as brusque as they felt tumbling out of my mouth. "I've trained and worked babies...but, no... I don't ride bulls."

Not anymore.

Chapter Six

Porch Swing Angel

QUINN

HALFWAY THROUGH DINNER AND I still couldn't puzzle together what I'd done to make Hux shut down like that. There'd been a definite shift in him when I'd brought up cowboys, but I didn't know exactly why. His expression, his entire demeanor turned guarded, closed off in an instant. And I didn't know him enough to know if I could push him for more explanation.

It was just as well, though. Whit might think that the entire purpose of this trip was to find hot cowboys and go *buckwild*, but I knew better. Not that she wasn't going to try her hardest to change my mind. She'd made us plans with Travis and the other hands—Wyatt, Dylan, and Brooks—to go out later tonight. And despite my best efforts, a teeny, tiny part of me hoped Hux went too.

If anyone noticed my silence during dinner, no one mentioned it. Georgette told story after story with the occasional chime in from my dad. Like how *serendipitous* it had been for them to have met at an ocean-side bar in Turks and Caicos. How they'd had the most magical night and felt like they'd met the other half of their soul. All of those were Georgette's words. Dad didn't say much on the matter, he just let her rub her hands all over him. Not in an overly gross way, but, like, they were *always* touching one another or holding each other's thighs, leaning into and pressing their head to one of their shoulders, pausing mid-sentence to smile and kiss.

Weren't teenagers the ones supposed to be so handsy? Didn't Georgette have any sort of decency? Didn't he? Like, this was my dad. Didn't he feel weird being so openly affectionate to his girlfr—fiancé in front of me?

I don't know if Whit was genuinely curious, or if she was keeping Georgette talking for my sake, but I was grateful I wasn't being expected to interact more than a nod or "wow" here or there.

"So, where are you guys planning on moving after the wedding? Are you going to stay in Texas or maybe come back to California?" Whit asked, sipping her wine. Her words snagged my attention. I'd been wondering the same thing.

Georgette's forever smile dipped for a moment. "What do you mean?"

A sense of unease simmered to life in the pit of my stomach. "Dad said that you guys were renting this place for the month of the wedding to make planning it on such short notice easier. He hadn't mentioned where you all were going after."

She glanced at my dad, her head tilting to the side as she said in that high-pitched, sugary-sweet voice of hers, "I thought you told her."

I cocked my head to the side, the unease turning to straight up dread. Why did I get the sense I wasn't going to like this conversation? This feeling had been manifesting, growing all throughout dinner, bubbling to life like water boiling in a pot. It started slow, but gained and gained and gained in intensity until all it could do was bubble over. "Told me what?"

My dad let out a nervous laugh as he leaned back in his chair, cupped a hand over his mouth, and rubbed at his chin. "I was uh...I was planning to tell you just you and me, but, well...this is as good a time as any." A luminous grin came to his lips as he threw his arms wide. "Surprise, Queenie. This is for you."

I froze, the only part of me able to move being my eyelids as I blinked over and over and over, trying and failing to puzzle this all together. "Um...what?" I finally managed to sputter out.

He swept a hand out at the gorgeous dining room. It gave off elegant, masculine men's club vibes with its dark oak walls, ornate chandeliers, and matching sconces that burned low and warm. A wet bar filled with a number of fancy glass decanters full of whiskey took up the entire western wall.

"I wanna turn this place into a full on destination ranch. Weddings, retreats, business trips, you name it. Georgie and I are gonna buy us some of those tiny homes and put them on the property to use as little guest cabins."

"There's a herd of about a hundred cattle," Georgette chimed in, a satisfied grin on her face. "And we're gonna offer small, all inclusive, elegant cattle drives to those who can afford it. And, well..." She rose from her spot beside my dad and made her way around to grab my hands in hers. Squeezing softly, she offered me a bright smile. "We don't see anyone better than you runnin' it, sweetie."

I know that she wasn't trying to be condescending, but I hated her so much in that moment. Her stupid smile, the way she held my hands, and how they didn't even ask me what I thought of this whole business venture.

I know most people would probably be over the moon about this opportunity, and even though I was grateful I found myself saying, "I...I have a job." Pulling my hands away, I looked across the table to my dad. "You were so excited for me when I told you I officially landed the gig."

Did he not believe in me being able to make it on my own? Even after putting in the hard work, the four years of college to get to this point, did he think I'd fuck up so royally that he felt the need to coddle me? Or was this some sort of left over guilt from Mom passing away and him basically going off the deep end, leaving me to all care for myself? Was this his way of trying to take care of me?

"I was!" Dad said, his words ringing with sincerity. "But I know you'll do fantastic running things for me."

His words hit like a punch to the face. He didn't even expect me to argue, but to just accept the offer. My heart pitter pattered in my chest like someone learning to tap-dance. Off key and too erratic. Disappointment welled inside me. I should have known that there was more to it than just the wedding. Now, things started to make sense.

Dad was always looking for a way to make more money. I swear, since Mom died, it was his main, driving force. And how convenient was it for him to have a daughter who could work his latest business venture? Yeah, a part of me was honored that he believed in me, even if it might be for selfish reasons, but running an entire event venue? I'd just gotten my BA in Event Management. I'd only just gotten a job with an venue in Beverly Hills, I couldn't imagine being in charge of an entire event ranch. Not to mention, I couldn't just drop everything in California and move here on a whim. I mean, I could, technically, but California was home. It was where Mom was buried. The thought of leaving felt like carving out a chunk of my soul.

Tears burned in my eyes. From anger, or frustration, or confusion, I didn't really know at this point. It didn't matter in the end, either. I scooted my chair away from the table and met my dad's stare.

The hopeful smile on his face faded at the emotion he found lurking on mine. "Queenie?"

"I…I need a minute," I managed to choke out. It was the only thing I could say that wasn't filled with expletives and made me sound like I was being selfish.

Without giving them time to respond, I walked out of the room. To where, it didn't matter. I ignored his shouted protest as I stormed out the front doors and off the porch, down the main gravel road leading toward the stables and the rest of the property. Now that the sun had dipped on the horizon, it was almost nice out. The humidity seemed to have lessened a bit, a light breeze picking up and blowing my long hair in the wind. It didn't stick to me like it had earlier, so that was a plus.

I didn't try to fight the tears that fell. I'd always been a crier. Something Dad hated, and Mom encouraged. She'd always been going on about being in touch with your emotions, feeling the feelings—all of them. Good and bad. Highs and lows. I wondered what she would think of all of this. Would she be on my dad's side or mine? She'd always been so good at making us both feel validated. What I wouldn't give to know her thoughts right now.

Movement caught my eye, and I looked up to find a dark-clothed figure making their way out of the ranch hand barn with a dog at their side. Even though I'd only met him today, I recognized the hat, the broad, muscular build, the shoulder-length hair. And while I was a crying, blubbering mess, I found myself calling his name.

He froze mid-stride, before turning my way slowly. I crossed the thirty or so yards between us, stopping a few feet away from him. "Hey," I said softly. "It's—"

"Quinn," he replied. "I'm blind not an idiot."

A laugh worked its way out of my mouth at the bluntness in his words.

"Sorry," he said, the lines of his face softening. "I didn't mean for that to come off so dick-ish."

"No worries..." I glanced down at the dog beside him, immediately recognizing it from earlier. "Is this your dog?"

"No."

I frowned. "Oh...sorry, I—"

"I'm just jokin'," he replied, holding a hand out at his side. The reddish brown dog leaned into his touch. "This is Rusty."

"Is he, like, your seeing eye dog?" Was that insensitive to ask?

Hux nodded, one of his shoulders lifting into a casual shrug. "Yes and no. He ain't registered or anythin' like that, but he's a good companion, and he helps me get around."

I smiled. "He's gorgeous. What kind of dog is he?"

"A Kelpie."

"I've never heard of it."

"They aren't too common. They're a workin' breed. Mostly herd and work cattle."

I liked to think of myself as a dog person, but I hadn't had a pet since I was a teenager and our old family Golden died. She'd been Mom's and after both of them passed, Dad and I just couldn't get another.

"That's cool. What were you doing just now?" I asked.

He was so attractive it was almost painful to look at him. I know it was probably indecent of me, but I liked being able to take him in without the weight of his stare. I could take my time examining his features without seeming like a creeper. Though, that definitely made me sound creeper-ish.

"Checkin' on the horses one last time for the evenin'. I thought you had dinner with your pare–your dad and Georgette?"

I appreciated the correction. Georgette wasn't and never would be my parent.

I rolled my eyes and blew out a breath. "I got upset and left."

"Why?" His brow furrowed as he turned to face me more fully. His sunglasses stare wasn't directly on me, but aimed in my general direction.

"I had no idea that my dad bought this place with the intent on running it as a destination ranch." I launched into the details of it all; all the while Hux listened silently. "I don't know if I'm being dramatic and a bit selfish, but I'm angry that he did this all without even talking to me about it first. And, well, I'm scared. This is…it's a lot more than I expected to take on so early in my career."

Hux lifted a shoulder in a shrug. "Ain't nothin' wrong with that. If it's too much, it's too much. You don't gotta please him."

"You don't get it, I hate disappointing him." Anyone in general. I was the epitome of a people pleaser. A perfectionist. And I had a problem with saying no. Dad knew it. That's why he expected this of me.

"Who gives a damn what he thinks? If you live your life for others, you're gonna lose yourself eventually." He said the words with such ease, such nonchalance. It should annoy me, he was so blunt and brusque it bordered on being rude or callous, at the very least, but it worked for him. There was a raw honesty to him that I could appreciate.

I huffed. "Easier said than done."

"Most things that are worth doin' are hard."

"You're probably right...actually, I know you're right, it's just..."

"Hard?" he offered.

I nodded, and we descended into stilted silence. I glanced up at him, finding his expression expectant, like he was waiting for me to say something. "Oh shit, yeah. You're right. Sorry," I breathed, a soft chuckle floating between us. "I nodded, but you..." my words trailed off, a wave of embarrassment flooding through me.

I'd have to remember to be more vocal. Mom and Dad always joked about how I didn't even have to say a word, I wore all my expressions on my face. That wouldn't work if I intended to be around Hux. Just the thought had butterflies fluttering in my chest.

"It's okay. I get it. Not many folks are used to talkin' to a blind person." There was a hard edge to his voice, but I got the feeling it wasn't aimed at me. More like himself. His circumstance.

I wondered if it was rude to ask him if he'd been born like that or if he'd gone blind. It probably was.

"You wanna know how it happened, don't you?" he asked, his rough, harsh voice filling the silence between us.

I gaped. "Can you, like, read minds or something?"

A smile cracked on his lips, a genuine laugh escaping him. The rich, deep sound did something to me. And that smile...maybe it was because in the time I'd met him, I'd mostly seen him broody or shut off, but that smile was like a setting sun.

How was it possible to be so attracted to a stranger? I swear, I was majorly crushing on him... It was a good thing he couldn't see me.

"Most people are curious," he replied, before sighing. "I wasn't born like this. I uh...I had an accident."

There was a finality to the words that gave me the sense that if I pushed, he'd just shut it down.

"I'm sorry. How long ago did it happen?" I asked hesitantly, wondering if that question was off limits too.

"Three years this August."

About a month from now. Holy God, I couldn't even imagine how hard that must have been for him. I voiced the thought aloud.

A muscle feathered in his scruffy jaw, and he flexed his hand once more. Rusty leaned into him on instinct. "It's...shit in a lot of ways. But, I'm not dead, so I guess there's that."

"I'm sorry." That seemed hollow, but I didn't know what else to say. What could you say to that?

He shrugged, petting Rusty for a long, silent moment. "Why are you apologizin'? It ain't your fault."

"I know, I just..." My words fell away again. Why did it feel like everytime I opened my mouth with him I put my foot in it?

"You goin' out with Travis and the rest of the group tonight?" he asked.

"Yeah, Whit would kill me if I didn't." I bit my lip, nerves trickling to life in me. "Are you coming too?"

"Me?" He shook his head. "Nah, probably not."

My heart sank. "How come?"

Another shrug. "Ain't really my scene."

I blew out a breath. "I get that. It's not really my scene either... but not gonna lie, I was kinda hoping you'd come."

He rocked back at that, his gaze still not quite fixed on me. The ever-present scowl on his face deepened. "Why?" Disbelief rang in the word.

I shrugged. More for my sake than his, and added, "I like you. You're easy to talk to."

"I am?" More disbelief.

I huffed out a soft laugh. "Yes, you are." An idea came to mind—one Whit might kill me for, but I'm sure she'd forgive me if I groveled enough. "Hey, what if I stayed here and you showed me around instead?"

Bars had always been more Whit's scene. I never understood why someone would spend so much money on a drink you could make at home for a fraction of the cost. Whit always mentioned something about that's why you got someone to buy your drinks for you, but that just made me feel...weird. Why would I let some random guy buy me a drink if I had no intention of getting to know him?

The idea of staying here with Hux, maybe walking the property, talking some more—I don't know, that sounded a lot more up my alley.

"Well," Hux replied, "You're, uh, in a much better position to show yourself around than I am. I don't know what the fuck this place looks like."

I know it was probably bad of me, but I laughed at that. He was so unapologetically blunt and honest. "I could tell you," I offered. "Take you around and explain what everything looks like, and you could tell me how it relates to you and your work."

Some emotion I couldn't quite place rippled over his features. His lips pulled up into a soft ghost of a smile aimed in my direction. "You'd do that for a stranger?"

I shrugged once more, quickly reminding myself after a silent beat that I needed to respond. "I'd do it for a friend."

He took a few steps toward me, close enough that I could feel the heat of him on my skin and the smell of his cologne. Something fresh and woodsy, with a hint of sweet. Maybe like teakwood and vanilla? I don't know, one of the manly smells. My heart fluttered in my chest at his closeness. He stirred something within me I'd never felt before. Not even with Devin. Hux's unseeing stare bore into me, and a little gasp escaped me at the intensity of it. And he was wearing sunglasses still. I couldn't imagine how much more intense it would be if he wasn't.

His words were a low rumble as he asked, "So, we're friends?"

Why did it feel like he was asking something much more serious? Was it how close he was? How attractive he was?

"I'd like to be," I breathed.

A grunt of...approval, maybe, escaped him. "I'd like that."

I bit my lip, completely overwhelmed by the closeness of him, the heat of him, the weight of his stare. He intimidated me as much as he enchanted me. He had a commanding presence, one that demanded all of my attention. I felt like a deer in the headlights. I didn't know whether to freeze or run. I'd never been around someone like him. Never felt so exposed, so vulnerable just by him looking at me. But as a shiver traversed down the length of my spine, I realized it wasn't at all the bad kind, but one that whispered of excitement. Adventure. Desire. "Good," I managed to squeak out.

The smile on his lips grew, pulling up at the corners. "I've changed my mind, let's go out tonight."

My brow furrowed. " But, I thought—"

"I wanna take you out. But *I am* goin' to take you up on that offer of showin' me around at some point." His words rang with finality. There'd be no convincing him otherwise, I could tell from the stubborn set of his jaw.

Another shiver went through me as I thought of going out with him. Honestly, just being around him in general. With a grin, I replied, "I probably should go get ready then."

Chapter Seven
This Ain't No Love Song

Hux

A LITTLE OVER THREE years ago, you'd be as likely to find me at a bar on a Saturday night as a rodeo. Funny how quickly things changed. I didn't go out much anymore. First, it was hard enough navigating the places that I spent most of my time in, unfamiliar places were a whole new level of hell. But secondly, I hated when people realized who I was. It wasn't everywhere, it wasn't all the time, but it was frequent enough to be a pain in the ass. I did everything I could *not* to think about my life before the accident. About rodeos and bull riding and championship buckles.

It sucked. All that time, all that money, all the blood, sweat, and tears I'd poured into making a name for myself, to have it gone in a night. In eight damn seconds, to be exact.

Quinn's friend, Whit, had gotten us all an Uber to one of the local bars in town. Worry pumped through my veins, making my heart stammer a bit in my chest as I got out. This had been a mistake. I didn't do this. Didn't go out with the guys.

I had half a mind to turn around and get back in the Uber and pay them to take me home.

"Hey, you okay?" Quinn's voice was gentle and warm, somehow cutting through the chaos of Main Street surrounding us. I felt the closeness of people as they milled about, the rumble of engines as they purred behind me while driving by. Music thumped dully from ahead of me in the bar—The Hitching Post, if Travis had anything to do with it. Then there was the sound of the group talking.

It was sensory overload. I hated when it got too loud. It fucked with my mind a bit. I made mistakes. Bumped into shit.

"It's loud," I found myself saying.

"I'm sorry. We don't have t—"

A flash of defiancé sparked in me, and I gritted my teeth. "No. I'm okay. Just tryin' to get my bearings."

I said I'd go out, and I wasn't a damn quitter. I could manage for a few hours.

"Here...can I at least help you?"

A warm hand settled in my right one, knotting through my fingers. Her already familiar scent drifted on the breeze. It settled around me, soothing some of my pent up frustration and worry.

I nodded.

She led me forward, careful to go slow, telling me where I was and the layout as we went. A lump lodged in my throat. I hated feeling so hopeless, but having her help—no one did that. Not that I really gave many a chance, but still.

She couldn't possibly know what her kindness did to me.

"I think they're heading for the pool tables, did you want to go with them?" she asked.

"How crowded does it look over there?"

I let the poppy country music wash over me, along with the familiar sounds and smells of the bar. I might not know the layout of this one, but there was a familiarity here. They all reeked of spilt liquor and the faint smell of cigarettes—even the ones you couldn't smoke in.

"It's pretty busy," she said over the music.

"What about the bar?" I asked, glancing to the left, trying to make sense of the layout Quinn had described.

"Basically empty. There's a couple at the other end, but that's it."

I nodded. "Wanna get a drink?"

"Sure."

I let her lead me forward. She went slowly, carefully, and I appreciated that. I hated nothing more than tripping over myself and looking like an idiot. I'd be damned if I used a fucking walking stick, and going slow was the only way I could get around. So opposite out how I'd been before. A knot of sadness sprung to life in my chest, but it didn't last long. Not as Quinn's soft voice cut through the chaos.

"Here's a stool right ahead of you." She guided my hand toward the seat. I didn't normally like having help doing things like this, but, I don't know, there was something about how gentle she was that I didn't really mind right now.

I managed to get situated in my seat when a sultry, feminine voice sounded from before me. "Hi, y'all. What can I get ya?"

"What'dya want?" I asked, reaching my right hand out toward where I thought Quinn was, coming into contact with her bare thigh. Something stirred in me. Damn, I hadn't meant to do that.

She didn't push my hand away, but I didn't miss the sharp hiss that escaped her. I wondered if that was good or bad. "Um...can I get a mudslide, please?"

I balked at that. A mudslide? Really? What was she, twelve?

"Can I see your I.D., miss?"

Huh. I wondered how young she was. She sounded young, but young enough to get carded? A trickled of worry stirred in my chest that I pushed back down.

"Sure."

After a couple moments of silence, the waitress made a satisfactory sound and asked, "And you, sir?"

The worry knotted in my chest eased. Thank fuck she was over twenty-one. "I'll take a whiskey on the rocks, please."

"You got it." The bartender's words were already drifting away, like she was walking as she talked.

Even though I couldn't see her, I turned to face Quinn in my seat. "A mudslide?" I scoffed. "Really?"

A soft laugh escaped her. "What? If I'm going to drink, I want it to taste good."

I chuckled, shaking my head. "At least you got somethin' with some whiskey in it."

She made a gagging sound. "Ew, whiskey and I do not mix."

"Darlin'," I huffed. "You do know there's whiskey in it right?"

"What, really? I don't usually like it."

"I don't know if this friendship's gonna work out between us if you don't like whiskey," I said with a soft laugh.

"What?" Her gasp drew the corner of my lips upward. "What are you talking about?"

"I got a real close relationship with my friends Jack, Jimmy, and Jameson. If you don't get along with them...well, I don't know if this can work."

A beat of silence. Two. Three. "I don't get it."

I dropped my head forward, wiping a hand down my face. She sounded so clueless. "You know... Jack Daniels. Jim Beam. Jameson whiskey."

Another moment of quiet, the only sound that of some shitty new country song blasting from the speakers. Couldn't they play some Garth or something from the King of Country himself?

"Oh! I get it!" she finally gasped, an embarrassed laugh bubbling out of her.

I shook my head, trying and failing to bite back a smirk. "Oh, well bless your heart, you sweet, innocent thing, you."

"Hey!" Her tone took on a defensive edge, and a soft, firm pressure pressed against my chest, nudging me backward slightly. *Did she just push me?* "That's not true! I am not all that innocent."

"Really?" I scoffed, my brow rising in question.

Something brushed against my leg, before settling there. I reached out a hand, feeling her thigh once more. Another spark. Another flutter in my chest. Did this girl have magic in her or something, or was I just that lonely that the simplest touch stirred something in my soul I'd thought long gone?

I pulled my hand away, even if a part of me told me to leave it. It was hard enough reading a woman's emotions, but now it was even fucking harder. I only had her voice and touch to go off of. And while both seemed inviting enough, I wasn't confident in pushing forward.

"When I was in tenth grade, I got invited to prom by a senior," she said, her voice rising as she spoke. "My parents let me go, but were adamant that I be home by midnight. I stayed out til two, though."

My head fell back, a laugh falling from my lips. Oh God, this girl really was innocent. "Shit, two hours late. Look at you, you rebel."

Another nudge to my shoulder. "It was a big deal! I got grounded for a week!"

"That's nothin'. I got kicked out of my prom for spikin' all the drinks at the refreshments station."

"Shut up! You did not?"

"Sure did," I chuckled, thinking back on a simpler time. A simpler world. Back when I'd been crazy and wild and full of mischief.

"Here's your drinks," The bartender's voice stopped our conversation. "Should I open a tab for you?"

"Yes, ma'am," I replied, fishing out my wallet from my back pocket before grabbing my card and handing it to her.

"Sounds good, I'll keep it open, Mr. Lane—Wait...you're Huxson Lane? Like, *the* Huxson Lane?"

Fuck. I blew out a slow breath, fighting the disappointment and annoyance welling inside me. I knew this would happen. Damn it.

"I used to be." I didn't know exactly where she stood in relation to me, but I made sure my face and tone told her everything she needed to know. I wasn't talking about this. Not now.

"O-oh...sorry, sir. I'll get that opened up for you. Let me know if y'all need anythin' else."

I nodded. "A shot of Jameson too, please. Make it a double."

Tonight was gonna be one of those nights.

"Right away, sir."

I reached slowly forward, my hand bumping into the plastic whiskey tumbler. I grabbed it and drained it in a single go—the burn a blessed distraction from the emotions writhing in me.

I wondered what Quinn thought. If she was confused or worried about the change in my attitude.

Her light voice drew my attention, chasing away some of the dark, angry emotions roiling in my soul. "I can't believe you spiked the drinks." If she sensed the shift in me, she didn't let on. For that, I was glad.

I nodded. "That was nothin'. I got a whole long list of dumb shit I did growin' up."

Her laughter was warm. "How old are you?" she asked after a moment.

"Here you go, sir," The bartender cut in. I heard the clink of the glass against the countertop.

I nodded. "Thank you. And another whiskey on the rocks, please." I turned my unseeing gaze back on Quinn, wondering more and more what she looked like? Was she a brunette? A blonde? Tall or short? Was she covered in tattoos? I doubted that. She seemed too innocent. But it wouldn't be the first time I'd been wrong about someone.

"I turn thirty-three in November," I replied to her.

"No way!" Her words shook with disbelief. "You don't look that old at all!"

I chuckled. "I feel that old. Older even." A career as a bull rider wasn't an easy one. I had the scars to prove it. Sometimes just getting out of bed felt like an insurmountable feat. I felt around for one of my shot glasses and threw it back easily enough. "How old are you?" I asked past the familiar burn.

A pause, and then nervously, "Not gonna lie, I'm kinda scared to tell you now."

Unease stirred within me once more. "You're over twenty-one, right? Or did you just give her a really good fake I.D?"

She laughed, the sound light and lyrical and enchanting. God, it did something to me. I hoped like I hell I wasn't flirting with some teenager.

"No. I just turned twenty-three in March."

I blew out a breath I hadn't even realized I'd been holding. "Thank fuck."

Another laugh, though there was a nervous edge to it. "It's not a problem for you?"

I shrugged, and with a confidence I hadn't felt a few moments ago—*whiskey must be kicking in*—I rested a hand on her thigh. "As long as you're okay sittin' here with my old ass, I'm fine with it. And...I don't know, you hold yourself together like you're older. I mean you're innocent as fuck, but I have a feelin' you got some fire in you."

The warm feel of her hand on mine sent a rush through me. "Good," she replied, low and sultry.

Yeah, she may seem all innocent, but there was something there. A flicker of desire just waiting to turn into a living, breathing inferno. And I didn't mind being the one to stoke the flames.

"I have an idea," Quinn said, an excited edge to her voice.

"Am I gonna like this?"

"I mean, it involves getting to know me and drinking, so you tell me?"

I shrugged, my lips curving upward. "Sounds good to me."

Her laughter warmed me from the inside out, more thoroughly than the liquor in my bloodstream. "It's a game. Kinda like truth or dare, but instead of a dare, you drink."

"Sounds easy enough…but it ain't fair that I'm over here drinkin' straight alcohol and your drinkin' some weak ass bullshit."

"Fair enough," she laughed. "But no shots. I can't shoot liquor to save my life."

I bet a bit of time with me and we could fix that. "Fine, how about another mudslide?"

"Deal."

I didn't even have to call the bartender over. As she delivered my whiskey on the rocks, I ordered another mudslide for Quinn.

"Alright, ladies first," I said, situating myself to face Quinn's direction more fully.

"Hmmm…okay, I'm going to start out easy. What's your favorite food?"

I huffed. Really? My favorite food? "Easy," I replied. "Steak and potatoes."

She laughed. "How come that doesn't surprise me at all?"

I shrugged, nodding in her general direction. "What? Let me guess, you like something like chips and salsa, tacos, and a marg with the girls?"

A gasp came from her, another light nudge to my shoulder. "Rude of you to assume!" Her voice was defensive, but also warm, happy. She couldn't obviously be too offended. "But it's also true."

I smirked, dipping my head in a nod and taking a sip of my whiskey. "I'm just gonna go ahead and drink for that."

She laughed. "Alright, my turn again." A pause, then… "What's the dumbest thing you've ever done?"

My head fell back, a huff of laughter escaping me. "Ah, shit…the dumbest? I don't know. It's all pretty dumb. But I think the worst was when I was, like, thirteen, my friends and I tried ridin' one of their dad's prize buckin' bulls. Thing was a fuckin' beast and had like an undefeated record. I lasted maybe a second before that sonova bitch bucked me into the fence. Shattered my arm and broke a couple ribs." I ran my fingertips over the scar along the outside of my left forearm from one of the surgeries I'd had on it.

"Oh my God!" The disbelief in her tone brought a smirk to my lips. "That is...far wilder than anything I've done."

Unsurprising, but I didn't say anything. I didn't need her to tell me what all dumb shit she'd done, I had questions of my own. "Alright, my turn... What do you look like?"

"Like, my hair color or—"

"All of it," I replied. I wanted—no, needed to know. I had so many different potential versions of her swirling up in my head, but I wanted to have an image of her. Even if I'd never truly see her. Even if it was the wrong image, I needed to know.

"Hmm...okay, well, I'm short, like, really short. I'm barely five feet tall, and I guess you could say I have curves. Like, I'm not straight up and down. I have a heart shaped—no, circular shaped face. Actually, I don't know, it might be a blend of both?" She let out a nervous laugh. "I have freckles on my nose and cheeks. When I was little, kids made fun of me for them, so my mom told me it was just left over fairy dust from the fairies who visited me in my dreams."

A soft smile threatened my lips at the image that came to mind.

"My eyes are a blueish green, but they have a ring of gold in them. Some, *stupid* people mistake them for hazel, but they absolutely *aren't* hazel."

Her adamant tone made my smile crack across my lips. Between the sound of her voice, the image I was conjuring in my mind of her, and the effects of the whiskey, I was feeling pretty good.

"I believe you," I chuckled. "What about your hair?"

She blew out a breath before a trill of laughter fell between us. Sounded like someone was feeling a bit tipsy. How was beyond me. She'd hardly drank anything. I was the one who should be buzzing. But that wasn't entirely surprising if her wild, rebel story was staying out a couple hours late for prom. "So, if you were asking Whit, she'd probably tell you something like vanilla swirl with a dash of almond butter," Quinn finally said, her words taking on a haughty tone.

"Sounds like you're orderin' a damn coffee," I muttered.

More giggles bubbled out of her and I found myself smiling as the sound washed over me. I liked her laugh. I liked that it wasn't one of those high-pitched fake ass laughs meant to sound sexy or cute. It reminded me of sunlight. And I wanted to hear more of it.

"It kinda does, doesn't it? It's blonde, though. But not like a golden blonde...more of like a pale blonde with warm lowlights. Does that make sense?"

I shrugged. "It's blonde."

She huffed a laugh. "Sure. Oh, and it's long. Like, really, really long."

"How long? Like down past your ass?"

"No! It brushes my hips when I walk. Here—" Her delicate hand clasped mine gently as she guided it forward. In the next instant, a soft lock of hair brushed against the inside of my palm. I ran my fingertips over it, feeling the length of it in its entirety, my fingers coming into contact with her body. Her hips.

There wasn't anything overtly, or really even remotely for that matter, sexy about this moment, but it pumped adrenaline and desire through my veins, lending to the intoxicating rush that the whiskey gave me. I wanted to touch more of her. All of her.

Hold your roll, idiot.

I thought of all the things she'd told me about herself, conjuring an image in my mind like a painter painting a masterpiece. The final result was nothing short of perfection. "You sound gorgeous," I blurted out.

More warm, heady laughter. "Thank you," she said softly, timidly, like she didn't quite believe it. I could envision her tucking a piece of hair behind her ear as she pursed her lips.

I ran my hand over her thigh once more and gave it a reassuring squeeze. "I mean it."

A soft little noise came from her. Not quite a gasp, but not a laugh either. It was an appreciative sound. "Who's turn is it again?" she asked, her voice slightly breathy.

I liked that I affected her. I liked even more that I seemed to be able to read her easily enough. "I think it's yours," I murmured.

"Hmm..." She drew the sound out for a while, her leg tapping against mine as she thought. After a moment, she blew out a breath. "Pass. I need a minute to think."

"You okay?" I asked, worry stirring in my chest.

"I'm fine," she giggled. "I just think the alcohol is kicking in a bit and I—well, let's just say you're distracting me."

I chuckled, reaching for my drink. My fingers brushed against the other I'd ordered. "What do you mean I'm distracting you?"

"Ugh, are you really gonna make me say it?" she groaned.

"Say what?" One of my brows quirked upward.

"Look—" Her tone turned more assertive. "You're really, really hot, and between me being a bit buzzed and your stupid, teasing touches...well, you're distracting me."

A smile stretched across my face, a sense of satisfaction bubbling within me. When was the last time I'd felt this good? It'd been a long time, that's for damn sure.

"How are you buzzin' off a fuckin' milkshake?" I huffed.

"It's strong, okay?"

"Sure it is." My words dripped with sarcasm.

Her answering laughter set my heart fluttering like hummingbird wings. I liked making her laugh. It warmed something in my soul—the dark, ugly, cold piece of me that had taken root after my accident.

"Alright," I said, steering the conversation back to the game. "What made you want to do event planning?"

"My mom passing away, actually."

"Really?" I remembered her mentioning something about her mom passing away when she was a teen. I wondered how that inspired her.

"Yeah. So, my dad was, like, a *total* wreck after my mom died, which, I mean, understandable. And my grandparents are, like, super, super old. They couldn't take on planning an event like that. With most of our family in Northern California, I just kinda took it upon myself to get everything done." A soft laugh spanned the brief silence where her last sentence ended and a new one started. "It was actually really...cathartic. On the day of her celebration of life, everyone kept saying how I'd done such a great job capturing my mom's essence. They felt like I'd brought a piece of her back to life. And well—" A pause "—that's when I realized I wanted to do this for a living."

I nodded and finished off the last of my whiskey on the rocks, draining it easily. "I like that. It's not easy lookin' at a shitty situation and findin' something positive in it." Fuck, I was still trying to do that myself. Then there was this girl who'd done it as a teenager. She might be younger than me, but she was a hell of a lot wiser.

"Exactly. So that's one of my big goals with planning events. It's so much more than that. It's a piece of someone. Whether it's as simple as a luncheon or a charity event, a first birthday or a memorial. I don't want to just plan events, I want to breathe life into them."

Something cracked in me.

I want to breathe life into them. That should be her catch phrase or something.

If I believed anyone could do that, it was her.

But Quinn's next words turned the warmth in my soul to ice. "What about you? Have you always been a ranch hand?"

I blew out a breath. "I grew up on a ranch, so it's always been in my blood..." And I don't know if it was the whiskey kicking in or the fact that she'd been so goddamn open with me, but I found myself saying, "There was a good amount of time, though, that I was pretty big into rodeoin'."

"Really?" Intrigue and wonder filled her voice, and I instantly regretted the decision to say anything.

Fuck. No amount of alcohol loosened me up enough to want to talk about this. It still hurt too damn much nearly three years later. I still felt the loss. Like a fucking phantom limb or something. That part of me was gone, but the pain from it all still remained.

Sometimes...on really bad days, I almost wished that I'd died. But I'd always been a prideful, stubborn sonofabitch and giving up just wasn't really in my blood.

"Is that...is that how you had your accident?" I didn't miss the trepidation and hesitance in her tone.

I bit the inside of my cheek, frustration mixing with the whiskey in my veins. A deadly combo. I went to reach for one of my drinks but they were all empty. *Fuck.*

"Next question," I said, the words little more than a growl.

"I'm...sorry." Her words were sincere, soft, as well as her hand on my leg.

"It's okay. You didn't know."

And hopefully she never would. I didn't need her to feel sorry for me. Didn't want her pity. It's why I never talked about it in the first place.

For the first time since getting to the bar, we fell into an awkward silence. I was still too hot to continue the game, and I could only imagine all the things going through her head, so I did the only thing that made sense: called over the bartender.

After ordering and pounding back another shot, the anger finally started to ebb, even as my words finally started to slur.

"I'm sorry," I murmured. "I don't like talkin' about my past."

To her credit, she sounded just as sincere as earlier. "You don't have to apologize, Hux. I get it...I mean, I don't get the extent of your injury, but you have no obligation to tell me what happened."

"There you two lovebirds are!" I recognized Travis' voice as it boomed over the music. A moment later, something heavy clapped me on the shoulder, startling the fuck out of me. *Goddamn.*

"We've been looking for you!" Quinn's friend, Whit, joined in.

"Obviously not very hard," Quinn replied, her voice taking on a sing-songy note. "We've been here the whole time."

Whit's tone bubbled with excitement, her words a bit breathy and high-pitched. "I hate to drag her away, but can I steal Quinnie for a moment?"

"She's her own person," I grumbled. "Why don't you ask her?"

"Oh...um." I could just imagine Whit looking at me with a blank expression on her face, unsure how to take my tone.

Quinn laughed, though, and brushed a hand against mine. "I'll be right back, okay?"

A shiver went through me at the whisper-soft touch, chasing away more of the anger—no small feat. Maybe I was onto something earlier. Maybe she did have magic in those hands of hers. Desire rippled to life in me. I nodded in her general direction, feeling the air shift as she moved. Her lemongrass and vanilla scent drifted away before disappearing entirely.

"Well, damn, weren't expectin' this for your Saturday night, right?" Travis said, followed by one of his goofy ass laughs. "Wonder what the fuck they see in us? They're way outta our league."

I huffed. "Speak for yourself, dumbass."

But his words stirred something in my soul. A tiny, traitorous fear that grew and grew the more I thought about it.

What *did* Quinn see in me? Was she truly enjoying herself or did she just feel guilty? It wouldn't be the first time that happened. The first pity date.

Fear sparked in that cold, dead part of me, igniting like kindling while being stoked by the flames of my whiskey-fueled anger. With Quinn not here to chase away the darkness, doubt crept in, mingling with my worries until I bristled with fury.

"Hey, man, you okay?" Concern rang in Travis' tone. But I didn't want his concern. His worry. His inevitable pity.

"I'm fine."

Travis and I had worked together long enough that he knew when not to push me for information. "Alright. Wanna come back to the pool tables with us?"

"Nah, I'm good."

"Let me know if you need anythin', okay?"

I nodded, offering him a dismissive wave. A moment later, I could make out the sound of his retreating footsteps. Turning myself toward the bar, I managed to get the bartender's attention.

"What can I do for ya, sir?" she asked.

"I wanna close my tab."

Maybe Quinn really was into me. Maybe she wasn't. But I didn't want to wait and find out.

Chapter Eight

One I Want

QUINN

WHIT KEPT ME IN the bathroom for entirely way too long as she talked about Travis and the other ranch hands. The whole time, all I wanted was to get back to Hux. Being around him, talking to him...I liked it. I liked it far too much for just meeting him earlier that day. There was no denying it, though. Something pulled me to him. Drew me in. Call it fate or chance, but there was a spark in my soul that I hadn't known was there until meeting him.

A terrifying, and yet oddly exhilarating notion, if I were being perfectly honest.

Between the little bit of alcohol I'd consumed and the excitement that thrummed in my veins, I practically bounced all the way back to the bar after leaving Whit.

Only Hux wasn't there.

Both our stools were empty, and the bartender had already grabbed up the drinks and was wiping down the countertop as if we were never even there. I glanced toward the pool tables, wondering if maybe he'd gone there.

"He ain't here, sweetheart."

I whirled at the bartender's smokey voice. "Do you know where he went?" I asked, making my way to the bar.

She nodded her head at the doors leading outside. "He closed out the tab and left a few minutes ago."

Worry and confusion ate at me, writhing in my stomach like snakes. "I don't understand," I breathed out, more to myself than anyone else.

I mean, I saw how upset he'd gotten when I'd asked about his accident. His hands trembled with anger as he'd downed my margarita like it was nothing but a glass of orange juice. But I thought we'd gotten past that. He seemed calm enough when I went to the bathroom with Whit.

"He's been known to be like that," the bartender replied.

My gaze snapped to hers, a frown drawing on my lips. "What do you mean?"

"Huxson Lane always had a bit of a temper."

"How do you know him?"

I'd noticed earlier when she'd recognized him. The awe in her voice, the look of excitement on her face had given me major celebrity vibes, but I didn't know of a Huxson Lane. Maybe he was like a local singer or something?

"Darlin'…just about every damn cowboy in Texas knows who he is. He was a two time World Champion bull rider before his accident."

I didn't know anything about rodeos, but *two time World Champion* sounded pretty important.

"You should look him up. He was incredible. It's a shame what happened." She offered me a wistful shrug.

My heart ached for him. He must have lost so much. But none of that answered *why* he'd left. I had to find him. First off, something told me he would be the sort of prideful to try and walk himself all the way home. And second, I couldn't just let him leave. I'd felt something with him. A spark. A connection. He may be stubborn and drunk and willing to throw it all away, but I wasn't, goddamn it.

So, after thanking the bartender, I hurried out of the bar, hoping, *praying* to God I found him. The moon had risen high into the night sky, but the town still teemed with life. I glanced right then left as I stood in the middle of the sidewalk before The Haystack. Oh God, he could have gone either way. *Uphill. Downhill. Left. Right.*

Biting my lip, I took a deep breath and headed downhill toward the right. *Please let me find him.*

I made it half a block before I found his dark figure leaning against the wall of what appeared to be another bar. This one had a band playing. Something country and a bit twangy from the sound of it. He bobbed his head to the beat and pressed something to his lips.

Relief flushed some of the worry from my veins, but a hint of it still remained. I still had questions. Like why he'd left?

"Hux," I said hesitantly as I approached.

He tensed as I came to a stop beside him, a cloud of smoke billowing out from his lips as he exhaled. The scent was sweet, not bitter like a cigarette. Tobacco, then. So it wasn't vanilla I'd smelled on him earlier. Made sense.

"What do you want?" His tone was brusque, uninviting. He didn't even look my way as he spoke, but instead faced toward the street, his gaze upturned like he was looking up at the star-flecked sky. I wondered if he missed seeing it. I know I would if I were in his position.

The coldness in his voice cut deep, but I did my best to ignore it as I asked, "Why did you leave?"

He just shrugged and pressed his sweet smelling cigar to his lips once more, taking a deep drag before blowing it out slowly. "Why are you here, Quinn?" He sounded tired. Defeated. And sad. So sad. But why? What had happened in the few minutes I'd been in the bathroom?

"When I came back you were gone. I wanted to make sure you were okay."

"I've been blind for damn near three years, darlin', and I've managed just fine. I don't need help and I don't need pity." He flicked the ash from his cigarillo before pressing it to his lips once more.

God, he was being a dick, but even as frustration sparked to life in me, I got the feeling his anger wasn't geared at me in particular. "Do you think that's why I came to find you?" I asked softly. "Out of pity?"

He shrugged, another cloud of smoke escaping him. "Wouldn't be the first person."

The admission broke my heart. "I would never do that."

"Why are you wastin' your night on me, Quinn? Why you botherin' with some washed up, deadbeat cowboy who ain't ever gonna be anythin' more in life than a blind has been?"

And there was the root of his anger. Presented with such harsh, raw honesty that it brought tears to my eyes. He hated his situation. Hated himself.

He might think he was worthless. Washed up. But I didn't see that. I saw strength. And grit. And perseverance. Even as my hands trembled with sadness, I grabbed his free hand in both of mine and settled before him. "I like you, Hux. You're honest and brash and you aren't afraid to speak your mind. I like how you make me feel. I feel...seen. Which may not make any sense, but I feel like I can be myself with you."

He huffed and put out his cigar, but something soft washed over his features as he faced my direction. "Yeah, I see you, Quinn." And the way he said it, so sad and quiet, I wasn't sure if he understood what I meant or if he was just being condescending.

"I would never ever lead you on," I whispered.

he huffed, though there wasn't much conviction. With a rush of confidence, I lifted a hand to his chest and bunched my fingers into the fabric of his shirt, drawing him down to me even as I pushed up on tiptoe.

I brushed my lips against his, the sweet taste of tobacco enveloping me. For a moment, he didn't move. Didn't so much as breathe. Fear trickled to life within my soul. Had I made a mistake? Had I taken it too far? Been too bold? Too forward? My heart fluttered nervously in my chest, beating against my ribs like a bird trapped in a cage.

Then one of his hands was in my hair, the other dragging my body to his, and he kissed me with a fierceness that stole the air from my lungs. I melted into his touch, riding the wave of desire that he created in me.

How could I feel this alive, this wild, this free with someone I'd just met? I'd been with Devin for years and never felt an inkling of this. Was this normal? Was this what it was supposed to feel like?

I pulled away first, breaking the kiss, my breath coming out shallow and rapid. Releasing his shirt, I pressed my palm to his chest and said softly, "Did that feel like a pity kiss to you?"

His hand slid from my hair before coming up to clutch my chin, tilting my face up toward his. And even though I knew it wasn't possible, it's like that sunglasses stare saw straight through me, down into the deepest, darkest parts of my soul. A ripple of desire went through me. "I think I might need more convincin'." His words were husky, low, deep.

Laughter flowed from me, along with a wave of excitement. Pressing up on tiptoe, I kissed him once more. There was an intensity, a ferocity to his touch, his kisses that made me feel like I was drowning, but I didn't mind one bit. I didn't care that we were making out in the middle of the sidewalk. I didn't care that any and everyone could see us. The entire world might as well not even exist right now. Not as his mouth moved against mine, and he held me as if I were a precious treasure.

I could get drunk off the lust that pumped through me. I wanted him. I wanted every inch of him that he was willing to give.

He broke the kiss this time, though he held me close. "What do you wanna do, darlin'?"

I'd never been one to think pet names were cute. Maybe because mine growing up had been *Queenie* or *my queen*, which just sounded so melodramatic and obnoxious. But there was something about the rough, deep sound of his voice and that sexy way he dropped the 'g' with his accent that melted me like butter.

"Wanna go inside? The band sounds kinda good." I pressed a kiss to his lips. "Or we could go back to the house and go on that walk?" Another kiss. "Or we could…" my words trailed off, but the implication hung in the air between us.

His grip on me tensed just the slightest bit. "You want that?" Disbelief rang in his words.

How could he not think of himself as a catch? So what if he couldn't see? He was still plenty capable. Plenty endearing. Plenty funny.

I'd just have to show him, I guess.

The realization hit me like a freight train. I wasn't usually a hook up kinda girl. I wasn't made for a one-night stand. Well, at least I hadn't been with Devin. I didn't have any experience other than him. Just the thought of standing here, wrapped in Hux's arms, kissing him in public—Devin never would have stood for that.

Good thing I'm not with him anymore.

If I were being honest, I'd definitely leveled up. And I'd be damned if I let this opportunity slip through my fingers. Not when Hux's touch scorched my soul and made me feel alive.

So, I kissed him once more, slow and deep, letting every unspoken emotion pass between us. When I pulled back, I nipped at his bottom lip teasingly before murmuring, "I want you, Hux."

The appreciative growl of approval that rumbled out of his chest sent a shiver down the length of my spine. "Let's get back to the house, then darlin'."

Chapter Nine
Nicotine

Quinn

IT ONLY TOOK US about fifteen minutes to get back to the ranch, but it might as well have been a lifetime. It didn't help that Hux wouldn't stop teasing me. Between his whisper-soft kisses, the gentle scrape of his rough hands on my thighs, the gravelly, hushed murmurs in my ear—my body zinged with desire and anticipation.

The main house was silent as I led Hux quietly through the back door. My heart thundered in my chest so loudly I'm surprised Hux didn't hear it. Surprised the entire house didn't hear it, to be honest. But we made it to the room I was staying in without incident.

"Here we are," I said, turning on the light and leading him into the middle of the room. I dropped his hand, a flood of nerves slamming into me so hard it made me falter. What if...what if I didn't have enough experience? What if I sucked? What if I left him disappointed? He was older than me, after all, and most likely more experienced.

My doubts withered away like ash on the wind as he reached for me. And then his lips were on mine, an intensity in his touch and kiss that left me breathless. My hands trailed over the planes of his muscled chest before sliding up around his neck. I pulled off his cowboy hat, spearing the fingers of my free hand into his dark shoulder-length hair.

He pulled away enough to warn, "Make sure not to put the brim side down."

"Why?" I asked, a frown sneaking its way onto my face. That's exactly how I had planned to put it down.

"Cowboy tradition. It brings bad luck. Just don't do it." His words weren't harsh, but there was a sense of urgency to his tone.

Breaking out of his grip, I placed it down the proper way on my nightstand and returned to him, gazing up at his face and frowning once more. Tentatively, I reached up toward his glasses. "Can I take these off?"

I hadn't seen his eyes yet, and the need to see him fully—no hat, no sunglasses—well, it burned so fiercely I couldn't ignore it.

He hesitated, a muscle in his jaw clenching, but after a moment he offered a single, curt nod. I went slowly, carefully as I pulled the sunglasses off, folded them, and placed them on the nightstand. He blinked a few times, his gaze settling in my direction.

Holy God, he was handsome.

I traced my fingertips along the corner of his brow, taking in everything about his beautifully chiseled features. His eyes—they were like twin pools of liquid amber, swirling with flecks of random gold.

"Your eyes are the same color as whiskey," I murmured.

He chuckled. "Beats shit-brown, I guess."

I scoffed. "Who said you have shit-brown eyes?" They were absolutely *not*.

"My dad."

"Well, he's an idiot," I blurted out before clapping a hand over my mouth. *Oh my God, did I really just say that out loud*?

But if Hux was offended he didn't let on. In fact, he laughed, the sound a deep rumble in his throat. Both of his hands moved to my hips before gliding up my body—following the curves of my waist, along the outsides of my breasts. His rough fingertips scraped gently along my chest as he trailed them up the column of my neck before finally cupping my jaw. The movement was slow, measured, as if he were memorizing every inch of me.

My breath left me in a whoosh, my legs turning all wobbly as a wave of desire so great, so terrifying, and yet so exhilarating swept through that I feared it might knock me out completely.

His lips twitched upward, but genuine curiosity rang in his words. "You like that?"

I nodded, biting my bottom lip as I tried to get my bearings and form a response. "The way you touched me...it's like you're trying to learn my body."

What the hell was I even saying? Did that make any sense? Probably not.

Hux laughed, though, pressing a whisper-soft caress to my lips before moving on to the corner of my mouth, then my chin, my jaw. "That's exactly—" A string of kisses along my cheekbone. "What I'm—" The gentlest touch of his lips to my nose. "Tryin' to do." He finished with the softest ghost of a kiss to my forehead.

Tears welled in my eyes. How was it possible that his admission both saddened me beyond measure and filled me with so much burning need? It was the ultimate paradox. He couldn't see me, had no idea what I looked like, and yet, I felt more desired, more wanted, more *seen* than I ever had in my life.

No one had ever touched me, kissed me, caressed me like that.

I wrapped my fingers around his wrists while he still held my face. "More," I whispered.

I wanted him to do so much more.

It's like a chord in him snapped, whatever restraint holding him back vanishing entirely. One of his hands knotted in my hair, and he pulled it enough to tear a moan from my lips. His mouth clashed with mine, his tongue brushing past my lips and demanding entrance. I gave in—happily, wholeheartedly, enjoying the possessive hold he had on me. Not breaking the kiss, I guided him slowly back to the bed, stopping when my legs came into contact with the edge. Pulling back, I tugged at his shirt, wanting—no, needing to see more of him. He had too much on. I wanted it off.

He obliged me, breaking contact long enough to rip his shirt off. I only had a moment to admire the expanse of tan skin, tattoos, and rippling muscles before he leaned in for me once more, but what I saw stole my breath. God, he was cut.

"Holy God," I breathed. "You're gorgeous."

He smirked, a grunt of approval rumbling in his chest. Then his hands found my shirt, and he pulled it off slowly, inch by inch—his hands roving over each and every curve of my torso and chest once he'd pulled it off. He pushed me back gently, a silent demand to sit, and I obeyed. His fingers trailed down my hips and along my legs before he pulled off each white cowboy boot and sock, using the same measured movements as before. This time he peppered kisses to my legs as well, the feel of his scruff teasing and tickling the sensitive skin of my thighs.

I writhed beneath him, a little moan falling from me as my body melted beneath his touch. I laid back on the bed when his hands found my waist, feeling their way for the button and zipper of my shorts. Lifting my hips, I helped him shimmy the fabric over the curve of my ass until I finally laid before him in nothing but my favorite black bra and thong.

I waited for the nerves. The trickle of typical fear. I'd always been a bit self-conscious. But the worry and fear never came. Not as he knelt before me and pressed a kiss to my inner thigh—like I was some sort of goddess he worshiped. Desire flickered throughout every inch of me, stoking the fires of my soul.

A sharp gasp wrenched out of me as my nerves ignited like fireworks. His warm breath tickled my skin as he chuckled in approval, his kisses continuing their dangerous path toward the apex of my thighs. It was too much. Too much tension. Too much teasing. And he hadn't even done anything yet.

"Hux," I breathed, my chest rising and falling to a fast, shallow rhythm.

He paused, kneeling between my legs. "Do you not want this?"

"No, I do. I just—I've never done this before."

He stilled, hands poised firmly on my thighs. "Are you a virgin?"

"No!" I replied quickly. Too quickly from the look of silent worry that blossomed across his face. Oh God, I was making a mess of this, wasn't I? "No, I'm not," I began again as I sat up and crossed my arms over my chest, feeling the sudden nerve to cover myself. "I'm not a virgin. I've just—"

"No one's gone down on you before?" He asked the question so casually it gave me pause. My cheeks burned with heat and, honestly, I was glad that he couldn't see me at that moment.

My only experience with anything involving intimacy was Devin, and he wasn't the most, well, intimate of lovers. I mean, we waited over a year before actually doing the deed, and then even once we did, it was infrequent at best. Which sounded really weird now, being that most of the photos on social media of him and his new fiancé showed them all over each other.

But that was *so* not what I wanted to think about right now.

I looked at Hux and nodded, but he didn't reply. Because— "Oh God, I'm sorry. I did it again. I nodded and you didn't see." I groaned, pursing my lips together painfully tight for a moment as a wave of guilt washed over me, fizzling out some of the desire. God, I was really making a mess of this, wasn't I? "Ugh, that sounded awful. I'm so sorry."

Hux let out a low, throaty chuckle and I just about died. Of course, I'd manage to take a hot, steamy moment and pour ice cold water onto it. If my cheeks had burned before, I wouldn't be surprised if I burst into flames from embarrassment.

Way to fucking go, Quinn. I groaned, falling back against the bed. But the groan turned to a gasp as Hux's hands tugged on my thong, sliding it slowly down my legs as he took his time caressing my skin as he did so.

I pushed up onto my elbows, glancing down at him. "What are—" My words fell away, dying in my throat as every nerve ending sang to life inside of me when he pressed his mouth to my clit. I cried out, my elbows giving way as I fell back against the bed. My eyelids slammed shut at the onslaught of desire surging through me.

Holy God, I burned. Every inch of me felt hot and tight, like my skin had become too small for my body almost.

He used those same measured, teasing strokes with his tongue as he had while exploring my body with his hands and lips moments ago. And each stroke. Each brush. Each lap of his tongue was like adding more kindling to a bonfire. I burned. Brighter. Hotter. Higher. So high that I didn't think I could go any higher. I hung there, poised on the precipice of my desire.

My fingertips held a death grip on the bed sheets and it took everything in me to simply *breathe*. My heart heaved and battered around in my chest, thumping so hard I thought it might crack a rib or something. I'd never felt anything like this. It was almost too much. Too much sensation and tension and desire. It hurt from the intensity, but a good kind of hurt. The kind that bordered right on that line between pleasure and pain.

"Hux," I breathed, forcing myself up onto my elbows once more as his tongue continued its delicious punishment.

His whiskey brown gaze snapped up to mine, and even though I know it wasn't possible, it's like his stare was focused solely on me. "Come for me, darlin'." Gaze still somehow locked with mine, he slid a finger inside of me, dragging his tongue over my clit in a slow, steady pressure that sent me hurtling over the edge.

I cried out as my orgasm erupted through me like an explosion. Every inch of me ignited, seared, burned as he pumped his finger inside of me, lapping at my pussy, prolonging that wildfire raging within me for what felt like an eternity. And as the flames slowly ebbed and withered away, as the heat licking at every inch of me started to subside, his mouth and hand left my core. But the touches didn't stop. They shifted.

"Good girl," he cooed, trailing his hands and mouth up over my hips, along my torso, before cupping a breast in one of his calloused hands, the gentle scrape of them against my skin sending a jolt of desire through me.

A weak moan fell from my lips. He chuckled once more and I felt his body settle beside mine, but I couldn't open my eyes. It was as if every inch of me had turned to mush. Like that orgasm had taken everything out of me. All I could do was just lay here and...*feel*.

Hux's voice in my ear was little more than a gravelly whisper. "Did you like that?"

I nodded. Words seemed so far away at the moment.

A soft laugh rumbled from him. "I'm gonna take your silence as enjoyment, unless you say otherwise, darlin'."

I forced my eyes open and found him propped up on an elbow beside me, his amber gaze aimed my way once more, but not focused on my face.

"That was..." I let out a content sigh. "I've never felt anything like that ever in my life."

"Have you ever come before?" The words weren't asked with condescension or judgment, just mere curiosity.

"Not like that," I said on a breathy sigh. Never like that.

"You want that again?"

And maybe it was the husky tone of his voice or the way his fingertips traced patterns over my side and teased the outer swell of my breast, but desire sparked low in my belly once more.

I pressed a hand to his tan, muscular chest. He had a tattoo right over his heart. A beautifully drawn black and white cow skull with some sort of snake slithering through one of the eyeholes. Connected to it, but looking like it had been carved out of his flesh was the outline of the state of Texas with an image of pastures in the outline. I wanted to trace my fingers over it, as well as the others marked into his flesh. His right arm was almost fully sheathed in more black and white artwork that I'd love to admire.

Later though. Right now I had more pressing matters to attend.

"What about you?" I asked, my fingers moving down his torso and toward his waist.

I watched his muscles ripple and flex at my feather-soft touches. He inhaled sharply. "Don't you worry about me, darlin'. Right now it's all about you."

I couldn't help but smile at that—from the way he called me darlin' to how invested he was in my pleasure. I can't say I'd ever been treated like this, but I could definitely get used to it. Though, as interested as I was in letting him continue his teasing, I wanted to give back as well. So, with newfound confidence, I brushed a hand over the front of his jeans, feeling the hard swell of his cock beneath the fabric.

"I want you to fuck me, please."

His resolve broke, shattering the cool calm he held on his facial features. Need and hunger shone in his light, amber gaze before he leaned in and consumed me in a soul-shattering, time-stopping kiss.

Chapter Ten
The Worst Way

Hux

"*I WANT YOU TO fuck me, please.*"

I don't know what I loved more, the fact that this sweet, sunshine soul had a mouth on her, or the fact she asked me to *please* fuck her. *Manners and a foul mouth*. One thing was for sure though, I was helpless but to oblige her.

There was something enchanting about Quinn. Maybe it was her innocence, her honesty, but *something* drew me to her. She was a beacon of light...of hope in a starless night-time sky.

I kissed her, enjoying the feel of her lips on mine and how reactive her body was to my touch. The hisses and moans and little gasps of pleasure did something to my soul, spurring me on.

Her hands fumbled with my belt buckle before moving on to my button and zipper. I broke the kiss, rocking back enough to grab out my wallet from my back pocket.

"Wh–what are you doing?" Quinn's tone echoed with concern and confusion.

I felt around for the condom Travis had handed me before we'd gone out tonight. Maybe he wasn't a complete dumbass after all. "I'm looking for a—" My words fell away, frustration taking over as I struggled to do the most basic fucking task. I'd just put it in there.

"Oh, a condom?" At least she didn't sound upset anymore. "I'm on birth control. So, if you can't find it..." Her words trailed off, but I got the implication easily enough.

Well, shit. I tossed my wallet, and a giggle escaped her as her hands found my waist again. Her soft, delicate fingers seared me as she dragged them over my flesh, but I didn't mind. I'd gladly burn for a taste of her.

I rose from the bed for a moment, shucking off my boots, socks, and jeans before returning to her. Peppering kisses to her soft, flawless skin, I slowly situated myself atop her. I know she'd said she wasn't a virgin, but a part of me wondered just how much or little experience she had. But despite her lack of confidence earlier, she moved with grace and a quiet surety as she guided my hips to her cunt

.

Her gasp as I slid slowly into her nearly shattered all of my resolve. Fuck, she felt good. So damn good. I picked up a slow pace, enjoying the feel of her beneath me. Quinn's hands slid up and down my back while she rained kisses on my chest, my shoulders, my lips.

I hated to sound like a damn hopeless romantic, but fuck...it's like she'd been made specifically for me. The way she fit and moved against me. The way her sweet, tight cunt fit around my cock. Each pump of my hips sent the sweetest damn moans from her lips, and that alone nearly did me in. Fuck, I wished I could see her. I wondered if the pleasure had gotten to her yet, forcing her eyes shut as she let the desire move through her. Or maybe she wanted more?

"This good, darlin'?" I asked, pressing a kiss to her jaw before trailing a path up to her ear. This close it was easy enough to almost feel like I wasn't blind. There were only so many places to caress and touch. "How are you feelin'?"

The appreciative little moan that fell from her lips as she arched into me sent a ripple of desire straight to my cock—enough to make me see stars. Fuck, I was close.

Her fingers continued their dance across my back, and her voice was husky as she spoke. "Harder."

My lips tugged into a grin against the column of her neck. "Gladly, darlin'," I growled out.

Grabbing the back of her left leg, I pulled it up high on my side, stretching her hips wider as I pumped in and out. The moan that came out of her sent another surge of lust through me.

Goddamn.

We moved in perfect tandem, her fingertips digging into my flesh as she clung to me. Each little sound from her, each pump of my hips sent my desire swelling and surging within me.

"That's it. You're doin' so good, darlin'. You're takin' me so well."

"F-fuck yes," she breathed, her voice a sultry melody I could listen to on repeat.

Her cuss was somehow both the most wholesome and sexiest thing I'd ever heard, and I liked what it did to me. The emotion that it brought as my heart thumped a fast, thunderous beat in my chest. I quickened my pace, ramped up the intensity, thrusting into her wet pussy in hard, deep strokes that sent that wave of desire threatening to break upon me at any moment. Her breathing had already turned ragged, her moans and cries picking up in volume. If those were any gauge, I'd say she was close as well. Dipping my mouth in the direction of her chest, I peppered kisses across her skin until I found the swell of her breast. Not slowing my pace, I nipped at her peaked nipple before running my tongue over it to soothe the hurt. She cried out, her body rippling beneath me, her fingernails digging into my shoulders.

"Hux," she warned, the word grated out, like she was clenching her teeth.

My name on her lips was like a siren song. I didn't think I could last any longer even if I tried. Repeating the action, I sucked her nipple into my mouth and slammed into her in a quick, brutal succession. Her body writhed beneath mine, her own orgasm taking her, her inner walls clenching around my cock tightly. Bursts of light erupted against the eternal blackness of my vision as I came hard and fast. So fast I didn't even manage to pull out.

Well, fuck. She was—that was...

"Fuck." I blew out a breath and my muscles turned to jello and gave way as I rolled off her and laid on my back. I hadn't come like that in a long, long fucking time. I could tell myself that maybe it had to do with the fact I hadn't gotten laid in at least two years, but I'd be a liar. This was different.

I was smitten. Enchanted. Enamored. Some would even say fucked. Call it whatever the hell you wanted, but I knew one thing for certain.

I wanted more.

Quinn snuggled up against my left side, resting her head on my chest as we both took a moment to control our breathing. For a time, silence lingered in the room—not the awkward, stilted kind, but the kind of content, peaceful quiet that reminded me of watching the sunrise or the stars bursting to life in the nighttime sky.

My fingers trailed lazy paths up and down her side and she let out a soft, appreciative sigh that both managed to soothe and exhilarate me.

There was something different about Quinn.

I'd never been with anyone like her. One so earnest, honest, innocent. The old me hadn't wanted to deal with someone like her, and inevitably breaking their soft heart. Too messy. Too many strings to detach and sever when I inevitably moved on. I'd be lying if I said I hadn't been wild and selfish, and treated my relationships a little too callously back then.

But since the accident, well, I hadn't dated much. At all, really. I'd tried once or twice, but most people only wanted to be around me because of who I had been, not who I was now. The two were night and day.

I wasn't Huxson Lane anymore. I wasn't a bull rider. I wasn't a rodeo cowboy.

I was washed up, used, broken.

Most people don't wanna take time to fix broken things. Not when it's so much quicker and easier to find something new, better even. Quinn didn't strike me as the type to be afraid of a little wear and tear, though. Not when she could breathe life back into something. I still remembered what she'd said at the bar. I don't think I'd ever get that out of my head.

"Truth for a truth," she said, breaking the silence.

I huffed. "Is this another one of your drinkin' games—that we failed at, by the way."

Her laugh was light and warm. "Speak for yourself. You're the one who wasn't playing by the rules and drinking out of turn."

Well, she had me there. "Alright, so what's your truth?"

"When you pulled out your wallet, for a second I thought you were planning on paying me like I was...like I was a whore or something."

I laughed. That explained her reaction then. "Why the hell would you think that?"

"I don't know," she laughed. "I have really weird intrusive thoughts, I guess."

"If you say so." I kissed the top of her head. "Alright, my truth now, I guess. I'm sorry but also not sorry for leavin' earlier."

I felt her head shift, and I could just envision her cocking her head to the side like a confused puppy. Probably an adorable golden retriever or something. "What do you mean?" she asked.

"Well, I'm sorry for stormin' off like that and worryin' you. I shouldn't have done that. But I ain't sorry for this... And I doubt this would've happened had I not left."

She pressed a kiss to my chest, the place her lips touched burning to life with desire. "Well, I'm sorry not sorry too, then. I'm sorry that you would think I would lead you on like that. But I'm glad that we ended up here as well."

Silence descended once more and my eyelids grew heavy. I focused on the sound of her breathing, the feel of her soft, warm skin on mine—like velvet or silk.

Her voice sounded far away when she spoke, and it was only then I realized I'd started to drift off. "Was that—was I okay?"

I stilled beneath her. The sound of her voice. The timidness, the fear—I clenched my jaw. Who the hell made her feel like she wasn't good enough? Some fucking asshat who probably didn't know the first thing about pleasing a woman went and made her feel like she'd done something wrong. That was the only explanation i could think of for her to ask that.

My hand found its way to her cheek, and even though I couldn't see her, I forced her attention on me. "You were fuckin' amazing, darlin'." The sound that came out of her was like a mixture of a sob and a huff. It pulled on my heartstrings. "Why would you think that you weren't good enough?" I couldn't hold back the anger in my voice, and I prayed to God she understood it wasn't aimed at her, but whatever fucking dickhead made her feel less than.

"I just...I don't know. I feel like I don't know what I'm doing. I..." The bed shifted and the warmth of her body vanished, her sweet, already familiar scent drifting away. I bit back a curse, instantly missing her touch.

So I sat up too, though I didn't reach for her. Not yet. Something told me she needed this moment. To sort out her emotions. Her thoughts.

When she spoke, her voice was small, weak. "I've only ever been with one guy, and, well...sex was always one of our weak points. I guess I'm just a bit self-conscious because of that."

"You got nothin' to be insecure about. Whatever problem that asshat had was on him, not on you."

Choked laughter escaped her, but sadness still lurked beneath the surface as she sniffled. "I'm sorry, I'm a stupid, sobbing mess."

Fuck, was she crying? What the hell?

No, I wouldn't allow that. Reaching forward, I scooped her up into my lap. She melted against me, fitting in my arms like she'd been made for them. Were soulmates a thing, or was I just so fucking whipped that I'd believe anything was a sign at this point? Was I so starved for a connection with someone that I was making shit up?

No, this wasn't me just being desperate. I didn't believe that. Maybe with someone else. But, I don't know, Quinn didn't strike me as the type to just sleep with anyone. Not when she clearly had a past.

"Hey...hey now, no cryin'," I murmured as she wrapped her legs around my waist and rested her head in the crook of my neck, right between my collarbone and jaw. Her body quaked with quiet sobs.

Well, shit. I hadn't expected things to take such a drastic turn. I found her face with my hands and cupped her cheeks. "Quinn, hey. What's goin' on?"

Another sniffle. "I'm sorry. I don't even know. I just—you're probably used to being with these super confident, super sexy women, then here I am, all self-conscious and pathetic and insecure."

"Who said you aren't sexy as hell?" I asked, pressing a whisper-soft kiss to her lips.

Her weak disbelieving laugh spoke volumes of what she thought of herself. "I'm not. Trust me."

I gripped her chin, not too tightly, but with a firmness that I hoped urged her to understand what I meant was important. "You don't get to tell me what I think is sexy, darlin'. You don't have to agree, but you got no control over what I think. I like you, Quinn. I like how you make me feel. I like that with you, the darkness doesn't seem so, well, it doesn't seem so dark. So fuckin' bleak." I blew out a breath. "More days than not, I think of how much I hate what's become of my life, but not today. So are you the most confident, experienced woman I've ever slept with? No. But you're the first I've slept with who's made me feel alive again. And I think that's pretty fuckin' sexy."

Her fingertips brushed against my eyebrow, pushing my hair off my face. I wished I didn't flinch at movement, but people touching my face always was a bit disconcerting now.

"Sorry," she murmured, before asking weakly, "You hate your life?"

And there was so much sadness, so much honest curiosity in her words, that I almost told her everything. About the accident. The months of rehab after. Learning to walk again. Learning to live again—if what you could say I did now was living. Some days it felt like I did nothing more than survive.

I moved my hand from her chin, sliding it back along her jaw and into her hair. It was soft and silky and smelled nice. I kissed her, slow and deep, before pulling away only far enough to whisper against her lips, "This ain't about me, Quinn. Right now's all about you."

"How are you even real?" she asked, a sense of awe in her words.

I brushed my lips against hers once more. "I could say the same about you, darlin'."

An appreciative moan escaped her. "I like when you call me that."

I let out a low chuckle and gripped her hair a little tighter, tilting her head back so I could rain kisses down her neck. She seemed to like that too. "Oh, yeah? How 'bout you tell me what else you like?"

Her voice was tentative, but husky as she whispered, "How about I show you?"

I grinned against the base of her throat, biting gently at her collarbone before kissing the hurt away. "I'd like that very much."

I took my time, learning every single inch of her. Her wants, her needs, her likes. What made her toes curl, what made her scream with desire. And when the two of us finally settled in for the night, when every nerve ending in my body was so awake and alive and burning that even the feel of her wrapped up in my arms was so intense it almost hurt, I knew that in the morning nothing would be the same.

Which was a terrifying, yet exhilarating notion, to be honest.

Chapter Eleven

Til You Can't

QUINN

I AWOKE TO A loud crash, followed by a muffled curse.

What the hell?

Bolting upright, I blinked the sleep from my eyes, taking a moment to adjust to the low light of the room. Where was I? *Oh, right*. Memories of the night before swirled to life in my head like tendrils of smoke. I glanced at the empty spot in bed beside me.

Oh my God. Hux. Was he okay?

I pulled the topsheet from the bed, wrapping it around me, and hurried toward the source of the crash—the bathroom.

It was dark in there as Hux's familiar growl echoed off the tiles. Flicking the light on, I found him in the middle of the bathroom, looking lost and pissed as all hell. His lips were drawn down into a scowl, his brows furrowed beneath his sunglasses. The curtain to the shower had somehow been knocked down. *Must've been the crashing sound then.*

"Hey, you okay?" I asked tentatively, so as not to startle him.

He stilled for a moment, every muscle in his body going rigid, before he loosed a breath and turned to me. "I was tryin' to leave and not wake you, but apparently that didn't fuckin' happen."

My heart sank. Why had he wanted to leave without me knowing? Did he not want to see me? The answer was like a shout in my head as doubt settled like stones in my stomach. "Oh," I said, defeat creeping into my tone.

"Wait—" Hux took a hesitant step toward me. Then another. And another. I reached out and pressed a hand to his chest so he didn't bump into me. "I didn't leave because I was tryin' to sneak out. Well, not cuz I didn't wanna see you or anythin' like that. I just didn't wanna wake you up. I gotta go feed and get to work for the day, and, well, it seems unfair wakin' you up at 5:30 on a Sunday mornin'."

And just like that, he pulled me against him, caging his arms around me. Relief blossomed in my chest. How was it possible to feel so at ease in someone's arms? How was it possible he could take away my worries in a heartbeat, like the tide erasing footprints in the sand? "I'm sorry," I replied, "I know I'm being insecure, I just—"

He stopped my sentence right in its tracks with a gentle, yet insistent kiss to my lips. Butterflies seemed to flutter behind my ribcage.

"I know," he murmured against my mouth. "You don't gotta explain or apologize."

Drawing back to look up at him, I grabbed his hand. "Here, I'll walk you out. You won't get very far in here. We're in the bathroom."

He huffed but let me lead him out into the room. After changing quickly, I grabbed his hand once more, partly to help him navigate, but mostly because I enjoyed the feel of his calloused hand in mine. And maybe, possibly, definitely, because I was terrified that after he left things would be different. So for now, for these next few minutes, I'd savor his touch and presence.

"So," I asked, glancing over at him as we walked down the quiet hallway. "What all do you do here for work?"

I wasn't trying to be rude, but I was genuinely curious because I didn't know the first thing about cowboys or ranch work or what all that entailed. And also because, well, I couldn't imagine having to do it without my vision.

"I feed, water, and work all the horses mostly, since none of these dipshit cowboys can train worth a shit. I can buck hay easily enough, and as long as one of the guys gives me directions, I can hold my own with most manual labor."

"You do all that without..." My words trailed off, uncertainty welling up inside of me. I didn't want to sound callous or rude.

"Without seeing?" he finished. "You can say it. It ain't gonna offend me."

"I just don't want to be insensitive," I said, pulling him to a stop for a moment as we came to the front door. Opening it, I led him onto the front porch.

He shrugged. "It's the truth. I can't see for shit. I'm blind. It's a part of me now, as much as I hate it. There ain't nothin' offensive about you sayin' it out loud."

He said it with such nonchalance that it both eased my fears a bit and made my heart hurt. But it was clear from his tone, from the way he talked about his situation, that he hated people making a big deal about it.

"I'm sorry." I gave his hand a soft, reassuring squeeze.

He pulled me into his arms and the butterflies in my ribcage started fluttering about once more. "Can we do this again?" he asked.

"The um—well, what part?" I sounded like an idiot, but the way his hooded, sunglasses stare bore into me made me nervous as all hell.

"All of it. Whatever you want. I could show you around—I mean, well, you could take me around and I'll tell you about what it means to me. I could take you to dinner too, if you wanted."

I smiled, warmth igniting in my chest. "I would like that very much."

He dipped his mouth toward mine and I kissed him, slow and sensual, enjoying the high I felt in his arms.

"How 'bout I pick you up right here around six-ish?" he asked as he pulled away enough to utter the words.

"Sounds good. Oh God, what should I wear?" The question was more for me than him, but he chuckled and answered anyway.

A wry grin came to his lips. "It don't matter to me, it all looks the same anyways. Wear what makes you comfortable."

I couldn't hold back the gasp that escaped me. It was going to take me a minute to get used to how casually he talked about his blindness. But he was right. It was a part of him. "You would think that would make it easier, but it doesn't."

He kissed the top of my head. "Don't overthink it, darlin'."

I blew out a nervous laugh. "Ha! You might not have noticed yet, but over-thinking is basically my entire personality."

He laughed, a low, deep, genuine sound that made my stomach do som-ersaults of excitement. "Well, I've always been partial to sundresses." His hand holding me against him slid down the small of my back and over the swell of my ass. Leaning in, he rumbled, "The shorter the better."

My head fell back, a husky laugh floating out of me as I wrapped my arms around his neck and kissed him. "I think I can make that happen."

"Good." His mouth descended on mine, and I didn't even mind that it was only 5:30 in the morning and it already felt so hot it was like I'd stepped into a bowl of soup. I got lost in Hux—in his touch, his scent, his taste. In that moment, it was just him and I. Nothing mattered, nothing existed but us.

"Ahem."

I startled at the sound of the masculine voice off to my right. Lurching back a step, but still wrapped in Hux's embrace, I glanced down the steps of the front porch to find my dad watching us. He'd thankfully traded in the obnoxious cowboy getup for something more familiar—one of his sleeveless t-shirts and a pair of workout shorts. He'd always been a jogger and an early riser. It was good to see that, at least, some things didn't change about him.

"Quinn, you're up early." His hard gaze landed on me, and I knew we'd be having a *conversation* later. But something darkened in his eyes as he glanced at Hux. "Huxson...shouldn't you be working?"

I scowled, my eyes narrowing to slits at his harsh tone.

Hux released me and nodded in my dad's direction. "I was just on my way to feed, sir."

"Well, I suggest you see to it." There was a layer of coldness to his words that he rarely ever used.

Anger bristled in my chest at my dad's callous tone. I mean, I'm sure it was probably a shock to see his daughter making out with one of his employees, but really, did he have to be such a dick about it?

Hux made his way slowly down the steps, each footfall measured and unhurried—it still amazed me how he could manage so easily without a walking cane. Turning back once he got to the bottom of the porch steps, he called out, "See you tonight, Miss Quinn."

I smiled. The way he said my name...it made my knees weak. "Have a good day!"

I waited until Hux was out of earshot before I glared at my dad. "Really, Dad? 'I suggest you *see* to it? Don't you think that was a bit, I don't know, tone deaf?"

He scoffed, pushing his sweaty, sandy locks back off his head. "What? It's just a figure of speech."

"Why were you so rude to him?" I sighed.

"I wasn't. I could've written him up for being late." Again with the harsh, cold words. Again, I didn't understand.

"Really?" I crossed my arms over my chest. "It's not even 6 AM on a Sunday, who cares if he's a couple minutes late?"

My dad wiped at his brow with the back of his arm. "What kind of precedent does that set for the other hands? It isn't fair for me to just give out handouts because of his..."

"His disability? It's called accommodations, Dad. Which he has every right to. He manages to do all of this without even seeing, cut the guy some damn slack! Besides, since when are you a stickler for the rules? Aren't you the one who used to always say that the rules are more like strong suggestions? That they're meant to be bent...maybe even broken?"

He sighed, and for a moment I thought I'd gotten through to him, but when he leveled me with a fierce, determined stare, I realized there was no winning this fight. I was familiar with a losing battle when I saw one. "I don't want you seeing him, Quinn."

"Why?" I scoffed, rocking back at his words. Dad always had been particular about anyone I dated. No one was ever good enough for his little girl. I know he hadn't liked Devin, so I'd kept their interactions to a minimum.

"He's too old for you," Dad said with a shrug, walking up the porch steps slowly. To anyone else, it just looked like he was tired, but I knew he took the stairs more carefully ever since he tore his ACL the year after Mom passed when he went through one of his midlife crises and crashed his snowmobile. This whole ranch business was the, what, third or fourth crisis now? I'd lost track at this point honestly.

I barked out a bitter laugh. "That's really hypocritical, don't you think, Dad?"

A flash of guilt flickered on his face before hardening to resolve once more. Dad was one of the stubbornest people I knew. I swear, he could argue with a wall and win. "It's different for Georgette and I."

"Yeah, it's arguably worse." I pegged him with a hard stare, my head cocking to the side. "Hux and I have about a ten year age gap between us...you and Georgette though, it's what? Like, twenty, twenty-one years?"

He opened his mouth to reply, but I cut him off. I closed my eyes and sighed. "Look, Dad, I don't want to fight. I like him, why is that so bad?"

It was too early for this, and I hated that he seemed intent on trying to tear down the high of happiness I'd been riding since last night.

He chewed on his lip for a long moment. "He's not good enough."

I couldn't stop my eye roll or the huff of disbelief that managed to come out of me. "Really? Let me guess, it's because of—"

"It isn't about that at all, Quinn. He's got a bad attitude. He's always picking fights with Georgette—"

"Have you heard how she talks about him, Dad? If she's as awful to him as she was when she was talking to us, I don't really blame him." I bit the inside of my cheek and clenched my fists at my sides. I understood that he was marrying her, but it pissed me off he could defend her so easily after only being with her for not even two full months. He would fight harder for her than his own damn kid?

My dad let out a frustrated growl, his nostrils flaring at the unexpected challenge. I *never* stood up to him. I gave in easily, I didn't push the envelope. I backed down when the water got hot, or things got tough. I didn't like to cause problems. But maybe it was the fact that I was fed up with keeping my mouth shut, the fact I felt fiercely protective of Hux despite just meeting him, or the fact that I was tired of my dad telling me what I could and couldn't do, but I wasn't going to back down or cower.

"He's got no drive," my dad snapped, anger finally boiling over and shining brightly in his blue-green gaze—nearly identical to mine. "He's the oldest hand here and he seems content to do this for the rest of his life. I don't know if you're aware of this, Quinn, but ranch hands don't make much, and you've been given a life of luxury. You really think he's going to be able to take care of you the way you're used to being taken care of?"

I shook my head, tears brewing like storms in my eyes. Angry tears that my dad always saw as weakness. Sucking in a deep breath of air and exhaling slowly, I pegged him with a harsh, furious glare. "First off, I don't *need* anyone to take care of me. It's why I have a job. I don't need him or you to fund my lifestyle. Secondly, Hux is a two-time World Champion bull rider. That takes quite a bit of drive, if you ask me." I didn't know the first thing about bull riding, aside from the little clips I'd seen on TV or online, but from what I did know, it was dangerous and hard and took guts.

Dad shook his head, letting out a weak laugh. "Yeah, and look where that landed him."

My breath left me in a whoosh, his cold, callous, hateful words hitting me like a ton of bricks. It was my turn to shake my head. "I can't believe you just said that." Each word was slow, measured, and quaked with so much emotion I couldn't quite figure out which it was more of—fury, disbelief, hurt, sadness. "How could you say something so—" A tear fell down my cheek. "So fucking horrible?" I shook my head, my vision blurring as I glared at him.

If only Mom were here. I could envision it now. Mom would glare at him, hiss out his name, and give him a ration of shit until she'd talked some sense into him. It didn't matter if there was an audience or not, she'd put him in his place if he was out of line. God, I wished she was here still.

My dad sputtered for a reply, but I cut him off. "Mom would be so disappointed in you," I choked out, stomping down the steps.

"Qu-Queenie. Quinn, please." His words wobbled and wavered. I'd cut deep. *Good*. Maybe he'd start to get his head out of his ass. My dad had always been a bit grandiose, materialistic, enamored by bright, new, shiny things. But he had a good heart—I knew he did. Right now, he wasn't acting like it, and I had no doubt I knew at least part of the reason why. It was a five foot something bleached blonde bimbo whose mind was smaller than her goddamn daisy dukes.

And I'm supposed to plan their wedding.

One crisis at a time though, right? I needed to get away. Blow off some steam. Anything as long as it was far, far away from my dad. As if summoned by my thoughts, Whit appeared, walking up the driveway from the direction of the hands' bunkhouse as I walked toward it.

"Hey, girl! Oh—" Her bright smile faltered. "What's going on?"

I noted her rumpled clothes from the night before, her bare feet and cowboy boots bundled in one hand with her loose bun piled atop her head. She was a whole hot mess of a vibe, and somehow she still managed to rock the hell out of it.

Confidence, she'd probably say. I swear, if I could bottle it up and drink it by the gallons I would. I could use a bit of her confidence.

"Wanna grab coffee?" I asked.

She offered me a soft, reassuring smile. "Let's go."

You'D THINK FINDING A place to grab coffee would be easy enough, but not at seven in the morning on a Sunday. We'd finally found a place—a little hole in the wall called Sunshine's that was only open for breakfast and lunch. It had a cheery vibe, with black and white checkered tables and a sunshine and bee painted mural on both of the main walls. Sunflower arrangements sat on each of the tables while soft country ballads played in the background.

It was an adorable aesthetic, but all it seemed to do was mock me and my terrible mood as I sat across from Whitt.

"I can't believe your dad was being such a dick," Whit said, scooping a spoonful of oatmeal into her mouth. I bit back a gag and took a sip of my iced coffee. I understood Whit's healthy food journey, and I was all in support, but oatmeal was just one of those things I'd never be on board with. I'd rather die than eat it. Seriously.

I'd told her about how Dad had caught Hux and I on the front porch and the argument that ensued after.

Sighing, I met her gaze. "I know. It makes me furious. Like, I know that my dad isn't perfect. He says stupid shit sometimes, but he isn't malicious. What he said..." I bit my lip, shaking my head. "It reminded me of yesterday when Georgette was talking down about Hux. And that's not him."

Whit offered me a sympathetic look. "You sure you want him marrying her?"

"It's not about what I want," I replied with a shrug. "What I think of Georgette doesn't matter in the end. It's his life. He deserves to be happy, and if she does that, well, that's all I can ask for my dad. I don't have to like her."

"You're a hell of a lot more mature about it than I'd be. She's..." Whit took another bite of her oatmeal. "About as awful as this oatmeal." Scrunching her nose up, she finally pushed the bowl away from her.

I laughed. "I don't know how you even ate that much of it."

She grimaced and grabbed her coffee, downing a few large gulps. "Sheer force of will, I guess." She steepled her cup between her fingers and pegged me with a knowing smirk. "So, onto more interesting things... Hux is famous?"

I nodded. "Yeah, at least that's what the bartender said. I guess he was a pretty big bull rider."

"That's so cool! I wonder why he doesn't do it anymore."

I frowned, my head cocking to the side. "I mean, it's pretty obvious. He can't see, Whit."

She gave me a no-shit kind of look. "Obvi! But like *how* did he go blind?"

I shrugged. "I don't know, when I asked, he shut down. He was really closed off about it and I didn't want to press." It made me sad though. Sad that he couldn't talk about it. That he struggled with trying to find a place in this world after his accident.

"Have you looked him up at all online?"

I huffed a laugh. "No, I haven't really had time."

Whit's lips pulled up into a wolfish smirk, her brown eyes twinkling with mischief as she pulled out her phone. "Well, now we do."

I swear, if Whit wasn't a phenomenal hairdresser, she'd make an amazing detective...or a stalker. In less than a minute, she'd managed to find all of his social media accounts—all of which hadn't been updated in about three years—as well as some of his most noteworthy rides, and an entire google search worth of articles about his accident. She even managed to find the video of said accident. Placing the phone sideways on the table, she pressed the play button.

It was him riding a bull. My heart thumped ridiculously fast as I watched him. I didn't know the first thing about what he was doing, but it looked amazing. *He* looked amazing. But then all of a sudden the bull moved and bucked in a way that threw Hux with so much force that he launched forward and smacked into the bull's horns. I think he lost consciousness at that point, because he didn't move. Didn't try to disentangle his hand. The bull ran and bucked and tried to get him off, and Hux just hung there, looking like he was a ragdoll. Looking like he was dead.

My heart faltered and my stomach clenched into tight knots as I clapped a hand over my mouth—to hide my gasp or to stop the nausea rolling through me in waves, I wasn't quite sure. The clip ended and Whit looked up from her phone to me.

"Are you crying?" she asked, though the words were merely curious and not judgmental.

I frowned, pressing a hand to my cheek. Wetness clung to my fingertips. "I guess so," I replied with a sad huff.

"That was crazy," Whit said. "I never realized bull riding was so brutal."

I nodded, still trying to fight the wave of unease pounding through me. I don't even know why I was so upset and emotional over it. It's not like I'd been there. Not like I'd dated him at that point or even known he'd existed. But maybe it was seeing just how much that moment changed him. From videos and reels and photos on social media he'd seemed outgoing, lively, a bit reckless. But the Hux I knew was not like that at all. The Hux I knew was closed off, harsh, brutally honest.

"More days than not, I think of how much I hate what's become of my life..."

I understood why he didn't want to talk about it now. I think if I'd gone through something like that, I'd want to forget about it too.

"I can't believe that happened to him." I sighed, grabbing Whit's phone and clicking on her Instagram to scroll back through his page. My heart cracked and shattered a bit more at each photo or video I saw of him. He smiled so easily, he looked so happy and carefree.

I wondered if he'd still be like that now had he never gotten hurt.

But then I'd probably never have met him. And the Hux I'd met was just as intriguing, just as amazing—probably even more so—than the version of him before the accident. And at the risk of sounding callous, I was glad to have met this version of him. Because he was broken and raw and beautiful. He was honest and attentive and kind, and he made my heart race in a way I'd never known before. Didn't even know was possible.

"You like him, don't you?" Whit asked, her tone and gaze turning serious—oddly unlike her. "Like, really like him."

"I just met him." I placed her phone back on the table and reached for my iced coffee, though I made no attempt to drink it. My stomach was still in knots.

"And you didn't answer my question." She pegged me with a knowing look.

But I didn't want to talk about the emotions that fluttered to life in my chest at the thought of Hux right at the moment. Because I did like him. Probably a little—okay, way too much, considering I just met him. And if I already felt this much after one night, what was going to happen after our date?

One thing at a time.

So, instead of answering Whit's question, I asked one of my own. "What about you and Travis? You've been awfully quiet about *your* night."

She laughed loudly and rolled her eyes. "I know you're just deflecting the question, but I'll let it slide. *For now.*" And then she launched into a play by play of what all had happened last night at the bar. She hadn't slept with him, but made sure to let me know she would ten out of ten hook up with him tonight if he'd quit being such a gentleman. In fact, she planned on it.

"I'm telling you, girl, there's something in the water here, or the air. These Texas boys are something else."

I couldn't argue with her there.

MY DAD AND GEORGETTE were nowhere to be found when Whit and I got back, thankfully, so the two of us had spent some time tanning by the pool before heading up to the rooms to figure out outfits for the night. As it turned out, Whit had managed to set up a solo date for her and Travis as well—even if Whit's stance on seeing him was much more casual than when I thought of the potential for my budding relationship with Hux.

Thankfully, I'd packed heavy for this month-long visit and brought a bit of everything. Had I depended on Whit's Tiktok hack, I'd be in serious trouble. As it stood, I had almost too many options to choose from.

A knock came on my door sometime in the mid-afternoon. I wasn't surprised to find my dad there. I figured he'd come around sooner or later. "Hey, Queenie. Can we talk?"

I glanced back at Whit and told her we'd be right back before turning to my dad. "Okay, that's fine."

Dad didn't launch into a speech right away, which wasn't entirely like him. He hated quiet almost as much as he hated being unproductive. So he talked and talked and talked normally. But right now he was quiet, so quiet it was painful. So quiet you could hear a damn pin drop.

We walked down the hall toward the entryway to the first floor, veering off in the direction of the back patio and the pool beyond. Each silent moment that passed made my anxiety ramp up higher and higher. What was he going to say? Would he still be angry with me? Would he act like nothing had even happened? Or would he try to lecture me and make me feel like I'd been the one who was in the wrong all along and that I owed him an apology?

"I'm sorry," he finally said as we came to the edge of the pool. He kicked off his sandals and took a seat on the side, putting his feet into the tepid water.

My mouth flopped open and closed like a damn fish gasping for air. I wasn't expecting an apology. Especially not one right off the bat. I hadn't even had a moment to slip off my sandals and sit down beside him before he continued on.

"I know what I said upset you, and I should have handled myself better. I truly was just trying to look out for you, Queenie." He blew out a breath, watching his feet as he kicked them slowly in the clear water. "It's hard sometimes...." Glancing over at me, he offered me a soft smile. "I still look at you and see my little girl. It's hard to remember you're an adult now, and can take care of yourself and make your own decisions."

I didn't know what to say. What to do. Surprise and disbelief swirled in my chest. My dad didn't apologize almost ever. And I don't think I could remember the last time he'd sounded so honest and genuine.

"Thank you," I replied, my words soft. I couldn't look at him. I think if I did I just might cry.

"I'm sorry for what I said about Hux as well. I was out of line."

"It's okay," I managed to croak out.

He sighed, and when I glanced at him, there was a heaviness to his gaze, his shoulders, his entire being that made him seem old. Older than I'd ever seen him. He'd always been incredibly active and fit when I was growing up, and it hadn't changed once Mom passed. In fact, he was probably more active now. To his credit, he didn't look like he was fifty-one. With his mussed up sandy blonde haircut, his youthful face, and his well toned physique, he could easily pass for his early to mid-forties.

But right now, with the sadness shining so brightly from every inch of him, he looked weathered. Broken. Soul tired. The tired that didn't go away with rest.

"It's not," he replied with a huff. "But I promise I won't say anything like that ever again."

I nodded and leaned into him. "Thank you."

He wrapped an arm around me, pressing a kiss to the top of my head. "I shouldn't have ambushed you last night. About the ranch. I just—I wanted to surprise you. I miss you and I want to be around more, but I just..." He blew out a breath, and when I pulled back enough to glance up at him, tears hung like star drops in his eyes. "I can't be in California. Everywhere I go, every place reminds me of her. I was hoping that I could have a new start here. I can't, nor do I want to erase your mom, but I can't move on when everything reminds me of her. I need somewhere different. Somewhere fresh. This—I think this could be really good. Great, even. I just... I wanted to share it with you."

My heart felt like it was nothing more than a piece of paper being shredded in half. It was almost like I could hear the actual sound of it tearing. I understood Dad wanting to move on. I understood him wanting to start fresh in a new place, on a new adventure. I even understood the want to involve me. I was all he had.

Dad's parents had been gone for a while now, and Meema and Grandpa had passed on shortly after Mom did. It was just him and I. So I got why he wanted me on this new journey.

But the thought of leaving California permanently... Of leaving Mom, even if she wasn't actually there, well, frankly it was kind of scary—okay, a lot scary. California was all I'd ever known. It was where Mom was buried.

Could I just give that up and start a life here?

"I know, Dad," I finally replied, blowing out a breath.

A few tense, silent moments passed between us until I finally looked at him and asked, "Do you love her?"

He nodded, a soft smile coming to his lips. "I do. She makes me feel alive again."

My heart panged in my chest, conflict welling to life there. A part of me—the little girl who couldn't imagine a life without her mom and dad together—hated that any woman, especially Georgette, made him feel anything at all. But the logical part of me understood that he deserved to be happy. Who was I to deny him that happiness?

I squeezed his hand again. "Then I hope you have to most fantastic wedding and life together."

He kissed my forehead. "I love you."

"I love you too, Dad." Blowing out a breath, I said, "Speaking of wedding, we should probably sit down and get started on figuring out all the details sooner rather than later."

"How about tonight?" Dad asked, brow quirking up. "We could do dinner here, or if you wanted we could go out. Whatever you prefer."

A wave of guilt crashed into me. "Actually, um, I'm supposed to go to dinner with Hux."

"He can come too. It'll be a good opportunity to get to know him more." Dad's tone took on his usual enthusiasm.

If only I shared that excitement. It was clear how Georgette felt about Hux, and I got the impression that the feeling was mutual on his end. Putting them together would likely end up being a dumpster fire.

"Um, let me see what Hux thinks after he gets here. I don't want to just assume—"

Dad cut me off. "It's okay. I know it's last minute, so if it doesn't work out that's okay! We got plenty of time."

I huffed. "We really don't, Dad."

He waved me off. "One more day won't hurt."

I kicked my feet in the water, enjoying the feel of the cool liquid against my skin. Right now, the heat wasn't so bad. "Where even is Georgette?"

He checked his watch. "She's probably just finished up kickboxing right now and has a hot yoga class for an hour after. She'll be back in another hour or two."

"How long does she work out for?" I scoffed. The idea of doing it for an hour seemed brutal, but multiple hours? God, no wonder she had the body of a goddess.

"Her Sunday workouts usually last three hours. Sometimes four."

I didn't even know how to comprehend, let alone respond, so I just nodded. Pulling out my phone, I checked the time. 3:30. I didn't need two and a half hours to get ready for my date, and it'd been a long time since Dad and I had a chance to catch up just us two. So, with a sigh, I laid my head on his shoulder and asked, "How have things been?"

Chapter Twelve
Fallin' In Love

Hux

IT WAS HOT, HUMID days like this that made me think of packing my shit up, quitting, and moving my ass as far away from Texas as possible. Somewhere cold most of the year. Maybe find myself some ranch work up in Montana—Travis had family up there I could go visit. But honestly, even Montana seemed too warm right about now, but it sure as hell beat here.

Texas was my home though, for better or worse. I was born here, and I'd likely die here as well. I almost had once already.

"Ho," I soothed as I sat deep in the saddle and drew Doc to a stop, letting out a sigh and wiping sweat from my brow.

I'd given up a lot of things since losing my vision, but I'd be damned if riding was one of them. It had taken a while to get used to, but growing up in the saddle definitely had its perks at the end of the day. In an arena or round pen it was easy enough to figure out the layout, and most halfway decent horses weren't going to run themselves into the fence, so I could manage easily enough.

I liked riding. It was one of the few moments in my day where I didn't feel like a hindrance, a burden, a waste of space. On horseback, I felt at peace.

"Hey, old man!" Travis's familiar voice echoed across the round pen, coming from the left.

"The hell do you want?" I asked, adjusting the reins in my hand and spurring Doc gently with my left leg to turn back in the opposite direction, starting up our circular pattern once more at a walk. He'd worked enough for today and I was done with this heat. It was about damn time I cooled him off. And myself.

"Ain't you supposed to be seein' that girl soon?" Travis' words came from my right, closest to the gate.

I thought of Quinn, a flicker of excitement sparking in my chest. She'd driven my thoughts all day long. Her voice, her scent, her touch. She was more intoxicating than any damn drug or drink.

"Yeah, what time is it?" I asked. I'd set an alarm on my phone to go off at 5 PM so I could clean up and get ready.

"It's 5:25."

"Fuck." Doc tensed beneath me for a moment before continuing his path around the round pen. What the hell had happened? I fished out my phone from my back pocket and asked, "Siri, what time is my alarm set for?"

"Your alarm is set for 5 AM."

"Fuck!" I growled out again, urging Doc toward the direction of the gate. I could have sworn I'd set the alarm for PM. But it didn't matter now. Fuck, I still needed to untack him and wash him off. I drew him to a stop and hopped off, feeling my way along the pipe-stall.

"I was wonderin' why you were still out here." Travis was close enough I could feel the heat of him and smell his familiar scent. He had a strong musky cologne that I never had a problem picking out.

"Why the hell didn't you say anythin' sooner?" I grumbled, though I wasn't mad at him, more so the whole situation.

"Oh, don't be grumpy, old man. You're lucky I noticed the time. I was just about to get ready as well."

I huffed as I heard the creak of the gate opening and followed the sound. Travis' work, no doubt. He settled at my side as I made my way toward the wash rack. Exactly six steps forward, and then fifty-seven paces directly to the right.

The packed dirt gave way to concrete as I led Doc into the crossties and started untacking him.

"Well, thanks for sayin' somethin'," I said with a huff, working at the rear and front cinch.

"No worries, man. Here. I can help." Travis' scent grew stronger as he came closer.

As much as I hated relying on the help, it sure as fuck saved me on time, so I begrudgingly let it slide.

"So, you got a date with Quinn's friend?" I asked, as I walked five paces straight back and reached for the hose. Thankfully, it was there. Some days—most days—the other hands left shit out of place, which royally fucked me. But at least something was going my way right now.

Travis' voice sounded far away—he must be in the tack shed then—but it gained in volume, accompanied by the echo of his footfalls. "Yeah. Girl's a fuckin' pistol, but she's hot as hell."

I nodded as I returned to Doc's side and made sure all his tack was off before turning on the hose. Quinn's friend seemed like a lot to handle, but Travis liked the ones with fire in them. The crazier, the better it seemed.

"Where are y'all goin'?" I found myself asking as I washed off the sweat and grime likely covering Doc's coat—whatever color it was. I hadn't the slightest idea. He was tall, that's about all I knew. At the end of the day, it didn't matter what color, what kind of breed he was, or the lineage he came from. All that mattered was how he worked, and he worked damn good for me.

"Think she like's dancin',so I'm thinkin' of takin' her to go do that," Travis replied.

"You serious about her?" I asked.

"I don't know. She and I don't feel like gettin' into anythin' heavy. I'm probably leavin' soon anyway. I ain't built for this hot as balls weather. What about y'all? What're you gonna go do?"

I shrugged, continuing my hurried, yet methodical process of washing down the horse. "I'm gonna take her to go see a movie."

"Really? What movie?" Travis asked.

I rolled my eyes and scowled in his general direction, unsure if I was even looking at him directly. "Really, dumbass? How the hell do you think that's gonna work?"

He chuckled. "Oh, yeah. Sorry, man. So what are you gonna do?"

"I'm gonna take her out to dinner, I think."

"Well, shit. Two nights out in town." He whistled. "You must really like this girl, don'tcha?"

The closed off, reclusive part of me bristled at Travis' prying words, but I knew he was asking out of genuine interest. At one point, before the accident, I'd easily have told him my plans. Hell, I'd have probably told the whole world my plans on social media, never missing an opportunity to meet a fan wherever I went, but now...well, now that hurt too much. The less people who knew who I was or where I was going the better.

I blew out a breath as I finished hosing off Doc. "I do," I finally admitted. From the minute I'd heard her singing I'd been hooked. And the thought of seeing her soon urged me to hurry.

"Well, you got damn good taste...even for a blind dude." Travis guffawed, smacking me on the back and startling the hell out of me. God, I hated when he did that. I wished at some point I'd get used to it. Maybe there was still hope, but so far, no such luck.

His words intrigued me, though. It didn't really matter what Quinn looked like—she could have lied about everything she'd said last night, though I doubt she had. I'd have never known the difference, either way. But the shallow part of me wanted to know if the idea of her I had in my head was real or made up. "Is she as pretty as she is in my mind?" I asked, walking the hose back to the rack. I could hear the faint sound of water splattering to the floor. Travis must have been wiping Doc down with the sweat scraper to get rid of the extra water.

"Well, I don't know what you got envisioned in that head of yours, but she's fuckin' hot," Travis replied, the words sincere. He was a shit liar, I'd learned real quick when he was trying to lie for my benefit. This, thankfully, wasn't one of those times.

I nodded, a soft smile coming to my lips. It shouldn't have mattered. It *didn't* in the end. It wouldn't change anything. The connection I had with Quinn wasn't based on looks at all, but how she made me feel. It was reassuring all the same, though. It made me feel like I still had a piece of that old me. I'd not been a bad looking guy—I couldn't say what I looked like now, but it seemed most people only interacted with me out of pity, not pure interest. So knowing I could land someone attractive did a little number on my confidence.

"Speakin' of her, you better get your ass cleaned up. You smell like sweat and horse. I doubt she's gonna be into that shit." Before I could even argue, he gave me a light shove in the direction of the house. "Go, I'll put him away."

"What about—"

He cut me off before I could even finish. "It's fine, old man. Take the help when you can."

I huffed, but blew out a "thank you" as I started counting out the three hundred eighty-seven paces to the house.

Chapter Thirteen

Next Thing You Know

QUINN

I PACED IN THE bedroom, anxiety rippling through me like a rising tide as I glanced at my phone for the twentieth time within the last few minutes. 6:03. "Whit, you look great. Now, hurry up."

I hated being late. Like, hated it with every fiber of my being. Whit, though, seemed to have no such qualms. Everywhere we went, everything we did, I could always depend on her to be late. And even though I wasn't going out with her tonight, I knew if I left her, poor Travis would likely be waiting for at least an hour.

"Are you sure about the black romper?" she asked, glancing at herself in the mirror for the eight-millionth time.

I fought the urge to roll my eyes as I sighed and pegged her with a hard stare. "Trust me, the black looks amazing against your tan. Now, *please*, let's go."

Hux was probably waiting for me, and every minute I spent in here meant another he spent outside in this god awful heat. Not to mention, another potential minute for my dad or Georgette, or both, to find him and heckle him.

"Ugh, fine! I'm ready," Whit replied, even as she proceeded to continue staring at herself in the mirror.

"I'm leaving," I finally huffed, already halfway out the door. Whit's laughter echoed behind me as I made my way down the hall. My hurried footfalls matched the pace of my heartbeat. I nervously smoothed out my sundress and fussed over my hair, trying to ensure that everything was perfectly tidy and in place. Not that it mattered, but still.

Between the blast of ungodly heat as I stepped outside, and how damn attractive Hux was, I didn't know which took my breath away more. His Levis were a dark wash, which contrasted well to the pale blue button up he wore with the sleeves neatly folded up to his elbows, leaving his tattooed forearm on full display. He wore a white straw hat again. I wondered how he managed to style himself so well if he couldn't see. Did he have help? Or was it just a coincidence? Either way, he looked—well, let's just say, I was already distracted. And with the way the tattoo on his right pec was playing peekaboo with the littlest movement he made, I wanted nothing more than to rip his shirt off and trace my fingertips ove r it.

Calm down, Quinn.

I hadn't even said a word, but he stood a bit straighter, his sunglasses stare aiming my way.

Travis spoke before he managed to get a word out, startling me. I honestly hadn't even realized he was here. I'd been so caught up in Hux. "Well, you sure look nice, Miss Quinn."

"Thank you. You look nice as well. Whit should be out in just a second, she was right behind me." I smiled at Travis before returning my attention to Hux, making my way toward him. "Hey," I said softly, pressing a hand to his chest.

He drew me against him as if I'd been specifically made for his touch, and this feeling of contentment settled over me like a blanket. Or a hug. It was peaceful, yet somehow ridiculously attractive at the same time, sparking my desire.

"Hey, darlin'," he murmured, dipping his mouth to mine for a soft kiss. I don't know what I'd expected, but the ease with which he held me, kissed me, honestly just interacted with me in general in front of Travis did a number on my heart. Devin would have rather *died* than touch me like this in public. And yet, Hux did it like it was as normal as breathing.

Was this normal? We weren't even together. Or were we? Was this just a hookup or did he want more? Did I want more?

I was so overthinking this. My heart jackhammered in my chest, the air all but vanishing from my lungs. My breath came out in shallow gasps when I finally pulled away from Hux's kiss.

He let out a soft, appreciative huff. "You smell nice."

I smiled. "You look...really, *really* good." My words were breathy and weak as I tucked a lock of my blonde waves behind my ear. Trying to recover, I glanced between us and laughed. "Oh my God, also, we match."

He scoffed. "Really?"

I nodded. "The dress I'm wearing is white with a light blue paisley pattern. It matches your shirt."

He let out a laugh, dropping his hold on me to grab at his shirt lightly. "Shit, this is blue? I didn't even know I owned anything with color on it."

"It's definitely blue," I giggled. "But I like it. It looks good on you."

Whit finally came out onto the front porch then, stopping our conversation for a moment as all four of us shared a few words before saying goodbye.

When it was just the two of us once more, Hux asked, "So, you wanna go grab dinner first?"

I sighed. "About that...So, please, please, *please* feel free to say no. Like, you absolutely aren't obligated to do this, and I know it's probably weird and way too soon and—"

"Quinn," Hux cut in, grabbing my hands and bringing them down. "You gotta stop with your hands. I just feel all the movement and it makes me nervous."

"I'm so sorry!" Guilt welled within me, only adding to my already growing nerves. What would he think of me inviting him to dinner with my dad and

Georgette? This was stupid. I should just lie and tell my dad that Hux said no. But I'd been an idiot and already opened my dumb mouth and said something.

"Now," Hux said, drawing me from my thoughts. "What were you sayin'?" He released my hands, but trailed his own slowly up along my curves until he cupped my face. And just like that, the nerves vanished, desire and lust and need igniting in my veins from his scorching touch. It's like he knew exactly what to do to set my heart aflame.

"Um..." What was I even talking about? My gaze fluttered to his lips then back up to his sunglasses stare. God, I wanted him. "I don't remember what I was saying," I admitted.

He chuckled, the sound a deep, sultry rumble in his chest reminding me of rolling thunder. A shiver of anticipation went down my spine. "We were talkin' about dinner."

"Right," I managed to breathe out as his thumbs trailed up and down my jawline, his rough hands scraping against my skin. It was one the most wonderful feelings I'd ever felt. "My—um, that, uh, that feels really good."

Another low laugh fell from him as one of his hands drifted to my hips before trailing down to the curve of my ass. "You feel really good, darlin'," he whispered against my lips.

I melted into the caress, opening my mouth for him and flicking my tongue against his. The appreciative growl that escaped him nearly turned my legs to jello. Did I think this time yesterday I'd be making out on the front porch of my dad's house with a hot AF cowboy? Nope, I sure didn't. Did I mind? Not one fucking bit.

"Queenie! There you two love birds are!" Though the pet name was from my father, it sure as hell wasn't his voice that called out over the sound of cicadas and birds singing in the trees.

I froze beneath Hux's touch, pulling away from him to look for the source of the voice. I fought the urge to scowl at Georgette. "Hi, Georgette."

"Girlie, how many times do I have to tell you? Call me Georgie! Or, you can start calling me mama if you want."

My lungs withered up and died right then, and I damn near choked on my own spit. What the hell had she just said? Was I hearing things? Hux let out a disbelieving laugh at my side.

"Well, look at you, sweetie, don't you just look precious in that little outfit? And, Hudson, was it?"

He cleared his throat, before replying in a cool tone, "It's Huxson, ma'am."

"That's right. How could I have forgotten? You sure clean up nicely." She waggled her eyebrows from the open doorway at me. "Queenie, you sure know how to spot a diamond in the rough, dont'cha?"

Was I going crazy or was she looking at Hux like he was a cool drink of water on a hot day and she wanted a sip? I leaned into Hux further, a protective, possessive stance, but I didn't care. I could feel his heart beating in his chest, felt the tension in his muscles. I was right, he didn't like her. And the more I was around her, the more I couldn't blame him.

"I was just comin' to find you," she said, sauntering out the front door before I could come up with a response. I noted her neon yellow shoe-string bikini along with the white silk sarong wrapped low on her hips. I mean, I guess when you looked as good as she did, why not flaunt it? "Your dad told me you two were havin' dinner with us."

I sputtered for a reply. He *what?* Frustration ignited in my veins, fueled by Georgette's annoying voice and behavior. "Oh, um, actually—"

But she cut me off before I could fully finish. "I was afraid y'all had left with your friend, Chelsie, was it?"

"It's actually Whit," I managed to get out without growling. It's like she was doing it on purpose now.

"Right." She waved me off before moving to the front door. "Well, come on. Get in here, you two. We're havin' some of Isidor's famous ceviche by the pool."

Fight it. Say no.

I wanted to say no. I *should* have said no, but I also didn't want to go and make a huge scene either. Maybe we could get this over with quick enough and then still go out to dinner just the two of us.

"We'll, uh—give us a minute, okay."

"Oh—" One of her perfectly manicured eyebrows rose, a mischievous grin lighting up her features. "I see. Gonna get a little quickie in, right? Don't worry, I won't tell your dad."

A groan of embarrassment escaped me, but I tried to hide it with a laugh. "Right. Yeah. Be there soon." I waited until the door latched closed before pressing my head defeatedly to Hux's chest. "I'm so sorry about that," I muttered.

If he was annoyed, he didn't let on. The chuckle that escaped him was genuine. He brought a thumb and forefinger up to tilt my chin up. "So, we're eatin' here tonight?"

"We don't have to. My dad wanted me to invite you. To apologize for how he acted and, like, get to know you since he saw us kissing, I guess. I told him I'd ask, but I never said it was a sure thing, I'm s—"

"Don't worry," he said, pressing a reassuring kiss to my lips. "It's fine, Quinn."

And the way he said my name sent a ripple of relief through me.

"Are you sure?" I asked softly.

He dipped his mouth to mine once more and I got lost in the feel of him for a moment. Pulling away, he murmured, "How bad can it be?"

Chapter Fourteen

Coal

Hux

I PROBABLY SPOKE TOO soon about things going bad, but I'd heard the panic and worry in Quinn's voice and all that mattered right then and there was trying to ease her fears.

Which wasn't at all like me. I didn't really do that shit. Didn't really take people's feelings into consideration. I told it like it was. I did what I wanted, consequences be damned. There was nothing tying me to her. No reason I needed to go to this dinner. But I'd do just about anything to be around her, I realized.

Fuck, I was in trouble. If I was this whipped now, I didn't know what another night with her would do.

Her hand fit perfectly in mine as she took it and led me forward. Cool air blasted across my skin as we went into the house. She led me in a generally straight line, across what felt like tile first, before giving way to hardwood. A brief stop and then I heard the soft click of another door opening, followed by an accompanying wave of thick, hot, heavy air and the cloying scent of chlorinated water. Music played over the sound of the outdoors and the trickle of water from the pool. It was some obnoxious pop tune—probably the future missus' Decker's music. At least I hoped, this shit was god awful, and I couldn't imagine Quinn's dad—let alone any sane person—listening to this.

"Quinn! You decided to come after all!" Her dad's voice came from ahead and to the right of me.

Quinn's response was light and breathy, but I didn't miss the layer of nervousness mingled in with her soft laughter. "Yep. Here we are."

"Well, come on over. Sit, sit."

And so we did.

Everything started out fine enough. Quinn managed to keep the general direction of the conversation light and seemed to turn any question aimed at me back Carl and Georgette's way, so that all they could talk about was the upcoming wedding and themselves. I don't know if Quinn did it because she knew I didn't like sharing about myself or if it was just a happy coincidence, but I appreciated her attempts nonetheless.

"Huxson, you hunt?" her dad asked.

Only my mom called me Huxson anymore really, but I didn't feel like correcting him. I shrugged. "Used to, sir." I couldn't even count all the dove and deer hunts I'd gone on with my dad and uncle while I was growing up.

"You and I should go sometime. I got a buddy who owns a helicopter and can take us boar hunting."

"Oh my God, Dad. Really?" Quinn all but gasped at my side.

I squeezed her hand gently in reassurance even as a huff of laughter escaped me. I didn't think her dad was trying to make a jab, most people honestly just forgot I couldn't see. I wouldn't expect him to remember something like that.

"What? I'm just trying to be friendly, Queenie."

"That sounds like a good time, Mr. Decker," I replied. "Afraid to tell you though, I ain't that great of a shot."

"Well, at least you have an excuse. I'm shit and I *can* see." He burst out laughing, even as Quinn leaned into me and pressed her head to my chest, a groan escaping her.

Fuck, she smelled good. Sometimes, people's perfumes or shampoos and sprays could be so overpowering. But not hers. Everything was soft, subtle, but somehow strong in a pleasing way. Kissing the top of her head, I murmured,

"It's okay, darlin'." It really was, though I appreciated her concern. I aimed my attention toward her dad's laughter. "Well, good thing is, sir, you could be a shit shot, and I'll never know the difference."

More raucous laughter from her dad, growing louder and louder. He was moving, the sound coming closer to me. I startled as something hard made contact with my right shoulder. "I like you, Hux." Nope, not just something hard. Carl's hand. What the hell was it with people clapping me on the damn shoulder? "How about you and I grab another round of drinks? You like whiskey?"

I forced my nerves to calm with a slow inhale and exhale before nodding. "I do, sir."

"Come on, then," he replied. "My friend just came out with a double barrel whiskey that's real smooth. I bought a few shares in the company. I think it's gonna be big. How about you and I have some so the girls can discuss wedding things?"

I'd dated enough to know this was the inconspicuous not so inconspicuous way of getting me alone to give me the talk. The one all dads gave to the guys dating their daughters. I shrugged. Might as well get it over with. Besides, I wasn't about to turn down a glass of whiskey.

"Sounds good, Mr. Decker."

Quinn's grip on my hand tightened for the briefest moment, but I offered a soft smile in her direction before feeling a light path from her hand up to her chin, gripping it between my thumb and forefinger. "Have fun," I whispered, brushing my lips briefly against hers.

I couldn't help it. It was probably indecent—no, I *know* it was indecent kissing her in front of her father like that, but trying not to touch Quinn was like trying not to breathe.

I just couldn't do it.

She mumbled something incoherent, the faint taste of alcohol on her lips from the mojito Georgette had demanded she have. Standing up, I turned toward her dad. "Ready when you are, sir."

Another smack to the shoulder. Another silent shudder through me. Fuck, I needed that whiskey at this point. The mojito I'd guzzled down hadn't done a damn thing.

I HATED FOLLOWING PEOPLE almost as much as I hated being in new places. Thankfully, Quinn's dad never stopped talking, so it was easy enough to follow his voice. Only problem was he walked fast, which led to me bumping into shit. Another thing I hated.

There was a lot of shit I couldn't stand about being blind, but at the end of the day there wasn't anything I could do about it. So, silently seething, I made my way behind him down what I think was a hallway leading to an open room. Our footfalls echoed louder here, and the sound of his voice traveled further. Yep, a room then. The darkness in the left side of my vision was just a tad bit...warmer. if I had to guess, there was a wall of windows somewhere over there.

"It's a nice view, isn't it?" Carl Decker's voice drifted off to my right, like he was walking away from me. I took a couple slow steps towards him.

"I'm sure it is," I replied, clenching my jaw. I wasn't sure if he was just oblivious or being a dick? Maybe a bit of both. He seemed aloof, reminding me of a cat kind of. Off in his own world and thoughts, but briefly coming around to interact when he wanted. He had just enough charm to not be obnoxious, but there was a steely edge to him beneath it all. He was probably a damn good businessman.

"Ah, damn, I'm sorry. I keep forgetting." At least that sounded genuine.

I waved him off. "It's fine. I'm used to it."

"You get around really well, though, you know. How come you don't have a dog or one of those canes?" he asked over the clink of glasses.

I shrugged, hating how vulnerable I felt. Anxiety rippled and swelled in my chest like a rising tide. "I got a dog back at the bunkhouse, but he ain't certified or anythin'. I only take him places I know they ain't gonna give me shit for it. I tried a cane before, but the urge to hit somethin' or someone with it was too strong, so I figured out how to deal without it."

"I can imagine how tough it must be."

I just nodded, a muscle feathering in my jaw. There was no way he could possibly understand what I was going through, and there was no point bothering trying to explain the depth of it. Better to just let it go.

Silence descended for a moment, before the sound of footfalls headed my way. "Here, try this."

I reached out hesitantly, my hand bumping into his for a moment before settling on the glass of whiskey. "Thank you, sir," I replied, taking it from him.

He clinked his glass against mine. "To Quinn."

I nodded, wondering how she was doing out there all alone with Georgette. She hadn't mentioned it, but I got the distinct feeling she didn't like her. Hell, I didn't like her, so I wasn't about to judge.

"To Quinn." I tilted the glass to my lips, enjoying the burn all the way down. Well, damn. Shit was good.

Carl's chuckle was low, full of disbelief. "You're supposed to sip it."

"I've never been one for goin' slow." All my life I'd been like a bullet out of a gun, a home-run hit—going, going, gone. Since the accident, I had to take almost everything slow. Something that killed me a bit more inside every day. But some habits just died hard.

"Well, I hope you slow down with Quinn."

I stilled, immediately regretting my choice of words. *Well that was stupid, Hux.* I opened my mouth to respond, with what I had no idea, but it didn't matter. Her dad cut me off before I could get a word out. Probably for the best.

"What are your intentions with her?"

I blew out a breath, nodding for a moment as I tried to gather my thoughts. "Look, sir, I honestly don't know. I haven't known her long, but I like how I feel when I'm around her. I like her company. I don't really plan my life out the way I should and think about the long run. It ain't me, and with my current condition, it's just best to take it one day at a time. I know she's heading back to California at the end of all of this, and I have no intentions of leavin' Texas." I shrugged. "But as long as she'll have me, I'm at her mercy."

A huff, and then, "I think that's one of the most honest answers I've ever gotten in my life. Most would have just blown smoke up my ass and told me what they thought I wanted to hear."

"I ain't one for doin' that, sir."

"Well, I appreciate the honesty." The air shifted and the ice clinked in his glass. "Well, damn," he hissed out a moment later. "That does have a nice bite to it when you drink it like that."

My brow quirked up, my lips curling at the corners.

"Look, I can't say I'm particularly happy about the situation, but in the end, it isn't about me, it's about her." He exhaled loudly, his cologne mixing with the scent of alcohol on his breath. "Please don't hurt her."

I nodded. "I won't, sir." Because in the end, Quinn was the one who had the power. The power to bring me back to life, or snuff out whatever light was left in me. He didn't need to know that, though.

Chapter Fifteen

Stay

QUINN

EVERY SECOND MY DAD and Hux spent in the house caused more and more dread to claw its way up my throat, making it hard to speak, hard to breathe. I hated being alone with Georgette. She hadn't done anything yet, but I just had this growing, horrible feeling the longer I was around her.

"How're you doing on that mojito, sweetie? You want another?" she asked, lounging on the couch like she was posing for Sports Illustrated or Playboy. I hadn't been around her more than a time or two before this, and even then it had been brief, so maybe this was really her, but she hadn't seemed so obnoxious when her and dad first met.

Whit's words burned in my mind from earlier today. *You really want him marrying her?*

More and more I realized I didn't. But again, it wasn't about me. It was about him. He genuinely seemed happy with her. Who was I to deny him that happiness?

I held up my half drunk mojito before placing it back on the coffee table before us. "I'm good... So, I figured we could hammer out some wedding details."

"Queenie, sweetheart, you need to let loose a bit. Sit back, relax, drink the mojito. And tell me about your boy toy!" She sat up, her gaze turning devious, the smirk on her face full of mischief. "You know, for a blind guy, he's pretty hot."

Anger simmered to life in my veins and I bit the inside of my cheek so hard I drew blood. Sitting on my hands to hide the trembling, I said with a calm I most certainly didn't feel, "You do realize him being blind has nothing to do with how attractive he is, right?" Was she really that ignorant? That stupid? Did she really believe that? But most importantly, how the hell were her and my dad together? Dad wasn't hateful like that. He wasn't mean-spirited and close-minded. Georgette...she might just be the most awful person I'd ever met.

You're doing this for Dad. Not her.

She at least had the decency to frown. "I'm so sorry. That came out wrong. I just—I'm sorry. I'm drunk. You must..." Her bottom lip even quivered. Oh my God, was she seriously criying? "You must think I'm awful."

I bit back an eye roll. This was such a shit show. I wondered how Hux's conversation with my dad was going. Was it as bad as this? Worse? God, I hoped not. Guilt bubbled in my stomach, making me feel sick.

I had just wanted to have a nice date with him, and now I was dealing with my dad's drunk, small-minded fiancé.

"I don't think that," I lied through my teeth.

Her brown gaze pegged me in place. "You're just saying that."

Shaking my head, I said, "No, I'm not. Honest."

Lies.

She sniffled, taking a drink from her already empty mojito, before glancing around the backyard and shouting for the poor cook who was grilling carne asada and chicken on the outdoor barbeque. "Isidor! Isidor! Another mojito when you get a moment." She hiccuped. "Please."

Well, at least she said please.

Even though every nerve ending in my body screamed not to, I rose from the couch and made my way over to her. "So, we really should start figuring out things for the wedding."

She leaned her head against my shoulder. "Wedding plans can wait, my head hurts. We've got time."

I fought the urge to point out maybe the headache had something to do with the four mojitos she'd had in the time I'd gotten here. Instead, I let out a nervous laugh. "Actually, we don't. The wedding is in two Saturdays from now. We need to get things going, like, yesterday, if we want everything to be smooth sailing."

I was under no such impulsion that there would be any smooth sailing with this event, but she didn't need to know that.

Isidor came a few minutes later with a drink in hand for her and set it down on the table. "Here you are, Mrs. Decker."

"Thanks, Isidor. How long for dinner?"

"Maybe fifteen more minutes, ma'am." He turned his gaze to me, a guilty look coming over his face. He was young, probably not much older than me, and looked so nervous and stressed as he stammered out, "I'm so sorry, ma'am, can I get you something?"

I offered him a soft, reassuring smile. "No thank you, Isidor."

An emotion shifted on his face, more guilt, I realized, as he leaned over and replied under his breath, "Actually, my name is Isidro, not Isidor, ma'am."

I clapped a hand over my mouth. "I am so, so sorry."

He waved me off with a genuine smile. "It's okay, ma'am."

I bit back the urge to glare at Georgette. Holy God, she really was the worst. She couldn't even bother to learn his name right? It was a miracle she even knew mine at this point. And as frustrating and hard as it was, I pushed the anger I felt towards her down for the moment. I still had a job to do.

After apologizing another couple times to Isidro, I turned to Georgette. Pulling out my phone from the hidden pocket of my dress, I said, "So, what I like to do is set up a Pinterest board with some images of what vibe you're going for." I pulled up the app and typed in *wedding inspo*. "If you find anything that catches your eye, just let me know and I'll save it in the folder so I can reference colors, themes, aesthetics."

She clapped her hands together before ensnaring my arm with hers as she leaned her head on my shoulder once more. "Ooh! That one, save that!" A gasp. "Ooh, and this one!"

Each photo that she chose for me to add to the folder left me more and more confused. The look she was going for was all over the place. One minute she was fawning over these ultra chic, modern wedding photos, and then the next a rustic farmhouse wedding vibe. None of it blended. It all clashed, and none of it made sense in the slightest.

I held back a frustrated sigh and turned to smile at her before pocketing my phone. "I think that's enough. I have *such* a great idea of what vibes we're going for."

More lies.

But if I spent another moment with her draped over my shoulder, reeking of alcohol as she contradicted herself from one breath to the next, I was going to go crazy. Or get ridiculously drunk myself.

I managed to shift so that she couldn't lean on me anymore, and aimed a grin in her direction. "So, what are those absolute necessities that you *have* to have on the day of? Like you can't imagine your big day without."

Maybe this would give me a better idea of where to go.

"Well, we *have* to have an open bar. And one of those super awesome 360 degree cameras for the guests. Oh and a DJ, ooh but what about a live band? Your dad and I just love live music." She pressed a hand to my leg. "Did you know that the first night you dad and I met, we were at this bar in Turks and Caicos and this amazing band was playing old eighties hits. Well, *Don't Stop Believin'* came on, and I caught him singing across the bar and he saw me, and it was just like fate brought us together."

I honestly don't really know what she said after that. My mind just completely ran away from me, and it was all I could do to nod and smile and insert a "wow" or "oh" every now and then to keep her talking.

How was I going to plan this wedding for her? I couldn't figure out what she wanted. Better yet, I don't even think *she* knew what she wanted. And why wasn't my dad being a part of this? This was his day too. I know most men argued that they'd rather just elope or do something small, but my dad loved a good party, and yet he wasn't here helping to plan it. The man who liked to have a hand in everything was just sitting back and letting Georgette call all the shots? It didn't make sense.

Thankfully, I didn't have to dwell on it too hard for too long. The sound of my dad's booming, obnoxious laughter floated across the backyard, and my gaze snapped to the door he and Hux walked out of. My dad wore an easy grin on his face, and even Hux looked laid back and at ease as he carried a tumbler of whiskey in one hand and an entire handle of amber liquid in the other.

Looked like their conversation had gone infinitely better than mine and Georgette's. At least one of us was having a good time.

I rose from the couch and moved toward Hux, like a moth to a flame. "Hey," I said softly, coming up to him.

"Hey, darlin," he replied, "how's it goin'?"

A weak half laugh half sob broke past my lips before I could stop it. "It's fine."

His brows furrowed, disappearing beneath his sunglasses, his mouth drawing into a frown. "You wanna get outta here?" he asked quietly.

"No, it's okay," I said with an involuntary shrug as I grabbed his wrist and led him back toward the couch.

Dad had already sat down, Georgette wasting no time to slather on the PDA. Her manicured fingers trailed over my dad's chest and I fought back the urge to gag.

"How was wedding planning?" Dad asked me as he hooked an arm around Georgette.

"It's going," I managed to reply with a feigned brightness. It was the closest thing to the truth I could give him.

He nodded, an easy grin lighting up his face. Oh, he was for sure buzzing. There was a glassiness to his gaze and a rosiness to his cheeks. "You know, I gotta say, Queenie, I wasn't too sure about Hux at first, but I changed my mind. He's got my stamp of approval."

That little revelation made my heart take flight and soar. I leaned into Hux, murmuring under my breath, "What did you do? No one's ever good enough."

Honestly, Dad hadn't approved of anyone I'd brought home. Not that the list was long. I think I'd introduced him to one other guy I'd dated for a few months before Devin.

Hux's low, relaxed chuckle eased some of the worry in my chest, replacing it with a warmer, lighter feeling. "I don't know. I guess my honesty."

He *was* really honest. That made me smile. At least my dad appreciated it as well. I know I did. I grabbed his hand and squeezed gently.

"So, Hudson—" Georgette began.

"Hux," I cut in, unable to rein in my annoyance any longer. "His. Name. Is. Hux."

Georgette rocked back at my tone, a little hiccup escaping her. "Sorry, I'm just the worst with names, sweetie."

I bristled, God, I was so tired of her calling me sweetie, acting like she was that much older than me when really there was only six years between us. Hux replied before I could say anything more. "Yes, ma'am?"

"So, Carl was telling me earlier that Quinn told him you were a bull rider. Is that true?"

Hux stilled beside me, and I swear it's like a blanket of silence descended on the backyard. He turned toward me, his voice low, sharp, as he asked, "You knew?"

Trepidation knotted in my stomach once more, guilt so great crashing like a tidal wave all around me. "Whit and I tried to look up your socials and I saw."

"Saw what?" he growled out, his grip on my hand tightening a fraction. I don't even think he realized it, but he trembled beneath my touch.

"Everything," I breathed.

And just like that, he let go of my hand. Just like that, it felt like a rug had slipped out from beneath me.

Chapter Sixteen

High Road

Hux

E VERYTHING.

She'd seen everything. She knew about my past. The accident.

Fuck.

I wrenched my hand from hers. Not out of anger, but because I trembled so fucking badly there was no way she couldn't feel it. Why hadn't she said anything about the accident? I mean, really we hadn't had much time to talk about it, to be honest, so maybe that's why.

Of course, she'd looked me up. I didn't blame her, I'd have probably done the same thing if I could see. I should have deleted my socials a long time ago. *Fuck.*

I unscrewed the cap to the bottle of whiskey and didn't even bother being polite as I pressed it to my lips. I'd more than likely spill more of it all over me while trying to get it in the tumbler, so, fuck it.

The whiskey burned a fiery path down my throat before settling in the pit of my stomach. Carl might have shit taste in women but he sure as hell had good taste in whiskey. I chugged down far more than was socially acceptable, but I needed the liquid courage if I was going to make it through the rest of this dinner.

Quinn made a little sound—so small and imperceptible I doubt she even realized she'd made it. It was like a mixture of a squeak and a gasp. I wondered what she thought. I'm sure she suspected I was mad at her.

Trying to calm the racing of my heart with a slow exhale, I reached for her hand once more. Her answering squeeze back eased some of the worry in my chest. As much as I hated the thought of talking to her about my past, of dredging up all the ghosts and skeletons in my closet, I'd tell her everything. Not that she didn't already know the majority of it. But it was always better to come straight from the source.

I fixed my attention Georgette's way and managed to get out, "Yes, ma'am. I used to ride bulls."

"Were you any good?"

Another sip of whiskey. Another scorching path trailing down my throat. At least it was kicking in. My limbs felt a bit lighter, my usual aches, pains, and hurts dulling to mere whispers. "I mean, I certainly wasn't one of the greats, but I was pretty big in my prime. Had two World Champion titles under my belt."

"Wow. And you chose a life as a ranch hand over fame?"

A muscle in my jaw feathered as I forced a smile to my lips. What a fucking ignorant bitch. I wondered if she even realized what she was saying or if she was just that stupid. I could honestly see it going either way. "I didn't choose anything. I had to give it up when I got hurt."

"Why?"

I paused at that. Was she serious? Maybe she *was* actually that stupid. "I mean...It's pretty obvious, ma'am."

Quinn quaked beside me, her body trembling so hard she nearly vibrated in her seat. She gripped my hand with both of hers.

"Oh, yeah, right," Georgette's words were slightly slurred as she continued, but it didn't give her an excuse for what came out of her mouth next. "But I mean, it's not like you got *hurt*-hurt. You're just blind."

Quinn's sharp intake of breath at my side made me tense. "Georgette." The word was little more than a vicious growl of warning. I honestly didn't think Quinn had that kind of anger in her. Didn't think she was capable of it.

And while I hated people feeling the need to defend or protect me, not gonna lie, it made a flicker of desire spark in me at her protectiveness. But in the end, the anger thrumming to life in my veins drowned out whatever need I felt for Quinn.

Maybe I shouldn't have drank so much. Whiskey was great when I was in a good mood, but things had the potential to go south real quick when my mood turned dark.

A bitter chuckle escaped me, my tone dripping with sarcasm as I replied, "Wow, you know, I never thought of it that way before."

"Maybe we should uh, change the subject, eh?" Carl's tone rang with false cheerfulness. But it seemed his fire-breathing bitch of a fiancé didn't like being told what to do.

"There has to be a cure, isn't there? I mean, I know this holistic doctor that works wonders. I could get you into contact with him." Her words were sincere and ignorant, and it made my blood boil all the hotter. God she really *was* that stupid.

I rolled my eyes, not even trying to hide my laughter. This woman had to be fucking with me. Well, two could play that game. Taking another swig from the bottle, I said, "Well, I'm afraid to tell you, Miss Georgette, but I've tried all the crystals and essential oils I can get my hands on and it still ain't helped."

A wave of silence settled over us, and for a long moment I could only hear the cicadas in the trees and the water from the pool trickling on the wind. Quinn's tense grip on mine was like a life preserver in the storm of rage I felt growing more and more violently in my chest.

"Well, you know what they say—" Georgette's words were nice enough on the surface, but they dripped with sugary-sweet venom. "Everything happens for a reason. God must not have wanted you to be a bull rider. It just wasn't your purpose."

Rage pummeled into me, so white-hot and intense that the black in my nonexistent vision all but turned red. I nearly threw the damn bottle of whiskey to the ground. But that would be a waste of alcohol. And this dumb bitch didn't deserve my anger.

I shot up from the couch, releasing Quinn's hand. "Thank you for the whiskey, Mr. Decker, sir." I turned toward Quinn. "Thank you for inviting me, but I'm gonna go." I didn't bother to wait for a response or even acknowledge Georgette. She could rot in hell.

I tried to remember the path Quinn had led me on out here and took a long swig before I made my way toward the house, the whiskey not even burning anymore as it went down.

I was in dangerous territory now.

Oh well, fuck it.

Chapter Seventeen

Wind Up Missin' You

QUINN

My emotions writhed and clawed their way up my throat—anger so boiling hot and potent that if I let it out I was terrified of what would happen. But also guilt and fear. Guilt because I'm sure Hux thought to some extent I was just as bad as Georgette—guilty by association, right? And then fear, because even though he'd silently reassured me by grabbing my hand, now he was leaving.

How could Georgette have said something so horrible? Better yet, how could Dad be with someone so horrible?

I stood up after Hux, trying to decide what to do. Help him get out and apologize profusely, or go off on Georgette for her inexcusable behavior.

I glared at her from across the way, sipping the last remnants of her mojito like she hadn't just insulted Hux. And maybe it was the ignorant smile she aimed my way, but I couldn't keep my mouth shut any longer.

"I can't even believe that you could say something so hateful and harmful. You should be absolutely ashamed of yourself." My voice quaked, and it felt damn near impossible to get the words out. I hated confrontation. I hated starting it even more, but *something* needed to be said. I fixed my gaze on my dad. "I—" My words fell away, tears burning in my eyes. I didn't even know what to say.

I was so far past disappointment I didn't even know what emotion came next. So, I just shook my head and hurried for the back door Hux had just disappeared into. But not before my dad's familiar voice echoed across the backyard. "Georgette, what the hell? That was out of line."

I ignored her excuses. A blast of cool air and a string of angry, slurred curses greeted me as I walked into the house. Hux loomed a few feet in front of me, righting a chair I assume he ran into.

"Fuck," he grumbled out, taking another swig of whiskey.

"Here," I said softly, coming up to his side and reaching out a tentative hand. "Let me help you."

He growled. Legit growled at me, but with an annoyed shrug he let me lead him through the house and out onto the front porch. I couldn't even begin to possibly imagine how he felt. He'd been insulted time and time again by some dumb, ignorant bimbo who literally knew nothing about his condition or predicament.

Biting back tears, I whispered, "I'm so sorry, Hux."

His body trembled beneath me like a mini earthquake—from rage or whatever emotions going through him, I could only guess. I honestly probably wouldn't ever truly know. Hux didn't seem like the type to talk about his fears and frustrations.

"It's okay, Quinn," he said tiredly. So tired it made my heart hurt.

I looked up at him, finding exhaustion and sadness and defeat carved into the brutally harsh features of his handsome face.

My heart cracked. "It's not. I...I promise you I don't think like her. She's awful. I–I can't even begin to tell you how angry I am at what she said." Tears burned in my eyes so fiercely I couldn't stop them as they dripped down my cheeks. "I just wanted to have a nice night with you. I'm sorry."

Some of his anger seemed to melt away, though I still saw it clearly in the hard set of his jaw. I'm sure if I could see his eyes, they'd be blazing with silent fury. "It's fine."

"It's not though. I'm sorry for saying something to my dad, and then not telling you I knew. I didn't want you to feel pressured or ambushed like tonight, so I wasn't going to say anything until you were ready to tell me." I bit my lip, struggling to look at him. I felt so awful and guilty for everything that had happened. My vision blurred as more tears welled in my eyes.

Hux's thumb brushed against the back of my palm, and I savored the feel of him. "I appreciate that," he murmured, though his words were still a bit clipped, almost like he was talking through gritted teeth.

I glanced up at him. Yep, his jaw clenched and unclenched. Over and over. More guilt crashed into me, making me feel weak and sick. "I'm sorry," I murmured once more. It was all I could say.

"Goddamn it, Quinn," he snapped, dropping my hand. For a second, I thought he was going to throw the bottle of whiskey to the ground.

I flinched, a gasp escaping me.

A heartbeat passed and he slowly lowered his hand, bending down to put the bottle on the ground. His lips softened from the scowl they were set in. "Fuck...now I'm the one who's sorry. I ain't mad at you." He blew out a breath and tilted his head skyward for a moment. He looked so sad and broken and tragically beautiful that it hurt to look at him. "I ain't mad at you," he repeated, the words softer as he reached a tentative hand forward to brush against my fingertips. He didn't grab my hand though. "I just...I'm mad at what went down, but not you. I promise... But I do think it's time I left."

I sighed, fighting and failing to hold back more tears. "O-okay, that makes sense. Can I w-walk you home at least?"

He shook his head. "No, I need some time alone. I ain't fit to be good company right now."

I nodded, wiping at my cheeks with the back of my free hand. "Well, here. Give me your phone and I can put my number in it. That way you can let me know when you get back so I know you're home safe."

He opened his mouth, shut it, opened it again, all the while my nerves climbing higher and higher. "I can't do that."

My lip quivered, more tears spilling down my cheeks, confusion sinking its claws into my heart. "Why?"

"If I have your number, I'm gonna call you. And if I call you, I'm gonna come back around, and I can't do that."

His words hit me like a freight train to the chest. "What...why?"

"Look, I can't even begin to explain the emotions I feel when I'm around you, darlin', but it's dangerous. You're leavin' in a few weeks, and I sure as hell am in no position to chase after you. Might as well stop this before it even starts. Because if I spend another night with you, I'm gonna end up missin' you."

My heart cracked at his words, shattering and falling to the floor of my stomach like a million broken shards. It didn't make sense to feel this way, but here I was, feeling like I wasn't just getting dumped by a hot stranger, but closing the door on one of the biggest moments of my life.

"Hux," I choked out, the word little more than a sob. I didn't care if he knew I was crying or not. If he thought me weak for it, oh well, it didn't matter. He'd really called this—whatever it was—off?

He let out a breath, and then his hands somehow found my waist before trailing up to cup my cheeks. And damn, but I loved the feel of him. The scent of him. The warmth and sense of belonging I felt in his arms.

"Go find someone to breathe life into, darlin'. Someone deserving of you and your love."

And then he kissed me.

It wasn't a soft, parting kiss. Or one that spoke of goodbyes or endings even.

It was the type of kiss from the movies where the music built and crescendoed while the rest of the world—every scent, every sense, everything faded away into the background.

It was a kiss of longing. Awakening.

A kiss that stole every ounce of air from my lungs. I could drop dead from the lack of oxygen and die content from that kiss.

And then he pulled away, shattering the perfectness of a moment like dropping a picture frame on the ground.

"Goodbye, Quinn," he whispered against my lips before pulling away and walking off into the night.

I WISH I COULD say that I pulled myself up by the straps of my super cute high-heeled sandals, fixed my makeup, and called Whit so I could go out dancing third wheel it and go out dancing with them, but that would be a lie. Instead, I decided to head to my room and try to go to sleep—even if it was only eight o' clock and the sun had only just started to set. I wasn't about to go hang out with my dad and Georgette, and chasing after Hux wasn't really an option, so I was limited.

In the end, I couldn't bring myself to slip out of the sundress I'd picked out for tonight. It was stupid and silly, but taking it off felt like I was fully putting

Hux behind me. And I didn't want to, goddamnit. I just wanted to get to know him.

Not that that was going to happen anymore.

With a sigh, I sunk onto the bed, snuggling up under the blankets as tears streamed down my cheeks. But sleep didn't come...because my stupid bed sheets smelled like the musky scent of his cologne mixed with tobacco. One night with him, and even my bed couldn't rid itself of his imprint. He'd left a mark on my soul, a stain on my heart, which might sound dramatic to most people, but it was t rue.

I didn't even care if people thought it was insta-love. Or infatuation. It wasn't. It was more than that. He meant something to me, and my feelings were valid, okay?

In the end, I ended up grabbing my phone and scrolling through Insta-gram—which led to clicking on his profile. And then his photos and reels. And then I watched like fifty-something of his most noteworthy rides.

Holy God, I was so, *so,* screwed.

Chapter Eighteen

Ode To Bourbon

Hux

WHY THE HELL DID walking away from Quinn give me the same feeling as when the doctors told me I couldn't ride bulls anymore? Each drunken step I took morphed from anger to regret. But Dad always said I was stubborn as hell. Even if I was wrong, I'd made my bed. Now I had to lay in it.

That kiss though. Fuck, the taste of her still lingered on my lips, her scent still ingrained in my lungs, in my soul. I didn't think there'd be any erasing her from my mind anytime soon. Maybe ever.

I'd dated my fair share of girls, but I'd never felt such a connection to someone so quick.

I needed another drink. At least I had the—fuck, I'd left the bottle of whiskey. Well damn, I couldn't go back. One word from Quinn and I'd spend the rest of the night wrapped up in her. I wouldn't be able to say goodbye twice.

So on stumbling feet, I aimed myself toward home. Which was a stupid idea, I came to realize, because apparently this drunk, I couldn't count right, and I kept losing track of how many steps I was on.

I have no idea how long or where the fuck I wandered. I could have checked my phone for the time, but I didn't care. Not like I had anything to do at home really. I could go paint, I guess, but the desire wasn't there.

The sudden, familiar smell of the barn and the soft nickering of the horses—no doubt hearing my footfalls and thinking they were getting a late night snack—helped me regain my bearings. I entered the barn and walked the twenty paces to Doc's stall, unsurprised to find his head hung over the rail as he let out a small huff of air.

"I don't have shit for you," I huffed right back, but I pet his muzzle softly before running a hand down his forehead. For a while, I just stood there, petting him. Coming out to the barn, being with the horses had always helped calm me down. They didn't talk, didn't ask questions, or give unwanted advice. With the horses, I usually found a level of peace.

But not tonight.

Thoughts of Quinn still plagued me. The feel of her soft skin against mine. Her smell. The lilt of her light, airy voice. Her laugh. Everything about her called to me. She felt so nice. So warm and welcoming. She felt like home.

I hadn't felt something like that, well, ever.

THE SOUND OF BOOTS scuffing against the dirt and Travis's god awful guffaw dragged me from sleep. What the hell? Where was I?

The familiar scent of hay and the angry grunts and whinnies from the horses made it obvious enough. Why the hell was I in the barn? Had I passed out in here? What time was it even?

"Well, good mornin', sleepin' beauty." Travis' voice sounded directly above me.

"Fuck you," I grumbled, slowly standing. Goddamn, I hurt. Every muscle, every bone, every goddamn limb. God, I hated getting old. Not that thirty-two was even old, but I *felt* old. Bull riding wasn't a forgiving sport though. The list of injuries I'd acquired over the years was long and extensive. Not even including my TBI or blindness. "What time is it, even?"

"It's—"

My alarm rang out, as if it had heard us talking about the time—sharp and loud. Well, that answered that. 5:30. Just like every morning. No wonder the horses were pissed. They wanted breakfast.

"Why were you sleepin' out here?" Travis asked, his voice light. "I figured you'd be with your girl."

My girl.

I bit back a curse. Quinn never was mine, nor would she likely ever be now. But it was just as well. I shrugged, not really in the mood to tell him the truth. "I don't know. Came out here to check on the horses and I must have passed out." Fuck, my head hurt. Whether it was from the alcohol or the fact I'd slept on the goddamn floor, I didn't know. Today was going to suck.

"You drank that much?" I didn't miss the hint of concern in his words. "Things not go good with her?"

Aiming a hard stare his way, I replied, "Don't ask."

"Well, shit man. I'm sorry." A clap to my shoulder, starling the hell out of me. *Really?* I could do without that this morning. "Here, I'll feed for ya."

I shrugged off his hand and shook my head. I didn't need handouts, especially when I'd done nothing to earn it. "It's fine."

"Dude, you look like death. Go grab a cup of coffee, some Advil, and take a damn shower, old man. Leave the hard work for us young ones."

I know I gave Travis shit all the time, but he was a pretty top-notch dude. Oblivious sometimes, but good-hearted. I huffed a laugh and waved him off.

"This new girl fuck the lazy outta you? That's twice now you've offered to help me."

Travis' obnoxious laughter followed me as I slowly made my way to the bunkhouse, but even that couldn't drown out the thought of Quinn.

Chapter Nineteen
In The End

Quinn

I'D HOPED THAT MAYBE some sleep would miraculously fix all of my feelings from the night before, but the next day I still felt just as shitty. I think the biggest issue I had with this all was *why*. Why the sudden change in Hux? Why was the thought of me leaving in a month now a problem when it hadn't even been a topic of conversation either of us had brought up at this point?

It couldn't be just that. I doubt he'd admit it, but I'm sure it had, at least, *something* to do with the fact that my dad was marrying that god awful woman and Hux would have to be around her now and then if he pursued me. I didn't really blame him if that was the case. I wouldn't want to come around and subject myself to her ignorance if I were him.

I glanced at my phone, which I'd forgotten to put on the charger last night, and bolted upright. 9:45 AM. *Shit.* Whit had a flight home in, like, a couple hours, which meant we needed to get our asses in gear to get her back into San Antonio on time.

I pulled up her name on my call log and listened to it ring until it went to voicemail, then proceeded to send her a text telling her to get her ass back here.

All I got back was an: **on my way.**

Which was annoying and vague and told me absolutely not enough details. Where was she on her way from? The bedroom across the hall? The bunkhouse?

A different place entirely? How long until she was here? Did I need to get her things ready? Speaking of getting ready, I needed to get myself ready.

So after asking her how long she'd be, I hopped in the shower, trying to wash away all of the feelings of the night before. Surprise, surprise, it didn't work, and I hated the fact that I was being mopey and sad and letting this affect me so much.

Hux was just a guy. One guy—a guy who managed to make me feel more wanted in a day than Devin had made me feel in the entirety of our relationship. One who was kind, and honest, and hot as hell, and really, really, *really* knew how to make a girl swoon—

Oh my god, stop. You're being ridiculous.

I could just imagine myself telling any of my friends back home about this and they'd probably all roll their eyes and tell me it was just an infatuation. That Hux was just a crush and these feelings couldn't possibly be real.

Why did it feel so real then? This was the problem with feeling things so strongly. It was hard to decide what was actually something big or small when every emotion pouring out of me felt *so* big. Mom always said it was a gift, Dad saw too much emotion as weakness though. So, as a result, I was constantly at odds with myself. Trying to feel my feels and temper my emotions all at the same time. It was exhausting.

By the time I got out of the shower and changed, Whit was in my room, packing up the last of her things into her carryon backpack.

"You know, when you sent me that panicky *where are you* text, I assumed you'd be ready when I got here," she said, turning to look at me. The grin she wore on her face fell the moment she took me in. "You okay?"

I shrugged, a shitty idea coming to mind. Walking over to my suitcase and tossing everything into it, I said, "I'm fine."

"Why are you packing?" Whit asked.

I refused to look at her as I retrieved my book off the nightstand and my charger.

"Quinn, what's going on?"

I sighed and turned to look at her, fighting back the sting of tears in my eyes. "I wanna go home. I don't want to be here anymore. I don't want to plan my dad's stupid wedding. I don't want to run into Hux every day and see him and be reminded that I royally fucked things up."

Whit was in front of me in an instant, wiping tears from my cheeks. "What the hell happened when I was gone? Why didn't you text me? Do I need to kick Hux's ass?"

I laughed through the traitorous tears that trickled down my cheeks and sniffled. "Please don't. It's not his fault."

"Why didn't you call me or text me? I'd have come back home last night."

I broke away from her and finished grabbing the last of my things. "At least one of us deserved to have a good night. I was okay. I *am* okay."

She gave me an *are-you-sure-about-that* look, which made me laugh.

"Really," I went on. "I promise."

"How about you tell me everything that happened on the way to the airport?"

"Or you could tell me about how awesome your date was with Travis?" I asked hopefully.

Even though a soft chuckle escaped her, I could sense her concern as she glanced at me once more. "*After* you tell me about your night."

"SO, WAIT, LET ME get this straight," Whit asked as we drove back to the airport. I hadn't bothered saying goodbye to my dad. I was still ridiculously pissed about what had happened last night and Georgette's inexcusable actions, and his, well, his lack thereof. I was pulling a trick from his book this time, and just up and leaving with nothing more than a text or a quick call from the airport. Guilt welled in me at the thought, but Whit's next words dragged my attention back to her. "Hux basically admits that he knows he's falling for you and doesn't want to dive into things for fear that you'll essentially break his heart when you leave, and then he kisses you?"

I swear, I could still feel the pressure of his lips against mine, the weight of that moment crashing around me. "I mean, yeah. And it wasn't even just, like, a peck or a forehead kiss. It was, like, in the book we're reading right now for book c lub."

"The one with the super hot, morally grey shifter?"

I nodded, while keeping my eyes on the road. "Yep. Whit, when he kissed me, it gave me those same kick-your-feet, heart stopping feels that I felt the moment that the couple realized they were soulmates."

"Spoilers! I'm not at that part yet."

I let out a weak huff of laughter, shrugging my shoulders. "Read quicker."

She laughed, but sobered a moment later. "Okay, being serious, though. So, your telling me that some hot as fuck cowboy kissed you like that, and you're *leaving*?" Her voice rose a couple octaves on the last word, complete and utter shock ringing in her tone.

"Whit, I can't leave California. My job's there."

"Quinn..." I glanced over to find her dark brown eyes burning with a seriousness that she never, ever wore. "I understand how much getting this job meant to you, but you have an awesome opportunity right now to work for your dad as well."

"I don't even know any detai—"

But she cut me off. "So, sit your dad down, have him come up with a business plan, a job title, a salary and all the back-end aspects, take the month to get to know Hux, see if this is something more serious than a hookup, and *then* make a decision."

"What about Georgette? I can't live with her. I can't plan her wedding."

"Fuck, Georgette," she huffed, before giving me a guilty grin and shrug. "Okay, but seriously. Think of it as a learning experience. You're not always going to like your clients, *trust me,* I know. So, this is an opportunity to show that you can be unbiased and work with someone you absolutely despise but still give them the best event ever."

I groaned, the thought already seeming like too big of a task. "She's so fucking awful though."

"I know. I mean, I haven't seen as much as you have, but from what I have, *I know.*"

I sighed and glanced her way. "This is crazy. I can't. What if it doesn't work out with Hux?"

"Then it doesn't! You'll have gotten to spend a couple weeks sleeping with a hot AF bull rider that you can think back on as some wild adventure. Not everything has to be weighed and measured and done only because it's beneficial. You're allowed to do some things just for pleasure, you know—" she waggled her eyebrows. "Like Hux. Multiple times a day."

There was no way to stop the laugh that bubbled out of my throat, but the minute I thought of last night, the light feelings in my chest withered to ash. "You really think I should stay?"

"Girl, you just had a guy give you a fucking mating bond worthy kiss and you're really asking me that?"

I blew out a breath, my mind going back to that kiss for like the umpteenth time. Okay, maybe Whit had a point.

The GPS spouted off instructions about the exit coming up and I glanced over at Whit. "I'm sorry that I dragged you all the way out here to Texas, and then we didn't even spend any time together."

"Girl, I am definitely not complaining. Besides, I've already booked myself a flight back out here Friday morning for a redo girls' weekend. By the way, can you pick me up from the airport?"

I loved that she didn't even try to pretend that I was getting a flight home today. She knew me more than I knew myself sometimes.

"Is that even a question?" I grinned. "So, are you and Travis an item?"

Whit smirked and offered a noncommittal shrug. "Nah, just keeping it casual. He's cute and kinda oblivious, which I like. he's definitely not boyfriend material, though, but he is nice to look at."

I shook my head and laughed. Well, in a world that was always changing and oftentimes overwhelming, at least I could always depend on Whit to make me feel better.

The world needed more friends like her.

I CHECKED MY REFLECTION in the mirror for like the tenth time. I'd picked out another sundress and gotten myself done up to go talk to Hux and ask him for a repeat date. One that didn't involve Georgette, or my dad, or talk of his past.

It was half past six, so I figured he'd be done working by now.

My heart fluttered in my chest faster than hummingbird wings. What if I walked all the way down there and he wasn't there? What if he said no? I don't think my heart could take a second rejection in just as many days.

You've got this. You're making it a bigger deal than it is. Just go talk to him.

I blew out a breath, smoothing out the skirt of my dress.

Well, here went nothing.

It was surprisingly nice out as I made my way toward the ranch hands' bunkhouse. It was still really sunny and warm, but there was a nice breeze that kept it from feeling too humid.

The motor of one of the Gators rumbled up behind me just as I heard a familiar voice shout out, "Hey, Queenie! Queenie!"

I held back a groan. The last thing I wanted was to talk to Dad right now. I was still raw and angry from last night, even if he hadn't specifically done anything. But in this case, doing nothing was just as bad. At least Georgette wasn't with him. I wondered where she was. Probably hot yoga again or something.

With a loud, outward sigh, I turned to face him. "What Dad?"

"What's wrong?" he asked, his face full of concern.

I waved him off. "Nothing. I'm fine."

"You sure?" His blue-gold gaze pegged me in place. Looking into his eyes was like looking into a mirror. They were the same as mine.

"Yep," I replied with a curt nod.

Maybe he'd just leave it alone, not push for answers, but when his head cocked to the side and he quirked his eyebrow, I knew he wasn't going to let it go.

With a sigh, I placed my hands on my hips. "I don't like what happened last night."

"I know, I'm sorry."

"You know, after Hux got mad and walked out, he broke things off with me and even though he'll never admit it, I'm pretty positive it has something to do with your gem of a fiancé."

"Queenie, I'm so sor—"

I cut him off. "Dad, what she said was absolutely fucking horrible. How are you okay with that? Like, that was mean and ignorant and completely unacceptable."

"I know, I know." Dad lifted his hands in a placating gesture. "She was drunk. Not that—" he said over me when I tried to cut in once more "—it makes it okay. We got into it last night and she feels awful. She plans to apologize."

I snorted. "That's the least she can do. Maybe she can spend a fraction of her time meant for working out trying to learn how to not be so damn ignorant and rude."

His gaze filled with sadness. "I don't want you to hate her."

A little ember of guilt welled inside me. Not for her. God, no. But for my dad. I knew what it was like to have someone I cared about not like my significant other. I didn't want him to feel that way, but I couldn't help it. She was horrid. "I don't hate her, Dad, but I can't really say I like her either. She hasn't given me much reason to."

He hung his head, rubbing the back of his neck with his hand, and when he looked up at me, he looked so much older than normal. Weathered and beat down, like all the fight had left him. "I know. I don't know what's going on with her. I've never seen this side of her before."

Maybe if you didn't jump this marriage so quickly you'd have noticed and thought twice. I bit back the urge to clap back. It wouldn't do any good.

Seeing Dad so sad and lost and beaten down hurt my heart. I wanted him to be happy, he deserved to be happy, and I hated that he was suddenly having problems with Georgette now that I'd come around. I couldn't stop myself from pegging him with a questioning look though. I found it hard to believe that Georgette was anything other than awful.

He huffed a weak laugh. "I'm serious. I've never seen her act like that before. She's usually warm and fun and lively. She's the light of every party. She makes me laugh, a lot. Makes me feel young."

My heart cracked a little hearing that. I sighed. "Look, I don't have to be her best friend or even like her. In the end, it's your relationship. If you love her, then it is what it is. But I didn't come here to plan *her* wedding. I came here to plan yours. I'm not doing this if you aren't going to be involved."

He sucked in a breath and for a moment I thought he would try to argue. That stubborn look he got when he was being confrontational flickered in his gaze for a moment, but after expelling a breath, he nodded. "That's fair. I wish you didn't feel that way about her, but I can't expect you to feel any different after the last couple days. You don't have to plan the wedding, Quinn."

I balked. He almost never used my name. It was one of those unspoken rules between us. As much as Queenie grated on my nerves, it was what I associated with my dad. Him calling me Quinn would be like me calling him Carl. "No, I said I would do it, so I'm going to do it."

"But you don't like her."

"So, you're my dad, and I want to help you."

The look he gave me let me know he wasn't convinced.

I offered what I hoped was a soft, reassuring smile and not a grimace. "I want you to have the day you deserve."

His gaze turned glassy, and I was so taken back by the honest emotion shining on his face that tears of my own welled in my eyes.

I took a deep breath. "I also wanted to sit down and talk to you about your business proposal."

Surprise replaced any softer emotions. "You want to work with me?"

With me. Not for me. That was a bit of a shock.

"I want to see what you can offer me and how it compares to my job back home," I replied, keeping my tone even, professional almost. Any tiredness that lingered in his limbs vanished in that instant, excitement and exuberance taking its place, making him instantly look ten years younger. I continued on before he could say anything though. "I'm not committing to anything long-term yet, but I'd like to treat the rest of my time here before the wedding as a trial run to see if we can work together and come up with some ideas for the ranch."

He nodded, and I knew I was losing him to his enthusiasm. He was like a kid in a candy shop. A dog with a bone. He only could focus on so many things at once. "That's a fantastic idea! It'll be great! We can..." he rattled on idea after idea but I wasn't entirely listening. Not to mention, he spoke so quickly even I couldn't keep track of what he was saying.

"Dad...Dad! Slow down." I let out a huff of laughter. "I was thinking, though, if I'm going to stay here, I don't want to be in the house with you and Georgette." The thought of spending one more night under the same roof as the woman, let alone an entire month did not sit well with me.

Dad gave a quick nod. "How about you stay in one of the guest houses on the property? They're both vacant. I've got the keys up at the house. Hop in and we can grab them."

I looked down the road, toward the general direction of the bunkhouse. I mean, I guess I could go get the keys *then* see Hux right? As much as I wanted—no, needed to talk to Hux, I got the feeling my dad needed this moment with the two of us more.

With a huff, I met my dad's gaze and nodded.

The wind blew my hair from the speed of the Gator as we made our way back toward the main house.

"So, this decision..." My dad said, glancing at me from the driver's seat. "Does it have anything to do with Hux?"

I scoffed, my heart squeezing tight at the mention of him. "I don't know what you're talking about."

His lips tugged up into a knowing smirk. "That's where you were headed, weren't you?"

I shrugged. I was so not talking about guys with Dad. I'd hardly even been comfortable talking about them with Mom before she passed.

My dad's grin turned wolfish. "I wasn't lying last night when I said I liked him."

"He's the first guy I've dated that you've liked. How come?"

"He's honest," Dad replied after a moment. "And I like that he doesn't let his circumstance keep him from living."

"So no more of this *'he's got a bad attitude'* bullshit?" My stare was hard and unyielding as I remembered dad's words from yesterday.

"No more."

TURNS OUT, GETTING THE keys became a whole damn night affair. First, Dad couldn't find them, so him and I searched his office for, like, an hour before finally, begrudgingly, I'd given in and let him involve Georgette, who was all but useless. But after another half hour of searching, we found them in Dad's garage with a whole key ring of spares for all the buildings on the property.

After that, Georgette apologized so profusely that I thought I might claw my eyes out if I had to watch her fake cry for a minute longer. Then she'd practically demanded that I stay for dinner, which as much as I hated it, went decent and served as an opportunity to get some wedding input from my dad.

By the time I managed to get away from them though, it was nearly midnight, and the thought of taking my things and settling into one of the guesthouses was just too exhausting. A part of me was still tempted to go find Hux and talk to him, at the very least, but would he or any of the other hands appreciate me knocking on the bunkhouse door in the middle of the night when they all basically rose with the dawn?

As much as I needed to talk to him at this point, that could wait until the morning.

Tomorrow, then. I'd make things right tomorrow.

Chapter Twenty

Hell On The Heart

Hux

WELL, ONE THING WAS for sure... I was fucked.

For the past two days, every thought—whether asleep or waking—was of Quinn. No matter what I did, no matter how hard I worked to drown her out with music or work, all I could think of was her.

You're the one who called it off, remember?

I still couldn't believe I'd done that. The action was so unlike me. So against my nature. Even before I'd gone blind, I'd lived life one step, one minute, one day at a time. Nothing mattered unless it was in the here and now. After losing my vision, that mentality only intensified.

No use worrying about the future. You had to live in the present—*one step, one minute, one day at a time*. Anything else wasn't worth worrying about.

I realized now, I'd just never had something I would regret losing.

Quinn—she was the kind of girl you thought of the future for. A woman who had the power to tame a man's wild heart. Bring him to his knees. Breathe life back into him. And I knew if I kept seeing her, I'd fall for her completely—if I hadn't already. And let's face it, first off, she deserved someone better than me. And second, I had no intentions of being the thing that kept her from reaching her dreams in California. She was so close. I wouldn't have her give it up for a broken, washed up cowboy.

Better to sever the cord before I caught any more feelings—it was already hell on my heart.

Good thing I was a resilient sonova bitch with a mean stubborn streak. I'd get over Quinn. It might take a minute, but I would... Once I forgot the feel of her soft skin, the sound of her warm, light laughter, and her intoxicating scent.

Fuck me.

Rusty and I walked into the bunkhouse, cool air replacing the blazing heat from outside, the sound of the guys' chatter filling the main room. I followed the voices, brushing my hand over the back of the leather couch to my right as I moved straight ahead. Ten more steps past that and to the left was a hallway that led to my room. I kept going straight, though, the rest of the twenty steps toward the kitchen, where the voices were loudest. Travis' being the loudest of all—as usual.

"Old man Hux!" Dylan shouted. He was the youngest and newest hire of the group—barely even nineteen, I guess.

Most of them left me alone. Not that I blamed them. I wasn't here to make friends. I was here because I didn't want to go home. Didn't want to face my dad's pity and my mama's fussing. I wanted to feel normal—as normal as I could now.

Wyatt's nasally twang and Brook's deep drawl greeted me as they let out a string of hellos.

"Hi," I grumbled back.

"You comin' out with us to Julio's?" Travis asked, a second before something smacked into my shoulder.

I shouldn't be surprised at this point. He did it so often it should be expected, but it still startled me.

The thought of not having to make myself something for dinner was enticing, but I had little to no desire to leave the ranch. I'd peopled enough the past couple days. Besides, I wanted to paint. Correction—I *needed* to. My fingers all but itched for the scratchy surface of the canvas and the cool, sticky feel of paint.

I wouldn't consider myself an artist—I mean, my mama would, but that's just the way with mamas, right? But I'd always found myself drawing or sketching when I was younger. Of all the heaps of therapies I'd been thrust into since my accident, finger painting had been the most calming for my soul. I didn't know if I was good at it or not, but I didn't do it for that. I did it for...well, I did it for the same reason I rode—it was a part of me.

"Nah, I'm gonna stay here."

I skirted my way around the kitchen island and felt my way over to the refrigerator, pulling out a tupperware of leftovers from the top shelf to take with me. Travis always made sure to put some up there for me so it was easy to find. I wasn't hungry at the moment, but this way I could take it to the guest house and use the microwave there to warm it up when I was ready.

After getting the things I needed, Rusty and I began the trek to the western guest house. I could have just as easily chosen the one closer, but that would have meant more potential foot traffic, more opportunities for people to see my work, which was a terrifying notion, and, I don't know, I just liked this place better. I don't know what it was. There wasn't anything really special about this one, it was a twin to the other, I guess, but the fact it was so secluded, and just the general feel of it called to me.

The picture in my mind of it was prettier too. I envisioned a little white wooden-sided house with river rock accents and blue or green shuttered windows and trim. Not that it was probably accurate at all.

The third step squeaked as usual as I mounted the stairs and walked the four and a half paces across the porch. I reached for the key beneath the mat and unlocked the door before getting to work.

I DON'T KNOW HOW much time passed since I started painting. I think I'd worked on three different canvases tonight, getting lost in the music playing from my phone and the calm that crept through me with each brush of my paint-covered fingers. Rusty had left my side a while ago, traipsing off toward the bedroom to probably curl up on the bed. He seemed to like it back there.

Painting had a similar effect on my soul that riding did. Sometimes I needed one or the other, or both. With what a train wreck the last couple days since Sunday had been, I needed both.

I was so lost in my work that I almost didn't hear the jiggle of the lock. Almost.

Every muscle in my body froze, and even though it didn't make a difference, I aimed my gaze toward the front door. Who the hell was here? Maybe Mr. Decker to check on the place? But he never came here. It's why I'd picked this place to keep my things after they'd moved in.

Muffled curses and general struggling sounded on the other side of the door for another moment and then it swung open hard enough to slam against the opposing wall, shaking the windows and making a loud bang, followed by a familiar, feminine voice. "Stupid suitcase. What's the—" A grunt as something scraped across the floor "—point of having *wheels...*" A heavy exhale "...if you. Don't. Fucking. Work?"

My heart skipped a beat. "Quinn?"

Chaos ensued then. She shrieked, and more curses flew, as well as a loud crash as something smacked against the floor. Rusty barked from the back room.

"Holy fucking God! Oh..." The way she dragged out the last word made it sound like she was blowing out a long breath. "Oh my God, you scared me." Another breath. "Hux, what are you doing here?"

I felt Rusty's presence settle at my side.

"Hi, Rusty," Quinn said softly, and his tail smacked against the floor happily in response.

I opened my mouth to respond to her question, wondering the very same thing about her, but her breathy, light voice filled the room. "Are—are you painting?"

The door shut, much quieter than a moment ago, and then her soft footsteps echoed against the hardwood. Her lemongrass and vanilla scent filled my nose, and every nerve ending in my body zinged to life. My fingers twitched at my sides as I fought the urge to draw her into my arms.

I shrugged. "That's debatable. A toddler could probably do better."

The air shifted as she moved, my senses going haywire at her closeness. Which fucking sucked. I didn't want to be around her—I mean, I did. Which was the entire damn problem. I'd never been great at self control. If I didn't stop this, sooner or later we'd end up with our clothes off, or with one of us leaving upset.

None of which helped this situation. But I couldn't find the willpower within me to move. It's like my feet had been covered in cement and I was stuck where I stood.

Quinn's huff of laughter was full of disbelief. "I highly doubt that. Let me see. What am I looking at?"

I quirked a brow, her question only reaffirming my thoughts. "Told ya. It's shit."

She let out an indignant hmph. "Oh, stop. Just give me a second." Her light touch on my shoulder should have startled me, but I don't know if it was just a coincidence or simply the calming magic of Quinn, but I didn't react quite the same as when Travis smacked me on the shoulder. Probably had something to do with how soft and tentative she was.

My mind and my senses were still reeling from her touch and the closeness of her so that I almost missed what she said next. "Wait...I see it now, I think. It's—it's a landscape. The greens and yellows and golds in the foreground are grass and hills, maybe? And I think the dark green and black smudges are supposed to be shrubs or possibly trees?" A slight pause and then, "But the background is definitely a sunrise or sunset. Though, from how soft the colors are, I'm guessing sunrise?" The last word rose up an octave, like she wasn't quite sure.

I huffed. I could see the image in my mind clear as day, so when I painted, that's what my fingers tried to capture. But no one had seen my paintings, let alone reaffirmed for me if what I painted actually was anything other than smudges.

But the cynical, sarcastic side of me couldn't let an opportunity go unmissed. "It's, uh, supposed to be a horse."

"Oh," she said, her voice falling in disappointment.

Shit. I guess maybe I was a bit too sarcastic. "I'm kidding, Quinn. You nailed it right on the head," I replied quickly.

"Really?" she murmured, that sense of wonder returning to her voice.

I nodded. "Yeah."

"Are the random patches of blue in the green parts—"

"Blue bonnets," I finished for her. "They grow wild in the pastures back home."

"This is your home?" Her tone was warm and held a hint of surprise. Almost like she hadn't expected for me to drop that little revelation.

I nodded, a wistful longing filling my chest. God, when's the last time I'd gone home? I think Christmas. Or was it Thanksgiving? Either way, a long, fucking time.

Quinn's scent was intoxicating with how close she was, her voice a siren song I was unable to ignore as she said, "This is amazing, Hux. How did you...?" Her words trailed off, whether it was because she didn't know how to finish her sentence or was still trying to figure out what to say, I didn't know, so I saved her the trouble.

"I drew a bit growing up. I mean, I don't think I was the next Picasso or whatever, really, but I was okay. One of the therapies they put me in was art therapy when I was at the rehabilitation center...to help with regaining dexterity and fine motor skills, or something like that." I could have stopped there, I *should* have stopped there, but I found myself wanting to tell her the whole reason. Which was dumb, but it's like my heart and my brain just stopped speaking the same language. "But—well, also for my anger and depression."

"Hux—" Her voice was timid and edged with a bit of sadness, but I didn't get the feeling she was sorry *for* me, but rather the situation. And then I felt her hand hesitantly rest against my chest, right over my heart. My breath hitched in my throat and I'd be surprised if she didn't feel my heart skip a beat. I expected her to bring up the anger, but one thing I was learning with her, is she didn't press me with questions. It's like she knew which ones I wouldn't want to talk about. "You're so talented," she said in a hushed whisper, "is there anything you can't d o?"

A soft chuckle escaped me. "Well, I mean, see." I couldn't help it. The words fell so easily from my lips, I wasn't about to miss an opportunity like that.

Laughter bubbled out of her, the sound like a goddamn melody. Why did everything about her call to me? It made it impossible to think, to focus, to breathe, even.

"Oh my God," she said, the last word muffled, like she'd cupped a hand over her mouth. "I'm sorry, it's not funny. I shouldn't have laughed."

I couldn't fight the words as they clawed up my throat. "No, please laugh. I love the sound of it." I raised a nervous hand and pushed my hair back off my face.

A quiet, light giggle escaped her. "You just got paint all in your hair."

I shrugged. "Ah, shit. Did I get it anywhere else?"

The heat of her consumed me as she moved closer—not even an inch or a breath apart it seemed—and when she pressed a finger to wipe at my brow I didn't even flinch—much.

"Here," she said quietly, her words taking on a husky edge.

And damn me, but I couldn't help myself from wrapping an arm around her and hauling her fully against me. A gasp escaped her, followed by the most feminine little sigh I'd ever heard. It sparked desire in my veins.

Trailing the backs of my knuckles up and down her spine, I asked, "Where else?"

Her fingers drifted down in a measured path from my eyebrow to my chin. "Here," she murmured, her touch disappearing a moment later only to be replaced with the softest whisper of a kiss.

A groan rumbled through my chest, and I brought my free hand up to cup the side of her neck. I trailed my thumb along the curve of her jaw. "Where else, Quinn?"

Her breath fanned against my cheeks, the heat of her mouth so close all I needed was to tilt my head down to kiss her. But I wouldn't. No, this had to be on her.

Her hands slipped up around my neck, knotting in my hair as she tossed my ballcap aside, and then her mouth was on mine, brutal and unrelenting and filled with so much passion and need that I knew I was completely and totally ruined, but didn't care one bit.

It was my damn undoing.

Chapter Twenty-One
Break Up More Often

QUINN

Hux's lips, his hands, his scent—let's face it, everything about him—left me reeling. My legs felt weak and wobbly, but it's like he was a mind reader or something, because just as I felt like they'd buckle or turn to jello, he lifted me in his arms as if I were little more than a feather, all the while his mouth never leaving mine. He sat me on the table, all of his paint supplies getting messed up and moved around in the process. My dress was probably ruined, but it was the least of my worries right now.

Not when his kisses left me feeling like I was drowning. But in the best way.

I pulled back just enough to look at him, my lungs screaming for air. Holy God, he was so painfully attractive, even covered in multicolored smudges. His unkempt brown hair was wild and falling around his face, and his scruff was thicker, closer to an actual beard instead of just a shadow of one. He wasn't wearing his sunglasses, I realized, and when he opened his eyes, it was like the soulful amber depths were seeing straight to the very essence of my being.

I raised a tentative hand to his brow once more, trailing my fingers along the lines of his brutally handsome face. He was rugged and hard and fierce, and I loved that about him. I loved that despite that, his actions could be so opposite—soft, gentle but no less intense.

I pressed a kiss to his lips, surprising myself when I whispered, "I'm sorry."

He stilled beneath my touch.

Damn. I didn't want him to stop, but I needed to get my thoughts off my chest. It was like now that I'd opened my mouth I couldn't help the words from coming out. I needed him to understand how I felt. So even though my heart pitter pattered in my chest, I continued on. "I know you said you couldn't do this, but I want you."

One of his hands slid up to grip my chin while the other trailed down my curves before coming to a rest on my hips. "I know, I can't get you out of my fuckin' mind, darlin'," he all but growled, the sound sending a ripple of desire through me.

I released my hold on his hair, sliding my hands down to rest on his chest, the black t-shirt he wore a thin barrier between me and his tattooed skin. I wanted it off, but I also—I don't know—I wasn't ready for the passion to overwhelm me yet. Once it did, there was no going back. It was probably stupid, but I'd been falling for him basically since the moment I met him, and after tonight, nothing would be the same.

I knew that without a shadow of a doubt.

So, I don't know, this moment, this pause, it was like those few gut-wrenching minutes when the rollercoaster makes its way up to the top of the drop off. That part was honestly more terrifying than the ride itself. It was the lead up. The tension. The stillness of the moment where you could hear your heart thumping in your ears and you were contemplating whether or not you'd made a massive mistake.

"I want you. Not just physically, but I want to get to know you. To learn about what makes you tick, what upsets you, what drives you. I want to know if this feeling I feel for you is real," I managed to get out quietly. "Because it feels real."

His grip on me tightened, and I watched in stilted silence as he bit his lip. He shook his head and my heart squeezed. Damn it, he didn't feel it, did he? Was this just a physical thing for him? Had I made a massive mistake?

"It *is* real, Quinn. I feel it too."

And then his lips were on mine once more. Urgent, insistent, unrelenting. There would be no more talking right now. And that was okay, because I don't think words could even accurately describe how I felt.

Hux's hand on my chin drifted to grip the side of my neck, his fingers tightening, but not to the point it hurt, just enough to make me feel wild and reckless. A moan tore up my throat, which only seemed to spur him on. His free hand drifted from my waist to dip below the fabric of my sundress, his callouses scraping against the sensitive skin of my inner thigh.

My head fell back as he peppered kisses to my mouth, my jaw, the curve of my neck. How could the simplest touch make me feel so alive? My body thrummed with desire, white-hot and all-consuming. I *burned* for Hux. Everything about him was like kindling to the fire within me, everything he did, every nip, every brush of his lips, his tongue, his teeth—*fuck*.

The moment his fingers dipped below the fabric of my underwear, the moment they found my pussy, it was like a supernova of light burst in my vision. My head fell back, my limbs turning weak, and it took everything in me to just *feel* as his hands worked their magic. A moan escaped me as I rode the burning wave of desire sliding through my veins.

"Hux," I moaned, his name all but a song, a prayer on my lips.

His chest rumbled with that sexy growl of his before he asked, "You like this, darlin'?"

Like it? I loved it. I loved the way he seemed to know exactly what I wanted and needed without any direction. I couldn't answer though, words were too far away from me, so I just let out a little, "mhm hmm." It was the best I could do.

He chuckled and wrapped an arm around to support me as he slid his fingers in and out of me.

Holy God, I was close. Already. With just a few strokes. Every inch of me felt like it was on fire. My veins, my lungs, my skin seared with the intensity of my burning need for Hux. But this wasn't all about me. This was about him too, and while I didn't think he particularly minded paying me all the attention right now, I was greedy for a taste of him as well.

I grabbed for his shirt, pulling it up, up, up over the taut muscles of his tan stomach. He paused long enough to rip it off with a growl, and then his mouth and hands were on me once more in a wild frenzy. I ran my fingers over the tattoo on his heart before trailing them lower and lower until I brushed the top of his jeans hung low on his hips. I pressed a hand to his rock-hard cock, eliciting a moan from him.

"I want you," I said, surprising myself with the confidence in my voice.

It's like the tether holding in his self-control vanished. He growled once more, and I gasped as he slid me to the edge of the table, all but ripping off my underwear and tossing them to the floor. He had the button and zipper of his jeans down in the next instant, his pants pulled down over his hips enough to expose his cock.

And despite all his intensity and desperation, he entered me slowly, gently, almost. Another moan found its way out of my chest as I rode the scorching desire that only Hux seemed capable of causing. His hips moved in slow, measured strokes, all the while, his hands roaming over my curves.

This. This feeling. This scorching passion, the searing kisses, the fire I felt...how was this real? Maybe soulmates were a thing. Or I was just so enamored and blinded by my lust that I thought they were.

"God, you feel so fuckin' good," he murmured as he kissed me.

I nipped at his bottom lip. I could say the same about him.

The action sparked something within him, further cutting at the tether holding back whatever shred of control he still possessed. One of his hands knotted in my hair, and he pulled hard enough to expose my neck before peppering kisses and nips to my flesh. My eyes fluttered closed at the feel of it.

"Yes," I breathed.

His groan of approval brought a soft grin to my lips. "What do you want, Quinn?" he asked, his words a deep, velvety whisper in my ear.

"I want you."

"I need you to be more specific." The hold on my hair tightened and I gasped as he picked up the momentum and thrust into me faster, his movements becoming harder, more punishing. And holy God, it felt good.

"I...I don't know. I just want you." I didn't know what I wanted. Was it pathetic to say that I'd never enjoyed sex this much until now? It had always felt more like a chore, like I was stumbling along in the dark. I didn't know the first thing I wanted when it came to sex. All I knew was that whatever he was doing, I wanted more.

He let out a huff—whether it was of approval or not I didn't know.

"What do you want?" I asked, hoping the question would distract him from whatever thoughts my last sentence caused.

"What do I want?" His words turned contemplative, even though every inch of him—every chiseled line and curve, every muscle, even the look in his eyes—silently told me he knew *exactly* what he wanted. His hold on my hair tightened another fraction, and his lips found my neck as he led a path up to my ear before whispering, "I want to lay you down over this table and fuck you til you're screamin' my name."

My cheeks heated at that, but the idea of it...yes. I wanted that. I *needed* it. "Yes. Please."

"Fuck, Quinn—" Hux moved then, pulling out of me and flipping me around to bend me over the table so quickly, I didn't even have time to think or breathe. His cock was poised at my entrance in the next moment, his hands once more knotted in my hair. "You don't know how much I fuckin' love that."

I leaned back into him, a breathy laugh coming out of me as I whispered, "Then fuck me, please."

He didn't possess the same amount of restraint this time around. He pounded his cock into me with brutal intensity, but I savored every thrust. Dipping a hand beneath the top of my dress, he grabbed one of my breasts, which he kneaded and squeezed, sparking even more desire in my veins. Between the punishing strokes of his cock, the tension of his hand in my hair, and now this...it was the perfect kindling for the fire blazing higher and higher within me.

"Hux," I breathed.

He growled out a curse in my ear, his hold on my breast vanishing as it trailed down along my curves and slipped beneath the hem of my dress. His breath fanned against my neck, sending shivers down my spine as he rumbled in my ear, "Be a good girl, and say it again, darlin'."

His fingers found the bundle of nerves at my core, his hand and cock both stoking me higher and higher and higher. And then he bit me. It wasn't more than a little love nip, really, but It was right at the tender cord of muscle where my neck and my shoulder met. I gasped as the most brutal, paradoxical sensation of pleasure and pain pummeled through me...

And then I was crashing, falling, plummeting down from the heights I'd just soared, my orgasm coming hard and fast and fierce. I screamed his name, my vision spotting and going black as I slammed my eyes closed and writhed beneath him.

He let out a curse, his thrusts turning wild and relentless—once, twice, a third time as his own release finally found him. His hold on my hair eased, and where his teeth had been just a moment before, he kissed now, sending a shiver through me. Hux's hands came up to cage around me as he pulled me back against him, finally slipping out of me. And despite the moment being so quiet, so simple, this was almost more magical than the sex. The intensity of this moment, the rightness I felt in his arms. It shouldn't be real. It couldn't be.

For a long moment I just stood there, our breathing matching each other's, but I wanted to look at him. Wanted to get an idea of what was going through his head. I was too scared to ask and shatter the perfectness of the moment. I turned to face him, trailing my fingers down his sleeve of tattoos taking up his right arm, admiring the artwork. It reminded me of an old Western. There was a desert landscape with a lonesome rider riding off into the sunset, barbed wire, cactus, some paisley filigree mixed in along with another cow skull, and a cross.

"I can't decide if I want you to stop that or keep going," he murmured, wrapping his other arm around me. His deep voice cut through the quiet of the room like thunder rolling in the distance. Powerful, yet subdued.

"Does it tickle?" I asked, looking up at him.

His lips were slightly upturned at the corners, his amber eyes warm and light. God, they were beautiful. I wish he didn't feel the need to hide behind his sunglasses so much. Though, I'm sure it was probably easier and felt more comfortable for him. He didn't have to hide from me, though.

"A little. But I'm more worried about how fast it's gonna make me want to fuck you again if you don't stop."

My laughter was little more than a breathy huff of air. "Would that be so bad?"

He chuckled, his grin widening. "I knew you weren't as much of a good girl as you let on." His lips met mine for a moment, stoking some of the desire that was little more than embers in my veins now.

I broke the kiss a moment later. "I don't know what you're talking about."

He chuckled, gripping my chin between his thumb and forefinger. "Sure you don't, darlin'." And the way he said it, Holy God. How was he so frikin hot?

"We should probably get cleaned up," I said, my voice weak.

"There's a bathroom down the hall and to the left. It's got a shower and tub," he replied.

I reached out and brushed my fingertips against his. "Wanna join?"

He pulled me to him once more, crushing me to his chest, but when he kissed me it was so opposite—soft and languid. "Is that a question?"

A few minutes later, I sat in Hux's lap, drawing lazy patterns on his chest while steam swirled around us from the bath. It was one of those fancy jacuzzi tubs with jets, so why not?

Hux's knuckles drifted up and down my spine in the most soothing, yet tantalizing way that both eased and drove my desire as he said, "Wasn't expectin' for you to come bargin' in here earlier."

I giggled. "Me? I wasn't expecting you! My dad said no one was staying in here so I could use the place. I thought you lived in the bunkhouse?"

"I do, I just keep my paint stuff in here. I'll have to move it, though, now that—"

"No!" I cut him off quickly. His brows furrowed, so I tried again. "No, you don't have to move your stuff. I don't mind if you paint here, in fact, you can come here whenever. My door's always open. Hell, you could even stay here if you like." Each sentence tumbled out of my mouth like word vomit. I couldn't hold it back even if I tried.

He stilled and I inwardly cringed. *Way to go, idiot. You invited him to live with you after one night. Desperate, much?*

"I mean, I'm not asking you to, like, move in or anything, I just don't like being alone and—" Oh dear God I was just making this worse. I let out a nervous squeak of laughter. "You know what, just forget I said anyth—"

His chuckle was low and deep as he drew me in and pressed a soft kiss to my lips, stilting any more words from coming out of me. When he finally pulled away, his voice came out as husky whisper. "No, I get it. As much as I like being on my own, feelin' lonely sucks. It's kinda why I like the bunkhouse. Reminds me of being on the ranch with my family. There's never a quiet moment." He paused, his next words more of an afterthought than anything. "Sometimes the quiet gets *too* quiet, you know?"

I nodded, a whisper of sadness stirring within my heart. "After my mom died, it was just my dad and I for the first three years. But I could tell he hated being there, so I was alone a lot while he worked and vacationed and did whatever my dad does for fun. I lived so close to campus for college that I didn't see a reason to stay in the dorms or rent a place, so I stayed at my parents, even if it was lonely and reminded me of my mom."

"I'm sorry. You still live there now?"

"No, I live with Whit. We met, like, a year or so ago while I was interning for this event company. She was the hair and makeup artist that the client hired for the wedding. We just kinda gravitated toward each other that day, and when the event was over, we just...stuck together. She was looking for a roommate and asked me if I wanted to move in, so I did."

"That's cool that you have her."

"Tell me about it. I mean, she's crazy, but a good kind of crazy. She keeps me on my toes, and the house is *never* quiet when she's home."

He chuckled. "That ain't surprising. She seems fiery."

"That's a good way to explain her," I replied with a soft laugh.

"So, how come you're stayin' here? I thought you had that job in California?" The way his hands moved up and down my spine, so soft, yet sure of their path, it felt absolutely amazing and more than a bit distracting.

"I haven't turned down the California job yet. It's still there, but my start date isn't until late August. I like the notoriety that would come with working for them, as well as how much I'd hopefully learn, but this business proposal from my dad could be interesting too. I'd get to essentially be my own boss, do things my way, and..." I pursed my lips, trying to figure out if I should tell him that he was part of the reason for staying? Would he think I was crazy—I mean, a part of *me* thought I was crazy—or would he understand? I know he said that he felt like this was real too, but... I don't know, what if it wasn't *that* real for him.

Hux frowned, and he asked, his voice tinged with a hint of worry, "Quinn?"

You know what...? To hell with it.

My heart beat a million miles a minute, but I pushed back the fear and said, "I'm gonna be completely honest with you, because, well, I'd rather know now if you think I'm crazy or not—" I blew out a breath. "I've never felt a connection like this before. Ever. And maybe it's infatuation, or that I typically have shit luck with relationships and you seem different than the rest, or maybe I'm just completely reading more into this than I should...but meeting you—"

My gaze dropped to rest on his tattoo; I couldn't meet his stare. Even though he wouldn't know what I was looking at, I felt too self-conscious. So I traced his tattoo with my fingers instead, as I continued on, "I know this is gonna sound super cheesy, and I'm fully aware of how crazy this is, but the moment I saw you, it was like my heart woke up and said 'mine'."

A peel of nervous laughter escaped me and I hid my head in my hands as my throat squeezed tight. I didn't know whether to laugh or cry. He probably thought I was a crazy person. And the fact he seemed so lost in thought, making no attempt to speak, was all the more nerve wracking. Biting back the familiar sting of tears in my eyes, since now I was an emotional wreck, I whispered with a fake cheerfulness, "Anyway, feel free to tell me I'm crazy. But I want to explore this. I want to see if this connection is as special as it feels before I go back home."

He was quiet—painfully quiet—for so long I thought maybe somehow, some way he hadn't heard me. Each second that passed sent my nerves skyrocketing, but he still held me, so I couldn't have completely screwed things up, right?

"Well, if you're crazy, I'm crazy too." The low timber of his voice was a balm to the fear burning in my chest.

I finally braved a look up at him, finding a softness to the set of his jaw. And this close, with the way his soulful amber eyes rested on me, it was easy to imagine him still having his vision. "How so?"

He lifted a hand to my face and slowly tucked a piece of hair behind my ear. "The minute I heard you singin' in the grocery store, I just—I had to find you. I think somethin' in my soul woke up then too. I hadn't felt warmth or anything like that for a long time."

Trying to stop the grin spreading across my lips was like trying to stop the sun from rising—impossible. "Really?"

A nod as he brushed his fingers tips along the curve of my jaw. A shiver went through me, a burning heat stirring once more.

I bit my lip and asked, "Do you believe in love at first sight?"

"Well, that don't really apply to me, now does it, darlin'?" His breath fanned against my cheeks with his answering huff of laughter. "But I guess you could say love at first...song? Speech? Fuck, I don't know."

I laughed and pressed a teasing hand to his chest. "Oh my God, Hux." Sobering slightly, I went on, "But yes. Like fate or soulmates?"

He gripped my chin, his unfocused gaze holding me captive as his lips drifted dangerously close to my mouth. "I believe this ain't somethin' I've ever felt before. Fate, soulmates, whatever the hell you wanna call it, I'm drawn to you, Quinn, like a moth to a flame. Like a sailor to the sea. All I can think, all I breathe, all I see is you."

A breathy gasp escaped me at his words. At the raw honesty in his tone. He felt the same. I wasn't crazy. I mean—maybe I still was, maybe we both were. But if being crazy meant exploring this with him...I didn't want to be sane.

More words tumbled out of his mouth before I could respond. "I've never been one for goin' slow or holdin' back. So, why start now?"

I pressed my forehead to his, our lips but a breath away from each other. "I'm not usually quite so reckless, but I like to think I follow my heart. And my heart wants you, Hux."

He kissed me. Slow and deep and sensual. It sent my heart fluttering in my chest, this feeling of peace overwhelming me so thoroughly it stole the air from my lungs.

Words, thoughts, everything but the feel of him became impossible to process as our mouths and hands explored one another. He made love to me in the tub, taking his sweet, sweet time, and then after we'd washed off the paint from each other, I'd led him to the room where we did it again.

I was wild. I was wanton. I was hooked on Hux.

Chapter Twenty-Two
Save My Soul
Hux

I LOST ALL TRACK of time with Quinn. I could have stayed in bed with her all night, but Rusty started whining at the foot of the bed.

"Oh my God, I completely forgot he was here! He's so quiet!" Quinn's voice rang with concern.

I whistled low and Rusty's nails ticking on the floor signaled his approach. I let my hand dangle over the edge of the bed, and a moment later something wet pressed against my palm. "Hey, boy," I said quietly, "you hungry?"

Quinn gasped. "Oh shit! That reminds me, I had groceries in the car! Oh my God, oh my God—" her words dissolved into a string of curses as the bed jostled. "Do you think it's still good?"

I felt the weight of her leave the bed. I stood up as well, trying to remember where the hell I'd put my clothes. "What all did you get?" I asked.

"Some meats and cheese. Ugh, that and the milk is probably for sure bad."

Probably, but I still asked, "How long was it out there for?"

"I don't know, I'd say a couple hours. It's dark outside now. Let me find my phone, I'll bring the clothes back."

She disappeared and I stood there for a moment stark naked just waiting for her, because it was easier and likely quicker for her to get my clothes than me struggling to find them on my own. I bit back a curse, my fists clenching at my side as a hint of anger filled me.

You take small shit like that for granted when you can see—being able to go find your clothes easily. Hell, putting them on even. Especially now that most clothing brands got rid of the damn tags on shirts, so now I had to fucking feel around for the small print on the inside of the material to find the back.

I heard her footfalls on the wood as she returned. "Here's your clothes." She placed them softly in my hands. "I just checked my phone and it's close to 10:30 right now. So the groceries have been in there for two and a half, three hours now. With this heat I doubt anything is good." There was a layer of annoyance in her voice. Not aimed at me, more like herself for forgetting.

I got the feeling this wasn't the first time she'd done something like this.

"I gotta go to the store tomorrow anyways. We can get you more stuff." My stomach growled at the mention of food. I had those leftovers in the fridge, but the idea of Quinn having to eat my leftovers didn't sit well with me for some inexplicable reason. "How about I help you bring in your stuff, and order us a pizza?" I replied, sliding into my jeans.

"What about Rusty, doesn't he need to eat?"

"Yeah, but he'll be fine til I take him home tonight." I pulled my shirt on next. The idea of climbing back into dirty clothes bothered me, but I didn't have much of an option. I'd be fine for the rest of the evening.

"You could...you could stay, you know? Oh wait, you just said you need to feed Rusty later never mind."

Fully clothed, I aimed for the direction of her voice, reaching out a gentle hand to find her arms out, waving around as she talked. She sure liked to use her hands, didn't she? A soft smile threatened my lips as I drew her into me. "Don't worry, I'll figure it out. Let's get your stuff."

About an hour and a half later we'd gotten her things into the house, the pizza delivered, and I'd managed to call Travis and convince him to bring over some new clothes for me and food for Rusty.

I stood on the porch waiting for him. Quinn was inside putting the last of her things away.

"So," Travis said, followed by a clap on my shoulder that made me stifle a curse. "I'm guessin' you ain't gonna be comin' home tonight."

I huffed a laugh. "That obvious?"

"Fuck, if a girl as pretty as her asked me to stay the night, I'd make sure I stayed forever."

My lips pulled up slightly, a sense of...not accomplishment but pride maybe swelling in my chest. I'd always been a confident bastard, but the past few years had left me feeling, well, less than. I'd lost my spark. Being around Quinn though, she made me feel confident again. She made me feel alive.

"She's pretty amazing," I finally admitted, unsure of how much to share. Travis and I were co-workers, friends, but I wasn't the type to share my thoughts and feelings with most people. The only one I'd done that with was Reid. And after the fight we'd had a couple years ago, mostly—no, all my doing, I was in no position to call him up and talk about a girl.

Travis chuckled and a familiar hard pressure smacked against my back once more. *Fucker.* Maybe one day I'd get used to it. One day. "You like her, don'tcha?"

I don't think there was a word in my vocabulary that accurately described what I felt for Quinn right now. It was more than like, but too soon for love. Even still, the feeling I got when I was around her surpassed that. Her talk of soulmates and fate had stuck with me. Quinn Decker stirred the ashes of my withered soul, sparking something in me that made me feel like the old me might just still be in there amongst the rubble and wreckage.

She was like a missing piece I hadn't known I'd lost. Hadn't even realized I'd needed until this moment. But now that I had her, I wouldn't give her up to save my damn life.

"I do," I finally replied.

"Well then, I won't keep you. See ya in the mornin'?" Another clap to the back.

I bit my lip, but nodded. "Sounds good, bud. Thanks again."

Making my way back into the house, I heard movement toward where I kept my paint stuff and then Quinn's soft voice. "I didn't want to start eating without you, so I figured I'd start cleaning up your supplies since we made a mess earlier."

"Ah, shit. Did it get all fucked up?" I asked, worry ringing in my tone.

"A couple of the paints fell out of the packaging. I think I put them back right, though."

I made my way over toward the sound of her voice, slowing as the shadows shifted just the slightest bit. I'd gotten to the table then. I put a hand out, feeling the cool wood beneath my touch before placing Rusty's bowl of food and a fresh pile of clothes down. "Can you tell me the order the paints are in? From left to right."

She rattled off the colors—only the yellow and orange seemed to be out of place, which she switched around for me at my request.

"So, that's how you know what colors you're using," she mused, a sense of awe in her voice. "I was wondering how you knew you were using the right ones. How do you guarantee that you're painting with the right colors though?"

"I mean, I can't. I try to put the paint set away the same every single time, and open it the same way. Every time I get a new set, I make Travis tell me the order of the paints so I can add it into a note on my phone."

"Wow. I admire the dedication. I don't think I'd have the patience to go through all those steps."

I huffed. "Yeah, well, bein' blind forces you to learn patience. It's just another part of the process If I wanna paint. I wasn't like this before. Completely opposite, actually."

"Really?" There was no mistaking the intrigue in her voice. I knew she wanted to know more about me. About the accident, but I got the feeling she was holding back.

Running a hand through my hair, I nodded. "Oh, I was the definition of impatient. Always in a hurry. Always goin' about a hundred miles an hour.." I blew out a breath, sliding my tongue over my teeth as a flash of annoyance swelled in me. "It was a hard lesson to learn. One I still struggle with, really."

"I'm sorry," she replied, just as her hand settled gently against my own. So opposite of Travis' shoulder slaps. "For the record, I'm absolutely amazed at how independent you are. And I'm not just saying that. I don't think I'd be able to function."

"You get used to it." Every fiber in my body felt like it was clamming up, freezing at the thought of sharing anything else about my situation.

"Come on, let's eat before it gets cold," she said, entwining her fingers with mine and leading me towards the couch, if I remembered the layout of the house correctly. I don't know if she saw my nervousness and chose not to push or if she genuinely didn't plan to ask me any more questions about it, but I was grateful for the moment to sort through my emotions.

A few seconds after I'd sat, she guided my hand to a paper plate weighed down by food. "I gave you a couple pieces. If you want I can feed Rusty really quick. He looks sad and mopey."

I thanked her for both, and then silence descended on us as we all ate. It wasn't stilted or awkward, but there was an undercurrent of tension present. Quinn had something on her mind—my accident, if I had to guess. But she didn't say anything about it or push me to talk. She'd been good about that, for which I was grateful. Despite setting my mind on telling her everything, I needed these quiet moments to prepare myself. It was a hard story to tell, an even harder pill to swallow. I was about to show her every ugly, broken part of me and lay it bare. It was scary as hell and fucking sucked.

I waited until it seemed like both of us were done eating before setting my plate down and leaning back against the couch cushions. With a sigh, I grumbled, "Well you might as well sit back and get comfortable, darlin'."

"Comfortable for what?" she replied, her words thick with confusion.

"You wanna know about my accident, don'tcha?" Fuck, the words were hard to get out. It felt like glue had replaced the saliva on the roof of my mouth.

"Hux," she sighed, and I felt the couch shift to my left. Her hand settled on my thigh a moment later. "You don't have to tell me."

I shook my head, angling my body toward her voice. "I do. If we're gonna explore this connection between us then you deserve to know why I'm the way I am."

A pause as more shifting unfolded beside me, the warmth of her body settling next to mine, and then. "Okay."

"Well, what all do you know? You said you and Whit looked me up." My leg started twitching at my side. Fuck, I hated talking about this.

A moment later, the weight of her hand rested against my leg. She squeezed gently. "I saw the video and read some articles talking about the accident. How you had a traumatic brain injury and went blind from it."

I nodded. "That's basically the gist of it. Had to learn to walk again. Spent the first year just tryin' to..." Blowing out a breath, I shrugged, "get back to normal, I guess. Not that this is normal, but well, it's my new normal. It was hard. Still is. Some days are better than others."

Quinn didn't say anything, though she did settle closer against me. Her scent, her warmth, it was like a salve to my soul, soothing some of the anger and hurt that still lingered. I don't think it would ever go away. Not fully.

"Do you miss it?" she finally asked.

"Every fuckin' day," I replied, blowing out a breath.

"Tell me about it?" Quinn asked, before quickly adding, "I mean, you don't have to if it's too hard. But... I don't know, it seems such a shame to hide a part of you that you clearly still love so much."

I chewed my lip a moment, conflict sloshing through me. On one hand it was painful, really damn painful, reliving my glory days, but I could see how it might be cathartic. So, even though every inch of me screamed not to, I told her. Everything. From the early years of just starting out as a kid, to the height of my career. The highs, the lows, the mountains and valleys. The in between even. She stayed quiet, so quiet I might have thought she'd left had I not felt her familiar presence at my side through it all.

"Damn, it's been a long time since I've talked about this shit," I finished, leaning back against the couch while wrapping an arm around Quinn.

She snuggled further into to my side, a soft sound escaping her. "I'm sorry."

I kissed the top of her head. "Don't be. It felt...well, I don't wanna say good, cuz that's a lie, but, I guess I feel lighter gettin' that off my chest. I've never really talked about this with anyone."

"Not even your family?"

"Especially not my family," I replied quickly. Just the thought of them stirred memories I didn't want to think about.

"How come?" Genuine surprise and confusion sounded in her tone.

I shrugged. "It's hard with them. My mama's always fussin' over me. Walker acts like I'm a ghost. And my dad..." Another shrug. "He never was the overly accommodatin' type, I mean for as long as I can remember he was the *if you're gonna be stupid you better be tough* kinda parent. But after I got hurt, he became just as bad as Mama. I don't know, I guess I just hate feelin' different. So, it's easier to not talk about it or be around them."

"I'm sorry," she whispered, moving beside me. A moment later, the feather soft feel of her fingertips against my cheek greeted me.

I grabbed her hand and kissed those soft fingertips. "You ain't gotta apologize, darlin'."

"I know, but still. I can't even imagine going through all of that... So, what made you decide to work as a ranch hand here?"

"I didn't wanna go home. It would have been the easier option. My parents own a ranch. My dad's a well known trainer, and I could've worked under him and had it made there, but I just didn't want them coddlin' me, you know?" I pressed my forehead to hers, returning her hand to my cheek where I held it against mine. "Here, I'm no one. I get no special treatment, I get left alone to my work. I don't gotta be reminded constantly of who I was."

She pressed the softest kiss to my lips and whispered, "I don't know who you were other than pictures and videos of you riding, and I'm sure you were awesome then, but I feel so honored to be here right now in your arms. Because this version of you is pretty damn amazing, Hux."

I swallowed, my lungs squeezing as they tried to get down air. Moisture pricked in my eyes, but I was quick to blink it away. Grabbing the back of her neck, I kissed her. I poured every ounce of emotion brewing within my soul into that kiss. All the pent up frustration, sadness, hope, and longing. I felt raw and broken, but Quinn's touches, her kisses, her presence, it was like glue as she pieced me back together, mending the shattered bits.

I had no doubt about it now—soulmates *were* real.

And Quinn Decker was mine.

Chapter Twenty-Three

Sad Songs For Sad People

QUINN

THE NEXT COUPLE DAYS were hectic to say the least. Between Georgette's inconsistent tastes and trying to find vendors with availability for less than two weeks from now, this wedding was going to be so much harder than I expected. Usually I had months to plan, not weeks, but I'd get it done.

This wasn't impossible. Just annoying. Mainly because Georgette was just so god awful. I'd finally settled on *not* having her and my dad come with me to meet with potential vendors, instead opting to just Facetime her or send her pictures of different things, because every single time I took her anywhere, without fail she stuck her foot in her mouth and made an enemy.

Honestly, the woman was truly horrible. Like, cookie-cutter villain horrible. The kind of awful that you couldn't believe existed until you met her. On the surface, she looked sweet enough. A little shallow and vapid maybe, but the minute she opened her mouth her ignorance and just downright awfulness were vile. I couldn't even begin to fathom what her parents were like to allow that sort of behavior.

Oh God, speaking of parents, I still needed to send out the invitations to them and everyone else, like, yesterday. Though that wasn't entirely my fault, since she hadn't gotten me the finalized list yet.

So far I'd gotten the food sorted, the flowers hopefully figured out—if Georgette didn't change the theme *again,* and her and my dad had an in-home cake tasting later that evening that I wasn't invited to, thankfully. Georgette's eyes had glowed with mischief at the mention of how romantic it would be to eat the cake at home. In bed. Naked. Off each other. I'd stopped listening at that point. At least Dad had the decency to look embarrassed at that.

Between all of that, and Hux working late the last day and a half to cover the other hands' responsibilities while they got ready for a rodeo in Bandera tonight, we'd hardly done anything nice together. But it was just as well, he'd been tense since the mention of Travis and the other hands competing.

I know a part of him wanted to do it. It was easy to see in the wistful set of his jaw, or hear it in the longing sound in his voice. I'd learned pretty quick, though, Hux was stubborn and prideful and he rarely liked to open up right away about something that upset him. He'd tell me eventually, or he'd get over it.

I wasn't about to ask and ruin the good thing we had going.

And it was a really good thing, even though I knew it was a bit—okay, a lot—premature. But the past couple days had been a dream overall. Hux had come over every night since Tuesday. Whether he'd stayed once I'd fallen asleep or not, I'm not completely sure. When I woke up each morning, he was gone, but with the whole slew of chores he had to do, it wasn't surprising.

Maybe tonight we'd get a chance to do more than cuddle on the couch for a couple hours before falling asleep. I knew the thought of the rodeo was weighing heavy on his mind. He could use a distraction.

A spark of guilt ignited in my chest. Whit was back out for the weekend, but I knew she planned to go watch Travis and the other hands at the rodeo. I doubted Hux would go. I shrugged off the thought. That was a future me problem. One

I wasn't going to worry about at the moment. Not as I navigated my way toward the arrivals area for the airport to pick up Whit.

"Hey girl!" she all but shouted as she opened the car door and slid into the passenger seat, tossing her jammed full backpack into the back.

"Hey!" I grinned, pulling away from the curb. "How was the flight?"

She waved me off. "Easy. I *finally* caught up in the book club book on the flight. Oh my god, girl! That mating bond kiss was—" She broke off, making a chef's kiss gesture.

I laughed. "It was pretty epic."

She eyed me heavily, a devious smirk on her lips. "And you're telling me your little boy toy kissed you like that and you were going to *leave* him?" Her words shook with disbelief towards the end.

A giggle escaped me even as I rolled my eyes. Leave it to Whit to be so damn dramatic. "It was a momentary lapse of sanity, okay? We figured things out."

"Good. You enjoying your time with him?" she asked, waggling her eyebrows.

I filled her in on any of the details I'd missed in our conversations over the last few days while we drove back to the ranch. "What about you? How's work been, and are you excited to see Travis?"

"Work's been the same as usual, busy, but I'd rather that than slow. I'm more so looking forward to going to our first rodeo and getting to check out dozens and dozens of hot cowboys!" The grin on her lips turned luminous.

My grip on the steering wheel tightened, guilt bubbling up in my chest as I turned my gaze toward the road. "About that..." My words fell away as I braved a look at Whit.

Her brown eyes shone with confusion.

Blowing out a breath, I said, "I can't go. I can't ask that of Hux."

"Oh—" Her face fell the slightest bit. "Yeah, no that makes sense. I probably wouldn't want to go either if I were him." A smile lit up her features—one of

Whit's super powers, her perpetual cheerfulness. "How about y'all come out with us after?"

"'I'll ask. That would be fun!" I added. But to be honest, the thought of a quiet night with Hux sounded nice. Maybe dinner and a movie? I don't know, something low-key and relaxing. But I'd ask anyway just in case.

B Y THE TIME WE got back to my dad's ranch it was early afternoon.

"Did you want to hang out for a bit, maybe tan by the pool before you go to the rodeo, or do you need to get ready?" I asked. "Also, how are you even getting there?" She didn't have a car, so—

Whit tossed her backpack onto my bed and laid beside it. "Travis is gonna pick me up in like forty five minutes."

I plopped down next to her. "How about tomorrow we do breakfast or lunch or something just us two? I need me some Whit time."

She laughed and rolled over to face me on the bed. "Aw, you missing me? Hux isn't as good a roomie, is he?"

I laughed and shoved at her teasingly. "He's only stayed the night. I'd hardly call him a roomie."

"But do you want him to be?" She quirked her eyebrows, that familiar mischievous smile lighting up her face.

"Whit! It's been like less than a week! I can't just have him move in."

She shrugged. "You and I moved in together after a day."

"It's not the same. You and I were never sleeping together. I'm afraid to make things awkward. I think this is a good thing."

"So you think you'll stay?" she asked, no hint of sadness in her voice.

Whit saw the positive in every situation. A forever optimist. But not the annoying kind who, like, reassured you that everything happened for a reason when you were down on your luck. She was just too upbeat and carefree and spontaneous to really be down for long. I could always depend on her to see things on the bright side. So it was no surprise that the prospect of me moving here wouldn't be a problem. She'd just see it as an excuse to visit all the time. Or uproot her life on a whim and start a salon here or something. Who knew with Whit.

I blew out a breath and turned onto my back, settling my eyes on the ceiling and not her expectant gaze. "I honestly can't even think about it right now. It gives me anxiety."

"Why?" Whit scoffed.

"Because, what if I decide to move here and make the wrong decision? What if my dad ends up selling the ranch at some point and I'm out of a job? What if Hux and I don't work out? What if—"

"What if you end up making amazing connections and finding your dream job? What if you fall in love with that gorgeous cowboy? What if you end up getting to run your dad's ranch? What if, what if, what if, Quinn. You don't know unless you try."

I rolled over and forced my lips down into a pout. "You're supposed to be the voice of reason, Whit. The one who tells me I'm being crazy."

She giggled and sat up. "Being reasonable is overrated. I'd much rather take a chance than stay in my comfort zone."

"Even if there's the potential of failure?"

"We learn more from our failures than we do from our success," she said with a shrug.

I rolled my eyes even as my lips curved up into a soft smile. "Where'd you get that from, a fortune cookie?"

She stuck her tongue out at me, before scrunching up her nose and grinning. "Actually, yes, I did."

"Of course, you did."

But deep down I knew she was right. What was that saying, there was no reward without risk, or something like that? Besides, I'd just turned twenty-three a few months ago. Most twenty-three year olds didn't have their lives together. Hell, one could argue Dad was in his fifties and *still* didn't have his shit figured out, so why was I being so ridiculously hard on myself? Life was wild and crazy and filled with so many twists and turns it was impossible to try and keep control of it all.

Maybe I should take a page from Whit's book and just learn to enjoy the ride.

Chapter Twenty-Four
The Painter

Hux

Tʜᴇ ᴀꜰᴛᴇʀɴᴏᴏɴ ꜱᴜɴ ʙᴇᴀᴛ down on me. One could argue it was too early to call it quits already, but this god-awful heat made it damn near impossible to do a good portion of my chores, and besides, with the entire bunkhouse gone at the rodeo—along with their horses—I only had a couple to clean and feed for the evening.

Normally, I didn't mind working, it was one of the few things that I could still do that didn't make me feel like a complete invalid. I guess all the muscle memory of growing up in the saddle and just sheer stubbornness had its perks. But the idea of getting to see Quinn sent my pulse rate quickening. I hadn't hardly spent any time with her the past few days, and I'd be lying if I said I'd been good company for most of it, what with all this rodeo talk going on around the bunkhouse.

It shouldn't have the pull over me like it did. It wasn't even like they were competing in one of the big rodeos. But still, just the thought of the word *rodeo* made my blood both freeze over and boil in my veins at once.

It had taken so much from me. Robbed me of my success, my younger years, my vision. Hell, it damn near took my life. But as much as I hated it, a part of me would always love it. It had shaped me, molded me into the man I was today—for better or worse.

My relationship with the rodeo was toxic as hell, but what a part of me—a deep, forbidden part of me—wouldn't give to have the chance to suit up and ride one more time.

I blew out an angry breath and a moment later a familiar pressure appeared at my right side. "I'm okay, boy," I huffed, even as I pulled a dog treat out of my back pocket and held it down at my side.

Rusty took it gently, not even skipping a beat or step as he continued trekking on alongside me. I'd owned quite a few dogs in my life, but none as smart as Rusty. He just got me. My mom and dad had gotten him for me shortly after the accident. He'd been about six months when they'd given him to me, so he was potty trained and had some basic obedience training on him, but any other training was from me. They'd urged me to get him properly trained, even so far as got into contact with an agency to work with him and I, but I didn't want a seeing eye dog. I didn't want a cane. I didn't want anything that let anyone know I was different. I didn't want to be singled out or judged or pitied, I just wanted to be left the fuck alone.

Silence descended on us as we walked the familiar path—and I mean silence in the loosest terms. Cicadas screeched in the trees, grackles cawed and flapped about, my boots scuffed against the ground, while Rusty's toenails clicked against the concrete or asphalt beneath my feet. From how goddamn hot the ground was, I'd say asphalt. But none of that would matter soon. Because soon, I'd have the sweetest distraction. Just the thought of Quinn had me quickening my pace.

I mounted the stairs of the porch and bent down to grab the key from beneath the welcome mat before the door. A random thought of what the welcome sign looked like went through my mind. Was it plain or did it have some cutesy little saying on it. Quinn hadn't replaced this one yet, I'd have felt the difference from all the wear and tear of it, but I bet if she got around to changing it, it'd have some cute little saying on it. Maybe not so generic as *live, laugh, love* but probably something like *Welcome. Hope you brought wine.* Which would be pretty ironic, since she was such a damn lightweight.

Feminine laughter trickled through the house from the back bedroom as I opened the front door, letting myself and Rusty in.

Sounded like Whit was here.

I liked the girl. She was a bit—okay, a lot much personality-wise for me, but she was nice and a good friend to Quinn, so who the hell was I to judge? Rusty's presence disappeared from my side, his footsteps echoing on the hardwood floor as he trotted away from me, no doubt to find Quinn. He was slow to trust, but not with her. Seemed she had him wrapped around her finger as easily as I was wrapped around hers.

Her excited gasp trickled through the house a moment later, followed by a drawn out "awww" by Whit. "Hi, Rusty. I'm guessing your dad must be home."

Home.

Was it preemptive and pathetic that the single word stirred a whirlwind of emotions in my soul? I might be an idiot, or a glutton for punishment at the very least, but I could envision coming home to her every night. I could envision a life with her. And it would be good. Amazing even to get to love her everyday.

Swallowing down the sudden lump in my throat, I shook off the wave of longing and closed the door. Two pairs of footsteps, accompanied by Rusty's claw taps, grew in volume as they made their way toward me. A ripple of anticipation welled in my veins moments before her scent hit me. It was the same as every day so far, but the calm that settled over me, curling around my limbs and wrapping around my heart, didn't cease to amaze me. No one had ever left such a visceral impact on me. Made me feel so deeply. I was painfully aware of Quinn, and I don't think it would ever change. Not that I minded. Not one damn bit.

"Hi, cowboy." Her voice was light and warm, matching her touch as she wrapped her fingers around my bicep and drew me into her.

A sigh of approval escaped me as I pulled her into my arms.

Holding Quinn was like holding a piece of heaven. The whole damn world could fall apart right now, but it wouldn't matter. Every worry, every fear or frustration turned to ash in her soft, soothing wake.

Whit's squeal of excitement gave me pause. "Ugh, stop it. You guys are just too damn cute!"

Drawing back, I pressed a kiss to the top of Quinn's head and aimed my attention in the direction of Whit's voice. "Howdy, Miss Whit. Pardon the intrusion."

She giggled once more, making my ears ring. *Fuck.* The sound was so opposite of Quinn's—louder, more high-pitched, whereas Quinn's laughter had the same soothing effect as listening to a soft flowing stream.

"You cowboys and your manners. Are you always so polite?" she asked.

I chuckled and removed my ball cap for a moment before running a hand through my hair—god, it was getting long. Righting it on my head once more, I replied, "I try to be, ma'am. Did you have a safe flight?"

For a few moments we just stood there talking—well, Whit talked, Quinn and I just listened, all the while, I held her in my arms, savoring the feel of her. A loud knock on the door interrupted us. Quinn withdrew from me, and then the door creaked open.

"Hey, y'all!" came a familiar, deep voice, just as Travis' fresh woodsy scent filled my nose. Hellos were tossed around, and even though I mentally prepared myself for his infamous shoulder clap, it never ceased to shock me with its intensity.

"Good luck tonight, man," I said, trying to shake the shudder that went through me.

If he noticed my nerves, he didn't let on as he squeezed my shoulder and said, "Well, shit, old man. I didn't think you approved of this whole thing?"

It's not that I didn't approve of it. Hell, I understood the want, the drive, the urge to compete. Even three years later, I *still* longed to. I'd always want to—as long I was alive and breathing. It was the fact that I couldn't that made me hate it so much.

I ignored the question in his words and offered my hand out between us for a handshake. "Go kick ass tonight."

He chuckled and clasped his hand in mine for a firm shake, and when he spoke, his tone lacked any of the humor he usually possessed, a raw vulnerability lingering there instead. "Thank you. If y'all want, we still got some time if you wanna tag along."

I ignored the guilty sting appearing in my chest and forced an apologetic grin to my lips. "Thanks, man. Maybe next time, though."

"If you boys are done with your little bromance moment..."Whit's teasing tone forced me to take a step back and clear my throat.

Travis' easy-going demeanor returned, any trace of gentleness or vulnerability disappearing as I felt the air shift as he moved through the room—closer to Whit, I assumed. "Aw, you jealous, sugar? Was I not payin' you enough attention?"

"Maybe." She gave an indignant huff before the sound of their hushed laughter and teasing filled the room. I fidgeted, feeling like I was intruding on a private moment. Had Quinn and I made Whit feel like this a moment ago, cuz damn, this was weird. It didn't last long though, and within a moment, we exchanged goodbyes and the two of them were off.

Not even a heartbeat passed after the door closed, and Quinn's arms snaked around my neck. God, she smelled so fucking good. "How was your day, handsome?" she asked, her lips brushing against mine.

"It was good, darlin'. And yours?" I replied, sliding my fingers in her soft, silky hair.

"Good. Just did some wedding planning stuff and picked Whit up from the airport. Wanna shower and figure out what to do tonight?"

And despite her tantalizing touch, despite the warm, seductive implication in her words that it wouldn't *just* be a shower, I found myself saying, "You should go to the rodeo, Quinn."

She stilled in my grip, and if I could see her face, she'd probably be scowling at me. As it was, I could feel the heat of her confused stare. "What? No. Why would I do that?"

"Your friend just flew here to see you, and you're gonna stay here, leavin' her all alone? I might not be the worst company, but I wouldn't blame you for pickin' a night of excitement over hangin' out with my old, boring ass."

She didn't move out of my embrace, but something jabbed into my chest—her finger I realized after a moment. "You don't give yourself enough credit. You're fine company. Besides, Whit can make friends with a wall. In fact, I guarantee that when they all come back tonight, she'll have made at least three new friends, and probably twice as many clients. She's going to be absolutely fine without me." The stabbing pressure on my chest disappeared as her soft palm replaced the spot her finger had been. "I don't want to go to a rodeo, Hux. Not unless you're going with me."

Her words, her tone, her touch, they were all so reassuring. It should've made me feel better, except the knot of guilt in my stomach writhed and tightened in response, like a snake coiling to strike. With a sigh, I asked, "Alright, so if you ain't goin' to the rodeo, what do you wanna do?"

A soft, feminine hum fell from her lips as the hand splayed over my heart began a lazy but sure path down my stomach and towards my pantline. "I can think of a couple things," she whispered against my lips.

Well, if she was trying to get my attention on something else, it was working. Desire sprung to life like a wildfire through my veins, my cock jumping at the touch. "You mentioned somethin' about a shower?" I asked.

Her warm, lyrical laughter floated around me as she grabbed my hand and led me along. But as she turned on the shower, as I peeled off my dirty clothes, as I stepped under the spray of hot water and Quinn pressed her plush, velvet lips to mine, a single thought kept swirling in my mind.

"We should go to the rodeo," I finally grumbled out begrudgingly.

She stilled beneath my touch, her words ringing with concern. "What's going on?"

I sighed and tilted my head back beneath the spray of water before pushing the excess back off my face.

How the hell did I explain this to her? I didn't even know what was going on, let alone where to begin. I'd avoided rodeos like the plague for the last three years. Sure, I'd experienced the familiar longing, the wistfulness that came along with thinking of my glory days, but never anything like this. The want, the need, the compulsion of being there, even if I wasn't competing was so strong and visceral I couldn't ignore it. It was an ache in my chest that I couldn' get rid of..

"You're in Texas, darlin', and what's more Texas than a rodeo?"

She humored me with a soft laugh, but I still sensed her confusion. Her hands splayed on my chest held more tension in them than usual. "Hux..." she began, but I cut her off.

"Besides, look at you goin' and plannin' this wedding for a woman you hate. If you can do somethin' like that, I think I can go to a damn rodeo."

She was quiet for some time—a really long time—the only reminder of her presence that of the soft feel of her against me. The hot water had started to cool a bit by the time she spoke. "You don't have to do this on my behalf. I promise."

I slid my teeth over my bottom lip before blowing out a breath. "I want to. Let me do this, Quinn."

Another moment of still silence from her. I felt her nod and then press a soft kiss to my chest. "Why? Why now?"

It was a good question. One I'd been pondering these past few minutes as well. Why now? I pulled Quinn into my arms, felt her soft skin against mine, inhaled the scent of her vanilla body wash mingling with the steam, focused on the reassuring pressure of her hands on my chest. I trailed my fingers up the curves of her hips, along the dip of her shoulder and the column of her neck before settling a hand on either side of her face. A satisfied smirk threatened my lips at the breathy gasp that escaped her.

It was all so clear now.

It was her.

With her, things felt easier. Brighter. Livelier. With her, I found myself *wanting* to do things. Wanting to go out, wanting to face a new day. Before Quinn's arrival, I'd just been existing—in the most basic sense. Wake up, go through the motions, contemplate the point of it all, drink myself to sleep a good portion of those nights, then start it up again. And I knew it probably seemed rash or forward or unbelievable, but in a couple short days Quinn had made me want to live again. I wondered what a few months with her would do? Years? Hell, maybe the rest of forever.

Dating had never really been my thing. I'd always been more driven by my career, by making it than finding love along the way. Not that I hadn't had any relationships, but I'd never dated anyone that made me think of *forever* when I thought of them.

I thought that with her. I felt it when I kissed her.

I wanted forever. And I wanted it with Quinn.

"In therapy," I managed to croak out, "Doc talked a lot about motivators for facin' our fears, and how it's different for everyone. For some people it's faith or religion. For others it's just time. And sometimes it's an event or a person." I blew out a breath, completely unfazed as the water continued to drop in temperature. "I thought it was a bunch of bullshit. I wasn't about to go to church and have people recognize me. It's been almost three years since the accident and time hasn't lessened the hurt of what happened. And no job or event or anything like that helped. But then you came along." I leaned forward, pressing a gentle kiss to her forehead before resting my head to hers. "I don't know what the hell you did, or what kind of magic you possess, but I want to take you to the rodeo. Show you that part of me...even if it hurts."And I knew it was gonna hurt. I swallowed past the lump in my throat before continuing, "But it's okay if it does, because I know...well, I know I got you to lean on."

The admission rocked me about as much as it did her, making my chest tight, and my pulse quicken. But if this stupid accident had taught me anything, it was that time was not promised, and if you wanted something, you should go for it. Who knew how long you'd have it.

The soft pressure of her hands cupping the backs of my wrists greeted me. "Hux, I...." her words washed away like the water down the drain. When she spoke next, her voice quaked, "I'm here for you. Through all of it. I want to see every part of you. Every single piece."

And then her lips brushed against mine with an intensity I happily matched. For a few long moments I lost myself in the feel of her and how perfect she felt in my arms. But as her fingers danced dangerously low on my waist, brushing against my cock, I let out a groan. "Fuck, Quinn," I breathed. "Careful, or I may just change my mind."

Her laughter was light, lyrical, and full of mischief as she toyed with my cock once more, eliciting another growl from me. "You sure you wanna go? We could stay here. I could make you dinner and you can fuck me all night."

She really wasn't the innocent little angel I'd pegged her for, that was for sure. And despite the fact that all of that sounded like a damn dream, despite every fiber of my being wanting to do exactly that, I grabbed her hand and pressed her up against the wall. "Darlin' as nice as that sounds, I wanna devote every single ounce of my attention to making you come again and again, and I want to do this."

My heart clamored in my chest. I hoped she understood. She lifted her hands to cup my face and I reveled in the feel of her slick body sliding against mine as she rose up on tip-toe to kiss me lightly before whispering, "Take me to the rodeo, Hux."

Chapter Twenty-Five
Leather

QUINN

I WAS GLAD WE'D been in the shower for Hux's revelation. The water washed away my tears before Hux could realize I was crying... Hopefully. Hearing him talk about how he'd just been existing before I came around...how I made him want to live again. It broke my heart that he could think so low of himself. He was so wonderful and brave and strong, and I wished he could see himself how I saw him.

Because he was nothing short of amazing.

I'm sure plenty of people might have seen that as a red flag. I could imagine my mom's mom saying something about how irrational I was being, throwing myself at a broken man, and what did that say if he needed me to feel alive again.

But he wasn't broken. Not to me.

At least I wouldn't get any flack from Dad. Him and Georgette had gotten together even quicker than Hux and I.

But I couldn't say we were actually together. There'd been, like, no defining the relationship or anything like that. Not that I was in any rush to do that. I didn't need a label; I was perfectly content with what we had going on.

My hair was still a bit damp from the shower, but I found that the humidity here did wonders for my wavy hair. Besides, I wasn't about to spend close to twenty minutes blow drying it for it to immediately go curly.

I glanced over at Hux as I drove us to the rodeo. He'd found a country station on my radio and hummed along to an older country song. Not gonna lie, I didn't know who it was, but I wasn't about to tell him that.

Holy God, he was so damn hot it hurt. His light blue long-sleeve shirt had a peach and navy colored chevron pattern. It was a shame it hid most of his tattoos, but I admired the few on the back of his hand and wrist that peaked from beneath the fabric as he gripped my thigh. The desire thrumming in my ears drowned out everything and made me almost miss more than a couple turns. He'd opted for his straw hat again, while letting me know that summer was officially straw hat season and it would be like this until Labor Day. I didn't care, I just liked that he looked so good in it.

"So, what can I expect tonight? What all events are there? Do girls rodeo too or is it just men?" I asked hesitantly.

He'd said he wanted to go, but I was terrified to set him off. This was such a monumental moment for him, the last thing I wanted to do was screw it all up.

He gave my thigh a gentle squeeze that just about melted me, and his face turned contemplative. "There's quite a few events. Two for women in PRCA—breakaway roping and barrel racing." I'd heard of the last one vaguely, but needed an explanation for the other.

"It's similar to tie-down roping for men, except the women just have to rope the steer instead of hoppin' off and tying it down after. Basically, you chase down a calf and rope it. It's real quick. Them girls are fast."

"Did you date any..." The words fell away like a whisper on the wind. God, did I sound as pathetic and insecure as I felt? What did it matter if he'd dated one? Well, I mean, I guess if there was the possibility of running into one of his exes it would be helpful to be prepared. Right?

Hux didn't seem bothered at all. A soft chuckle and another reassuring squeeze came from him before he said, "Don't worry, Darlin'. I didn't date any rodeo girls."

"Oh." Well, that made me feel a bit lighter. "How come?"

He shrugged. "I don't know. Rodeo girls are fuckin' nuts. Walker says it's just cuz I could never handle women, but that's a damn lie."

I laughed. "So, what about the men's events?"

He gave me the total run down, from what the rough stock events were and how they were different from the timed ones. Bull riding was apparently a rough stock event, along with saddle bronc and bareback bronc riding. Then you had the timed events, including team roping, steer wrestling, which apparently one of the ranch hands, Brooks competed in. I hadn't really had the opportunity to interact with much, but he seemed nice enough. A bit shy and bashful. Or was that Wyatt? There was also tie-down roping. That was Travis' event. Hux even told me about mutton bustin', what sounded like an adorable, albeit a bit dangerous event for the little kids involving them riding sheep.

I don't know if he realized it, but the longer he talked the more the tension just washed off of him like mud rinsing away in a rain shower. There was this lightness, this easiness that took over his voice, settled into the marrow of his bones. His harsh features had smoothed out, and the softest whisper of a smile toyed on his mouth.

But hearing him talk about the rodeo was *nothing* compared to actually seeing him there. It wasn't a quick, obvious thing. In fact, at first I was worried that we'd made a horrible mistake. He'd gotten ridiculously quiet, his grip on my hand vice-like in its intensity. His breathing was sharp and shallow as he walked at my side, the only sound that of his leather cowboys and my, well, white fashion one s scuffing against the dirt. I was glad I'd opted to wear them even if I was worried I'd stick out like a sore thumb and look like a fraud. I hadn't expected the rodeo to be outside, which was probably stupid, but I'd never been to one before.

"This is a small rodeo," Hux clarified when I'd asked. "Not all of 'em are indoors and in fancy arenas."

An announcer and loud music blared over the speakers surrounding the place, mentioning something about five minutes until starting. A few stragglers still filed into line behind us as we made our way through the short line.

"Two tickets," Hux said, fishing out his wallet as we settled before the pay station. I hadn't even had time to grab for my purse. How had he possibly known we were at the front of the line? Was I just oblivious to my surroundings or was he hyperaware of things now? Probably a bit of both, but the latter seemed to be very true. He was always much more aware of things than me.

"That'll be twenty-four dollars, sir," the older woman replied.

"You take card or just cash?" he asked.

"Either, sir."

He handed her his card, and I watched the moment recognition washed over her. Her eyes lit up, her mouth forming into a shocked "O". "Well, goodness me. Jack—Jack, get over here! It's Huxson Lane!"

My heart clenched as every muscle in Hux stiffened. A muscle in his jaw feathered and his grip on my hand tightened a fraction. He was so still, I wondered if he was even breathing.

"I'm so sorry, sir, but my husband's such a huge fan."

Oh God. This was going to end poorly. I braced for the...I don't know what to come, but from Hux's stance, the stillness, the barely breathing, it couldn't be good.

"Debby what the he—" The man's words died on his lips as he took in Hux. "Well, I'll be damned. You're—you're..."

And then Hux surprised the hell out of me. He reached out his free hand and offered it between him and the older man. "Huxson Lane, sir. How're you doin' tonight?"

He spoke with such ease, held himself with such confidence it made my heart squeeze. This wasn't the same gruff, closed-off, bitter cowboy I'd met a week ago, this was someone new. Or old, I guess. Maybe he was both now, but this was like getting a glimpse into the past. Into the man who I'd only seen in interviews and reels. At first I thought it was just a ruse, but as Hux stood there and chatted up the old man and his wife for a couple of minutes before paying for our tickets then making our way toward the grand stands, I realized this wasn't an act. This was him. The real him.

And God he was beautiful.

The place was packed, and my worries about standing out wearing my cowboy boots were for naught. There were so many more girls in far flashier outfits than my sage green sundress and white cowboy boots. Hux's hand never left mine as I helped him navigate through the crowd, but honestly, it was more like he was leading me.

Walking through the rodeo grounds had been like walking through a portal or something to an alternate reality or the past.

Hux moved with purpose, confidence, holding his head high. If he was aware of the growing number of hushed whispers, he didn't let on. Or maybe he just didn't care anymore. Either way I was proud as hell of him.

We made our way through the throng, stopping for a few minutes as the National Anthem was sung and a red, white, and blue clad cowgirl galloped across the arena on a beautiful pearly white horse while an American flag billowed behind them. Not gonna lie, it was pretty epic to witness. As the song ended and they announced that bareback bronc riding would start in five minutes, we continued on to find Whit or some open seats, whatever we could find at this point

.

"Well, shit. They just lettin' any old rabble in here these days?" An older gentleman scoffed, stepping into our path. His voice was deep and raspy, reminding me of the sound of gravel. He was probably in his mid sixties or so, and handsome, if not a bit rough around the edges.

I rocked back at his harsh tone, but Hux's lips pulled up into a wide grin as he held out a hand. "Shit. Bad Mooney! Man, it's been a minute. How're you, sir?"

The man gripped his hand and shook it hard. A solid handshake. "Doin' good. Didn't expect to see you here."

"Trust me, that makes two of us, sir." Hux tugged on my hand gently, pulling me closer to his side. "I wanna introduce you to Quinn. She's um…" He chewed his lip a moment and my heart thumped as I waited with bated breath for his next words. What did he think we were? "Well, she's mine."

Mine.

I bit back a gasp, a chord thrumming to life in my chest at his little admission.

I wondered if he'd even realized the significance of that four letter word. If it meant as much to him as it did to me. Did he remember when we were talking the other day and I told him it's like my heart woke up and claimed him as mine?

I'm sure some people would see that as another red flag. Him claiming me as his own. But I didn't see it that way. It felt fitting for us, to be honest.

I squeezed his hand in silent reassurance and smiled at the older cowboy across the way. "Hi, it's nice to meet you, Mister Mooney, was it?"

He appraised me with a cool, hazel stare, a soft, appreciative grin finally coming to rest on his lips. "Pleasure's mine, Miss Quinn." Then he turned to Hux. "Now how'd your ugly mug wind up with someone as beautiful as this girl?"

From the light in his eyes and the smirk I knew he was joking, but his tone was so harsh, so unrelenting and brutal it was hard to remember that. I wondered how they knew each other.

Hux laughed, the sound rich and warm, warmer than I'd ever heard it. "I don't know. Probably for a similar reason you landed yourself with a gem like Mrs. Mooney. Luck of the draw."

The man laughed once more, a sudden, deep sound reminding me of the crack of a whip, or a clap of thunder. "Can't argue with that. Have your parents met her yet?"

Something rippled across Hux's face at the mention of his parents. It wasn't as intense as anger or as wistful as sadness. I wanted to say maybe...guilt?

"Not yet," he replied. "Haven't had a chance to get back there." Mr. Mooney nodded and before he could say a word, Hux asked, "Speakin' of the missus, where is she? I don't think I remember her ever missin' one of Cash's rodeos."

"She's back home helpin' the girls with the kids. It's a boys' trip, accordin' to Cash."

"Cash settled down and had a kid?" Hux asked, surprise written plainly on his face.

Another bark of laughter fell from the old cowboy. "That'd be the fuckin' day. Nah, Maverick and Ryder both have kids now. You remember them, right?"

Hux nodded. "Yeah, I remember 'em. Good for them. Cash still his usual self?"

Mr. Mooney chuckled. "Well, he's got himself a girl now, believe it or not, but it ain't gonna last. He ain't ready, and until he is, he'll continue chasin' tail." He nodded at me. "If you're smart you won't let Cash meet her."

I didn't know who Cash was, but I gave Hux's hand a reassuring squeeze once more and leaned in closer to him. I wasn't going anywhere.

"Don't let me meet wh—hot damn!" The sound of an unfamiliar voice drew my gaze and I took in the handsome, if not a bit gaudily-dressed cowboy who walked toward us. He was handsome, like, unfairly handsome with a chiseled jaw dusted in a five o' clock shadow beard, cropped, caramel-colored hair, and a physique that must've been sculpted by God himself, making the discussion about him earlier make much more sense.

No wonder he had no plans of settling down. He probably could get any girl in this place. Even in his obnoxiously bright pink outfit, complete with rhinestones and all.

His hazel gaze swirled with mischief and temptation as he flashed me a dazzling, lopsided grin. "Well, hello there, sweetheart. Aren't you just as pretty as a damn present? The name's Cash. But you can call me Big Daddy."

I glanced at Hux who fidgeted at my side. Was he nervous? Worried I'd be affected by this guy's charm? It was odd seeing him anything but the cool, confident cowboy I'd met.

"Thanks for keeping her company, bud," Cash went on to Hux, his entire being rippling with confidence, "but it's time for her to take a ride on a real cowboy." He glanced at me, offering me a wink. "Don't worry, sweetheart, I don't buck...much."

I couldn't help but laugh. Now *this* guy was a walking red flag. It should be illegal to be that charming and that good looking. But lucky for me, I already had my own hot as hell cowboy, and found him plenty charming.

"Sorry, *sweetheart*," I tossed back with a sugary-sweet voice. "But I don't consider eight seconds a long ride." I might not know much about rodeos, but Hux had let me know eight seconds was the magical number when it came to staying on a bull or bucking horse.

The cowboy was unfazed, that smug, perfect grin of his pulling wider on his face. Seriously, how was this guy not a model or something? "Not all my rides are eight seconds, darlin'."

"Yeah, kid, sometimes you only last four," Mr. Mooney chimed in, his words cutting to the bone even as a charming smile lit up his handsome features. Looking at him and his son side by side...wow. The Mooneys had some amazing genes.

Hux huffed out a laugh and pulled me tighter into his side as he kissed the top of my head. I glanced up at him, completely ignoring Cash and his father bickering back and forth. As entertaining as that was, seeing Hux so happy and light...it was magnificent. I couldn't help but wonder why he'd stayed away from the rodeo for so long. Especially when just being here clearly mended some of the shattered parts of his soul.

"Didn't they just call bareback ridin, dipshit?" Hux asked.

"Yeah," Bad added, a frown forming on his face. "What the fuck are you doin' out here? Better yet, what the hell's wrong with Mav if he let you go?"

Cash brushed his dad off with a dismissive wave. "I need my lucky light."

My brows furrowed together even as Mr. Mooney growled out some incoherent curse. "What the fuck are you talkin' about, dumbass?" he managed to get out.

"Well, I like to carry a pack of smokes in my bag to light up right before some of my rides. I'm out, and Mav ain't smokin' now since Chey had the baby and I figured since Mama ain't here, you'd be lightin' up like a damn chimney."

Seemed like a bit of an over the top pregame ritual if you asked me, but his dad just shrugged and felt around in his chest pocket then both of his back jean pockets. "Fuck," he all but snarled. "Where the hell did I leave 'em?"

I bit back a grin at the following string of curses that fell from his lips. And I'd always thought cowboys were the epitome of manners and gentlemanly behavior, but apparently they had the mouths of sailors. It was okay though, I didn't mind at all.

Hux shifted, his hold on me vanishing as he reached into his back pocket. "Here, I got ya."

Cash's grin was luminous as he grabbed the cigar in one hand and clapped Hux on the shoulder with the other. I noted the slight shudder that rippled through Hux, but it did little to dim his own grin. "Well, damn, look at you comin' in clutch like that? Thanks, man. I'll let it slide that your girl hurt my pride." He chuckled, more to himself than anyone else. "I gotta run, but y'all should come out with us tonight."

"Oh, I don't know," Hux replied, but Cash was already disappearing through the crowd as the first bareback rider was announced.

Chapter Twenty-Six
Dear Rodeo

Hux

I COULDN'T RECALL A time in my life where I'd sat in the stands of a rodeo and not competed. Even when I'd been out for injuries, anytime I watched, I was down in the thick of it, there to cheer on Reid or whatever other buddies I knew were competing.

This...this was new. Different. But it didn't have any less effect on me. The sounds, the smells, the air I breathed felt so familiar that it was easy to conjure up an image in my mind. And just like that night at the bar with Quinn—and every moment with her since—it's like I could see everything clearly.

And so much joy filled my heart, so much calm settled over my soul like a warm blanket, that I wondered why the hell I'd waited so damn long to make my way back here.

The rodeo always had been and always would be in my bones—whether I could compete or not. Trying to ignore it was like trying to ignore part of my soul.

The sweet familiar scent of Quinn's lemongrass and vanilla perfume drifted on the soft breeze that kissed my cheeks and I took the opportunity to pull her tighter against me. None of this would have been possible without her.

I don't know if she realized how big of a moment this was, or just how much of an impact she had on me, but I would forever be changed because of her.

Bad Mooney had insisted we sit in his box with him. *"I don't need all this goddamn space, and you ain't gonna get shit for seats now. So shut up and accept the offer."* Bad words. Whit had found us about halfway through the lineup of bareback bronc riders when she'd gone to get a drink. How she could get up during an event, willing to miss any of the action was a mystery to me, but this was her first rodeo after all, so I'd forgive her. Though I might not if she didn't stop talking. I could understand if it were about the damn rodeo, but apparently she was more interested in people's outfits and hair.

Quinn impressed the hell out of me though, which wasn't surprising at this point. Everything she did seemed to impress me. God, I really was whipped.

"So, what exactly determines the score?" Quinn asked. "I know part of it is lasting the entire eight seconds, but some guys get higher numbers than the others? Why?"

I nodded toward where I knew Bad was now sitting. "That's a question for a legend himself." Sure, I could tell her, but I knew Bad enjoyed getting to relive his glory days any chance he could, and it wasn't everyday you could ask a famous bronc rider tricks of the trade.

"You were a rodeo cowboy?" That was Whit—surprise ringing in her voice.

"Damn right, I was. I got buckles older than you, girl."

A smirk threatened my lips. Ever humble Bad. Some things never changed, and I found solace in that.

Bad and my dad went way back. Back to their youth rodeo days. My dad used to rope, but his heart was never in rodeoing, it was in training. But the two stayed close through the years. Hell, they talked more than I talked to my family at this point.

Bad cleared his throat and aimed his next words at Quinn beside me. "Scorin's got a lot to do with spurrin'. Your toes should be turned out with the spurs, and you can't let up on it or else you're gonna get a shit score. Rhythm and control play into it as well. There's a hundred points total. Fifty for the rider, and fifty for the horse."

"The horse?" Whit asked. "The horse gets points? For what?"

"For the way it performs. How much does it buck? How athletic is it? Did it just rock back and forth or make it damn hard for that guy to be in the saddle?"

Quinn and Whit took turns asking Bad questions about the difference between saddle and bareback riding and which was harder, but all conversation died when Cash's name was called over the speakers. The air felt charged around Bad—it's like I could feel his focus. It was sharp and hot on my skin, like burning coals.

And despite how loud everything was—between the crowd and the music—I heard the gate slam open, *felt* the power in that horse's hoofbeats in the loose dirt. Kid Rock's "Cowboy" came on, but it only lasted eight seconds before the buzzer sounded. Bad didn't shout out or make an excited fuss. He simply grunted out a soft, "Getcha some money," under his breath.

I clapped, even as Quinn squealed in excitement. "He did it! That was so amazing!"

The entire crowd cheered, but none did louder than fucking Cash himself. His familiar crow and tagline of "Big Daddy's in the house" echoed across the arena.

"Holy shit!" Whit said, her voice full of awe.

A wave of newfound cheers and claps erupted, and I rolled my eyes even as a grin pulled on my mouth. "Bastard just did a backflip, didn't he?" I huffed.

"How did you—" Quinn began.

"I rodeoed with Mooney on more than one occasion. It's his trademark move after a winning ride." He always was such a fucking showboat. It always seemed to work for him though. Still seemed to from the way women were shouting his name.

"He damn near broke his neck tryin' to learn how to do that," Bad grumbled from my side. "Violet hates that he still does it."

"She still match him when he rides?" I asked.

"Does a bear shit in the woods?"

I laughed, and Quinn said, "She matches with him? That's so cute! Makes me feel bad for thinking how obnoxious his clothes were."

Bad chuckled. "His clothes *are* obnoxious as fuck. But his mother loves it. And Cash may be a fuckin' pain in my ass, but one thing is for certain. That boy loves his mama."

Honestly, I didn't know a soul who didn't love Mrs. Mooney. She was the kind of woman who was everyone's mama. It didn't matter if you were hers or not, if you needed something, she took care of you. Don't piss her off though. She was kind, but she was fierce, and if you crossed her, you better hide before she lit your ass up like a firecracker on the Fourth of July.

Most of the rodeo went like that.

Quinn and Whit—well mostly Quinn—asked questions about the events, while either Bad or I explained it to them. Quinn seemed to hold a genuine interest in everything revolving around the rodeo. Whether it was because of my involvement in it or her own curiosity, I didn't know, but I was happy I'd brought her tonight. Everyone deserved to experience the magic of a rodeo at least once in their lifetime. Whit seemed to be enjoying herself easily enough, but I don't think she appreciated the same aspects of the rodeo that Quinn did.

The closer time crept toward bull riding, the more my emotions went haywire. By the time barrel racing ended, leaving no other events aside from bulls left, my heart sped along faster than a runaway train.

Quinn leaned into me, her warm, gentle touch settling some of my nerves like putting a salve over a burn. "Are you okay?" she whispered in my ear, so quiet I almost didn't hear it.

Had she read my thoughts or something? Or was I just that easy to read? I opened my mouth to respond but the words lodged in my throat. I didn't even know where to begin with explaining how I felt. Every muscle in my body was taut and full of tension, and my heart pounded so wildly in my chest I'm surprised she didn't hear it. As it was, it damn near drowned out the sounds of the rodeo.

I offered a silent nod and squeezed her hand once before adjusting my attention toward Bad. "Are the bull chutes still over to the left?" I asked, my voice thick with an emotion I couldn't—didn't want to quite place.

"Yeah. Want me to get Cash and have him take ya back into the thick of it? Let'cha feel it again?"

I cleared my throat and shook my head, fighting the appreciation that battled with the fear and wistfulness swirling in my chest. "I'm gonna head that way," I managed to get out as I stood, disentangling my fingers from Quinn's.

She resisted for the shortest moment, concern reverberating in her words as she asked, "Want me to come with you?"

I shook my head, and suddenly the lump in my throat was back, and no matter how hard I tried, I just couldn't get the word out. I didn't want her to worry about me, but I didn't want her with me for this either. Not because I didn't want her to see that part of me, or because I feared she'd pity me or anything like that, but I just...I needed this moment alone. To go through the wave of emotions, to ride that tide without her there to witness it. It was just something I needed to do. My hands trembled so badly I clenched them into fists as I finally forced out a gruff, "No."

"O-okay." I instantly regretted my tone. I hadn't meant to sound like that. I reached out a hand and drew her to me, slowly reaching up to cup her face. "Thank you, but no," I whispered against her lips.

And before she could say a word, before I let her soft warmth or her sweet scent keep me there, I walked away.

Each footfall of my boots on the wooden grandstands reverberated through my bones as I made my way down the center aisle toward the left half of the arena. I slid my hand along the handrail, following as the aisle dipped downward, until nothing but empty air and the crunch of gravel and dirt beneath my feet greeted me. I reached out my hand and made a few steps to the right before coming into contact with the pipe-stall fencing of the arena.

My heart raced as I settled my arms atop the middle wrung and leaned forward, my unseeing gaze resting toward where I assumed the bull chutes were. I could hear them easily enough. The crashing of horns against pipe, the excited din of chatter from the contestants. The cowboys working behind the scenes to get the bulls loaded into the proper chutes. Adrenaline and terror pumped through my veins, so intense it was almost like I was competing again.

Why was it this hard? How was simply standing here such a damn big deal?

Because it mattered, a little voice whispered in my head. Because this was who I was for so long. This was what I did. This was my life. And even though I'd given it up, I'd never moved on. I'd never addressed this part of me. And it was hard and it was terrifying and as much as I was tempted to just walk away, stomp my ass back to Quinn's rental and wait for the rodeo to be over, I wouldn't. I couldn't. I *had* to do this.

The commentator announced the first rider and bull—Ryder Wright and some bull I'd never heard of. Only reason I knew Ryder was because he and Cash were buddies. Back when I was professional rodeoing, he'd still been making a name for himself—competing in two events. From the sound of it, he was doing pretty good for himself and was looking like a potential candidate for NFR, according to the announcer. I'd done my best to erase anything about PBR or rodeos from any aspect of my life for the past three years. I didn't know what the latest standings were or who was in the running for heading off to NFR this year. A thought of Reid popped into my head. I wondered how he was doing.

But all thoughts of Reid—or anything really—vanished as the gate slammed open with a thunderous crash. And then the strangest thing happened. The music died—vanishing on the breeze until it was nothing more than whispers in the wind, and even though I was at least twenty yards away from the actual action, I could hear the bull's snorts, the slap of leather against its thick hide. I could *feel* its hoofbeats as they pounded against the earth with each rock and buck and spin.

I wasn't an onlooker, I wasn't standing outside of the arena. For eight seconds, I was atop that bull. The phantom feel of the bull rope appeared against my right hand, and I felt myself clinging to it for dear life. I rode that rush of adrenaline that thrummed through me like a shockwave to my heart, wondering how the fuck I'd ever thought I could give up this part of me.

Then the buzzer went off, and sound returned—the music blared and the crowd was going absolutely nuts. Reality set in then.

"Well, hot damn ladies and gentlemen. This kid sure knows how to ride 'em right, don't he? That was another spectacular performance by Ryder Wright with a–holy cow! A ninety point five ride. That one's gonna be tough to beat, folks. This kid just got himself sponsored last year and his future's lookin' bright."

I blew out a shaky breath I hadn't even realized I'd been holding in, my lungs searing as I sucked down hot, humid air.

I wiped at the moisture pricking in my eyes. Fuck. That was...I still didn't know exactly. One of the hardest, yet most freeing things I ever had the opportunity of doing. I'd fought so hard to forget about the rodeo, but having this moment made me realize that there was no forgetting. No moving on. No letting go.

I'd stopped living three years ago. I was alive, but I wasn't really living, ignoring who I was at my very core. And that was a rodeo cowboy.

And even if I never competed again, my accident, my blindness, couldn't take away the fact that I was, and always would be, two time World Champion bull rider, Huxson Lane.

I found myself glued to the spot I stood in. Despite wanting to get back to Quinn, my feet may as well have been roots spearing into the ground, holding me in place.

One more time. What I'd give for just one more time. To gear up. To climb into the chute. To ride out eight seconds.

"Well shit, man. Did you just come, cuz I just came." I jumped at the closeness of the voice, recognizing the cocky, suave tone immediately as I tried to hold back the shudder of surprise that coursed through me and set me on edge. How the hell had I not heard him?

"What the fuck, Mooney?" I grumbled.

He laughed, and I felt the air shift as he settled at my side. "Got another smoke?" he asked, his tone carefree and casual. He was always like that. Always so laid back. Before the accident I'd been more like him, but even then, no one was quite like Cash fuckin' Mooney. He was as offensive as he was charming. And he knew it. Yet somehow it always worked out in his favor.

I fished in my back pocket for my pack of cigars and pulled two out, along with my lighter. I lit mine and pressed it to my lips, before handing everything to Cash.

For a moment there was nothing but relative quiet surrounding us as a wave of sweet tobacco billowed around me, but then Cash said, "You miss it, don't cha?"

My chest squeezed painfully tight, and it had nothing to do with the smoke in my lungs. "Course I fuckin' do."

"You should be out there." Cash's voice held an honesty to it I'd never heard before. Or maybe I'd just never really talked to him on a deeper level. He'd never really been the guy to have a heart to heart with, and three years ago, I sure as hell wasn't that kind of guy either.

I huffed. "Yeah, well, fate had other plans."

"You really think you'll never do it again?"

I took a puff from my cigar before blowing out. "Doctors said one hit to the head and I may not walk away next time."

"Yeah, that's what doctors are supposed to say. But what they say and what you decide to do don't always align. What do *you* want?"

My hand trembled as I took another drag of my cigar. Fuck. Was I shaking that bad? I opened my mouth, that annoyingly familiar knot lodging in my throat once more. *What did I want?* The list was surprisingly short.

Two things in particular: I wanted Quinn, and I wanted to ride.

The first I could have. If she wanted me—which I wasn't ever the smartest kid in school, but I was pretty damn sure she'd have me. But the second…the risk was so high. As wild and reckless as I'd been before my accident, I just didn't know if the risk outweighed the reward now.

I opened my mouth to speak, closed it, opened it again. "What I want and what I need are two different things. I wanna ride, but one wrong move and I can't have her." I raked my teeth over my bottom lip. "And I need her."

I needed her warmth and light. I needed her laughter and kindness. I needed her like a desert needed rain.

Chapter Twenty-Seven
Am I Okay?

QUINN

"Did I…did I do something wrong?" I asked, watching Hux walk away and disappear into the tide of people. I glanced at Whit, who looked just as confused as I felt—her brows furrowed and a frown scrunching up her face.

What had happened? He was doing so good. Great, even. At least, he seemed like it. What had I missed, or not noticed sooner?

Every inch of me screamed to go after him, but Mister Mooney's warm, heavy hand on my shoulder kept me rooted to my seat. "You didn't do anythin' wrong, Miss Quinn. Some demons you just gotta fight alone."

I chewed on my bottom lip, shifting my focus between where Hux had just gone and Mister Mooney. "I hate that," I admitted with a huff.

His gaze turned contemplative as he looked off in the distance and nodded. "Yeah, but I wouldn't worry about him too much. Kid's tough as nails."

Something about Mister Mooney's words eased some of the worry knotted in my chest. Not much, but it was enough to keep me from running after Hux.

My heart hurt at the thought of him going through this alone. He'd come here because of me. Because he wanted to show me this world. This part of him. And even though Mister Mooney's logic made sense, I still felt like I could—should be doing more to help than sitting here.

I cast my gaze to Whit once more, sharing a silent *what-do-you-think* look with her. Her lips tugged upward into a soft, hopeful smile. "Give him some time, Quinnie," she whispered, reaching over to squeeze my hand gently.

With a sigh, I set my sights forward on the arena. Mister Mooney explained the ins and outs of bull riding as they went one by one through the lineup of contestants. Watching them compete was equally as terrifying as it was magnificent. How they rode these gargantuan animals and didn't die was no small miracle. But not only that, they did it with such ease and grace. It was baffling.

Of the eight riders who competed, only three lasted the full eight seconds. Three impressive rides, but the highest score went to a cowboy by the name of Ryder Wright—yes, you read that right. Whit and I giggled like school girls at that wonderful innuendo of a name.

Mister Mooney went on to explain that his son, Cash, and Ryder were best friends, and that Ryder was a potential candidate for NFR this year, which was, I guess, the *"big daddy rodeo of all rodeos"*. His words. An annual ten day rodeo for the top fifteen competitors in each event.

Hux had gone to that. And won. Not once, but twice. He'd been working on a third.

"Alright, Miss Quinn," Mister Mooney said as the commentator announced the end of the rodeo. "Let's go find your cowboy."

My cowboy.

Butterflies fluttered against my ribcage at that.

The rodeo erupted into chaos as people filed out of their seats and down the main aisleway. We followed the throng, my heart thumping faster and faster in my chest. I wondered what state Hux would be in. If he'd still be open and happy like earlier, or as closed off and shut down as when he'd left me.

As I followed the throng of people and made my way down the aisle into the main rodeo grounds, my gaze settled on a section flurrying with excitement. My heart skipped a beat. Two, three as I got my first glimpse of Hux.

I'd expected—well, I don't honestly know what I'd been expecting, but certainly not this. Not him smiling and laughing and conversing with fans. My boots felt like they'd been filled with cement, keeping me rooted to my place. For a long moment, all I could do was watch. Watch as fan after fan walked up to either say hi to him or ask for a photo or autograph. He never said no. Never looked annoyed.

"Holy shit," Whit gasped, "He's like a *really* big deal."

Mister Mooney let out an appreciative huff. "You don't become a two time World Champion by bein' mediocre, miss."

I liked Mister Mooney, he was brusque and the type to not sugar coat things, but would tell you like it was. He reminded me of Hux.

The weight of his hand rested on my shoulder. "Told ya he'd be okay."

I nodded, awe replacing any of the worry left in me. "I shouldn't have doubted you," I replied, offering him a soft smile.

He winked and nodded toward Hux and Cash, who stood a few feet away, talking to two other rodeo contestants. "Come on, now."

I was only a few feet away from him when a family approached Hux—well, approached was a nice way of putting it. The couple had tried and failed to hold back their kid—couldn't be older than nine or so—as he barreled for Hux. Their younger daughter hung back though, too shy to follow her brother.

"Mister Lane! Mister Lane! Can I get your autograph?" The little boy all but bounced from foot to foot as he came to a stop before Hux. And Hux, the gruff, shut off cowboy I'd come to know, crouched down before the kid and aimed a grin in his direction. "Sure, kid. Where do ya want it on?"

"My hat!" the kid exclaimed. "Can you sign my hat?" As the kid thrust his cowboy hat into Hux's hands, I noticed the sharpie Hux held. I was only a few steps away and saw his immaculate signature as he put it on the bottom of the brim of the kid's hat.

"You were my favorite bull rider. I wanna be like you one day."

Hux chuckled, the sound soft and deep. He reached out and tentatively placed the hat on the kid's head. It took a moment, and a minor adjustment from his mom, who pushed him more into Hux's line of fire. "Can you promise me something...what's your name?" Hux asked, standing up once more.

"My name's Hayden, sir!"

"Hayden, I don't want you to be just like me, I want you to be better. I want you to be the best version of you that you can possibly be. You do that, and you'll be just fine."

If my ovaries weren't already a puddle of mush, they were now. Hot, brave, and good with kids?

"Well, that was just about the cutest thing I've ever seen," Whit squealed under her breath.

I tried and failed to bite back a grin, then proceeded to wait until the family had said their goodbyes to Hux before stepping forward and saying, "Hey, cowboy. Have a minute for your biggest fan?"

Recognition rippled through him, a broad, brilliant smile coming to his lips. It was a miracle my heart didn't beat right out of my chest with how fast and hard it thumped.

Holy God, he was gorgeous. And he was *mine*.

When he held his hand out, I reached for it easily, melting into him as he dragged me to his side and pressed his lips to the top of my head. Seeing him like this, so open and happy and carefree, it brought tears to my eyes. Tears I'm so glad he couldn't see, because I didn't want him to mistake them for sadness. I'd always been one of those happy criers. Honestly, just a crier in general. But most people didn't understand how I could get so ridiculously happy that I'd make myself cry.

This was definitely one of those times.

"Sorry for leavin', darlin'," he murmured, quiet enough so only I could hear.

I kissed him, whispering back, "you don't need to apologize."

"Well, shit, man," a cocky voice called out from a few feet away, dragging my attention. Cash Mooney's million-dollar grin lit up his face, bright and luminescent like the sky on the fourth of July. "He didn't even compete and he's gettin' a winnin' kiss. I wanna kiss from someone as pretty as you."

Hux chuckled, but before he could even spout off some smart ass remark, I found myself meeting the handsome cowboy's stare, saying, "I'm sure there's a mirror in one of the bathrooms you could kiss if you're feeling left out."

Everyone got a kick out of that, especially the two cowboys closest to him, who burst into laughter. Well the shorter of the two did, a wide grinning pulling on his scarred face. The other, more stoic one let out a low chuckle, the ghost of a smile peaking through his harsh features, but the movements looked like they were foreign to him. I recognized the first as the bull rider who won—Ryder Wright. The other was Cash's partner in his timed event of team roping. I couldn't remember his name though.

"Damn, sweetheart," Cash chuckled, lowering the obnoxious rose gold sunglasses he wore to peg me with his intense hazel gaze. "Cuttin' me down twice in one night?"

I laughed. "If anything I gave you a compliment. Let's be honest, you're the prettiest person here."

His grin pulled wide. "Aw, shucks. You're makin' me blush now."

Hux huffed at my side, drawing me in closer to him. "Don't make his head any bigger than it already is."

I grinned, reveling in the feel of Hux. I'd never thought of myself as a touchy person, especially because of my time with Devin, but turns out I loved it. Craved it. Needed it. Or maybe it was just Hux I needed. He talked about me having magic, but I think he had a magic all his own.

"And who is this pretty little lady?" Cash's voice dragged me from my reverie.

Oh my God, I'd completely forgotten about her. Which sounded horrible, I know, but she was being so quiet compared to her normal self, and well, I'd been distracted with Hux.

Gaze flicking between him and my best friend, I said quickly, "This is Whit, my bestie. Whit, this is Cash Mooney."

Cash's smile turned even brighter—if that was even possible—as he took Whit in. He stepped forward and reached out to grab her hand, pressing a kiss to the back of it. "Whit, huh? Thank God, cuz my wits abandoned me the minute I saw your beautiful face."

Chaos ensued then.

Ryder and Hux both burst into fits of laughter. Even the tall cowboy cracked a smile, his shoulders rising and falling in silent mirth. Mr. Mooney appeared to have choked on his own spit and dissolved into a fit of coughing.

I couldn't help but smile even as I rolled my eyes. God, that was the most cheesy, corny, yet clever thing I'd ever heard.

There was no doubt about it. Cash Mooney was terrible. Terribly charming. Terribly attractive and terribly dangerous. He was the epitome of a playboy. A cowboy casanova. And a walking red flag if there ever was one.

"Where'd you get that shit," Mister Mooney replied, having recovered enough from his coughing fit to speak. "Outta a Cracker Jack box?"

Cash didn't even have the sense to blush. He probably didn't even know how to. He was so ridiculously confident. Just like Whit.

"Well, you sure know how to charm a girl, don't you?" she replied just as confidently, grinning right back at him.

If she hadn't come here with Travis, the two would make a fantastic pair. Her and Cash together could be trouble. I mean, he was gorgeous, but he had heartbreak written in bright neon letters hanging above his head, along with approximately eight million red flags.

Cash's lips tugged into a lopsided grin. "Come on out with us tonight and I'll show you a real good time."

His best friend, Ryder, smacked him across the chest, breaking the moment. "You got a girlfriend, remember?"

Cash shook his head, the smile on his mouth faltering as if he'd just been shaken awake out of a daydream or daze. "I know," he replied, his voice holding a mock defensiveness as he clapped a hand over his heart. "I ain't plannin' on doin' anythin'. I *am* a gentleman, after all."

His father snorted, falling into another coughing fit, while everyone else had a good laugh.

The tall cowboy spoke this time, his voice low and deep. "The only thing you are is an idiot." His words were harsh, but there was warmth swirling in his bright jade eyes.

Cash shook his head before sticking his nose up in the air, giving off the facade that he was offended. Honestly, I doubted he got offended or embarrassed, like, ever. "Y'all are assholes," he huffed.

Hux chuckled. "Takes one to know one, Mooney."

Cash shrugged and then clapped his hands, going so far as to rub them together as he said, "So, what's the plan? We goin' out and celebratin' tonight or what?"

His friends and dad both grumbled their agreement amongst themselves before Cash aimed his gaze mine, Whit, and Hux's way.

"What about y'all?" he asked, clapping Hux on the shoulder hard enough that I felt it reverberate through me.

Hux just laughed. A deep, genuine sound that made my heart flutter in my chest like butterfly wings. He'd hardly even flinched, which absolutely shocked me. It didn't take a rocket scientist to know he didn't like people unexpectedly touching him. Crazy what a little bit of closure could do to his confidence.

"What'dya say, darlin'?" he murmured in my ear.

Shivers danced up and down my spine at the feeling of his scruff scraping against my skin. God, he was so incredibly hot.

I squeezed my arm around him just a little tighter, leaning further into his embrace. "I'm down," I replied, before glancing at Whit. "You coming too?"

Her grin and eyes glimmered with mischief. "Duh."

D ECIDING TO GO OUT might not have been a good idea.

"Are you sure you want to be here?" I asked Whit as we followed our new group of friends toward the main bar of Roughie's, a little honky tonk in town that hadn't been open for very long. It was everything I envisioned when I thought of a cowboy bar. Cool rodeo posters, a whole western aesthetic complete with wagon wheels, saw dust on the floor, and lots and lots of cowboy boots and hats, and a massive dance floor. They even had a mechanical bull that a large number of people stood around, cheering on whoever rode.

Hux and Cash walked together, and even though I doubt Cash noticed the tension in Hux, I did. He hid it well, but his shoulders were stiff, rigid, his back ram-rod straight. Worry wriggled like a worm on a hook in my stomach. I'd check on him as soon as we got settled and the two of us had a moment alone.

Despite her little argument with Travis, Whit still seemed to be in exceptionally high spirits. She flashed me a warm grin. "Of course, I want to be here. A night with my bestie, new friends, and dancing...what more could a girl want? Now, all I need is someone to buy me drinks."

I laughed. "I'm sure Cash would be more than happy to."

She grinned, her gaze flicking to him for a moment. "He's hot as fuck, but I think that's a ride that I'm not ready for."

"So what are you gonna do about you and Travis?"

"I don't know. We aren't a couple. I mean, he's cute and sweet, but I don't like sore losers, and I'm not down for someone trying to control what I do. The way I see it, he's free to do whatever he wants and so am I. And as far as tonight goes, I don't want to hear another word about him." She pushed her long waves over her shoulders as we came to a stop at a table that Hux, Cash, and the others had settled around.

"Fair enough."

Drinks were ordered—well, shots. Cash demanded that everyone *had* to have one, save for the tall cowboy. Cash hadn't even tried to get him to drink. Despite the fact he completely fit in looks wise here, he stuck out like a sore thumb. He kept quiet, checking his phone every now and then while watching the crowd. When his appraising jade gaze met mine I offered him a soft smile. He only tipped his hat in response before scanning the room once more.

I turned to Hux, who stood beside me, and leaned into him, placing a hand on his forearm that was rested on the table. "Hey, do you know who the other cowboy with Cash and Ryder is?" I asked quietly.

"That's Maverick Holstrom. Cash's cousin. They're more like brothers though."

"How come he doesn't drink?"

"He ain't the drinkin' kind. Or the talkin' kind really."

"Why?"

"Just never has been."

"Must take a lot of patience for him to come out and be sober," I mused.

"Yeah, let alone deal with Cash. Don't think there's a more patient man on the earth."

I glanced at the cowboy once more, but he was busy scanning the room as if looking for a potential threat. I turned back to Hux again. "How're you doing, cowboy?" I asked quiet enough for hopefully only him to hear, but it was hard to whisper over the loud Country music.

He grabbed my hand and squeezed gently. "Some liquid courage will help," he replied back. "But overall, I'm good. Really good."

Pressing a soft kiss to his cheek, I whispered in his ear, "Good."

Chapter Twenty-Eight

Belong Together

Hux

I HADN'T FELT THIS good in a long damn time. So long I didn't even know I could feel like this again. Not even the fact I was in a new place, surrounded by a shit ton of people could dwindle how I felt—much. The nerves still fought back a bit, but the moment I'd felt Quinn at my side, they'd just, well, disappeared. The alcohol helped too.

A couple shots and a beer or two in, and my worries were like ash on the wind.

"Wanna dance, darlin'?" I asked Quinn.

"You dance?" Surprise rang in her voice from my side.

I chuckled. "I used to, a lot."

"Really?"

I nodded. "I might not be able to do those fancy turns and dips anymore, but I can spin you round the dance floor a few times."

"Well, aren't you just full of surprises." Her hand slipped into mine, a silent yes as she led me to what I assumed was the dance floor.

Her hands settled into position, one of them coming up to my shoulder, and I instinctively placed a hand on her hips, drawing her in close as I started up to the beat of the song. It was slower. Exactly why I'd picked this one. I wanted to ease back into it. It'd been a while since I'd danced.

"It's nice to get a moment alone with you," Quinn said softly.

I swayed to the music and spun her around before pulling her against me once more. "It's been a pretty wild night, hasn't it?"

A giggle. "It has. I still find it a bit crazy that this is the real you."

"You don't like this side of me?" I asked, a hint of worry sprouting in my chest like a weed.

"Oh my God, no, no, no. That isn't at all what I meant. I love this version of you. I'm so happy that you've found yourself again. I'm just blown away that you're, like, a *big* deal."

I huffed, some of my tension easing, even as a sense of wistfulness settled in my bones. "*Was* a big deal."

"Hux, you had a line of people waiting to meet you at the rodeo. At least a dozen more have come up and asked for an autograph since we got here. You *are* a big deal still."

I'd forgotten how good it felt, meeting fans and interacting with them. Just being back in the rodeo world. I missed it. Missed it with every fiber of my being.

"It's just cuz this is the first time anyone in this scene has seen me in three years. This'll pass."

"You don't want it to, though, don't you? Tonight...you came alive."

I dragged her hand up to my lips and kissed the backs of her knuckles gently as we danced our way across the floor. "Because of you."

Her words were soft and light. "No, Hux. It wasn't because of me. It was the rodeo."

"I wouldn't have gone had it not been for you."

"True," she replied, placing her head on the spot right between my collar and jaw. We fell into silence for a few moments, until she finally asked, "When you introduced me to Mister Mooney, you called me yours. What exactly did you mean by that?"

A smile tugged on my mouth. "You noticed."

"You seriously thought I wouldn't?" she said with a scoff.

I shrugged, pulling her closer to me. Ignoring her question, I said, "I ain't known you long, but I think in this little time I have, I've made my feelings for you pretty clear. I want you. I'm better with you. And if I have to move my ass to California to be with you, I'll do it. I'll take you in any way you're willin' to give m e."

A sharp gasp escaped her, the faint smell of alcohol on her lips. "Hux." My name was little more than a whisper almost drowned out by beat of the music.

Goddamn, I loved the way she said my name. "I ain't one for goin' slow, or plannin' things out. I think with my heart, not my head. But every inch of me, every piece of my heart, head, and soul are in agreement about you, Quinn. I'm yours. I've been yours from the moment I heard you sing."

My heart squeezed at the feminine sound that escaped her. One of surprise and adoration and some stronger emotion—maybe, possibly even love. "I—I'm not taking the job in California, Hux."

"What? Why not?"

"Because I want to stay here. With you. I don't care how long or how short we've known each other. I want you too. And I'm yours. For however long you want me."

The power of her words hit me straight in the chest, forcing me to let out a huff of relief. I'd figured, well, hoped, that she felt the same, but it was nice to hear her reaffirm that if I was crazy, she was right there being just as crazy too.

Without another thought, I settled a hand around her neck and drew my mouth down to hers. I put all I had into that kiss, every emotion that told her without words exactly how I felt about her. She kissed me back with just as much fervor, matching me in intensity. The music and the sound of the bar peeled away, 'til all that was left, 'til all I could think of and feel was her. We stopped dancing, and for a long moment I just kissed her, uncaring of who all saw.

I'm sure there'd be some sort of article out tomorrow about my return, and likely this moment, but I didn't care. In fact, the idea of the world—even if just the rodeo world—knowing about my relationship with her sent a spark of desire through me.

Quinn broke the kiss first, though she remained close enough that I felt her breath on my cheeks as she murmured huskily, "Kiss me like that again, cowboy, and we may need to go home."

I chuckled, rubbing my thumb along the curve of her jaw as my fingers slid into her hair. "Don't tempt me with a good time, darlin'."

She laughed, pressing a feather-soft kiss to my lips before saying, "As much as I want that, I want at least another dance or two with you."

I chuckled, squeezing her tight, a wave of pure happiness flowing through me. "I think I can manage that."

SOMETHING LIKE FOUR OR five songs later, Quinn and I finally got off the dance floor. She left me at the table along with the guys to go to the bathroom with Whit.

"How 'bout another round, old man?" Cash asked as he clapped me on the back. Either the alcohol was its intoxicating magic, or I was getting over my aversion to people touching me. It was probably the former.

"I ain't gonna turn down free alcohol."

Ryder's laughter, followed by Maverick and Bad's quieter chuckles surrounded me, but they were drowned out by Cash's crow of excitement. "Atta boy." Another clap to the shoulder. A moment later he pushed a shot glass into my hand. "Here, a little liquid courage, old man."

"Me?" I asked. "Why do I need liquid courage?"

"I put your name in to ride the mechanical bull. You're up next, buddy."

A flurry of emotions erupted in my chest. I know it wasn't a real bull, but just the thought of doing something like that left me feeling some sort of way. Because it wasn't some big secret—I wanted to ride again. I wanted it so fucking bad; it didn't take a rocket scientist for anyone else to see that. But I also didn't want to die. Not when I finally had something worth living for. And if I hurt myself again and jeopardized anything with Quinn, well, if the fall didn't kill me, that just might.

And even though I'd ridden a mechanical bull before, worry clenched around my stomach. "I don't know, man."

"Come on, it ain't a real bull. You got this." Cash's voice held an excited, encouraging note to it.

"Yeah, but how the fuck am I even gonna get on the thing? You gonna walk me up there, help me on up? What if I fall and hit my head? I can't see what I'm doin'. I fall wrong and I could be dead."

A gentler, yet no less firm hand settled on my left shoulder. "I took a nasty fall last year, and I know it ain't at all the same, but I get the fear and worry." I recognized Ryder's smooth voice.

I huffed, pulling off my hat to run a hand through my hair as I fought to come up with words, but Ryder beat me to it.

"There was a guy I heard about, I think he was a cutting horse trainer or somethin', and he lost his leg and everyone told him he wasn't gonna cut ever again. But that didn't stop him. He built himself a prosthetic and rigged up some way for him to cue the damn horse with his left leg... What I'm sayin' is, bull ridin's in your blood, man. It ain't just a want, it's a need. Trust me, I know."

I found myself nodding, because he was right. It was a need.

"Look, you got both hands and both legs. You fall just as hard with your vision as you do without. You're a bull rider, man. You're used to ridin' two thousand plus pounds of pissed off, rank sons of bitches. You can manage a fuckin' mechanical bull."

I blew out a deep breath. He was right. About all of it. My head and heart warred within me though. My heart because it just wanted to feel that rush one more time, even while the logical part of me knew it was a dumb idea. I didn't need to prove anything to anyone.

But what about proving it to myself? That I was still something. Someone.

"It's a stupid idea, son," Bad said from my right. "And you *could* get hurt…"

"Yeah," I replied, "So, you sayin' I shouldn't do it?"

"I said it's stupid and you could hurt, but I don't think you're gonna find an argument from any of us. You need this moment. To prove to yourself you're still you. Ain't none of us can do that for you. You gotta do that for yourself."

A huff of laughter escaped me. Bad sure knew what to fuckin' say. Sucking in a breath, I tossed my shot back, excitement laced in my words as I said, "Hundred bucks says I can last longer than you, Mooney."

"Make that two." Bad's gruff tone held a hint of approval in it.

"Well, damn, Dad. Thanks for the confidence," Cash defended.

I chuckled and rubbed my hands together in anticipation. It wasn't a real bull, but it would do.

Chapter Twenty-Nine

Wild As You

QUINN

W HIT AND I MADE our way out of the bathroom, my gaze falling to the empty table our group had been at just a few moments ago. I wondered if they'd gone to the bar, or to have a smoke or something—I knew Hux, Mister Mooney, and Cash at least smoked. A wave of excited shouts coming from the mechanical bull area floated on the air above the sound of the music.

"Where are we going?" Whit asked as I made a beeline in that direction.

"I bet they're—" Cash's unmistakable crow of excitement rose over the cacophony in the bar. I glanced back at Whit. "They're over by the mechanical bull."

The crowd was thick, but Whit and I managed to wiggle our way to the front.

And then I saw him. Not over by Cash and the rest of our group, but atop the mechanical bull. Left hand held up over his head, while his right firmly gripped the loop meant for holding on. He rocked and twisted and spun with such ease.

He was mesmerizing. Amazing. Magnificent.

His harsh, brutal face was a mask of concentration, his gaze focused on the mechanical bull's horns. He'd taken off his glasses, but left the hat. And my God, what a sight he was.

My heart swelled, like waves rolling toward the shore. I'd told him that he'd come alive tonight, and I hadn't lied. Right here, right now... This. This was him.

Who he truly was at his core. I was so proud of him for conquering this fear that had plagued him like a demon these past three years.

I didn't know the first thing about he'd gone through, and I'd likely never know the true extent of it. But he was proving that just because he'd physically lost a part of himself, didn't make him any less. In fact, it made him more.

I could have watched him forever. I think the crowd could have too, honestly. But somewhere around the three minute mark the guy controlling the mechanical bull finally called it quits and announced over the mic they had a new winner for the longest ride. After Hux got himself off the bull, begrudgingly letting Cash help him out of the padded arena, he was awarded a Roughie's t-shirt and a round of shots for his party. Cheers and shouts from myself and the rest of the bar rose over the music, but none were louder than Cash as he clapped a hand on Hux's back. Ryder, Maverick, and Mister Mooney even joined in with the revelry of it all

.

I don't think I'd ever seen Hux smile so brightly, so openly. It's like it was plastered to his face. My heart pitter-pattered excitedly in my chest with each step I took toward him.

"That was a hell of a ride, cowboy," I said, settling at his side, wrapping an arm around his waist.

He snaked a hand through my hair, dragging my mouth to his. I melted at the fierce intensity of his kiss. The possessiveness in his touch.

"You were...magnificent," I said, trying and failing to convey just how amazed I was by him.

"I don't know how I looked, but it sure as hell felt fuckin' good," he said, a wide grin pulling on his mouth.

I think in that moment, seeing the happiness and hope and warmth on his face was when I fell completely for him. This had to be love, right? The elation I felt just thinking about him was unlike anything I'd ever experienced. It wasn't just butterflies or excitement. It wasn't lust or infatuation.

When I closed my eyes, when I thought of my life in a year, five, fifteen from now all, I could see was him. He was like a shining beacon in the dark, promising warmth and safety and love.

"You looked good, cowboy. Really fucking good," I said a bit breathlessly.

A low, appreciative hum rumbled in his chest as he captured my mouth in the whisper of a kiss. "Oh, yeah? How good?"

I giggled, wrapping my arms around his neck. It's like I had a second-hand high from his happiness. It was infectious. And I was greedy and wanted more. "Like fuckable good."

"Well, damn. If I looked that good on a fake one, I wonder what you'll think of me when I ride a real one."

"Wait, what?" I pulled away and searched his face. He wanted to ride a real bull now?

"Yep, I'm comin' back." His voice picked up in volume as he shouted over the crowd. "'Y'all heard it first. Huxson Lane is comin' outta retirement."

The crowd erupted into more cheers, Cash going so far as to rip the mic from the DJ's hands as he shouted, "Y'all here that? Two time World Champion bull rider, Huxson Lane is comin' back!"

My heart thumped in my chest and knots coiled tight in my stomach like a dozen snakes. I was all for him chasing his dreams. I was all for him riding again, but wasn't this a bit quick? Rash? He'd just told me the other night the doctors said one bad fall could literally kill him.

Hux squeezed me tight, his deep voice breaking through the fog of worry in my mind. "What'dya think, darlin'?"

I bit my lip, glancing around at all the excitement and buzz from his statement. I wanted him to ride, I really did, but somehow the words tumbling out of my mouth were, "Are you sure?"

He stilled against me, and when I looked up at him, anger flickered to life in his whiskey colored gaze. "Of course, I'm fuckin' sure. You don't want me to ride?"

The knots in my chest constricted tighter somehow, making it hurt to breathe. "No! No, that's not it at all. I do. I just—maybe this is a decision to make sober?"

Hux pulled out of my grip fully, barely restrained fury rippling across his face. Holy God, he was pissed. "I ain't drunk, Quinn."

The way he said my name was like a stab to the heart.

Oh God, why had I said anything? It wasn't that I didn't want him to ride. It truly, honestly wasn't. I was allowed to be worried for him, right? I mean, riding a mechanical bull and a real one were similar, but the danger was infinitely more with the latter. Was that wrong of me to think that maybe this revelation was just a bit preemptive?

"I'm sorry," I croaked out. "I want you to ride, I just—"

"You what?" His tone was clipped, hinting at the anger lurking just beneath the surface. Any warmth or light or happiness he'd worn on his features moments ago had vanished, cold, wild fury replacing it.

Tears welled in my eyes. "I'm just a little surprised and scared, okay? I want you to ride again. I really do. But am I not allowed to also be a bit worried that you made this decision after I don't even know how many drinks in?"

"You're just scared I can't do it because I'm blind, right?" It was phrased like a question, but I heard it for the statement, the accusation it was. And it broke my heart. Broke my heart because I knew that at the root of it, this was *his* insecurity.

A tear leaked down my cheek. "What? No. No, Hux. You're—"

"You are. You think I can't do it cuz I can't see."

Anger rippled to life in me, fueled by the alcohol and adrenaline pumping through my veins. I didn't think he couldn't do it because he was blind. He'd proven time and time and *time* again that he was fully capable of anything he set his mind to even without his vision. I *knew* he could ride. But I just wanted him to be smart about this. To think it through. Was that so much to ask?

"I know you can do it without your vision, Hux. That isn't even the issue. I—"

"Then what is it?" he all but growled at me.

"I don't want you to die, okay?" I shouted. "I don't want you rushing into something you aren't ready for. Riding a mechanical bull and a real one aren't the same. And I don't—"

"I'm fully aware of the difference, Quinn." He spoke with such vehemence, such venom that it cut to the bone.

"Then stop being a stubborn idiot. I'm not saying I don't want you to ride. I will be your loudest cheerleader in those stands when the day comes. But you're more than just an eight second ride, Hux. You don't have to prove to anyone that you can do this. We all know you can. Everyone is amazed at your resilience, your strength, your bravery. When are you going to realize..." I sucked in a choked sob as I pressed a hand to his chest. "That the only person who thinks you aren't good enough, is you."

Some emotion I couldn't quite place rippled across his face, shattering the angry mask he wore. His jaw loosened, those beautiful whiskey-colored eyes guttering as most of the fight seemed to leave him. "Quinn... I—"

My vision blurred and I wiped the moisture from my eyes, trying to stop my bottom lip from trembling more than it was. I noticed the quiet that had settled around us, the ridiculous amount of eyes on him and I. *Well, that's just fucking great.* I glanced back at Hux one more, whose gaze was aimed my way but not directly on me.

"I'm gonna go. I'm sorry," I murmured before walking away.

"Quinn, wait!" There was a desperate note to his tone. Gone was the anger, worry and fear, I realized, in its place. But I kept walking—-too raw and broken and angry to try to talk it out right now. We'd both cut deep. And I didn't have it in me to continue this argument, I just wanted to crawl under a rock and hide.

How could the night start on such a high and come crashing down the way it had? I should've kept my mouth shut. Whit's arm entwined with mine a moment later. "You okay?" she asked softly.

"No," I choked out as I made a beeline for the exit. I needed fresh air.

We'd just gotten outside when someone called my name. I turned, my heart breaking just a bit more when I realized it wasn't Hux. Mister Mooney walked toward us.

"Are you alright?" he asked, true concern ringing in his gravelly tone.

"I didn't mean to upset him. It's not that I don't think he can ride. I know he can. Am I not allowed to be scared?" More tears fell down my cheeks.

"You absolutely are, Miss Quinn. I know you love and support him. Hell, even he knows. But one thing you gotta know about us cowboys is we're stubborn sons of bitches to our very core. Don't like bein' told no. Especially not with an audience. Go on and add in the fact that the boy's been drinkin' and he's got a bit of a temper, and, well, now we gotta fire to put out."

I blew out a dejected breath. "I should never have said anything."

He shook his head, those hazel eyes so similar to his son's pegging me in place. "Answer me this. If he had his vision and randomly said he wanted to ride again would you still be worried?"

I didn't even have to fully process his sentence to know where he was going. "Yes. A hundred percent I'd still be worried."

"That's what I figured. I know this ain't about him bein' blind. You know it too. But that boy's more stubborn and tougher than a two-dollar steak. He needs time to cool down. Let the alcohol and anger wear off tonight. Talk to him tomorrow."

I bit my lip to try and stop the tears hanging in the corners of my eyes. "Thank you for coming out and checking on me. Will you make sure he gets back to the ranch?"

He nodded. "I promise, Miss Quinn."

I offered him what I hoped was a smile and not a grimace. "Thank you. It was nice meeting you. I hope to see you again."

"I'm sure I will, and it was a pleasure meetin' you." Mister Mooney glanced at Whit and tipped his hat. "You as well, miss."

A warm arm wrapped around my shoulders, and the scent of Whit's familiar perfume enveloped me. "Wanna see if we can get some ice cream and watch some cheesy rom-coms at the house?"

I sniffled and nodded.

But in the end, not even a night with Whit had helped. My fight with Hux haunted my thoughts, awake and asleep.

Were things screwed up beyond repair?

God, I hoped not.

Chapter Thirty

My Fault

Hux

M Y SKULL FELT LIKE a stake had been driven through it, but the sharp, throbbing pain was nothing compared to the guilt squeezing around my heart as I thought of last night.

Fuck, I'd been an asshole. I'd been drunk and high off the feel of riding again, and when Quinn had questioned my decision I'd lost my temper like an fucking idiot. Losing my temper made it seem tame. I'd yelled at her. In front of our friends. In front of the entire bar. Even worse, I'd let her walk away.

Fuck, I was an asshole.

I understood her hesitance. Her worry. At the heart of it all, she was just being supportive and looking out for my own well-being. But I still couldn't help the sting in my chest at the doubt in her words when she'd said "Are you sure?"

Which wasn't fair, I knew that now that I was sober. But at the time, I'd only seen red. Because those words struck such a chord of doubt in me. My own doubt. In the end, I was the only one who had an issue with my circumstance. Everyone else talked about how strong and brave and resilient I was, but I didn't feel any of that. I felt useless, broken, and I *hated* it. With every single fiber of my being. And last night, for those few minutes, I felt wild and free and capable. And I wanted that feeling again.

But I wanted Quinn more.

This wasn't just a fling with her. This was the real deal. I felt it in my bones. In my soul. The way I felt reminded me of the way my mom and dad still looked at each other. Quinn was it for me. I had no doubt about that.

And if having her meant giving up that part of me, I'd do it. In a damn heartbeat. Because she was all that was good and light and beautiful in this dark and lonely world and she deserved more than a drunk, hotheaded cowboy who belittled her in a bar.

After I finished my morning chores, I'd go talk to her.

I was already moving slow because of last night. We'd left shortly after my temper tantrum. Mister Mooney called the night and Cash's cousin, Maverick, drove me home. I'd been a stumbling mess trying to get through the bunkhouse and into my room. Every part of me had wanted to go to her place, to make things right. But not as a drunken mess.

Letting out a weary sigh, I grabbed Doc's halter from the hook just outside his stall on the wall to the right. My phone rang from my back pocket, making me wince at the loud noise. It was too early for Ghost Riders in The Sky. But that made me frown as I recognized the specific ringtone and who it must be. Why was Dad calling? He wasn't the talk on the phone type. Really honestly, the talking type in general.

"Hello?" I said, answering the phone.

"You got about thirty seconds to explain what the hell is goin' on, son. Your mama's a downright wreck."

"What the hell are you talkin' about, Dad?'

"It's all over the local news. On The Cowboy Channel. Hell, Walker even said you broke rodeo...click clock or tick time—"

"It's rodeo-tok, Dad!" My sister's voice sounded warped and distant, like she was shouting from further away. But in the next instant, her words were loud and clear through the phone as she said, "Hi, Huxie. First off, your girlfriend's really pretty, and second, you were a real asshole to her."

"How the hell do you—" The words died on my lips. There'd been a bunch of people there last night. Likely one of them, if not more, videoed my ride or the argument that ensued after. Fuck, word traveled fast. I'd forgotten that part about bull riding. God, I was a fucking idiot. It's like I got a taste of my old life and forgot how far I'd come since then.

Dad was already back on the line, hissing at Walker to leave him alone before he said, "You got some explainin' to do, Huxson. Comin' outta retirement? Fighting with your girlfriend? When the hell were you goin' to tell us about her, by the way?"

I blew out a breath and nodded. Great. Mama was likely furious, and I didn't miss the disappointment in my dad's tone. "Yeah. I 'spose you're right. Let me finish my mornin' chores and talk to my boss about leavin' early. I'd rather explain it all at once to y'all in person."

Dad's words came out muffled, and it took me a minute to realize he wasn't talking to me but to my mother, relaying what I'd just said. After another moment, his voice rang clear. "Your mama says to bring your girlfriend too."

"Alright," I said with a sigh. "Can you ask her to make fried chicken?"

It'd been too long since I'd had one of Mama's home-cooked meals, and at least if today was a shitshow, the food would be good.

Despite my dad's obvious annoyance, a low chuckle came through the line. "Alright. Let me know when y'all are comin'."

"Alright, Dad." I hung up, blowing out a breath.

Well, now I really needed to talk to Quinn.

A THIN LAYER OF sweat covered me from head to toe by the time I'd finished working horses. It couldn't be later than 10 AM maybe, but it already felt like being in an oven. I'd already sent Rusty back inside. It was too damn hot for him out here to be watching me work horses.

A shower sounded nice right about now. The memory of Quinn and I showering yesterday before the rodeo swirled to life in my mind. God, had that only been yesterday? With how much had happened, it felt like so much more time had passed.

What I'd give to take a shower with her right now. Wash away the argument between us like washing the sweat off my skin. But Whit was probably with her and who fucking knew how talking with Quinn would go. No, I'd shower real quick and head over to her place.

I shut the stall door of my last horse and replaced the halter on the hook outside the mare's stall before turning in the direction of the bunkhouse. Little embers of excitement and then worry warred in my chest as I thought of Quinn. What if she was pissed? What if she didn't want to talk to me? I wouldn't exactly blame her after last night.

The sweet scent of perfume filled my nose, and my heart skipped a beat. Had she come? But as I inhaled deeply, I all but gagged on the cloying, overpowering smell of some floral scent that was way too goddamn strong.

I bit back a snarl as I clenched my fists at my side. "Georgette," I ground out. "What can I do for you?"

"I just...I wanted to apologize. I feel like we got off on the wrong foot." Her sugary-sweet voice put me on edge, the closeness of it forcing me to step back. Why was she so close? And better yet, why had she come all the way down here just to apologize?

"Oh...kay," I replied, stepping to the side of where I felt the heat of her to walk out of the barn. My nerves coiled tight and every inch of me felt on edge, trepidation swirling in the pit of my stomach. "Apology accepted. Now, if you'll excuse me, I gotta meet with Quinn."

"Why are you in such a rush?" A warm hand pressed to my chest. "I was hoping you could help me with something."

Warning bells in my mind went off like a tornado siren. Her hand drifted lower down my abdomen.

I took a step back out of her reach, and said darkly, "I can't help you, Georgette. Now, I'm gonna leave, and I suggest you do too before I mention something to your fiancé."

"He'd never believe you." The words were confident, smug even, as her hand found my chest once more.

Once more I stepped out of her grip. "Yeah, well, Quinn will believe me, and I know for a damn fact her dad will take her word over yours."

"I wouldn't be so sure about that, *Huxson Lane*. I didn't realize how famous you are here. Your little temper tantrum is all over the news. I doubt she wants to talk to you after last night." Suddenly I felt the heat of her right before me, and I backed up until I hit the wood of one of the stall doors. "She might not like your temper, but I wouldn't mind taking a ride on you, cowboy."

"Not interested, Georgette." I tried to get around her, which was really fucking hard, being that I couldn't fucking see, but she pushed me back to the stall door with more force than I'd expect from her.

"But I'm interested." I'm sure that sultry voice worked on others, but it might as well have been acid on my skin.

I huffed. Well, this was just fucking great. On top of all the shit that had happened last night, now I needed to deal with this. I needed to get away from Georgette and talk to Quinn. Before this dumb bitch had the opportunity to spin some sob story, painting me as the villain. Girl was a spider, spinning webs of lies to get what she wanted.

Quinn's dad deserved better than her.

The heat of her enveloped me in a sudden wave, followed by the firm pressure of something against my mouth. No, not something, her lips. The overwhelming taste of her lip gloss made me want to gag.

"What the fuck, Georgette?" I wiped the back of my hand over my mouth, spitting, as if I could get any lingering bit of her off me.

Shoving her out of the way, I started walking in the direction of the barn doors, but I ran into one of the fucking wheel barrows used for mucking stalls, spilling the entire contents and stumbling over myself.

She was there in an instant like a locust. Or a spider going in for the kill. To do what, I don't know. But before she could sink her fangs in, a familiar voice called out from somewhere ahead of me, "Do not. Fucking. Touch. Him. Again."

Chapter Thirty-One
Homewrecker

Quinn

I HADN'T SLEPT. SHOCKER. And with each hour that passed by this morning, the pit of worry in my stomach only seemed to grow wider and wider. I'd worked out, showered and gotten ready, even tried to read some of my new book, but nothing could distract me from thoughts of Hux.

I was still hurt and upset at how he'd blown up at me, but more than that, I missed him. I didn't like that I didn't know where we stood. I shouldn't have left like that last night, but you could argue he shouldn't have yelled at me in front of an entire crowd. We'd both made mistakes. We both needed to take responsibility for them. I didn't want to bother him at work though. He'd likely be riding horses right now while it was still—relatively—cool out.

By 10 AM I couldn't take it anymore, though.

Whit was still sleeping, so I figured I'd just send her a quick text later instead of wake her up. It didn't take a genius to know where I was headed.

I shouldn't even have bothered with showering. By the time the barn came into view, I was dripping with sweat. Not the way I wanted to go into this conversation that was likely going to be hard and frustrating and might involve more than a few tears.

Steeling my nerves and taking a deep breath, I left the main road and strode down the path for the barn. Muffled voices echoed from within. Great, I didn't want to interrupt him if he was busy with one of the hands or something. But then a familiar, obnoxious voice drifted on the wind. I couldn't make out what was said, but my gut churned all the same.

Georgette.

What the hell was she doing in the ranch hands' barn? Her and Dad didn't have any horses. And aside from the grand tour I got on the first day, I'd never once seen her out on the grounds in the last couple weeks.

Hux's deep timbre sounded far off, but I could at least make sense of the words. "I'm not interested, Georgette."

My stomach did a somersault, and I thought I might just throw up right there on the pavement.

"But I'm interested."

Okay, what the hell was going on?

I hurried toward the open barn doors and slipped inside only to feel like I'd been hit by a ton of bricks. Hux stood against one of the stall doors while Georgette kissed him.

What the hell was happening? Why was she kissing him? My mind and heart had gone into overdrive and it's like I couldn't comprehend what I was seeing.

Hux pushed away immediately, revulsion written plainly across his face as he wiped the back of his hand over his mouth. "What the fuck, Georgette?" he snapped.

Before she could do anything else, he was stomping down the barn aisle toward the doors I stood in. He didn't get far as he crashed into the wheelbarrow and stumbled over himself. Georgette was there before I could even take a step forward, ready to sink her claws in. To do what exactly, I wasn't sure, but if she'd already tried to kiss him, I don't know what else she'd try to do while he was vulnerable.

God, I really hated that bitch.

Anger boiled like lava in my veins as I stepped forward, finally making myself known. I'd seen enough. "Do not. Fucking. Touch. Him. Again," I spat, the words like venom on my tongue.

"Quinn! I—he. He kissed me! He came at me and—"

"I know *exactly* what happened," I said with a calm I most certainly didn't feel. My hands trembled at my sides, tears of anger burned in my eyes, but I wouldn't let them fall.

"Quinn." Hux's tone was a mixture of shock, relief, and a twinge of fear. I flicked my gaze to him, finding the look on his face pleading as he gazed in the general direction of my voice. He looked so vulnerable and scared in that moment. Like he thought I'd actually believe Georgette's words. "I didn't. I promise."

And even though I was still angry with him, even though we still needed to talk about last night, I made my way to his side and slid my hand into his.

Aiming my gaze at Georgette, I said, "I think you need to leave."

"Quinn—I. Please."

"Now." Even I was impressed with the finality in my tone. "I don't suspect my dad will be very happy with you when he finds out what you did."

She didn't cower or balk at my words, instead puffed herself up like a goddamn rooster and sneered at me. "Who's he going to believe?"

"He won't believe you over me, that's for damn sure."

Georgette raised her nose high in the air, her dark gaze vicious and sharp as daggers. "We'll see about that."

I huffed a laugh and shook my head. God, she really was delusional. "Yeah, I guess we will."

She let out a squeal of rage before stomping her foot—yes, a thirty-year-old woman *stomped* her foot—and marched herself out of the barn, making sure to aim a hate-filled gaze mine and Hux's way. Pretty sure I heard her mumble something about me being a haughty bitch, but I didn't even deign to respond. She'd get her comeuppance for being a shit human being soon enough.

When she finally disappeared through the door, I let out a deep, shaky breath, but it did little to quell the anger inside me. "God, what a stupid, fucking cunt!" I shouted, unable to hold the words in any longer.

Hux's soft huff of laughter drew my attention. "You'll find no argument from me there."

He seemed to have recovered a bit. The revulsion had disappeared, leaving him looking stone-faced and tired. I squeezed his hand and turned to him.

"Are you okay?" I asked softly.

His brows furrowed beneath his sunglasses. "Me? What do you mean?"

"Hux, she—" Just the thought of what she'd done made bile rise in my throat. "She sexually assaulted you. She cornered you. Tried to take advantage of you." Each word that came out of my mouth escalated in volume and turned more hysterical. I hadn't even realized I was talking with my hands so much until Hux brought them down to my sides.

And then I was crying. Sobbing, more like—with rage, with disbelief, with devastation. Honestly, at this point so many emotions barreled into me I didn't know what exactly had set me off. All I kept thinking was how terrified I'd have been in his position.

Hux drew me in, dragging me against his chest, and I fell apart in his arms as tears flowed down my cheeks and stained his dark t-shirt. He shushed me quietly, running the backs of his knuckles up and down my spine in a slow, soothing motion.

"I'm okay, darlin'. I promise." When his reassuring words failed, he settled on cupping my face in his calloused hands and forced me to look up at him. "Breathe, Quinn. Breathe."

I was helpless but to listen, following his orders and taking in slow, deep breaths before holding them in for one second, two, then letting them out.

"Good girl. Again."

It took a few tries, but with each inhale and exhale it got easier to breathe, to think. "I'm sorry," I finally managed to whisper.

He wiped the tears spilling down my cheeks with his thumbs before pushing my hair back off my face. "You ain't got nothin' to apologize for. I'm just glad you came when you did."

I sniffled. "What happened?"

"I was just about to come find you, then she was there gettin' all handsy. When I told her she needed to leave she just got more aggressive."

I blew out a breath. "I'm sorry."

"It's okay, Quinn. Really." His tone was stern but gentle. "We should probably go talk to your dad, though. Get this all sorted before Georgette spins more lies."

"Let her. If my dad believes her over me, then I want nothing to do with him." There was no way in hell that my dad would buy her bullshit once I got involved. She could weave the most extravagant tale, but at the end of the day, my dad wasn't an idiot. Besides, I didn't want to leave until Hux and I had figured things out. I hated this feeling. This hollowness in my chest that I'd felt after last night. I needed to know where we stood.

Looking up at him, I said softly, "You hurt me last night."

His hands dropped to his sides and he let out a defeated sigh as he looked skyward. "I know. You don't know how much I regret what I said, what I did, how I treated you. I was—" He swallowed hard and raised his hands toward his head, pulling his ball cap off with one hand and spearing his fingers through his hair with the other before righting it once more. "I was a fuckin' idiot. I was drunk and belligerent, and I promise you I ain't ever gonna do that shit ever again."

"Drink, or ride, or yell at me?" I found myself asking.

"Any of it. All of it. Whatever you want."

My eyes welled with tears once more. "Was that the real you last night?"

"No. No, I promise. I ain't gonna lie though, I've gotten too drunk on more than one occasion, and my anger is something I fight with daily. But last night... That ain't me. I don't want that to be me. I swear, Quinn." There was a desperate note to his voice I'd never heard before, and it broke me.

"I'm not going to be your punching bag, Hux. I'm already that for everyone else, it seems."

"I don't want you to be that. I fucked up. Never again, I swear."

Did I believe him? I wanted to believe him. I think I believed him. But doubt lurked in the shadows of my mind. What if this was just the start?

Chapter Thirty-Two

Save Me

Hux

EVERY MINUTE THAT TICKED by felt like I was losing her. Second by second. Inch by inch. I'd seriously fucked up. The sadness in her voice, the way she seemed so closed off and just...dead inside. It's like she'd lost all her light and warmth.

I had made her feel that way.

"I'm not going to be your punching bag, Hux. I'm already that for everyone else, it seems."

That broke my heart. That she felt she was nothing more than that to people. That she'd come to expect that type of treatment from others. And I'd gone and proven I was just the same as everyone else.

I longed to reach out and touch her. To draw her into my arms, hold on tight and never let go. But the brokenness in her voice gave me pause. I didn't want to push her away when everything we had was so up in the air.

"I don't want you to be that. I fucked up. Never again, I swear."

She blew out a shaky breath that danced across my skin. "I want you to know that I have no doubt you'd be able to ride again. I believe in you. I always have. You are brave and talented and so, so incredibly resilient and capable, and you'll excel at anything you set your mind to. But at the end of the day Hux, that's not enough for you, is it?"

My brows scrunched together, her words hitting me like a sledgehammer, knocking the wind from my lungs. *That's not enough for you.*

She was done, wasn't she?

I opened my mouth to respond, but no words came out. It didn't matter though, in the end, as she continued, "Me believing in you isn't enough. You need to believe in you. That's the root of your anger, isn't it?"

A lump lodged in my throat, and my lungs screamed for air that I couldn't manage to suck down fast enough. My eyes stung. How fucking right was she? It wasn't some secret how much I hated my circumstance. How much I hated what I'd become. It didn't matter if I could navigate a grocery store decently without my vision or that I could ride a horse, or feed, or paint. None of that mattered, because at the end of the day, I was still the blind guy. I didn't want anyone's pity or them saying I was so brave because of my circumstance. I just wanted to be me.

And the prospect of riding again, getting on a bull felt like a start to bringing that old me back.

But that version of Huxson Lane was gone. Dead. He died the day of my crash.

"It ain't that I don't believe in myself," I whispered. "It's that I don't think I'm worthy. I—I hate myself, Quinn."

A quiet, choked sound escaped her. "Why?"

"You don't know what it's like goin' from bein' independent and capable and feelin' on top of the world to watching it all shatter around you in a heartbeat. It's gotten easier, but most days, at the beginning..." I swallowed. "I wanted to die. I wished I'd died. I didn't want to live if I couldn't do the thing I loved most. You don't—" A deep breath in and then out as I tried to force words I'd never spoken aloud to anyone before fell from my lips. "You don't know how often I thought about endin' it all. Killin' myself."

"Hux." She all but sobbed the word, and then I felt the soft pressure of her fingers against my cheeks, wiping away the moisture leaking down them. Her warmth seeped into me, chasing away some of the darkness tainting my soul like the sun breaking through the clouds after a nasty storm. I hadn't even realized I was crying.

I couldn't help myself any longer. I reached out, trailing my hands up her curves before settling them on either side of her neck. I scraped my thumbs along her soft jawline. God, I wished I could see her right now, but the image of her in my mind would have to do. And it was beautiful. Sad, but no less beautiful.

As much as I hated opening up and talking about this, I needed her to hear it. I needed her to see just how broken I was. If she couldn't deal with it, I wouldn't blame her. Hell, most days it was hard for myself to. But before she decided to stay or leave, I wanted her to see all of me.

Her touch gave me the courage I needed. "I had it all planned out... I was still in the rehab center at the time. But in the end, I just couldn't go through with it. I thought it made me weak, a coward. And I'd rather be a broken, pathetic mess, than have anyone ever call me a coward." I huffed. "I'm a stubborn bastard, after all."

"I'm glad you didn't," she croaked out. "But why didn't you try riding a bull until now if you missed it so much? The way you talked about the rodeo...I thought that you didn't want anything to do with it until yesterday?" Her words were soft. As soft as her.

I continued tracing lines along the curve of her jaw. "I thought if I could convince myself I hated the rodeo, I could give it up one day. But it's like a phantom limb. The memory of it never leaves entirely. It dulled a bit. I'd drowned it in enough painkillers and alcohol, learned to keep myself busy with ridin' and paintin' to keep it mostly at bay." Blowing out a shaky breath, I continued. "Then you came in, seein' me for me, not for the mess I am. You thought so good of me, and I wanted to be that good. I wanted to be better. I wanted to be someone deservin' of you. Not some blind dude you needed to lead around. Bein' a cowboy's all I know, and after last night, after feelin' myself come alive again because of everythin' you helped me through, I wanted to prove I was... Well, that I was worthy."

"Hux...don't you understand? You *are* worthy," she whispered, her words breaking. Warm liquid trickled down my fingers. Damn, I'd made her cry. "You've always been worthy. You don't have to ride a bull to prove that to me or anyone else."

"What if I need to prove it to myself?" I asked, my own words choked out and thick.

She pressed both hands to my chest, followed by the softest, barest hint of a kiss right over my heart. "Then I'll be right there, cheering you on in those stands."

I swear, my lungs seized for a moment, making it impossible to get a breath in. If I hadn't fallen for her completely already, I would have right then and there.

Cupping her face like she was some precious treasure I'd found, I kissed her softly. "I love you. I know it's early and I have no right to say it, but I do. You are everythin' to me, darlin'."

The sound that came out of her was half sob, half gasp. The pressure on my chest disappeared, and then her hands were wrapping around my wrists. "Hux..."

I kissed her forehead, murmuring softly as I pulled her into my arms, "You don't gotta say it back. I just needed you to know. And, if you don't wanna be with me anymore, I get it. I understand."

She huffed, her breath fanning against my cheeks. The familiar feel of her lips brushed against mine. "You are all I want. All I need, Hux. I'm not going anywhere." Her tone turned a bit stern as she added, "but yell at me again in public like that and it's over."

Well, it wasn't an I *love you,* but in a way it was so much more. Either way, I'd take it.

I snaked a hand back through her hair and kissed her. Like the world was ending. Like it was the last thing I'd ever do. I put every single piece of me into that kiss, hoping, praying that it would always be enough for her.

Chapter Thirty-Three
From Austin

Quinn

I**T WASN'T EVEN NOON** and I felt so emotionally drained. It was like a tornado had come through and sucked everything out of me. From the fight last night, to that encounter with Georgette, and then the talk with Hux. That had gone the smoothest of them all, but finding out just how low he thought of himself absolutely wrecked my heart. I'd do anything I could to help him realize his worth. Because he was so much more than what he gave himself credit for.

My stomach roiled with anger and worry as Hux and I made our way to my dad's house. We hadn't even made it onto the front porch when I heard Georgette's sobs.

"Dear God," I huffed. "She's the fucking worst."

Hux squeezed my hand gently, even as a soft chuckle fell from his lips. "Don't worry, she'll be gone soon enough."

I sure as hell hoped so.

With a groan, I squeezed his hand back. "Let's get this over with."

We followed the sound of her loud, obnoxious wails throughout the first floor until we came to my dad's study. The door was ajar, so I made my way into the doorway and knocked on the frame.

"We need to talk," I said, not even bothering to wait for my dad to greet us.

The room gave off gentlemen's club vibes with the rich, mahogany accents, dark wood floors, and leather furniture. A wet bar took up most of the right side of the room, while most of the left wall was made up of glass windows that let in a view of tall oak trees and rolling pastures. Georgette and my dad sat on a sofa directly ahead of us—her body splayed across my dad's chest, her head hidden in the fabric of his shirt as she sobbed. My dad stared out the windows, barely even glancing my way as I led Hux into the room. His jaw was clenched tightly, and every muscle in his body looked way too tense.

Georgette's cries rose as she snapped her head in our direction. "You!" she spat, her wild gaze landing on Hux and I. "You brought him here? After what he did!"

"Oh, cut the bullshit, Georgette," I snapped, white-hot anger boiling over like water in a pot. I was so over her antics. So over her hatred and stupidity and ignorance. I didn't even have the sense to be decent anymore and veil my disgust. "You literally—"

"Enough." My dad's tone was cold, final, his gaze even icier as he pegged it on me.

"But, Dad. She's lying!" I took a step deeper into the room. "She—"

"I said *enough*, Quinn."

I rocked back at the fury swirling in his light eyes.

Did he seriously believe her? Over me? After how awful she'd been in the time since I'd come here? I bit back tears, knowing they wouldn't move him, more than likely just anger him further.

"Come here, Hux," my dad said, stone-faced and devoid of any emotion. So unlike him. Dad wore every emotion, no matter how big or small, on his sleeve. He was an open book. Easy to read. To gauge.

"Yes, sir." Hux dropped my hand and made his way forward on measured steps. He'd done his best to angle himself in the direction of my dad's voice.

"I want you to tell me what happened."

With a deep breath and a nod, Hux launched into a retelling of earlier. "...then she placed her hand on me and I told her she should leave, before I said something to you."

"Lies! Baby, I *never*—"

"Goddamn it, Georgette! Enough!" My dad's booming voice echoed through the room.

Georgette bolted upright, disbelief and shock shining in her shit-brown eyes. She opened her mouth, shut it, opened it again, looking like a fish gasping for air. Looked like someone was finally able to leave her speechless. I didn't even know that was possible.

My dad didn't give her the time of day as he settled his sights on Hux once more. "Continue."

"Well, sir, she said you wouldn't believe me and kept gettin' more and more insistent. I told her I wasn't interested. When I tried to walk away, she pushed me back against a stall and kissed me."

Violence blazed in Georgette's eyes as she sucked in a breath and opened her mouth to respond. My dad didn't speak as he shushed her, just held up a hand toward her face. I bit back a sneer. He literally just gave her the hand.

"What did you do?" he asked.

"I got her off me, sir, and tried to get away. Fell over a wheelbarrow...and then Quinn walked in." He took a deep breath. "Look, sir. I don't know why it happened, or what made her come in there. I know it might seem like I'm makin' this up, it don't even really make sense to me either. But if there's one thing I ain't, it's a liar. And I would never jeopardize my relationship with your daughter by doin' somethin' like that."

My lips curved upward softly, and I closed the distance between us, snaking my fingers through his as I leaned into his shoulder. A silent show of support as I met my dad's gaze.

I hated that I couldn't tell what he was thinking. Did he believe Hux? Or had Georgette sunk her claws so deep into my dad that he'd believe anything she said? God, I hoped not. I don't think I could forgive him for this if he chose her over me.

"What did you see, Quinn?"

Quinn. Not Queenie or Quinnie, just my name in that cool, clipped tone.

I shivered at the unease trickling down my spine, but shook it off quickly as I explained my side of the story.

Each thump of my heart felt like a ticking time bomb that was about to explode, and my fears and doubts started to paint terrible pictures in my mind with each stilted moment of silence.

Dad finally took a deep breath, and on the exhale he stood up and walked himself over to the bar. Back to all of us, he poured himself a drink, and said, "You know, I remember seeing this place for the first time and thinking, I want my family here. I saw so much potential. A way to start new, fresh. With the woman I loved and my daughter." He turned to face us as he poured himself another drink. "But since the fucking moment we've all been here together it's been one damn argument after another. I'm over it. I'm done. It's too much fucking work."

I chewed my bottom lip, trying to make sense of what exactly he was saying. Was he mad at me? Had I ruined this dream for him? A wave of disappointment stirred to life in my chest.

He drained another glass, his sights set on the fields beyond the windows. "You've got fifteen minutes to get your things and leave."

My heart stopped, fear igniting in my chest. Was he firing Hux? Was he telling Georgette to leave? Or me?

He didn't even bother pouring another glass this time, he just took a pull straight from the decanter. His ice cold stare fixed on Georgette. "Leave the keys to the car I bought you. Leave my credit card. Just go. I'll get an Uber for you."

"Carl!" Georgette's cry pierced through the silence of the room like a banshee's shriek. I didn't even fight to conceal my disdain as she shot from the couch and desperately tried to reach for him. "Please, baby. Please. It's not true. It's not. Please!"

A trickle of pride shot through me as he batted her hands away and said, "Can you just stop fucking talking for once, Georgette? Jesus Christ! It's done. *I'm* done. The wedding's off."

She stopped moving, the look of complete and utter disbelief shining in her teary eyes as her lip trembled. "Please..." she squeaked out.

My dad turned back toward the bar and leaned his elbows on the polished, wooden countertop. "You have fifteen minutes." And then my Dad pulled his phone out of his back pocket and scrolled through it, completely dismissing her. Any weak sense of composure she possessed crumbled then, downright fury replacing it.

"Fuck you!" she all but screeched. "And fuck your perfect, princess daughter. Fuck this fucking ranch. Who do you fucking think you are, old man, turning me down? I am the best you'll ever get. You'll regret this, Carl Decker. I will fucking ruin you!"

His only answer was to take another enormous gulp of alcohol. He didn't even wince or flinch as it went down. My stomach turned at the thought of shooting whiskey in general, but to just drink straight from the decanter like that? Ew.

She shrieked, her tiny, toned body quaking with rage. "Fuck you," she spat, snatching the bottle from him and throwing it at the wall as she stomped for the exit. Glass and liquid rained down on the floor. She disappeared through the doorway, crashing, shrieks, and curses resonating through the house in her furious wake.

I blew out a shaky breath, a wave of relief washing over me. "Good fucking riddance," I huffed under my breath.

"You guys want a drink?" my dad asked, turning to face us.

I shook my head, even as Hux shrugged and said, "A drink sounds pretty good right now, sir."

My dad nodded, stood, and grabbed another glass and decanter before filling it up with whiskey and walking toward Hux and I. "I'm sorry about what happened," he said, placing the drink near Hux's hand.

Hux grabbed around for it and nodded. "I'm sorry to have caused any problems, sir."

My dad sucked in a deep breath and sighed loudly. "Well, here's to endings." He clinked his decanter to Hux's tumbler and took another strong pull.

Holy God, he was going to be trashed if he kept this up. I mean, understandable, but still.

"Dad..." The word trailed off into nothingness. I didn't know what to say. I'm sorry didn't seem adequate enough. As relieved as I was that he'd called things off with Georgette, I knew what it was like to lose someone they loved. And even if that love was misplaced, he *had* loved her—at least the idea of her.

My dad looked at me, and once more I was shocked at the age that lingered in the corners of his eyes and across the planes of his face. He looked old, broken down, lifeless. "I guess you can keep that job in California, Queenie. No point keeping this place anymore."

My breath escaped me in a sharp whoosh. "What?" He wanted to sell this place? "But I thought... What about the destination ranch? The events and retreats?"

He shrugged, taking another pull from the decanter. He swayed on his feet a bit now. Looked like the whiskey was finally catching up to him. "I don't know the first thing about ranching and I don't wanna be here anymore. I should have just bought a boat or something," he grumbled more to himself than anyone else.

I felt like I'd been hit by a truck.

I understood him not wanting to be here while feeling so raw, but he was just going to up and sell the place just like that? After promising me a job. A home. "I'm giving up the job in California, Dad. I thought you wanted us to do this together."

"Qui—" But my name died on his lips as his phone buzzed on the countertop. He closed the distance to it and cursed. "I gotta take this," he said.

"But, Dad. Wait. What do you want me to tell vendors? We can't cancel. The event is in two weekends."

He already had the phone to his ear as he backpedaled towards the open door. "Throw us a farewell party, Queenie. I don't know. I don't care…. Hello? Yeah, Bill, sorry, just talking to my daughter. No, I'm not busy. What's up?"

And just like that, he disappeared through the door. Just like that, my entire career path seemed to be blown up in smoke. Because I didn't want the job in California. I wanted to be here. With Hux.

Chapter Thirty-Four
Pick A Place

Hux

Quinn's footsteps echoed throughout the living room of the guest house. A fast, yet rhythmic pace as she walked from one side of the room to the other. I stood against the kitchen counter in silence, Rusty's warm presence at my side—we'd stopped by the bunkhouse to get him on the way back from the whole shitstorm up at her Dad's.

Crazy how so much had happened and it wasn't even the afternoon yet.

"What am I going to do?" she asked, her words urgent and high-pitched. She'd been quiet most of the walk back to the guest house, but the moment we'd crossed the threshold and she realized Whit wasn't here, she'd not stopped fretting. Or pacing. So much pacing it put me on edge, but I didn't want to tell her to stop. She needed an outlet for her anxiety. Unfortunately, it just spiked my own.

"You really think he'll sell the ranch?" I asked.

I didn't know Carl Decker enough to know if he'd just been pissed and drunk and lashing out in the moment, or if he was dead serious.

"Who knows?" Quinn huffed, and a smack echoed through the room, almost like she'd tossed her hands up in the air and let them fall at her sides. "My dad is literally the definition of *flying by the seat of his pants*. He makes every decision in his life based on how he feels in that moment. So, is there a chance that by tomorrow he's chilled out and willing to possibly figure something out? Yeah.

But it's also just as likely he'll be ten beers deep, acting like a pirate as he parties it up in the Caribbean."

She didn't even give me the opportunity to respond as she launched into another thought, all the while, *pacing, pacing, pacing.*

"What am I going to tell the vendors?" Something in her voice broke, and I sensed that this was right around the time when the tears would start to fall. "I mean, we can cancel, but that's literally thousands and thousands of dollars down the drain."

I pushed off the counter and followed the sound of her voice. Thankfully, the house was still pretty bare and I had a clear shot from the open kitchen to the living room. "Hey. Darlin'," I said over the echo of her steps.

She must not have heard me, or been too lost in her thoughts and pacing to notice. My chest constricted, thinking about how much shit she'd gone through in the past twenty-four hours. We both had, but, I don't know, for some reason, I didn't care about anything other than that I had her.

I could fight any battle, climb any mountain, deal with any problem as long as I had her.

So right now, I could be her anchor. Her tether. Her lighthouse in the shitstorm that was her life.

Reaching out a hand, I finally made contact with her. She paused long enough for me to find her arm and pull her into me. "Quinn, look at me."

And just like that, she stilled in my grip.

"You lookin' at me?" I asked.

A soft, weary laugh escaped her. "I'm sorry, that isn't funny. Yes, I'm looking at you."

I cupped the side of her neck in one hand, running my thumb over her cheek. "We'll get this sorted. I promise."

"But—"

I cut her off, noting the anxious edge in her voice. "Look, there's nothin' we can do right now. Too many unknown variables. And until we sit down with your dad, we ain't gonna know what exactly's goin' on. He just found out his fiancé was kissin' his employee. Hell, she's probably been cheatin' on him all along, for all we know. Give him a day to process."

She blew out a breath, her words little more than a whisper as she asked, "So what are we supposed to do now then?"

"Well, bein' as you could use a distraction..." I trailed my thumb over her jaw once more, a wave of nerves washing over me as I said, "My parents want to meet you."

A sharp gasp escaped her and she stilled in my grip. Fuck. What if she didn't want to meet them? What if that was too much for her today? Too quick. I just...I wanted to distract her from the problem at hand, but what if it only caused more problems for her.

"They know about us?" she asked.

I nodded slowly, blowing out a deep breath. "Yeah, so does most of the rodeo world."

"What? How? Oh... Oh god. Social media." She fumbled around for something, and then another gasp escaped her. "Oh my God, I have, like, fifty DMs. People I've not talked to in years. Apparently, it's not just the rodeo world who knows."

Another soul-weary sigh left my lips. I should've known this would happen. It hadn't been the first time I was in the news or tabloids. I guess being so removed from the rodeo world for so long made me forget just how quick news traveled.

"Yeah," I huffed. "Walker, I guess, told my dad I broke rodeotok. She thinks you're pretty, by the way."

"Wait, who's Walker?"

"My sister."

"You have a sister?"

"Yeah, I've mentioned her before, right?"

"You'd only mentioned her name. I assumed she was your brother."

I chuckled. "She gets that a lot."

Quinn's voice was as soft as the press of her hands to my chest. "You want me to meet your family?"

"I do, but if it's too soon—"

My heart thumped a wild, erratic beat in my chest. I know we were okay, but what if she didn't want to move as fast as I did? What if she wasn't ready for this next step?

"No, I want to. You've met my dad. I want to meet them." Her lips brushed softly against mine. "I would love to meet them."

I slid my hand into her hair and dragged her mouth to mine. I kissed her. Slow, deep, savoring the feel of her in my arms.

She pulled away first, a curse falling from her lips, "Oh shit, what about Whit? I can't just leave her here."

"I'm sure she'll be back soon. Let's find out what she's doin' and we can go from there."

"Well, what should we do until then?" I didn't miss the suggestive, sultry note in her words.

Desire sparked like fireworks in my veins. I gripped her hair just a little tighter and kissed her again, before gently biting her lip as I pulled away to say, "A shower would be nice."

An appreciative hum floated on the air between us as her hands slid up my chest before hooking around my neck. "A shower does sound nice."

I let her lead me down the hall and into the bathroom where she slowly—so damn slow that I swear to God I was shaking—pulled off my clothes, one piece of fabric at a time.

Chapter Thirty-Five
Cowboy Kind of Love

Quinn

"**I** can't believe that dumb bitch did that!" Whit exclaimed as she plopped down onto my bed. "I mean, it's not entirely surprising because she looks like a whore, but I can't believe she did that to Hux! I'm surprised he didn't punch her, doesn't he hate her?" She added with a huff.

"Right?" I laid down on my stomach beside her, propping myself up on my elbows while dangling my feet in the air behind me. "But, like, the thing I can't wrap my head around is why? Why target Hux?"

Whit's gaze held a sad look to it. "I mean, he's an easier target than most because of..." Her words trailed off, like she couldn't stomach saying the rest. *Because of his blindness.*

My stomach flip flopped, even as anger boiled my blood just at the thought of what Georgette had done. She was awful. Disgusting. Truly vile. Thank God she was gone.

Whit pursed her lips then added, "There's also the fact that since you came back here the dynamic between her and your dad has shifted. I wouldn't put it past her to try and do that to get rid of you."

I frowned. What did she mean? "I'm not following."

Whit crossed her legs and pulled a pillow into her lap. "Just think about it, if you thought Hux cheated on you with her, you'd break up with him, he'd get fired when your dad found out, and then there'd be no reason for you to stay and help your dad here on the ranch. She'd have been able to have him all to herself without you being there to guide his moral compass."

I'd never thought of it that way, but I could absolutely see Georgette as the scheming type. I mean, she had to be if she'd gone and tracked Hux down to assault him. "That does make sense."

Whit offered me a hopeful smile. "At least that dumb bitch is gone now. I wouldn't be surprised if she was out on the town tonight trying to find her next sugar daddy. She seems like a gold digger."

I huffed. She was right about that. How Dad could have put up with her for as long as he had was beyond me—and it hadn't even been two full months.

Whit's warm, dark brown gaze met mine. "How are you feeling right now, girlie?"

I let out a loud exhale and dropped my head against the mattress for a moment. "Stressed. Worried. Anxious. This entire morning has been one spectacular shitstorm. The only positive to come out of this is that Hux and I were able to talk."

"You two were doing something..." Whit offered me a wolfish grin and waggled her eyebrows. "And it sure didn't involve talking when I came back."

My cheeks burned with embarrassment as I remembered mine and Hux's little bathroom hookup, and how I'd led him into my bedroom only to find Whit sitting on my bed, the biggest shit-eating grin on her face. "We really were just talking."

She cackled. Like, full on cackled and smacked me with the pillow playfully. "Oh, so that's what we're calling it these days?"

I tore the pillow from her grip and tossed it back at her. "You're terrible."

A giggle escaped her before she sobered enough to ask, "So, you guys are okay now?"

I thought of everything. Of our talk after the encounter with Georgette. How he'd bared his soul to me. Told me he loved me. Just the thought of it all made tears sting in my eyes. "I think I'm in love with him," I whispered.

I know it was crazy and sudden, but it was true. I did. I knew it deep in my bones. In my heart of hearts. He'd said that I was it for him, and I couldn't help but feel the same. I had no doubt about it. He'd been made for me. Was he perfect? No, but he was mine, and I loved every broken, raw, shattered piece of him, and I'd spend the rest of forever piecing him back together if I needed to.

"Fuck, he's got the body of a damn god. I'd be in love with him too."

I sat up, swatting teasingly at her. "Oh my God, Whit! You're horrible!" My smile faded. "I'm serious though, I love him."

Whit reached over and grabbed my hand before giving it a gentle squeeze. "Girl, I think the only one who didn't know that was you."

Really? Was it that obvious?

"He wants me to meet his family," I said, meeting her stare.

Excitement rippled across her pretty features. She clapped her hands together in excitement. "Really? When?"

Guilt welled in the pit of my stomach. This was two weekends in a row that we'd planned to be together and ended up separated. "Today. But I told him I needed to talk to you first and see what you were doing. I'm not just leaving you here when you came out here to visit me."

Another reassuring squeeze of my hand. "Quinnie, you aren't skipping out on meeting his family for me." She sat back, waving a flippant hand through the air. "I'll probably see if the ranch hands want to go out to The Hitching Post or something."

"Did you talk to Travis?" I asked, sitting up on the bed. God, I was a terrible friend. Not even asking her until just now about her problems.

She pulled a note out of her pocket and handed it to me. "Apparently, he left for Montana early this morning. Says it's too hot here, and his parents need help with their ranch."

I laughed. "So, he just up and left? Did he tell any of guys? Wyatt or Dylan, or Brooks?"

"Brooks said he left around three this morning."

"That's crazy. I can't believe he didn't even say goodbye to Hux."

"Right?" She gave me a sad, wistful look, before sighing. "No more talk about him. What am I going to do without my roomie?"

My heart tugged tightly at that. I didn't want to think right now about Whit living basically halfway across the country. "You could always move here?" I offered hopefully.

The grin on her lips had me guessing she was already working up a plan.

"Come on," she said, bouncing off the bed and standing. "If you're going to meet his parents you better look your damned best. Thankfully, you have your super amazing and talented hairstylist bestie here to glam you up."

I grinned. "Want me to make mimosas?"

She was already halfway out of the room when she turned back to peg me with a tense stare. "Quinnie, is that even a question?"

The drive to Hux's family ranch was absolutely gorgeous. Just a two-lane highway winding through some of Texas' gorgeous hill country. Trees and golden fields stretched from horizon to horizon, the sky a brilliant cornflower blue interrupted by big, random, fluffy clouds that reminded me of cotton balls. It was honestly so beautiful it looked fake.

Okay, I could see why Dad bought a place here. The weather might be shit, but the land was absolutely gorgeous.

Hux held my hand from his spot in the passenger's seat, gaze turned outward toward the window like he was imagining or remembering what it looked like.

"So, what are your parents like?" I asked over the music coming softly from the rental's speakers. "Anything I need to know?"

A grin tugged on his mouth and he aimed his stare my way. God, he looked good in sunglasses. In anything really. "Mama will talk your ear off, and can be fussy, but she means well. Dad's real quiet, though. He probably won't talk much. Not because he won't like you, just because he don't like to talk to anyone but his horses, really."

"Will your sister be there?"

He huffed. "She sure will. She'll probably tell you a whole bunch of bullshit about me, but none of it's true. Don't listen to her."

I laughed, wondering what their sibling dynamic was like. Honestly, what the whole family dynamic was like. "How old is she?"

"She's about to turn twenty-one."

"Oh wow, that's a big age gap between you two."

Hux nodded, a wistful look clinging to his features. "Yeah. my mom and Dad had a hard time gettin' pregnant after me. And then the ones that did take, she lost pretty early on. They'd given up for a good long while, but then out of the blue, Walker came along."

I squeezed his hand reassuringly. "My parents struggled too. It's why they only had me. My mom used to call me their rainbow baby."

"Mama calls Walker that sometimes too."

"What else can you tell me about them?" I asked.

He told me everything. Big things, little things. Stories of growing up and everything in between. I listened in relative silence, taking in every detail I could remember as if my life depended on it. I loved how open he felt he could be with me. It was a nice change from how closed off he usually was.

Before I knew it, we were there—stopped before the most beautiful flagstone arch with an ornate wrought-iron gate. I didn't even get a chance to ask what the gate code was, he just rattled off the numbers to me.

"Wow, this place is beautiful," I breathed, taking in the gorgeous tree-lined road before us. Twin pastures spanned on either side of the road, and up in the distance loomed a house, though I couldn't make out major details yet. "What kind of trees are they?" I asked, admiring the purple blooms that hung from the branches and littered the ground.

"Jacaranda," Hux replied. "Mama's favorite color's purple, so Dad had 'em planted."

I glanced at him, noting the soft, almost contemplative look on his face. It's almost like he was remembering it all in his mind.

My heart clenched as I thought of how hard it must be. Remembering all of these places and sights, but not getting to see them anymore. Even then, I couldn't imagine it. Grabbing his hand, I squeezed it gently. He squeezed back before lifting my hand up to his lips and kissing the back of my knuckles.

The main house came into view as I drove further down the drive—a pretty flagstone ranch style home with large windows and a red tin roof.

I hadn't even fully put the car in park when the front door opened, three figures gathering onto the front porch. A wave of nervousness settled around me. I wasn't usually so anxious meeting people. Maybe it was the fact that his parents had seen me in videos online. I wondered what they thought about me? About the fight? Had they seen it? I'm sure they had.

As if sensing my anxiety, Hux reached over and wrapped a hand around the back of my neck, pulling me towards him. "They're right outside, aren't they?"

I blew out a breath. "Yeah."

"Figures. Mama's probably been watchin' the drive for the last half hour." He brushed his lips against mine softly. "They're gonna love you, Quinn. I promise."

The way he said my name sent a shiver through me. "How do you know?"

"Because I love you."

Okay, well, heart completely melted and worries *mostly* eased. How did he know exactly what I needed to hear in that moment?

An I love you of my own nearly tumbled out of me, but I bit it back. It wasn't because I didn't feel that way or I was afraid to say it, but the helpless romantic in me wanted to drop that little bombshell back on him at the perfect moment.

So, I kissed him instead, with enough intensity and love that I hoped showed what I hadn't repeated aloud.

If the appreciative hum that rumbled from him was any indicator, I'd say mission accomplished.

We got out of the car, and I found my way to his side once more as we walked toward the house. It's like he knew exactly where everything was and didn't have any trouble navigating across the gravel drive to the porch steps.

We'd only barely made it up the last step when Hux's mom exploded from her spot by the front door, wrapping Hux in a tight hug. "Oh, I've missed you," she said, before pulling back to hold him at arms' length and look up at his face. "My goodness, look at you. You look like a grizzly bear with all that hair and scruff. When are you gonna cut it all off, Huxson?"

Hux laughed. "Hi to you too, Mama." He looked my way and held out his hand. I grabbed it reassuringly, intertwining my fingers. "This here's my girlfriend, Quinn.... Quinn, this is my Mama, Dorothy."

I smiled. "Hello there, Mrs. Lane. It's nice to meet you."

She was a pretty, petite woman with shoulder length dark brown hair streaked with golden highlights and warm honey-brown eyes that glinted like they were always happy. The complete opposite of her husband, who shared Hux's tall, strong build, hooded gaze, and a stern look on his face.

Like father like son, I guess.

But that wasn't exactly true. Hux was almost a perfect blend of the two of them.

"Oh, no need for the formalities, sweetheart. Call me, Dotty. Everyone does."

She surprised me, reaching out to wrap her arms around me in a tight embrace. I choked on a surprised gasp as I hugged her back. "Thank you for having me."

She released me, waving a flippant hand in the air, a soft smirk on her lips. "The pleasure's mine. I couldn't miss the chance to meet Huxson's girlfriend." Gesturing at her husband, she added, "This is my husband, Paul."

Mister Lane's amber gaze met mine, and he removed his hat as he stepped forward, holding out a hand. "Hi, miss."

I offered him a soft smile. "Hello, sir. It's nice to meet you."

He nodded once more and replaced his hat on his head.

"I'm Walker. And you're even prettier in person," the brunette standing next to her father said. She wrapped me in a hug before I could even utter a reply.

She was young and beautiful, and reminded me so much of Hux it was crazy. They were like carbon copies of each other, but, like, not in a weird "they looked like the same person" way, it was more so that the features they shared were perfectly suited to their genders. They had the same dark, warm-toned hair, but Walker's long, wild waves were tipped in blonde like they'd been dipped in sunlight. They had the same complexion, the same eyes even. But while Hux's whiskey-colored gaze always seemed more pensive, Walker's swam with amusement and a hint of mischief.

"I'm Quinn," I replied as I pulled out of the embrace. "And you're the pretty one."

She flashed me a smile before launching at Hux. "Hi, Huxie," she giggled into his chest.

I didn't miss the way his body tensed for a minute, but just as quickly as the tension appeared, it disintegrated, withering away like dust on the wind when he hugged her back. "Hi, sissy."

"Well, come on in, y'all. Dinner's almost ready. Quinn, sweetie, would you like a tour?" Mrs. Lane said, ushering us toward the front door when Hux and Walker finally broke apart.

"Oh, I'd love to Mrs. L—I mean, Dotty," I replied with a smile.

Hux huffed as he settled beside me once more, slipping his hand into mine. He leaned into me, the scruff of his shadow beard tickling against my neck as he whispered, "I hope you're ready for this, darlin'. She's gonna take you into every single room in this house and have a story to go with each."

I bit back a chuckle as I looked up at him and whispered, "Really?"

"Oh, I guarantee it," he replied.

I followed Walker and Mrs. Lane into the house, making sure to thank Mr. Lane, who held the door for us. Surely, Hux was being just a tad bit dramatic. A story for every room?

HE HADN'T LIED.

His mom did have a story for each room. And turns out the house was *a lot* bigger than it looked. But it was fine, all of the stories made me laugh, sometimes hard enough to bring tears to my eyes. Though, it was probably only so funny because Hux and Walker teased each other relentlessly. And when they weren't teasing each other, they were ganging up on Mrs. Lane for being so fussy or remembering things wrong.

Being around them made me long for the days when Mom was still here, when we'd been a family. But the memories were so old, it was hard to remember a time when Mom wasn't sick.

My face hurt from laughing so hard by the time we finally made it back to the kitchen.

It was a pretty kitchen, with warm-hued granite countertops, rich cherrywood cabinets, and chicken and rooster decorations everywhere. Chicken valances, rooster salt and pepper shakers, oven mitts, hand towels, soap dispensers...you name it, it had a chicken on it.

"Oh, perfect. Cobblers are done." Hux's mom bustled around the kitchen, grabbing the over mitts before pulling the pies out of the oven.

"Cobblers...?" Hux asked, "As in plural?"

"Well, I didn't know if she'd like peach or mixed berry more, so I made both," Dotty said matter-of-factly as she sat them on the long, rectangular island directly in the middle of the kitchen.

"You could've just called and asked," he huffed.

"Speak for yourself, Huxie," Walker said, leaning toward the delicious-looking peach cobbler with eyes full of excitement. "There's always room for more cobbler." She reached out a finger, like she was going to swipe some of the filling that had bubbled over, but Mrs. Lane swatted her hand away.

"Now, you stop that, Walker Rose. You know damn well to wash them hands of yours."

Walker scrunched up her nose and made a pouty face at her mom, the motion accentuating the dark freckles flecking her nose and cheeks. I nearly burst out laughing when Mrs. Lane made the same face right back at her.

"Go on, go wash them hands and make sure the sweet tea set up well."

Mr. Lane, who'd remained so quiet this entire time that I'd completely forgotten he was here, finally spoke up, his voice gruff and stilted, like he wasn't used to talking. "Maybe, uh, Miss Quinn can, uh, help you." He shared a look with his wife before training his gaze on Hux. "Your mother and I need to speak with you, Huxson."

I could feel the tension ripple through Hux at my side. It was like a shift in the air. He seemed to straighten a bit as he let go of my hand. "Yes, sir." To me, he said softly, "I'll be right back."

"Be right here," I offered.

My stomach tightened a bit, but I pushed it away. I'm sure this was about last night, and wanting to get the facts straight before we sat down for dinner and wasted the whole time talking about that. And it's not like I couldn't spend a few minutes getting to know his sister. She seemed nice, reminding me a little bit of a younger, somehow more playful Whit.

Hux followed his mom and Dad out of the room. Leaving me alone with Walker. She pounced quicker than a cat on a mouse.

"So, you and my brother, huh?" she asked over her shoulder as she washed her hands.

I probably should wash my hands too. Walking around the island, inhaling the mouth-watering scent of the cobblers, I replied, "Yeah."

She turned to take me in, her whiskey eyes appraising. They still held a playful edge to them, but there was a seriousness in the depths that hadn't been there earlier. "He's never brought a girl home before."

I scoffed. "What? I don't believe that."

A playful smirk pulled on her lips as she faced away from the counter and rested her elbows back on it. "I'm tellin' the truth. He has this rule about girls and meeting Mama."

"What is it?" I asked, stepping up to the sink and nodding to it, silently asking permission.

She dipped her head and looked toward the hall her family had just disappeared into. "Mama gets attached to things real easy and she feels things a lot deeper than most. She don't deal well with loss. He promised her he'd never bring a girl home unless he intended to marry her."

My chest squeezed. For, like, so many reasons. First, because that was so precious and considerate of him. And second, that meant... He wanted to marry m e?

We'd hadn't even been together a few weeks. People would think we were crazy. Like totally crazy. But, I mean, it's not like bringing me to his parents was literally him getting down on one knee and asking me right here and now. It just meant that someday, maybe a few months or a year or two from now, he intended t o.

I washed my hands in silence for a long moment, trying to get a hold of the wild beating of my heart against my ribcage.

"Are you that serious about him,? Or is he just a few minutes of fame, or better yet, a charity case?" she asked, her tone full of accusation. Like she had me all figured out.

"What, no?" I rocked back at her words. "I would never."

"You'd be surprised how many girls tried to weasel their way into his heart for all sorts of reasons. You seem different—you're kind and warm and you don't look at him with any sort of expectation or pity. I just...he's my big brother—" Her words wobbled a bit. When I looked at her, I noticed how glassy her eyes were. "He spent so much time when I was growin' up watchin' over me. I wouldn't be a good sister if I didn't do the same for him."

I grabbed the hand towel and faced her fully, meeting her dark stare. "I've never felt something like I feel with your brother. I don't need money, I don't want fame. I didn't even know who he was when I first met him. And while that part of him is amazing, it's not the part of him I fell for."

A single tear slipped down her cheek, even as a bright smile pulled on her lips. She moved with lightning fast reflexes, drawing me into a hug. "I knew I liked you," she whispered into my hair.

A blanket of relief settled around me, easing my worries, as I let out a giggle. "Thank God."

She pulled back, the seriousness in her gaze that had been there only moments before vanishing entirely, warmth and excitement replacing it as she hopped up onto the counter and said, "So, not gonna lie, I kind of insta-stalked you. Your entire aesthetic is such a vibe and I'm so here for it."

I laughed once more. "You sound so much like my best friend." I leaned against the island opposite her. "So, what do you? Are you in school?"

"I just graduated from Texas A&M with a Bachelors in Kinesiology. Probably gonna take a semester off then go back for my Masters."

"That's awesome. What made you choose that?"

She glanced once more toward the hall Hux disappeared down. "Him. I took him to therapy a lot after his accident. I wanna be able to help others in situations like him."

My chest tightened at the love and thoughtfulness in her tone and words. "I love that. I think you'll be amazing."

She smiled. "Thanks. And what about you?"

"I'm an event planner. It's how I met your brother. Well, not exactly *how* I met him, but the reason why I am here in Texas in the first place."

Her face lit up. "You have to tell me how you met. I want every. Single. Detail."

I laughed. Well, I'd probably spare her quite a few, but since Hux and his parents still hadn't come back yet, I had nothing but time.

Chapter Thirty-Six

Beneath Oak Trees

Hux

MY HEART FLUTTERED UNEASILY in my chest as I stood in what I was pretty sure was Mama's crafting room, if the onslaught of scents was any indicator. It was sensory overload, but I ignored it as best I could. This wouldn't take too long, I presumed. Dad liked to give lectures like how you'd rip off a band-aid. Quick and with purpose.

"What the hell were you thinkin', boy?"

I huffed. Some things never changed with my old man. "About what exactly, sir? You're gonna have to be a bit more specific."

"Gettin' all drunk and belligerent in public!" Mama said. "Yellin' at that poor, sweet girl out there."

Dad's words nearly drowned hers out as he said at the same time, "Tellin' the whole damn crowd you're coming out of retirement."

Their replies couldn't be more them. Mama had always been more worried about my drinking and how my actions affected others. Dad had always been more worried about me and my career. Not that they didn't share all of those fears together, but it just highlighted their thought process so clearly to me.

I blew out a breath and addressed my mother first. "I know, Mama. I was an idiot and she didn't deserve that. It ain't gonna happen again, I promise."

She sighed heavily. "I sure hope so. She seems good for you."

I thought of Quinn, and how much it meant bringing her here. Meeting Walker and Dad and Mama. Especially Mama. She didn't know about the silent promise I'd made back when I was just a teen, but I'd kept it all this time.

I had every intention of marrying Quinn one day. If she'd have me. And I was willing to wait. However long it took.

"She is," I replied. "She's kind and patient. She believes in me."

Mama's sharp inhale of breath squeezed at my heart. "Oh, my sweet boy. That's wonderful."

Dad's brusque tone still held anger in it. "I suppose the talk of comin' back was just you being drunk, too?"

Well, if this talk was like ripping off a band-aid, might as make it quick. The good thing about Dad is he didn't stay mad long. Better to get it over with. "No, that was true. I am comin' back."

"Huxson!" Mama gasped.

"Fuckin' hell," Dad growled, the sound of his boots loud on the hardwood as he paced a path back and forth. "What the hell for?"

"Look," I sighed, pulling my hat off for a moment to run my hands through my hair. "I don't expect y'all to get it. I don't expect y'all to support it, or agree with it even, but it's...well, it *is* happenin'."

There wasn't any reprieve from the accusation in Dad's words. "And what does she think of this?"

Mine and Quinn's conversation echoed in my mind from earlier. Of the undying support she offered me. "She understands."

"Does she know you can die?"

I nodded. "She does, sir."

Dad scoffed, his boots never slowing their pacing. "You're willin' to risk your life, whatever you got goin' on with that girl, to ride again?"

I didn't expect him to understand. Hell it was hard to fully comprehend and grasp it myself. But I wasn't changing my stance on this now. "Dad, I just...I gotta do this."

He blew out a breath. I braced for his disappointment. It wouldn't be the first time I'd felt the scalding heat of his ire, and it probably wouldn't be the last.

"Well, I guess you better start trainin' then, you ain't in ridin' shape. And you *will* tell us when you ride. We wanna be there." I'd never know how he could sound so harsh while his actual words were anything but. He might not understand, but I could always depend on them to support me. To believe in me, even when I didn't believe in myself.

A soft, appreciative smile tugged on my lips. Holding out my hand, I said, "Thanks, Dad."

His strong, calloused one gripped mine tightly as he pulled me into a hug. My throat tightened. I could count on one hand how many times he'd hugged me. He just wasn't that kind of guy. So these random bursts of emotion were just as unexpected as they were meaningful.

Mama made a little gasp. "Huxson..." Oh God, was she crying? "Are you...are you sure?"

I pulled out of dad's grip and aimed my words toward her. "I am, Mama."

A sigh and then, "what changed?"

"She came in." My voice turned thick. I rubbed the back of my neck. "She makes me want to be better. She helped chase away the darkness." I thought of her words on that first night we'd met. They'd never been more true. "She breathed life back into me."

Another little gasp from Mama as she wrapped me in a hug. "Oh, Huxson. I like this girl. How long have y'all been together?"

"About a week," I admitted with a shrug.

I expected her reservation, or at the very least surprise, but I didn't expect her next words. "Well, if this girl's done that much for you in a week, I can't even imagine what good she'll do in a couple months, a couple years from now."

I smiled softly. "I intend to find out, Mama."

Chapter Thirty-Seven
Silence

QUINN

EVERY MOMENT I SPENT with Hux, I learned something new about him. Like, how he grew out his hair when he was a teen so Walker could play hair salon with him. Or that he'd been massively understating his artistic abilities when he'd told me he drew as a kid. He'd won multiple art contests at school, apparently, and had even been awarded a scholarship that he turned down for his rodeo career. Each revelation added another deep, complex layer to him that made me love him all the more.

We sat in the dining room around a massive dark-stained wooden table. Mr. Lane took up the head, while Mrs. Lane and Walker sat to his left, Hux and I to the right. Dinner had been delicious—fried chicken, fresh bread, roasted veggies, and mashed potatoes. But dessert had been divine. Hux's mom might be the best cook I'd ever met.

"You want another slice, sweetie?" Miss Dotty asked me.

I smiled, but shook my head. "Thank you, but I'm okay. If I have another piece I might go into a food coma. They're both absolutely delicious, by the way," I added with a giggle.

She smiled, scooping the slice she'd been poised to give me onto her husband's plate instead. He opened his mouth to argue, but a single look from her and he sighed before digging into his third piece.

I guess there were some battles not worth fighting.

"So, Quinn," Hux's mom asked, "how did you and Hux meet?"

"Oh." I let out a nervous laugh, remembering the incident in the grocery store. "It's actually kind of funny, I guess. We met twice, you could say."

"Twice?" She offered me a quizzical look.

Hux chuckled, placing a hand on my thigh beneath the table. A shiver went through me. "The first time she didn't actually talk to me—well, not really. I was in H-E-B and I heard this girl singin' from the aisle over. I just..." I looked at him, noticing the soft look on his face. "I had to find her." He squeezed my leg.

I took over the story, adding, "I hadn't realized anyone in the aisle was with me and I turned around and found him standing there watching me, or so I thought. I waved at him, not realizing—" I paused, "Well, you know, and I thought he was offended by my singing so I basically ran away."

"What?" Miss Dotty's eyes twinkled with excitement. "Did you chase after her, Hux?"

"I mean... I tried. But I didn't get far."

"Well then how—" she started, but Hux cut her off.

"Turns out her dad is the guy who bought Broken Creek."

"Really?"

I laughed. "Yeah, that's why I came back to Texas in the first place. I am—was planning my dad's wedding and staying at the ranch. When I went to go meet the ranch hands, I saw Hux and realized he was the guy from the grocery store." I left out how I'd embarrassed myself yet again, before thankfully fixing the situation—she didn't need to know that.

Hux's mom giggled. "What a cute story."

"You said you were plannin' your dad's wedding," Walker said. "What happened? Is it no longer happenin'?"

Dotty batted at her daughter. "Walker Rose, you don't ask that!"

"What, it's just a question?" she defended.

I blew out a breath, taking comfort in the silent feel of Hux's hand on my thigh. "No, it's okay. My dad and his fiancé broke things off today. Now it's kind of a scramble of what to do. It's too late to cancel the event and get any sort of refunds from the vendors or anything like that. And now my dad is talking about selling the ranch and, I don't know, everything is kind of a big mess."

I bit back a groan at the amount of unneeded information I'd just word vomited. They didn't need to know all my problems. They hadn't even asked. I guess at the end of the day, even the prospect of meeting Hux's parents couldn't quell the anxiety I felt over this whole debacle.

Hux's mom offered me a sympathetic smile. "I'm sorry to hear that, sweetie."

I returned what I hoped was a reassuring smile and not a grimace. "I'm sure it'll work out in the end."

Hux slid his hand up and down my thigh in soft, soothing strokes, but even as the conversation shifted I couldn't shake the worry burrowing deeper and deeper into my heart.

I wondered how Dad was. I hadn't heard from him. Not that I expected to, really. I hoped wherever he was, whatever he was doing, he was okay. Maybe I'd call him after dinner, check in on him.

Yeah, that sounded like a good idea.

There was no such luck getting ahold of my Dad, though. Again, not surprising, but at least I could say I tried. I offered to help Hux's family with dishes after dinner, but Miss Dotty shooed me out, all but demanding that Hux show me some more of the property.

"Come on, let's check out the barn," Hux said as he led me through the house with ease and out onto the front porch.

THE BARN WASN'T QUITE as fancy as the main one on my dad's ranch, but you could tell this one actually saw use. It was accented with warm-hued wood, flagstone, and black wrought-iron, much like the front gate. Almost all of the horses knickered and whinnied as we came in. Hux muttered something to them about not having anything to eat.

"So, are all of these your family's horses?" I asked as we walked down the right-hand aisle, filled with horses on either side. To the left was a large, indoor arena, and then to the left of that was another aisle of stalls.

"Most of 'em in this aisle are my dad's. The left are his horses in training or ones he's gonna sell."

"That's a lot of horses." There had to be at least twenty, if not more in the barn.

"You ever ride before?" he asked, threading his fingers through mine as we walked deeper down the aisle.

I shook my head as I replied, "I mean, my dad and I rented horses for a day in Griffith Park a couple times when I was growing up, but no. Horses never really were my thing."

"What was your thing?" he asked, as we continued walking. It's like he knew exactly where we were going.

What was my thing? Did I have one? I tried to think of what hobbies I'd had that I felt as passionately about as he did in regards to rodeoing, but I kept coming up short.

"Um...I don't know, honestly. I did sports growing up. Gymnastics, cheer, volleyball. But I was never, like, super into it, you know?" I pursed my lips. "The only thing I can think of that I've always liked to do is read."

We stopped before the final set of stalls and Hux turned to face the right, close to where the stall door was. "You like to read? What kind of books?"

"Oh, um..." I tucked a piece of hair behind my ear. "Lots of stuff. As long as it has a love story and happy ending, I'll read just about anything."

"Walker likes to read too. She tried to get me to listen to some audiobooks of her spicy books, she called 'em."

"Really? Did you like them?" I asked tentatively.

"Reading' really ain't my thing." He leaned in and whispered, "But I wouldn't mind doin' what some of those guys do to their girls in those books," he said before reaching a hand out toward the stall.

My cheeks heated, but all thoughts of spicy books and Hux and I reenacting scenes from them died in my mind as I watched as an oddly-colored horse padded from the back of its stall into the light of the aisle. Holy God, it was huge...and beautiful. It was tall. Like, crazy tall and seemed thicker set than most of the horses in the barn. Its coat was a pretty grey color, while his long mane and tail were black as midnight.

The horse blew out a soft huff of air as it bumped its muzzle into Hux's hand. A soft warm smile illuminated Hux's face. "Hey, bud. You miss me?" Hux pulled me closer and lifted our intertwined hands up, before letting go enough for me to press a hand to the massive horse's cheek. "Darlin, this is Church. He's the best horse I've ever had."

My heart fluttered as I ran a hand gently up and down his cheek. I didn't know the first thing about horses, but I think he liked the attention. "He's gorgeous. And huge. Like, really huge compared to the others."

Hux laughed. "Most of the horses my dad trains are Quarter Horses. Church, here, is a Mustang Percheron mix I found at an auction my dad and I were at about ten years ago. Poor guy was gonna be sent off to the glue factory—"

"Glue factory?" I asked.

He aimed his gaze in my direction. "Slaughter."

I gasped. "People actually do that?"

Hux shrugged, rubbing a hand up and down the length of Church's neck. "You'd be surprised how common it is. Some people are fuckin' assholes..." He shook his head. "Anyway, best six hundred bucks I've ever spent. This guy's bomb-proof. You can put anyone on him, take him anywhere. He'll do anything you ask of him. He don't know how to hurry if his life depended on it, but if you need to get somewhere, he'll get you there...eventually."

I looked up at the horse, noting his kind, dark eyes. "He sounds amazing."

"He is." Hux patted him a couple times on the neck softly before taking a step back, gaze still focused toward me. "I'd offer to take you for a ride, but it'll have to wait 'til next time. I wanna show you somethin'."

"What is it?" I asked, my heart beating quicker in my chest.

"Can't tell ya. You ever driven a truck before?" he asked.

"Um, no. But as long as it isn't a stick-shift, I can make it work."

He held out a hand to me, and with a final pat goodbye to Church, we walked out of the barn.

"You notice a truck with a flat bed?" Hux asked. "Walker said she parked it outside the barn."

I looked around and noticed a large black truck with a weird looking truck bed. "Does it look like just a big sheet of metal instead of like an actual truck bed with a tailgate?"

"Yes."

"Okay, then it's just over there to the right."

I led him over, and he made his way slowly around to the passenger side while I hopped into the driver's seat—no easy feat in my sundress and high heeled sandals, I might add. I'd never ridden in a truck this big, let alone driven in one, and I had this weird, nervous tick about driving cars that weren't mine. At least we weren't going off the ranch—I hoped. Oh God, what if we were? Why was I freaking out about this? It's not like I'd never driven before. I'd be fine.

It's fine.

"Alright, there should be a road just east of the barn. You're gonna take—"

I interrupted him before he could say anything else. "Which way is east?"

He chuckled. "You don't know the cardinal directions?"

I scoffed, adjusting the rearview mirror to better suit my ridiculously short self. "I struggle with following GPS with step by step directions, you expect me to know my cardinal ones?"

Another laugh rumbled out of him as he placed a hand on my thigh and surprised the hell out of me by leaning over and pressing a deep, insistent kiss to my lips. I melted into his touch, loving the confidence in his caress. When he finally pulled away, my lungs screamed for air and my chest fell in heavy breaths.

"What was that for?" I managed to breathe out.

"No reason at all, darlin'." He settled once more in the passenger seat, but his grip on my leg remained. "Alright, I can still get us there, even if you ain't good with your directions. If you look toward the barn, there should be a dirt road off to the right. You see it?"

I looked out the windshield and spotted the road he was talking about. "Yes."

"Okay, head that way for about a quarter mile."

I did as he said, cautiously urging the truck forward. His fingers started up a soft pattern along my bare thigh, sending sparks of desire igniting low in my belly. *Fuck.*

"If you keep doing that, I can't be held liable when I accidently crash your dad's truck," I said, my voice a bit high-pitched and breathy.

He chuckled, the sound sending another spark of desire straight to my core. His fingers slid up higher, higher, dangerously close to slipping beneath the fabric of my dress.

"Hux...where...where do I go?"

God, a few simple touches and I couldn't even talk straight. His touch really was magic, and I was helpless to it.

His tone rang with amusement, and when I glanced his way, a satisfied smirk curved his mouth. "There should be a dead, black tree that's comin' up on the left, right next to a gate leading into an open field." His fingers continued their teasing.

I tried to ignore it as best I could—which was nearly impossible—as I focused on his words. There it was. "Okay, I see it."

"You're gonna stop there. I'll hop out and open the gate for you, then drive on through so I can close it back up."

I followed his directions, my body all but screaming out for him as he left me alone in the truck. I didn't have to wait long until he was back, though, picking right back up with where he'd left off, stoking the flames of my lust higher and higher with each teasing touch.

I don't even know how long it went on like that, but by the time we finally came to a stop in the middle of an open field of mostly golden grass with trees dotting the distant horizon, my body felt like it would spontaneously combust at any minute.

"Here?" I asked, my voice little more than a breathy moan.

His hand finally paused its lazy, teasing pursuit of my inner thigh as he leaned over and brushed his lips against mine. It was soft and slow, almost taunting with its gentleness. Which sent a surge of annoyance through me. He'd gotten me all worked up, to the point my body all but vibrated with need, and now he was going to stop?

Nope, I wanted him. Right now. I grabbed a fistful of his shirt and pressed my lips to his harder.

He chuckled, gripping my chin between his thumb and forefinger. "Easy, darlin'."

"Easy? You're the one over here teasing me this entire drive. I want you. Please."

The groan that escaped him sent spears of desire straight to my core. "Fuck...I love it when you say please."

I hummed, capturing his lips with mine. "I know," I whispered, reaching out to trail my fingers down his chest, along the hard muscled plains of his stomach, before toying at his belt buckle.

His free hand gripped my wrist. "I want you just as bad darlin', if not more, but I wanna show you this first."

"Show me what?" Some of the desire stilled in my veins, curiosity replacing it.

"Hop on out and I'll show ya."

With a huff, I did as I was told. I hopped out of the truck and made my way to his side. He was rummaging through the back seat for something.

"What are you—" But even before I could finish my question, he took a step back, holding what looked like a couple pillows and a blanket in his arms before he closed the door.

My heart did little somersaults. How had he gotten those in there?

Walker. I remembered how he'd said she had parked the truck by the barn. My heart fluttered wildly in my chest. What else had he secretly planned without me knowing?

"Can I help with anything?" I asked.

"Help me spread this out?"

I did, and he grabbed his phone out of his back pocket once we'd finished. "Hey, Siri," he said, waiting for the robotic voice to respond. "Play my Country playlist."

A moment later, some soft music played from his phone as he placed it on the blanket.

Okay, this was seriously the cutest, most romantic thing anyone had done for me. He held a hand out and said, "Come here, darlin'."

Like I needed to be told twice. I melted into his embrace and we swayed to the beat of the song for a few long moments. How was he this attentive and romantic? All day, he'd gone out of his way to reassure me and make me feel wanted.

"Thank you," I whispered, pressing my chin to his chest as I looked up at him.

He kissed my forehead. "For what?"

"For this distraction, as you so called it earlier today. Thank you for introducing me to your family. For bringing me here. For giving us this moment."

He stopped swaying, one of his hands remaining on the small of my back while the other came to cup my cheek. "Thank you for comin' with me. I've never brought anyone home before."

"I know," I whispered. "Walker told me."

He chuckled softly. "She did, did she?"

I nodded, gazing up at him. He still wore his sunglasses, and I found myself wanting to see his eyes. I wanted to see the emotion lurking in the amber depths. "Can I take your sunglasses off?"

He stilled, but nodded after a moment. I took them off gently before disentangling myself from him only long enough to put them safely on the blanket by his phone. I turned to go to him when the sun sinking low on the horizon gave me pause.

A gasp escaped me, realization settling over me as I looked around the field. The pale pinks and oranges and blues of the sky. The random splotches of green and brown—the shrubs and trees. Miles and miles of golden fields. And the pops of blue. *Bluebonnets.*

Tears welled in my eyes, blurring my vision.

"Oh my God," I breathed. "It's the...it's the painting. This—" I swallowed past the lump of emotion in my throat. "This is what you painted that day."

The smile on his handsome face was soft, appreciative, and a little surprised. "You noticed."

I honestly don't know how it took me this long to piece it all together. The similarities between his painting and the actual real deal were impeccable. "I remembered you'd said this place was on your parents' property, but I didn't think you'd actually bring me here."

He held out a hand in the direction of my voice and I crossed the distance to him, letting him pull me into his arms. "I've wanted to bring you here from the moment you saw that painting," he murmured as he picked up a slow pace to the music once more.

"Really?" My heart went from fluttering to full on pounding around against my ribcage now. He was so sweet and kind and thoughtful. Did he even realize how amazing he was? Probably not. Actually, I knew he didn't. Which was such a damn shame. I'd just have to show him, I guess.

He nodded, stepping away from me and forcing me to twirl around before bringing me back into the safety of his embrace once more. "As soon as you said you'd come with me today, I got a hold of Walker and planned it all out."

Tears welled in my eyes once more at his thoughtfulness. "Hux..." I didn't know what to say. Thank you just didn't feel like enough. "This is the most romantic thing anyone's ever done for me."

He tipped my chin up with his fingers and pressed a feather-soft kiss to my lips. "You deserve it, darlin'."

"I wish I could do something for you too," I admitted quietly.

We slowed to a halt, and Hux asked earnestly, "Can you tell me what you see?"

I cocked my head to the side. "Like, the clearing?"

He nodded. "The clearing. You. Me. All of it. I want an image in my mind that's as close to this moment as possible."

My throat bobbed and tears sprouted in my eyes. Emotions pummeled into me, so hard and fast it was near impossible to keep them all straight. I never realized how much I took for granted with my sight. I couldn't even comprehend what he went through, but he did it with such ease and grace that sometimes, most of the time, it was too easy to forget he couldn't see.

And him not being able to see this moment, well, it broke my heart. But, if I could do this for him, if I could help him envision this moment in his mind, I would do my damned best.

"The fields are golden, but not like a bright, burnt gold, more like a–a soft buttery color. Right here it's not too tall, but off in the distance it's long enough to sway in the breeze. There's pops of blue all around us, just like in your painting. Dark shadows of trees fleck the horizon."

He nodded, a soft appreciative sound rumbling in his chest. "And you, darlin'?"

"I–I'm in a blue sundress with a white paisley design and thin straps—" My breath hitched in my throat as his hands began to trail up and down my body, like he was trying to memorize every line and curve.

I looked at his outfit, taking in his tall, powerful build. "We're matching again," I said, laughing when he frowned. I remember he told me he thought basically everything he owned was black. "Your t-shirt's a light sky blue, it goes well with the dark fade of your jeans. I like that I can see your tattoos today."

"Oh yeah?" The rumble in his chest sent shivers through me. "Got a favorite?"

All of them, I almost blurted out. I reached out and traced my finger tips up and down his sleeve. My lips tugged upward as I felt him shudder under my touch. "It's hard to choose, but the one on your heart will always be my favorite." It encapsulated everything that represented him so beautifully.

He slowly brought a hand up to grip my chin. "And the sky?"

I only dared take my gaze from him for a moment. As beautiful as the sunset was, it had nothing on him. With his fierce jawline that could've been carved from stone, or his intense stare that reminded me of finely aged whiskey. He was harsh and brutal and beautiful—like a wildfire or a storm. Devastating, yet gorgeous.

Reaching up on tiptoe, I whispered against his lips, "I'd rather look at you, cowboy."

Another low chuckle escaped him as his arms caged around my waist and he pinned me to his chest. He kissed me. Hard and fierce and with enough force to rip the air from my lungs. But I didn't care. Not when his touch felt like fire, searing me to the core.

Our mouths moved in time with one another, a seductive dance that left me shaking with need. God, I wanted him.

"Hux," I breathed against his lips. "I want you."

And that was all it took.

Chapter Thirty-Eight
Whisper

QUINN

WHATEVER SHRED OF CONTROL either one of us possessed vanished in that moment. Our mouths clashed once more, a battle of tongues and teeth as our hands grappled at clothes and tangled in each other's hair. I urged us back toward the truck bed on stumbling feet—it was hard to maneuver us both when neither one of us could keep our hands off each other for more than a second.

The cold metal of the truck bit into my back as Hux grabbed the back of my legs and hoisted me up onto it. I clung to him, my fingers knotting in his hair as I kissed him like my very life depended on it.

It might have.

Nothing mattered, nothing existed in this moment but Hux. The entire world could be ending right now, but I didn't care. Not when each touch felt like he was worshiping my body, his kisses filled with a ferocity I couldn't help but match.

One of his rough, calloused hands scraped up the sensitive skin of my inner thigh and dipped beneath the fabric of my lacy underwear.

"Fuck, darlin', your so damn wet for me." His words were like a purr in my ear.

A whimper ripped from my throat as he swiped a finger over my clit. I arched into the touch, wanting—no needing more. I needed him. All of him. Anything he would give me. "Please, Hux," I breathed.

A growl of approval reverberated in his chest. "That's my girl. Use those manners of yours and tell me what you want."

His finger teased and taunted me, sparking my desire like throwing a match into a vat of kerosene. I burned. Burned so brightly, so damn high that I hoped I never came back down.

I gazed up into his face, the smirk on his lips, the look of fierce determination blazing in his amber eyes. I pulled his mouth down to mine and kissed him, dragging my teeth over his bottom lip as I finally pulled away. I reveled in the growl that escaped him. "Give me more, please. Give me everything you've got."

A shiver rolled through me as he groaned and forced me to lay back on the blanket. Pulling my underwear off, he rumbled out, "Then be a good girl and hook your legs up over my shoulders."

I didn't hesitate, obeying the command in his voice. My eyelids fell shut with the first brush of his lips against my thigh, his stubbled jaw tickling my skin. And when he dipped his mouth to my pussy...

Fuck.

I moaned, my fingers darting into his hair as I held him to me. My back arched up off the blanket and little stars winked in and out of existence in the corners of my eyes. "So good," I breathed, unable to even form full sentences anymore. Not when his tongue did wonderful, dangerous things.

Each stroke was like fanning the flames, until every nerve ending in my body felt like it was on fire.

"God, you taste so fuckin' good, darlin'," he murmured, head still between my thighs. His breath tickled as it washed over me, the words a hum that sent shivers dancing over every inch of me.

I'd been reduced to nothing more than a whimpering, trembling mess, hovering right on the precipice of an orgasm. It was so close, it almost hurt. My hips rolled as he dipped his mouth to my pussy once more and all but fucked me with his tongue.

So close. So damn close.

But Hux didn't seem to have any plans on letting it end. Not as he worked me up, up, up, before drawing back enough to let me slowly simmer down only long enough to catch my breath. Then he'd start the infuriating, seductive process again. It was maddening, and so fucking hot.

"Baby, please," I begged as I shivered beneath him. It hurt. It hurt so good, and I wanted, needed, to crash and burn.

I think he sensed that too. He slid a finger inside of me, pumping in slow strokes as he lapped at my pussy. My head fell back, eyes rolling shut as a cry fell from me.

Holy God. Yes. Yes. This was just what I needed. The cliff I teetered on the edge of cracked, and I waited for the inevitable fall. For my orgasm to overwhelm me.

Except, he paused.

My gaze shot to his face and I swear, the sexy, satisfied smirk on his mouth was almost enough to make me come. "You wanna come, darlin'?"

"Yes. Fuck yes."

"Foul words from such a pretty mouth." With an approving growl, he descended on me once more, his tongue darting over my clit as he slipped not one, but two fingers inside me.

A scream tore from my throat. And then I was falling, crashing, burning as my orgasm ripped through me and my very soul. My vision flooded with black, every nerve ending in my body igniting as I rode the wave of pleasure. All the while he never relented, prolonging it all as his fingers pumped in and out of me.

"Good girl, come for me, darlin'...just like that."

When my orgasm finally ebbed, I found myself paralyzed in place. My skin felt like it was on fire, but the cool breeze floating on the wind sent a shiver through me. Hux gently, so gently, lowered my legs and righted my dress. I felt the truck shift as he hopped up beside me, and then he was pulling me into his warmth. Cradling me to him as he peppered kisses along my shoulder and neck.

My eyes fluttered open and I turned to face him, embers of desire already sparking once more in the wake of his teasing touches. I wasn't done. The need, the want, the thirst for him was insatiable.

With a newfound ferocity, I sat up, pushed him onto his back, and kissed him while fiddling with his belt buckle and then the button and zipper of his jeans. I managed to pull them down enough to let his cock spring free before straddling his waist, the rock hard length of him poised against my entrance.

The groan that escaped him and the punishingly tightgrip on my hips left my body trembling once more.

"Fuck, Quinn."

My name—the way he said it... A shiver rolled down the length of my spine and I slowly seated myself onto his cock. Inch by inch, reveling in the growls and hisses and curses that escaped him.

He tried to sit up, probably to kiss me or pull me into his embrace, but I found myself rather enjoying the view. Of him struggling with the lack of control, struggling with letting his desire overtake him completely. The first rock of my hips had his mouth falling open and his eyes rolling back into his head. By the third, he slammed a fist down onto the truck bed.

I giggled at the lack of restraint. I'd never seen him like this. At my mercy. It was always the other way around. I feel like I normally melted with just the simplest touch for him. It was nice to know I had this effect on him. It was empowering, even.

"You like this?" I asked, my voice far more confident than even I expected.

He gripped my hips, helping me pick up a steady rhythm as I rode his cock. "Fuck, yes. You're so fuckin' good at this."

I hummed, his approval warming me to my soul. I never realized how much I needed his praise. But being showered in it, being loved and worshiped like I was a goddess...it did wonders to my confidence. "Yeah?"

"Oh yeah, darlin'. Keep doin' what you're doin'. Ride my fuckin' cock."

With a hand still gripping my hip, his other drifted up to grab one one of my breasts. A ripple of desire speared straight to my core, forcing a moan up my throat. My head fell back to the darkening sky.

"Fuck...that feels...so good." I could barely get the words out as a new orgasm flared to life and rose from the ashes. He kneaded and squeezed my breast, only stoking the flames more. God, I was so close again.

So, fucking close.

He shifted, sitting up fully, and then his mouth met the column of my neck before trailing down, down, down over the curve of my breast. When his mouth found my nipple, his tongue swirling over the peaked bud, I nearly came undone.

"I'm so close," I managed to bite out as our hips rolled in time with one another.

His teeth grazed over my nipple before he released it with a pop, sending a surge of pleasure so white-hot and vicious through me I almost fell apart right then and there. I didn't know whether to sigh in relief at the slight reprieve of sensation it gave me or cry out in mourning from him stopping his unrelenting teasing.

"Wrap your legs around me, darlin'," he growled out, the words low and husky.

I did as I was told, pleased with how filling this position left me feeling. It put him in more in control once more, but I didn't mind. Each thrust of his hips sent my orgasm blazing brighter. Any second I would catch fire completely and combust. I liked the intimacy of this position too. The closeness I felt to him. He peppered kisses along my jaw, my neck, my chest, while one of his hands stroked up and down my spine gently, while the other speared into my hair, tilting my head up to give him better access to my throat.

"You feel so fuckin' good. I love the way you ride me."

His words flooded me with warmth. "I'm so close, Hux."

Black dots dotted my vision once more, and my body quaked with the need for release. His thrusts sped up in tempo, turning more rushed and violent.

"Come on, darlin'. Come for me," he murmured against my skin, before nipping at the chord of muscle on my neck.

The mix of pleasure and pain was like an explosion of sensation that detonated through me. I screamed his name as my orgasm tore through me with a vengeance.

I writhed on his cock, clutching to him as if my life depended on it as I rode the blaze searing through every inch of my body. He roared his own release a moment later, his hips bucking and twitching as he came inside me.

We sat there, tangled up in one another. My body had turned to jello, putty, mush. Every limb in my body was suddenly too heavy to move even an inch. Resting my head into the crook of his shoulder, I listened to his racing heartbeat. His fingers brushed up and down my spine—soft, reassuring strokes meant to calm and soothe.

I don't know how much time had passed, but when we'd righted our clothes and laid out on the blankets and pillows night had fully taken over the sky. Stars shone like diamonds against a canopy of black. I'd never seen so many stars before. His music still played softly, accompanied by the soft chirping of crickets and an owl in a nearby tree. It didn't feel real how perfect the moment was. One of his strong arms cradled me to his chest, while he had the other propped behind his neck, his gaze toward the stars.

But even though I had a the most beautiful night-time sky above me, all I could look at was him.

"It's rude to stare," he huffed, a lopsided grin pulling on his lips.

"I wasn't staring, I was admiring," I teased.

He chuckled, running his fingers lazily through my hair.

I bit my lip. I probably shouldn't ask this, but I was curious. Watching his face to gauge his reaction, I said, "I'm sorry if this is rude. You don't have to answer if it makes you uncomfortable. But...well, what do you miss most about seeing?"

He didn't even miss a beat. "Tits."

I gasped, bolting upright and pegging him with an exasperated stare. "What?" I giggled. "*That* is what you miss most?"

He laughed. "What? It's true." He pushed up onto an elbow and traced my curves with his calloused hands as his mouth found mine. I got lost in him so thoroughly I almost forgot what we were talking about. His hand skimmed up my breast before cupping and kneading it, sending bolts of desire straight to my core.

"I bet yours are fuckin' gorgeous," he murmured against the curve of my jaw as he kissed a path down toward my throat.

As turned on as I was, I found myself laughing. "You are terrible."

"I'm honest." His mouth dipped lower, his teeth scraping along my collarbone.

"So, tits is your final answer?" I asked, the words a bit breathless.

Another laugh rumbled out of his chest and I reveled in the way it floated over me. I don't think he realized how incredibly sexy he was. Everything he did made me want him. All the time.

He blew out a sigh, some of the playfulness sobering within him as he settled onto his back once more and said, "I used to love watching the stars at night. This... What we're doin' now. It was my favorite thing to do on a nice night like this one."

I smiled softly, glancing up at him. There was a wistful twist to his lips, a sad smile, like he was remembering those nights. I placed my hand on his chest, the steady pulse of his heartbeat thumping beneath it. "It's beautiful out tonight. I've never seen anything like it."

"Are the stars shining?" he asked, and I didn't miss the longing note hidden in his words.

My bottom lip trembled as I tried and failed to imagine how I'd possibly feel if I could never see the stars again. If I could never see again in general. He was so much stronger and resilient than anyone would ever be able to comprehend. I sat up and leaned over him to kiss him gently. "Brightly, Hux. So brightly."

I settled back against his side, and for a time we just laid there once more, content to enjoy the peacefulness of the evening.

"So, I've been thinkin'..." Hux's voice startled me with its depth after so long in silence.

I traced patterns with my fingertips over his chest. "About?"

"About if your dad sells the ranch." He sat up higher, propping himself up against the back of the cab of the truck.

I stilled, my gaze flicking to his. "What do you mean?"

"I could buy it." He said the words so casually I almost thought he was joking. But something in the set of his jaw gave me pause.

"What? How?"

With a shrug, he said, "I've got quite a bit saved up."

I mean, I had no doubt he'd made a lot from riding, but... "My dad paid like ten million for that place. You have that?"

He nodded, completely unfazed by the disbelief coating my words. "I've made a lot over the years, and you've seen this place. My parents didn't need the money. They helped me invest it. If your dad wants to sell the ranch, I've got the money to buy it."

Holy God. He was that wealthy? I couldn't help but wonder why he would even choose to work, but the thought was so painfully obvious I could have slapped myself. He didn't work for the money, he worked because it made him feel useful. It gave him a purpose. But then a bigger, heavier realization struck me square in the chest. He was willing to buy my dad's place for me. Just because. My heart clenched tightly in my chest to the point I couldn't breathe.

"You...you can't do that for me," I whispered.

"Yeah, but it wouldn't just be for you, darlin'. I've worked there since after the accident. That place means something to me too."

How was he real? How did he exist?

"You'd really buy it? What would you do with it?"

"*We.*"

That made my heart skip a beat. Two. Three, maybe. *We.* I mean, I knew we were together. Knew that what we shared went so much deeper than the short amount of time we'd been together, but still. Hearing him so casually talk about us as a pair, it hit me on a whole new level.

"I liked your dad's idea to do events at the ranch, but I have another idea as well. A bigger one."

"Like..."

"Like makin' it an in-patient therapy center focused around equine therapy. Ridin's helped me more than I could ever explain. I know the healin' effects it can have on a person's soul. We could convert the main house into a therapy center, but I'd rather build a new structure on the property somewhere. That way you'd still have the main house to use for whatever you want. Us, events, retreats. Whatever."

The plan was... It was brilliant. There was so much thought and care already put into it, and just looking into his eyes made me realize how much he wanted this. Needed this.

"You thought this all up today?"

He nodded.

I sat up, chewing my lip as I thought of the possibilities. I still couldn't believe he'd come up with such a brilliant idea, but.... "It'll be a lot of money to expand building, not to mention hiring more employees to upkeep the ranch, buying horses for the program, and getting all the permits and licenses and all that. Can you...can you afford all that?"

"Well, that's what got me thinkin' about the party too."

"What about it?"

"I know your dad said to throw a party, but...I don't know. That just seems like a waste of money to me. Why not have something good come out of an ugly situation? I was thinkin', let's put on an event to help with some of those funds? Between me, my dad, and the Mooneys, we have an awful lot of connections in the rodeo and horse world. When people find out I'm hosting an event, especially after announcing my comeback, everyone'll wanna be there. We could have an auction—my dad would probably throw in, like, some lessons, or, hell, maybe even a stud service from one of his roping horses. Mr. Mooney would probably throw in something as well. Hell, Cash would probably auction off himself if we let him."

I snorted. "That's honestly not a bad idea. He'd probably fund the entire damn thing all on his own."

Hux chuckled. "Fuck, never mind, we'd never hear the end of it. He'd think he was god's gift to the damn earth or something."

"Doesn't he already?"

He laughed once more before turning more serious. "And if we raised enough money, I'll ride my last ride."

My brow furrowed. "Last ride?"

He nodded, and I watched in silence as a myriad of emotions rippled across his face, the strongest of them all being the resolve shining brightly in his eyes. "I realized today that I don't need to ride bulls the rest of my life. I just want the chance to face my fear, get on its back, and ride the hell out of it one more time before walkin' away."

My heart squeezed at that. With a hint of sadness, but mostly heaps and heaps of pride. What he'd just said couldn't have been easy. Giving up that part of himself. But I was so, so proud of him. "Are you sure?" I asked, the words little more than a whisper drowned out by the crickets.

He chewed his lip a moment before nodding, reaching out to touch me, like he needed the reassurance. I grabbed his hand and held it in both of mine, kissing his scarred knuckles as he said, "You know, for the last three years I've been strugglin' to find my place, my reason for livin'. I didn't know what the hell I was doin' other than just existin'. I couldn't understand why I was spared that day, while still losin' so much of myself. I couldn't see, couldn't ride bulls. What was the point of livin'? Then you came here and you made me feel good. Alive. You made me wanna be better. And after the rodeo...well, it's all I've known my whole life. I felt like ridin' again was my purpose." He blew out a breath. "But I don't think it's my purpose anymore. Not in the long run, anyway. The more I get on bulls, the more of a chance I don't make it out of the arena back to you. And I don't wanna—no, I *can't* lose you, darlin'."

My breath caught, tears springing to life in my eyes before slipping down my cheeks. I held his hand like it was a life preserver and I was lost at sea. There were so many things I wanted to say flowing through my head, but it's like the connection between my mind and my mouth had been severed. "Hux..." I choked out, my voice wobbly and weak with emotion.

Hux reached out a hesitant hand, searching for my face before wiping at the tears on my cheeks. "So, that got me to thinkin'—"

"Lot's of thinking today," I managed to say past the lump in my throat, earning a chuckle from him.

He kissed the tip of my nose. "I was thinkin' of how far I've come since the accident. How much therapy I've been through—both physically and mentally... And I don't know, I like the idea of creatin' a place for people like me to come and heal. I'd get to ride and work still, and I'd come home to you every evening and not have to worry about dyin' and never seein' you again. I think... I think this can be my new purpose."

I couldn't see him clearly through my tears anymore. They fell unbidden; it was like trying to hold back a waterfall. I didn't have words to adequately explain how fiercely proud I was of him. Of all of this self-reflection he'd gone through in just a few hours, and the strength and courage he possessed.

A broken sob escaped me.

Hux's voice was a soft rumble, but I heard the hint of worry in it. "Well, what do ya think?"

I sniffled, wiping my tears and leaning forward to kiss him softly. "I think that your idea is brilliant and beautiful, and I am...so, so incredibly proud of you. I think that regardless of if my dad ends up wanting to sell the ranch, you should pitch this idea to him. And if he doesn't bite, then hell, I'll help you find another ranch. You deserve that dream."

"We, darlin'." He pulled me into his lap so that I straddled him. One of his hands danced paths up and down my spine while the other cupped the side of my face, his thumb wiping at the tear stains left behind. "I can't do this without you, Quinn."

If I had even a shred of doubt that soulmates were real, it would be gone now. Turned to dust or ash fluttering away on the wind. How was he so perfect and kind and reassuring?

And even though I wanted everything he said, even though I couldn't imagine my life without him despite the small amount of time I knew him, a trickle of worry filled me. What if he got tired of me? Would he always feel this way?

I looked at him. Really looked at him. The earnest set of his mouth, the warmth and desire written into the brutally handsome curves and lines of his face. But the look in his eyes—the determination, the need, the *love* in his whiskey-colored gaze erased any lingering doubt.

"You sure you want me to be a part of it?" I asked, even though I knew the answer. But I needed to hear him say it.

"I'm positive, Quinn."

My heart just about exploded in my chest. I kissed him—slow and soft, but no less intense—before resting my forehead against his. "Good. Because I want to be part of it. Wherever you go, I'll go. They can say we're crazy, they can think whatever the hell they want, but what we have...it's different. It's special. And it's real. I... I love you, Huxson Lane."

Chapter Thirty-Nine
Closest to Heaven

Hux

"*I LOVE YOU, HUXSON LANE.*"

My chest swelled at the admission, knocking the air from my lungs so thoroughly, it took me a minute to catch my breath. How the hell had I lucked out with her? I might have been dealt my fair share of shitty hands in the past, but meeting Quinn, loving her...and having her love me back was like having a royal flush.

And her admission. Well, damn. If I could drive, I'd already be finding a pastor, preacher, or wedding chapel to marry her right now before she changed her mind.

I slid a hand up along the curve of her neck and into her hair, knotting my fingers in her silky tresses. "Well, hold on now. Maybe I was a bit too hasty about changin' the wedding into a charity event. I'll marry you next weekend, darlin'. You just say the word."

Quinn's laughter was the most beautiful melody. A song made specifically for me. One I could—and planned—to listen to for the rest of my life. "You know, I would've totally entertained that notion had I planned it for anyone esle beside fucking Georgette."

I couldn't help but laugh at the venom in her voice. Angry Quinn reminded me of a kitten—but I'd learned she had claws and could use them when she needed. Thankfully, Georgette—the bitch—was out of the picture. But then the weight of Quinn's gaze struck me. "You'd really get married next weekend?" I asked.

"Possibly. But the event I planned for her was too obnoxious. Too grandiose. I don't want a big wedding."

"But you're an event planner. Don't you—"

She huffed. "That's exactly why I don't. I see all the drama and stress included in planning a wedding of that size." The familiar pressure of her hands on my chest seared straight through the fabric and down to my very soul. "At the end of the day, when we get married, I just want it to be you, me, a small group of our close friends and family in a pretty open field—actually..." she paused. I could feel her body turning this way and that, like she was looking for something. When she spoke, her voice rang with a note of excitement. "I want to get married right in this field."

I chuckled, a rush going through me at her eagerness. Because her words conjured images in my head that made my heart pound in my chest like a stampede of wild mustangs.

I knew most would think us silly and stupid. They'd call it puppy love. They'd call it infatuation or an obsession or some other bullshit like that.

But I didn't care.

They didn't feel the rush I felt when she spoke, the peace that overcame me when I smelled her lemongrass and vanilla scent. They'd never know how her touch stoked the flames of my desire, or how her presence was a balm to my broken and battered soul.

I'd told her before, if she was crazy, I was crazy. We could be crazy in love together. And to hell with the rest.

I tugged her toward me so that our lips brushed as I spoke. "Let me get you a ring first, darlin'. I promise I won't make you wait long."

I reveled in the feel of her hands sliding through my hair as she pulled herself closer to me, as if she needed the contact as much as I did. "I'm gonna hold you to that promise, cowboy," she murmured softly before dragging her mouth to mine.

Chapter Forty

Girl Who Drank Wine

QUINN

S O, AS IT TURNED out, I was wrong about my dad partying it up in the Caribbean... But when Hux and I ventured up to the main house Sunday morning, we found him packing his things to head off to the Bahamas instead.

Hux and I had stayed at his parents house late the night before, figuring out details for the event next weekend, as well as logistics for Hux's dream for the ranch.

Not gonna lie, I was a tiny bit disappointed when Hux hadn't even gotten halfway through his proposal and Dad said, his words a bit rushed, albeit a bit hopeful, "You want the ranch? It's yours."

Hux and I had worked so hard on the proposal, and I was more than prepared to have to fight my dad on this to convince him, so his quick acceptance was a bit—okay, a lot—of a let down.

But in the end, we got what we wanted.

My dad had mentioned he'd work with his loan company, work up a fair deal, and get it to Hux asap. Perks of being a realtor, I guess. He also said he'd help make some calls to get the ball rolling on any of the permits and licenses and other things we might need to turn this ranch into a therapy center.

The rest of the week was chaotic and hectic, but really productive, thanks to Hux and his family. But even as Saturday morning rolled around, my nerves wouldn't settle. Not completely unheard of. I always got a bit nervous on the day of an event.

But this was different. This was *my first event*. If anything went wrong there was no one to take the blame but me. Anything forgotten: my problem.

"Okay, the florist should be here within the next half hour," I said, walking into the living room of my guesthouse. Whit, Walker, and Dotty were already there, chatting quietly amongst themselves. "Caterers are coming around 4. The party rental company is getting the pool planked, while Hux and the guys set up chairs and tables. Oh, the DJ should be here around 3:30 to set up, and the mechanical bull and 360 camera thingy should be here sometime this afternoon as well." I blew out a breath. "What am I missing?"

Whit stood from her spot on the couch and came over to me. "Nothing, Quinn. You got this, girlie. You just need to sit back, have a mimosa, or, like, five, let the hair and makeup artist doll you up in a bit, and just relax!"

So why wouldn't the knots in my stomach lessen? I was missing something. I had to be. If it wasn't any of the things I'd already mentioned, then what was—

"Oh my God, it's my dress. I need to pick it up at the drycleaners." The realization was like a weight off my chest. *Thank God.*

Whit waved it off like it was no big deal. Which, in the grand scheme of things, I guess it wasn't. "Eh, that's no problem. One of us can go get it really quick, or if you want to go catch a break for a moment, we can hold down the fort while you're gone. Actually—" She strode forward and pressed warm, reassuring hands to my shoulders. "You go get yourself a coffee, take a breather, and get your stuff. We can manage."

I frowned. "Are you sure?"

Dotty's words of reassurance settled whatever dwindling remnants of anxiety I had left. "Quinn, sweetie, go take a moment for yourself. You've done an amazing job. Between the three of us, we'll keep these boys in line."

"Okay, okay. Does anyone want anything from the coffee shop?"

I'd just put the orders into my phone when I got a call that made my stomach drop and twist, forming tight knots once more. By the time I hung up, my heart fluttered like hummingbird wings in my chest.

Taking a deep breath, I looked at everyone's expectant gazes. "So, that was Isidro. His mom's in the hospital and he's no longer going to be able to work the bar tonight."

"What about one of the hands?" Walker asked.

"We've already got them tasked out doing things." I began pacing once more, willing my mind to think of another angle. This wasn't anything more than a setback. *I can make it work.* "Okay, I'm gonna go into town, grab my dress, the coffees, and see if I can find any servers who want to make some extra cash. Tell Hux I'll be back."

I checked my phone for the time as I grabbed my car keys. 12:30 PM. Okay, I could make this work. *I got this. I got this. It's all going to be okay.*

I hoped.

I PICKED UP MY dress without a problem, but trying to find someone to bartend seemed to be an impossible task. Everyone either was under twenty-one or way too old. I'd honestly resigned myself to just working behind the bar myself by the time I gave up my search and headed to get coffees—I'd worked as a server for a bit, and while I wasn't great, I could make it work if needed.

I sat at one of the tables in Sunshine's by the little pick up counter, waiting for my order, and shot off a text to Whit about how I hadn't found anyone and was heading back. The bell above the door dinged, announcing a customer, but I didn't look up, too distracted on how the hell I was going to pull off serving alcohol all night to about a hundred or so guests. I didn't know how to make any specialty drinks other than a gin and tonic or a jack and coke.

God, I was so fucked.

Jimmy, the old man who owned the little coffee shop with his wife, greeted the newcomer before telling her he'd be right with her.

"You guys wouldn't happen to be hiring, would you?"

I glanced up at the owner of the smoky, feminine voice and stopped dead in my tracks.

Holy God, she was gorgeous. Not in, like, a classically pretty way, but more of a sucker punch to the throat kind of way. She had a predatory grace in the way she moved, reminding me of a panther.

Long, midnight colored hair with a single chuck of icy blonde that gave off the illusion of a split dye fell in thick waves down to her full, hourglass shaped hips. She had the most gorgeous deep, coppery tan that made her look like her skin glowed against her dark clothes. Her right arm was covered from shoulder to fingertips in gorgeous grey and black ink. I couldn't tell what from the distance, but I think I saw some feathers and flowers mixed in there.

"We aren't currently, miss. There might be a couple places in town, though. What all can you do? Maybe I can point you in the right direction."

I tried to be discreet as I watched the conversation unfold. Mostly because I was just being nosey at this point, but also because, well, she was just so damn striking.

She shrugged, tossing her hair back off her shoulder. "I can do basically anything. I can serve, I can cook. Clean. I've worked on cars, worked in customer service. I can make deliveries. Basically, whatever you need done, I can do it."

Jimmy's gaze flicked up and down her, as if measuring her up. He nodded. "The Hitching Post doesn't open up until 3 PM, but you might find somethin' there."

"Thanks, sir," she replied, flashing him a grin before her gaze fell to the glass display full of pastries. "Are those chocolate croissants?"

He nodded. "The missus makes them fresh daily."

I could hear her little hum of approval all the way from the other side of the room. "I'll take one please—actually, make it two."

Jimmy nodded once more with a chuckle as he placed my order of drinks on the pickup counter. "Here you go, miss Quinn. Have a nice day."

"Thanks Jimmy, you too."

I grabbed my things and looked at the girl once more. She was probably around my age, if not a couple years older. Definitely old enough to serve alcohol. And she clearly needed a job if she was asking around town.

"Would bartending happen to be on that list?" I asked.

Her gaze settled on me and I finally got a full view of her. She had light eyes, but there was something odd about them. The more I looked, the more apparent it became. Her eyes were two different colors. The right was an icy blue, so light it looked more silver than anything, while the left was more of a golden hazel color. It was a striking combination.

Her mismatched gaze turned assessing as she took me in from the top of my head to the tips of my toes. I shivered. "Who wants to know?" she asked, her words oozing with a confident, almost playful edge. Her full, pouty lips seemed to tug upward of their own accord, as if stuck in a permanent smirk.

"Oh, um, hi. That was really rude of me," I replied, stumbling over myself. "I'm Quinn Decker. I have an event tonight, and my bartender called out. I'll pay you, and whatever tips you make are yours."

She pursed her lips a moment, her eyes narrowing in contemplation.

"It's a big event," I added, " there's gonna be at least a hundred people there. You'll make good money. And if you need a place to stay, I have room on the ranch."

Her eyes twinkled as a smile formed on her lips. "I'll follow you on my bike. My name's Ollie. Ollie Ravenwood."

B Y THE TIME WE got back to the ranch, it was nearly 2 PM. All things considered, it hadn't set me back much. At least I still had enough time to introduce Ollie to everyone, get myself ready, and be there to oversee all of the last minute preparations. I found Whit, Dotty, and Walker with the ranch hands and Hux, helping put tablecloths on all the tables and setting up some of the decorations.

"Hey, guys!" I called, trying to get everyone's attention. "Can you come over here for a second?"

Whit was the first over, her dark gaze fixed on Ollie with interest. Dylan, Wyatt, and Brooks looked like they were about to start salivating at the mouth over her. As obnoxious as it was, I couldn't really blame them. She really was something to look at. But Walker's reaction to her was probably the most honest and wholesome of all.

"Holy shit, you're like...scary pretty," she said, coming up to stand beside Whit.

Her mother tsked her, chastising her under her breath. "Walker Rose, don't be rude."

"What? It's not rude. It's true."

If Ollie was annoyed from all of the attention she was getting, she didn't show it. A smoky laugh fell from her lips as she placed a hand on her hip and asked, "Do you mean it's scary how pretty I am, or that I'm pretty in a scary way."

Walker's head tilted to the side for just a second before she shrugged. "Both, I guess."

Ollie laughed again. "I'll take it as a compliment either way."

"You guys," I said, getting everyone's attention. "This is Ollie. She's here to save our asses tonight."

If I had any reservations about Ollie settling in with the group and having any problems, they dwindled away with each passing moment. She had the ranch hands all but eating out of her palms, and had a get-the-job-done attitude that I seriously appreciated. Between her and Dotty, I didn't know which one was more bossy. But they were so effective that within an hour we were ahead of schedule. Enough so, that I felt comfortable enough to go inside and have my hair and makeup done.

MY HEART FLUTTERED AS I walked through the backyard, getting my first look at everything finally finished. This was always my favorite moment of an event. The few quiet minutes before all the guests came in, where I got to simply soak up all of the magic I'd helped create.

The flower arch and arrangements had turned out beautiful—a mixture of blushes and rusty reds, with pops of mustard yellow and burnt orange here and there. All of the details—subtle rustic nods with the whiskey barrels, the western stitching on the napkins, the rope accents and wrought-iron touches—couldn't have come together more beautifully. Georgette had been an evil bitch, but at least something good came out of her wedding.

"You out here, darlin'?"

I shivered at the sound of Hux's deep, silky voice, and turned to take him in.

Holy God, he looked good. The cream colored suit jacket against the soft, sage green of his long sleeve shirt was the perfect combination to go with the light wash of his Wranglers. His hair was slicked back underneath a straw hat.

"I am," I said, making my way over to him.

Some of my pre-event nerves eased as I placed a hand on his chest and melted into his touch. I think I had the same effect on him as he had on me. He inhaled deeply, some of the lines of his face softening. "You smell nice," he said, pulling me tighter against his chest.

Pushing up on tiptoe, I smiled and kissed him. "So do you. And you look great. I like this color combo on you."

His head cocked to the side and he stilled beneath my touch. "What color is it?"

"Your jacket is cream-colored and the shirt is a light sage."

He huffed a soft laugh. "I thought I was wearing black."

It was probably rude of me, but I couldn't help but laugh. "Hux, I don't think I've ever seen you in black other than the first time I met you. And even then, I'm pretty positive it was like a navy color."

He shook his head, pulling his hat off to spear a hand through his hair before righting it once more. "Mama had one job..."

"What do you mean?" I asked, running a hand over his heart.

"Since the accident, Mama gets my clothes for me. I told her to just get me black so I wouldn't have to worry about not realizing if I'm matching or not." He chuckled.

I pushed up on tiptoe once more and kissed him. "Well, your mom has impeccable taste. I have been so impressed with the outfit choices you always make."

One of his arms wrapped around me as he kissed me back, while the other slid down the soft satin of my dress, sparking little embers of desire to life along my flesh. "And what are you wearin' tonight, darlin'?" he murmured, his hand drifting down to cup the curve of my ass.

God, he was being a tease tonight. I found myself leaning further into the embrace.

"My dress is like a dark blueish-green. Kinda like my eyes, if I'm being honest. It has a really low back and the straps form this, like, crisscrossed, braided pattern."

His calloused hands slid up, up, up before scraping against the skin of my back. "Mmm, sounds nice."

I laughed. "That's only part of it. The way the front fits...well, it makes my tits look really nice."

The deep rumble of laughter that erupted from his chest had me melting under his touch. "Is that so?" he asked, even as his hands slid up my waist, creeping up toward my breasts.

"Behave," I warned, even though the words came out a bit breathless.

He captured my mouth in his, kissing me so deeply that for a moment I forgot where we were or what we were doing. Nothing mattered, nothing existed, except him and I.

It was a preview. A promise of what was to come.

Hux broke the kiss first, though he kept his arms caged around me—thank God. My legs had officially turned to jello. "Behavin' is the last thing I wanna do with you right now, Quinn."

I bit back a grin, trying to force air into my lungs while willing my heart to stop hammering in my chest. The way he affected me, so quickly and thoroughly with just the simplest touch would never cease to amaze me.

"How would that look, you and I hooking up on one of the tables when all of these people come walking in?" I asked.

He chuckled, brushing his fingers through my hair. "It would make headlines, that's for sure." I laughed and he pressed a kiss to the tip of my nose. "Alright, fine. I'll behave." Hux grabbed my hand. "Tell me what everything looks like. I wanna have an idea in my head."

We only had a few moments until people started coming in, so I settled against his side and walked him around, explaining everything to him, all the while savoring the feeling of peace I felt in his arms.

Chapter Forty-One
I've Got Friends

Hux

I THINK THE PARTY was going well. It *seemed* to be going well. I wasn't typically on the hosting end of these types of things. Usually, I was the one enjoying all the amenities and getting one too many drinks from the open bar.

It had been a whirlwind of activity since it started. I felt like a broken record, saying the same shit on repeat to almost every person I talked to. *Hi. Thanks for coming...* Then I'd tell them a bit about the goal of tonight and what all we were trying to achieve.

Without a drop of alcohol to give me a little bit of liquid courage, I was anxious and feeling slightly out of my element. I didn't want a repeat of last week. Not that I intended to get that drunk again, but I didn't want to do anything to fuck up tonight. Not for Quinn. Not for me. Not for my parents. We'd all worked our asses off this past week to make things come together. I wasn't going to throw that shit down the drain because I was a drunken fool.

I managed to find a moment of peace amidst the chaos, trying to gain some composure for the auction coming up.

"Well, there you are."

A soft smile curved my lips even as I silently mourned the loss of quiet that I'd been so enjoying. "Hi, Mama. Havin' fun?"

Mama placed a soft hand on my arm. "This event is truly magical, Huxson. I'm so impressed with Quinn and all she's done for this. She's really something else."

My smile grew at the thought of Quinn. It still amazed me that she'd even bother with someone like me. I'd never know what she saw in me, but I was sure as hell glad to call her mine. "I know. I'm gonna marry her one day, Mama."

"You say that like I'm supposed to be surprised," she replied, her words warm with laughter.

Well, shit. Was it that obvious? I blew out a breath. "Do you believe in soulmates? Or fate?" It felt silly asking such a thing. Like I was a kid or something. But Quinn felt the same way, so I couldn't be that crazy.

"I believe God works in mysterious ways. I think he sends certain people into our lives when we need them most. Miss Quinn..." She let out a little hum. "I have no doubt in my mind that she was meant for you, baby."

As much as Mama's words were meant to soothe, a knot of doubt formed in my chest. What could Quinn possibly need from me? It was clear how much I needed her, but what did she get out of this? I hoped that she'd need me always. That this wasn't just a phase or something. But as long as I had her, whether it was a day or the rest of forever, I'd cherish every moment.

I huffed. "Thanks, Mama."

She left me not long after, and I dove back into the fray of the party. Not much time passed before I came across a familiar crow of laughter.

"Shit, man!" Cash Mooney called out, the air shifting before me. I held out a hand, bracing myself for the vigorous handshake about to come. Cash's firm grip shook my entire body with the force of it as he said, "You and your girl sure know how to throw a party."

I chuckled. "Thanks, man."

"Ryder and Mav are here too."

I offered a hand to shake to both of them.

"The girls are off gettin' drinks or somethin' with Mom and Dad."

"You brought a girl tonight? I thought that was one of the rules in your rule book for datin'," I huffed.

He laughed. "Yeah, tell me about it. I'm already regrettin' it. But she was beggin', and I just couldn't say no."

I nodded, a grin tugging on my lips. I wondered when he'd find a girl. One who could tame the stallion. Maybe he wouldn't find one at all. Honestly, I think secretly he'd prefer that.

"Who's that bartender, though?" Cash's voice dipped low—a feat I didn't know was possible. "You know her? Is she single? I've caught her side-eyein' me all night."

Ryder's words were full of humor. "Sure, bud. You're the one who's been slack-jawed and droolin' every time you look over there."

"Shut your damn mouth!" I could imagine Cash trying to shush Ryder or something as he looked around for his girlfriend. "Jacie Lynn's gonna be pissed if she hears."

"When are you gonna cut that girl loose?" Maverick's voice dripped with concern.

"I've tried!" Cash defended. "It's fuckin' hard. She's just so damn sweet."

"All the more reason to break it off before you break her heart," Maverick went on.

"Enough about me. We're here for Hux and Quinn," Cash replied, ending the conversation. "So, tell us about what you're plannin' for this place."

They all seemed eager enough to listen as I talked. Surprisingly, the most vocal of the entire endeavor was Maverick. He'd never been a talker, but he seemed the most interested in the plans. But soon talk of the ranch turned back to Cash and women. Honestly, by that point, I didn't even mind. It was nice to have a moment just hanging with some friends.

Chapter Forty-Two

Finally Stop Dreaming

QUINN

EVERYTHING WAS GOING WELL. Thank God. Everyone seemed to be enjoying themselves and people were excited about the auction coming up. My nerves were still a bit strung tight, though. I didn't typically host the events I planned. Honestly, I hadn't done that since Mom's memorial. And Mom's hadn't been anywhere near as big as this.

There had to be, like, two hundred guests here—more than I'd thought would come. All wondering about my relationship with Hux, or what exactly this event was about. There were. So. Many. Questions.

I was so tired and my feet hurt. The boots Walker helped me pick out at Boot Barn were adorable, but it probably wasn't my smartest move to wear them without breaking them in first. After excusing myself from the latest round of questions, I angled my way toward the bar, where Ollie worked.

Whit appeared next to me, as if sensing my need for a moment, like the perfect best friend she was. "I saw Ollie making this yummy looking drink," she said. "Something sweet. It looked right up your alley."

I smiled, my lips forming a wry grin. She knew me too well.

Whit snaked her arm around my elbow. "I think Ollie was a good choice. She seems to be doing well."

"Yeah, I like her." My gaze settled on her once more, noticing Cash saunter his way on up to the bar. The way he looked at Ollie...and the way she looked at him. *Holy God.* I was too far away to hear what he said to her, but I saw her offer him a feral smile that I think would send most men running.

It wasn't surprising that Cash didn't balk or cower, but instead leaned further across the bar. He seemed the type to see a girl like Ollie as a challenge.

"Looks like Cash might have met his match," I mused, watching the two of them interact.

"Isn't his girlfriend here?" Whit asked.

I thought of the pretty strawberry blonde he'd arrived with on his arm this evening. She was perky and sweet...too sweet for Cash. I'd only met him a couple times now, but he didn't seem to be the settling down type. At least not with this girl.

"Yeah, she is," I replied, spotting her talking to the two women who'd come with Cash's friends, Ryder and Maverick—a gorgeous redhead and beautiful blonde. Cash's girlfriend kept glancing at the bar, apparently aware that he was there, but when she saw Ollie and him talking, there wasn't any anger or shock written on her lovely face. I wasn't sure what the emotion was.

"This might sound mean of me, but I just don't really see him and her together," Whit said.

I glanced at Whit, offering her a guilty nod. "I know. Same here. She seems really sweet."

"I think that's the problem. Cash doesn't strike me as a sweets guy."

I glanced back at the bar to where him and Ollie still spoke. "You think he wants someone a bit more like Ollie?"

"I don't think Cash knows or cares to know, for that matter, what he wants."

"True."

Cash and Ollie were still talking at the bar when we came up and interrupted them.

"Ladies," Cash said, tipping his hat while offering us one of those million-dollar smiles of his. I wondered how many girls fell victim to it? Probably too many. "Y'all are lookin' particularly pretty tonight."

"Well, thank you. You're looking particularly—" I took in his pink and white paisley colored suit jacket, his white washed denim Wranglers, and expensive boots. He had such a vibrant, flamboyant style, but if anyone could get away with it, it would be him.

His grin pulled wider. "Handsome? Debonair?"

"Spell debonair," Ollie snorted from behind the bar.

Cash chuckled. "Now that's a bit too big of a word for a humble cowboy like me."

"Humble?" Whit burst into a fit of laughter. "So that's what you're calling yourself nowadays?"

He scoffed, mimicking offense, but there was no hiding the playful glint in his hazel eyes. "Miss Quinn, tell them they're wrong."

I grinned and gently patted his arm. "I wish I could."

He scoffed, more of that mock disbelief escaping him. "Y'all are mean."

We all laughed as another newcomer approached the bar. "Hey ya, Cash."

"What can I get you, sugar?" Ollie asked.

"Coors, please." He glanced at us only a moment before setting his gaze straight ahead, like he was nervous or something. He even fidgeted with something in his pocket.

He was older—like, as old as, if not older than my dad—but that didn't do anything to diminish how attractive he was. Short, wheat blond hair mostly hidden beneath a white straw cowboy hat. A fit build, and an impeccable sense of fashion. Even amidst this sea of money at this event, everything about him screamed wealth—from his fitted navy sports coat, his pale pink button up peeking out from beneath it, to his heavily starched jeans, and a pair of cowboy boots that were probably made out of some exotic animal. Maybe snakeskin or crocodile.

"Who is that?" Whit breathed, quiet enough that the man hadn't heard her.

My gaze whipped to my best friend then back at the cowboy. There was a youthfulness to him, making him seem younger than his years. All around he was incredibly attractive, but he was easily a good twenty-five years older than Whit, and that was being generous.

Ollie handed him a cold beer with a wink, before aiming her attention back our way.

Cash's gaze turned quizzical as he glanced between Whit and the newcomer. "That's my Uncle Goodie. Why?"

Whit smoothed out her black, body-hugging gown and stood a bit taller, her gaze flicking to the older cowboy once more. He noticed her stare and fumbled with his beer, on accident knocking it over on the bar top.

"Oh, shit!" he exclaimed, trying to mop up the mess with napkins. His gaze flicked back up to Whit and the look of surprise, then downright bafflement that crossed his face was the most wholesome thing I'd ever seen in my life.

I swear I heard her murmur under her breath, "He's so cute."

Okay, was I, like, in the Twilight Zone, or something?

Without another word to any of us, Whit moved toward the man. "Hi there, I'm Whit. Wanna buy me a drink?"

The man opened and closed his mouth once, twice, glancing between Cash and Whit, almost like he couldn't believe what was happening. "I um... I..."

Cash flashed his uncle a sly grin and nudged him with an elbow. "Well, order the girl a drink, Goodie. Damn." He glanced at Ollie and tipped his hat to her, something flickering in his light gaze. "Have a nice night, Miss. Lovely party, Quinnie girl."

"It's Ollie, not miss," she clarified as he walked away.

He turned back to wink at her. "See you around, Miss Ollie."

And then he left. Past Ryder and Maverick and the rest of their party. Past his girlfriend. He kept walking, disappearing into the mass of people. I glanced at Ollie, noting the intrigue in her mismatched eyes.

"Well, that was interesting," I said, blowing out a breath.

Ollie pegged me with her intense gaze and I shivered under the weight of it. She could be terrifying sometimes. This...this was one of those times. "What are you talking about?"

"I think he likes you."

She huffed. "That's not hard. He likes anything with a pretty face and a pussy."

Thank God I didn't have a drink or it might have come out of my nose or something. "Ollie!"

"What?" She shrugged, brushing her midnight waves back over her shoulder. "It's true. I am fully aware of his kind. Always on the hunt for his newest catch." Even as she spoke, she watched the place where he'd disappeared.

"But...do you want to be caught?" I asked hesitantly.

She laughed, flashing another feral grin. "No, Quinn. I'm a hunter as well."

It all made sense now. I think Cash really had met his match.

By the time I made it back to Hux's side, I realized I'd forgotten to get myself a drink. I'd been too caught up in everything.

"Where've you been?" he asked, pulling me against him.

"Watching the weirdest things unfold," I admitted, before launching into what all had happened. The connection I swore I could feel between Ollie and Cash. The strange encounter between Whit and Cash's Uncle Goodie. "She's still over there talking to him, by the way," I went on, my gaze flicking to them for, like, the dozenth time. And what was even more unexpected was how happy and at ease she looked. He still came across as nervous and fidgety, but there was intrigue and a bashful smile on his face, so I think it was going well.

"Maybe she's into older guys," Hux offered.

"Yeah, maybe." Except I'd never known. She was my best friend. Shouldn't I, like, know or something? It wasn't like I was weirded out or anything like that. Though, the thought that she might be into someone as old as my dad was a bit surprising. But hey, whatever floated her boat.

Shaking my head to clear it of my thoughts, I pressed a kiss to his cheek. "You ready for the auction?"

He blew out a breath, and I felt him tremble beneath me a bit. "Is it weird I'm nervous? It's not like this is the first time I've been up in front of people. But...I don't know. This feels bigger. More important."

I reached up on tiptoe and brushed my lips against his. It amazed me how quickly the tension in his muscles and limbs melted. As if my touch held that much power over him. I know he held that much power over me.

"It's gonna be amazing," I whispered against his lips. "And I'll be right by your side."

He cupped my face in his hands, scraping his thumbs along the curve of my jaw. Butterflies danced in my chest. "Love you, darlin'."

I hummed in approval and kissed him once more. Slow and deep, like we were the only two souls on the planet. "Love you too."

"Wait, who the hell is gonna auction things for us?" he asked as we made our way toward the DJ's table to grab the mic.

"I already got it covered. Cash said he'd do it."

"Oh shit," Hux cursed.

Trepidation welled in my stomach. "Is that a bad thing?"

He'd seemed like the perfect candidate. He was witty, charming, and a bit aggressive, which I figured were all attributes that someone trying to sell things would possess.

Hux blew out a breath and laughed. "I guess we'll find out, won't we, dar-lin'?"

NOT MUCH LATER, HUX and I made our way to the center of the dance floor. He gripped my hand like his life depended on it. I didn't mind, I probably held on just as tight, especially with all the eyes on us.

Hux rolled some of the tension out of his shoulders and held the mic up to his lips. "Thank y'all for comin' out tonight. I hope y'all've been havin' a good time."

A chorus of claps and an all too familiar crow of excitement erupted from the crowd—Cash. I bit back a grin as I found him close to the front with their group. Mr. Mooney met my gaze and offered a reassuring wink. I smiled and nodded. I liked him.

"I know that I've already talked to quite a few of y'all here about the uh...the significance of tonight, and what we're plannin' to do with this place," Hux said, pulling my attention to him once more.

"The first night I met Quinn, she told me she got into event planning because she wanted to breathe life into things. Well—" Hux cleared his throat, his gaze dipping toward me. It was moments like this when it was easy to think he was actually seeing me. Maybe he could, in a way. "Not only has she breathed life into this event, but she managed to breathe life into me as well."

He kissed my forehead and I melted, tears stinging in my eyes. "I love you," I whispered, quiet enough for only him to hear.

He peppered another soft kiss to my forehead before continuing on. "Quinn and I want to create a place for people to come and heal. To have the life breathed back into them. The Broken Creek Ranch Equine Therapy Center will allow patients to recover and heal here through the power of horsemanship and other forms of therapy. And as you can imagine...that's gonna cost a pretty penny to get started. So, all proceeds from tonight's auction will be goin' towards that."

A wave of approving murmurs traversed through the crowd.

"Now, before we begin," Hux went on, "I know that an awful lot of you wanna know if I'm comin' out of retirement. And I am...on one condition."

I swear, the roar of cheers and excitement was so loud it was deafening. It went on so long Hux had to shush everyone.

With a chuckle, he said, "If we can raise enough money tonight...if we can reach our goal, I'm gonna ride one more time. So, how about we get this auction started? Cash Mooney, you wanna come on up?"

After another long bout of cheering, Cash Mooney sauntered from the crowd, grabbing thanks mic from Hux.

"Thanks, bud," he said with a grin and a clap to Hux's back. "I'll take things from here."

Hux and I moved off to the side where Walker and Dotty prepared whatever was necessary to present each of the items as Cash took a deep breath and readied himself to take on the task of being the auctioneer. Apparently, he'd done a few auctions himself and was really good—according to him.

Except he wasn't. Oh my god, he *so* wasn't. Not that I knew much about what all went into it, but the unintelligible jargon falling from his lips was evidence enough that I'd royally fucked up.

"What the hell is he doing?" I hissed. "He said he knew how to do this."

Hux shook his head, a disbelieving chuckle falling from his lips. "You actually believed him?"

"Oh my God, we have to stop him. No one knows what the hell he's saying."

"Well, I can't do it. I wouldn't even know what the hell I was auctioning off."

Neither would I, but not because of my lack of vision, just my complete and utter lack of horse knowledge. Most of the things we were auctioning off were trainings, stud fees, things I knew nothing about.

A warm hand on my shoulder startled me. I turned, glancing up into the face of the older cowboy who'd caught Whit's eye. "Miss. I apologize about my nephew. I can, um... well, if you need someone to do this for you, I can do it."

"Are you sure?"

I was not ready for someone else to say they could do it and screw everything up.

He tipped his hat to me and nodded. "Yes, ma'am."

I sighed and glanced in Cash's direction. "Thank you. That would be helpful."

Turns out Cash might not know a thing about auctioneering, but his uncle sure did. The fidgety, nervous looking man who'd spilled a drink at the bar earlier had vanished entirely, a cool, confident, fast-as-hell talking cowboy replacing him. I didn't miss Whit's approving smirk on her lips as she watched him. Wow, she really was into him, wasn't she?

My nerves and excitement mingled and danced in my chest as each item was auctioned off. With each *"sold"* that fell from the cowboy's lips, we ventured closer and closer to our goal. One hundred fifty thousand dollars might have been a bit lofty, but in the end, we'd take whatever we could to make this dream become a reality.

When the final item—a stud service from one of Mr. Lane's famous roping horses—finally sold, we were still five thousand dollars short. My heart sank as I glanced at Hux, noting the lines of disappointment etched into his face. I knew he'd ride regardless, but this meant so much to him. He was so determined to make this goal.

"Well, damn," Hux huffed, hanging his head low. "Guess that's that."

"Actually..." I said, "There's one final item."

I'd known there was a chance that we might be just shy of the goal, so I'd planned to have one final item. Just in case.

Hux frowned. "What is it?"

Chapter Forty-Three
East Side of Sorrow

Hux

WORRY CREPT THROUGH ME at the tone Quinn used. It was hopeful on the surface, but lurking just beneath was a hint of hesitance. Almost like she was afraid of what I'd think.

"I wanted to make sure we had a backup item in case we were shy of the goal. So, I um...I brought up one of your paintings."

My heart stuttered in my chest. I shook my head. "No. No one's gonna want that."

Emotions roiled within me. Not necessarily anger, but maybe frustration for sure. That and, let's face it, a hell of a lot of anxiety. No one but her had seen my paintings. Not even Mom and Dad. Sharing that part of myself with the world...I don't know. It scared the hell out of me.

"You don't know that, Hux," she replied back, a note of desperation thrumming in her words.

"I do. No one's gonna pay five grand for a finger painting." My words came out low, bitter, little more than a growl.

Quinn's soft hands slid up the planes of my chest before trailing up the column of my neck and resting on either side of my face. "Hux, your artwork is beautiful. I'm not just telling you that."

Her soothing touch warred with the anxiety writhing in my chest. Something about the feel of her...I was helpless to it. My hands drifted to hold her waist. "Quinn..."

"Do you trust me?" There was no missing the desperation now. But she sounded determined too.

I didn't even have to stop and consider her words. I did trust her. Whole-heartedly. Sighing, I raised a hand to cup her cheek, savoring the feel of her smooth skin against mine. "I do."

I felt her nod. "Good. Because it *will* sell." There was a fierceness to her words that made my lips curve upward.

I kissed her before asking, "It ain't the picture I—"

"No," she cut in, not even letting me finish. "I'd never sell that one."

Good. That painting she'd seen me making had a special place in my heart. And since we'd spent the evening in that exact same field a week ago... I couldn't imagine giving that one away.

"Which one is it then?" I asked.

"It's a bull."

I painted them a lot. But I wondered which one exactly. "You're gonna have to be more specific. Actually, here, let me have it real quick."

She left my side, and a moment later I felt the weight of the canvas against my hand. I held the painting in one hand and brushed my fingertips over the dips and curves, the rises and falls of the paint strokes. A wistful smile formed on my mouth. "This is Lights Out," I murmured. "The bull who made me go blind."

It seemed kind of ironic, selling this painting. Lights Out ended my career three years ago, and very well could be the reason it started back up again.

"Well, let's see what we can get for it."

"DO I HEAR FIVE thousand once? Five thousand twice? Sold to...well, I'll be damned? Is that Reid Wilson? I'm a huge fan."

I think my lungs seized up on me. No matter how hard I tried, I just couldn't get air down my throat. I hadn't talked to Reid in years. Not since that last day he'd come to visit me at the therapy center. I'd been a fucking prick to him. To be fair, I was a prick to everyone back then, but I was by far the worst to him. Which wasn't fair. He'd been by my side through it all. In the ambulance taking me to the ER. He'd been the first person after my parents in my hospital room. He came and watched me at therapy. Brought me anything he could think of to help.

And I'd driven him away because I was a jealous asshole. Jealous that he could still ride. That he could still see. Jealous that he'd gotten my spot as top rider and made it to NFR that year and won the whole damn thing.

I'd pushed him away because he reminded me of everything I should have been, but wasn't.

I didn't even know when the auction ended, I was so far into my own thoughts. Applause and cheering finally broke through my mind, drawing me back to the present. I didn't know why exactly they were cheering, though.

Quinn's presence disappeared from my side for a moment, and then her voice rang clear over the din of the crowd. "Well, that's all for the auction. Will the winners come forward to claim their prizes? The dance floor will be back open in a few moments. Get yourselves a drink and some desserts, and thank you so much again for coming tonight and spending your time with us."

I could sense movement all around me as people went back to conversing with one another.

"You okay?" Quinn asked, her tone as gentle as the soft hand she placed on my arm.

I opened my mouth to respond when I heard a voice drawing near. "Well, damn...I didn't know you painted too, man."

I swallowed past the lump in my throat and turned in the direction of Reid's familiar, lighthearted tone. Holding my hand out, I said, "Reid."

His handshake was firm, but he went even further and pulled me into a rough embrace. "It's been too long, man."

I tried to speak, but nothing came out. I didn't know what to say. So many different things swirled around in my mind, but when I tried to get them out, they just wouldn't come. "Um..." I cleared my throat. "It has. Thank you for comin'..." I pulled out of his embrace and reached for Quinn. She was there in an instant. "Uh, this is, well, this is my girl, Quinn. Quinn, this is uh...this is Reid Wilson."

"It's nice to meet you, Reid," she said back sweetly.

"This is a beautiful event you put on."

"Thank you." Quinn's name was called and she sighed. "Excuse me really quick. Walker needs my help." She brushed a soft kiss to my cheek. "I'll be right back."

My body mourned the loss of her warmth, and I found myself wishing I'd gone with her. Shame hung like a shroud around me at the thought of facing Reid.

"She's beautiful, man." A sense of awe coated Reid's tone. "I always figured you'd settle down at some point. She seems good for ya."

"Thanks. She's really something. I'm lucky to have her."

We fell into stilted silence for a moment, the weight of what I needed to say hanging like a storm cloud above me.

"Look, man," I began, "I'm sorry for—"

"Hux, you don't have to apologize."

I held out a hand. "No, I do." I swallowed past the lump of guilt in my throat. "I do. I was an asshole to you. I was bitter, broken, and I fuckin' hated everythin' about my life. And I wanted to hate you too," I croaked out, my words breaking a bit at the end. "You represented everythin' I wanted, but didn't have anymore. And you always came around, you were always there for me, always tryin' to make me feel better. And I just…" Blowing out a breath, I shrugged and hung my head. "I'm sorry."

Reid's grip on my shoulder was firm. "I appreciate it, but I'd probably react the same way if I were in your position. I don't blame you pushin' me away. I didn't stop comin' because I was upset with you or anythin' like that. I stayed away because I knew that's what you needed." He gave my shoulder a reassuring squeeze. "You're always gonna be my best friend."

My throat squeezed shut tight, and unshed tears stung my eyes. Fuck, the last thing I wanted or needed, for that matter, was people to see me getting all sappy and shit.

I cleared my throat and clapped him on the shoulder before pulling him into a hug. "Thanks, man," I whispered, before pulling away. "So, uh…how've you been?"

"Good. I've been good. Got signed with a PBR team this year."

"Well damn," I scoffed. I remembered one of our last conversations before he'd stopped coming around. He'd been talking about wanting to get onto one of them. "Which team you ridin' for?"

"The Twisters. They're new. Based outta Oklahoma."

"You livin' there now?"

"Fuck, no. I mean, at least not full-time. I go there to train and then go on tour with them, but I always come back home."

I nodded. "That's awesome, man. I'm happy for you."

"When are you gonna ride again?" he asked me.

With a shrug, I blew out a breath and said, "I'm not sure. I gotta get back in shape first. Talk to someone and figure out how to get me on a bull. I want it to be somewhere big. Somewhere loud. I want it to feel as real as possible."

I could practically feel the excitement coming off of Reid as he said, "Let me talk to my team manager. He's a good guy, and I bet he could get us some answers."

I couldn't stop the smile spreading across my mouth.

"Reid Wilson! Is that you?" Mama's voice rose over the commotion of the party.

Reid chuckled beside me. "Hi, Miss Dotty. You're lookin' beautiful as ever."

"How're ya doin, sweetheart?" she asked, hijacking the conversation.

"Doin' good. Just, um…wait, is that…" His voice filled with disbelief. "Is that Walker?"

Walker laughed somewhere off to my left, the sound getting louder with the footfalls of her boots against the ground. "Hi, Reid."

Was I hearing things, or did he sound a bit breathless as he said, "Well, damn. You're all grown up."

I didn't have time to dwell on it further as the familiar scent of lemongrass and vanilla drifted on the breeze followed by a soft, lyrical voice that made my heart hammer in my chest. "Sorry about that. I'm back."

I reached out for Quinn, drawing her against my side to press a kiss to the top of her head.

It was crazy how quickly things could change. I was no stranger to that, and yet it still amazed me that the tables could turn, the winds could shift at the drop of a hat.

A few weeks ago, I hated my life, and now…well, now I was on cloud nine.

None of this would have been possible without her.

Chapter Forty-Four

Home is Wherever I'm With You

QUINN

THE COOL CONCRETE KISSED the bottoms of my sore feet as I helped clean up. It was well past midnight, all the guests were gone, leaving our little crew once more. Well, minus Whit, who I hadn't seen in a while. Something told me she was off somewhere with that older cowboy. We'd gained another cowboy though, the one who'd bought Hux's painting—Reid. Turns out they were, like, best friends. They'd been almost inseparable since talking after the auction.

Ollie had already finished cleaning up the bar and was in the process of pulling all the table cloths off the tables and cleaning up any trash she came across.

"Hey," I said, approaching her with a smile.

She glanced up at me, the thick blonde chunk of her hair falling into her eyes for a moment before she brushed it back off her face. "Hey. What's up?"

"You did good tonight. Thank you again for saving my ass."

She flashed me a confident grin. "Thanks for the opportunity."

I started helping her clear the table she was working on, tossing whatever I could into the trash. "So, what are you going to do now?"

She rose to her full height, and even though she was maybe an inch or so taller than me, she had this larger than life air about her that made a shiver skitter down my spine. Blowing out an exhale, she shrugged. "Not sure. I'll probably see if anywhere else is hiring in town. If not, I'll probably start making my way up toward Dallas. Or I don't know, Wyoming's nice this time of year."

"If you wanted, you could stay here," I said, a bit hopeful. Her head cocked to the side in question, but I didn't give her time to respond before I launched into the proposal I'd been planning in my head all night. "One of our hands just up and quit last week, and Hux will be taking on more responsibility with the ranch now, so we could use another hand. And hopefully soon I can start using your help for more events once we get that up and running."

Ollie's brows scrunched together, her lips pursing for a moment. "I don't know much about horses. I've only ridden a couple times."

"Something tells me you'd be a natural," I huffed. "Besides, there's more to this ranch than just the horses."

Her mismatched gaze was full of contemplation, and each moment that ticked by had me more and more convinced she'd turn the offer down. Which was fair. But, I don't know, I liked her, and I thought she would be a good fit here.

"You can stay in the other guest house too. That way you don't have to be in the bunkhouse with the boys."

She waved me off dismissively. "As long as I have a bed, I don't care where I sleep."

"So, is that a yes?" I asked, trying not to sound too hopeful.

Her lips pulled up into a lopsided smirk. "Sure."

I smiled brightly back.

Hux had been right when he'd talked about making something nice out of a ugly situation. Tonight had opened up the doors for so many new opportunities. New friendships and some rekindled ones. New dreams, and the prospect of maybe a couple new relationships.

Overall, I was so happy and impressed with what we'd achieved. And above all else, thankful. I was eternally thankful for everyone who'd helped me make tonight magical

I SWEAR, I BLINKED and two months flew by. So much had changed in that time.

I'd officially moved to Texas. Whit was in the process of finding a place to have her own salon and would likely be fully moved here after the holidays, which was her busy season. Hux and I were navigating through all the legal things we needed to do to get the therapy center up and running, while managing the new build on the property. I'd gotten quite a few inquiries about hosting and planning some events and weddings, which I was really excited about.

All in all, life felt pretty amazing at the moment.

Smoothing out my dress, I knocked on the door to Hux's changing room. Reid's team manager had been eager to make some calls and pull a few strings to get Hux one more ride. And at the PBR Teams Championship in Las Vegas, at that. Which I'd learned from having so many cowboys in my life now, was a pretty damn big deal.

It was a sold out show tonight, and even from down in the depths of the arena I could hear the rumble of the crowd and the echo of the music bouncing off the concrete walls.

Hux's gruff, muffled voice called from the other side of the door, "It's un-locked."

I turned the handle and made my way in before shutting the door gently behind me. Leaning against it, I couldn't help but admire him as he slid his left arm into a sky blue button up.

He'd been working out a ton in preparation for this. I'd thought that he was cut when I first met him, but now...dear God, he might as well have been sculpted from marble.

Embers of desire sizzled in my veins. I don't think I'd ever tire of looking at him.

"Hey, cowboy," I managed to breathe out, cursing myself internally for how easily he affected me even two months later.

A smile softened his harsh face. "Darlin'."

Some of the tension in his my muscles eased as he held a hand out to me. I was helpless but to go to him. We were like magnets. Drawn to one another by an invisible pull. His touch was both scalding in its power and intensity, and a balm to my soul. I loved the paradox.

"How're you feeling?" I asked, resting my chin on his chest as I gazed up at him.

His fingers brushed a path up and down the curve of my spine. "Nervous. Excited. A bit terrified."

I kissed his chest gently, pulling back enough to trace my fingers over the tattoo on his heart. "I can't even imagine. But you." I kissed his chest once more. "Are." I kissed his collarbone. "Going." Along the curve of his stubbled jaw. "To be." I rose up on tiptoe, brushing a kiss to the corner of his mouth as I wrapped my arms around his neck. "Amazing," I finally murmured against his lips.

His arms caged me against him, one of his hands knotting in my hair. I didn't miss how his body shook beneath my touch. Whether it was from nerves or desire, I wasn't quite sure.

"Thanks, darlin'," he whispered back before capturing my mouth in his.

I reveled in the feel of him. In the scent and taste of him. These past two months had been the best of my life, and I had him to thank for that.

He pulled back, breaking the kiss and the quiet moment, and asked, "Will you do me a favor? Can you grab me the box over on the table to the left. It's got my belt buckle in it."

I nodded. "Sure."

I found the box easily beside his sunglasses and hat box, but frowned as I picked it up. "Um…is this supposed to be so light? It doesn't feel like there's a belt buckle in here?"

"I'm sure. You can open it up and check."

I shrugged. Why not? I wondered which one it was. He'd won a lot during his time rodeoing, and with this being such a monumental moment, I figured he'd probably wear one of his gold buckles.

Only when I opened the box, there was no belt buckle inside.

Time froze, leaving me paralyzed in place. The air left my lungs in a loud gasp, and tears blurred my vision so badly that I couldn't even focus on the soft velvety pillow where a buckle *should* have been.

Because in its place was an engagement ring.

"Hux…" The word was little more than a choked out squeak. I blinked, letting the twin tears slide down my cheeks and clear my vision, before turning to him.

He knelt before me, the softest, most earnest look on his face. "I figured it'd be easier for you to put it on yourself. I'm just as likely to lose it tryin' to put it on the right finger."

Laughter bubbled out of my chest even as more tears fell freely down my cheeks. "Hux."

Oh my God. Oh my God. Oh my God. He was proposing.

He reached out a hand, and still holding the box with the ring in my one hand, I gripped his with my free one.

"I told you I wouldn't make you wait long for a ring." He lifted my hand and brushed a kiss to my knuckles. My heart might as well have had wings, the way it soared from his words and touch didn't seem possible. "I know this might not be, like, the most romantic setup. I'd been hopin' to do it back on my parents' ranch, but we just haven't had time to get back there. And, well—" He blew out a breath and ran his free hand through his hair. "There's a decent chance that I don't..." his words wobbled, "that, uh, I don't make it out of this arena tonight. And if I don't, I wanna know that I've given myself to you completely. Irrevocably. So, Quinn—darlin', will you marry me?"

My knees gave out as wave after wave of emotion pummeled into me. Happiness and excitement and terror and worry, but mostly—yeah, mostly pure undiluted joy. I nodded, words too hard to form as I tried to bite back sobs.

"Is that a yes or a no, darlin'? I'm gonna guess that your silence is a yes?"

I laughed through my tears and leaned forward to brush my lips against his in the ghost of a kiss. "Yes, Hux," I managed to whisper. "Absolutely yes."

He dragged me against him, claiming my mouth in a soul-scorching kiss. God, he was so perfect. Somehow in what were probably the most terrifying moments of his life, he managed to switch the focus to me. I know he'd argue that he didn't deserve me, but that wasn't true. We deserved each other. We were made for each other. And now I got to spend the rest of forever calling him *mine*.

Officially.

I gasped, remembering the ring in my other hand. "Careful, I haven't put the ring on yet."

He chuckled. "Well, hurry it up."

"Okay, okay!" I giggled as I plucked the ring up and admired it for a moment. It was vintage in nature, and the large center diamond was cut into an oval, with diamonds and swirling filigree on the rose-gold band. "Wait...are you sure you don't want to put it on me? I won't let you drop it, I promise."

"O–okay." The word trembled as much as his hand did as he held it out for me.

I placed the ring in his palm and helped him grasp it so that I could slide my ring finger through the band. My heart danced in my chest as I watched the emotions playing out on his handsome face. The love and need and want burning in his whiskey brown eyes.

"I love you, Quinn Lane," he murmured as he settled the ring on my finger.

I smiled through happy tears. "I love you too... And I love the sound of that."

He pulled me to him, kissing me deeply, fiercely, enough to steal my breath away. "I do too, darlin'. I do too."

Resting my head against his, I knotted my fingers in his shoulder length hair and whispered against his lips, "Go ride that bull. Face your fears, Huxson Lane. Then come back to me. We got a wedding to plan."

He squeezed me tighter to him, and I swear, I'd never felt so happy in my life.

THE ARENA THRUMMED WITH music and cheers as I made my way to the private box we'd been given for the night for Hux's performance. The whole crew had come to support him. Hux's parents, Walker, all of the ranch hands—Dylan, Wyatt, Brooks, and Ollie. Whit was there, along with Cash and the Mooneys, as well as the rest of the Mercenary Ranch gang, which they liked to call themselves: Ryder, Maverick and their fiancés, Charlie and Cheyenne. Their adorable babies even tagged along for the event.

Oh, and how could I forget Cash's uncle, Goodie?

Crazy how in just a couple months, these strangers had practically become like a new family to me.

The only one missing was Reid, and that was only because he was also riding tonight.

"How's our boy doin'?" Mr. Mooney asked, noticing me first. I swear, nothing got past him.

"He's ready," I said with a soft, but no less confident grin.

He and Mr. Lane—Paul, I needed to stop calling him that. He'd told me time and time again Paul was fine—exchanged looks and nodded.

I greeted everyone, taking a few moments to fawn over Charlie and Cheyenne's babies, before making my way to the front of the box where Whit, Ollie, and Walker stood. The last two had quickly become my closest friends back here in Texas. They hadn't replaced, nor would they ever replace Whit, but I was so glad to have them here these past two months when Whit had been busy back in California.

All the while, tension rose and rose through the box. I mean, I guess it was understandable, with Hux's ride coming up as one of the first events to kick off the evening, but still. It left me wanting to tell them all the amazing good news just to make things feel more normal. But as much as I wanted to tell someone, *anyone* at this point about my engagement, I didn't want to make this night all about me when it was supposed to be about Hux.

Even Cash was unusually quiet, which was practically unheard of.

And what was worse, was that everyone wouldn't stop looking at me. I could feel their stares like the heat of a thousand suns—just staring, staring, staring. It was maddening.

What were they expecting? Did they think I was going to break down or something? Why was everyone being so damn weird?

When I couldn't take it anymore. When the weight of their stares turned suffocating, I whirled to face them all and asked, "What's going on?"

Dotty swooped in like a vulture, settling before me in an instant. "Well, let us see it!"

"See what?" I asked.

"The ring, sweetheart! Let's see the ring."

The entire box erupted into a fit of chaos then as everyone converged on me to see the sparkly diamond on my ring finger—well, mostly the women, though Cash was there, because, of course he was.

They'd known? How had they known? I took them all in, unable to say anything, just silently shaking my head. "What? How?" I managed to finally get out.

Dotty wrapped me in a warm hug, squeezing me tight. "Oh, honey. We all knew. How do you think he managed to pull it off?"

Walker giggled and drew me into a hug the minute her mom let go of me. "Why do you think I kept badgerin' you all week about us gettin' our nails done?"

"Or why I made sure you looked cute as hell," Whit replied with a wink, squeezing me tightly after Walker.

I glanced at Ollie. "Did you have anything to do with it?"

She offered me a wry grin, before pulling me in for one of her awkward one shoulder hugs she wasn't very fond of handing out. "The guys and I loaded up the room with little hidden cameras so I could get some pictures and video of it. I'm gonna go through it tomorrow and edit a video for you."

My eyes stung, and my throat tightened as tears slipped down my cheeks. "You guys," I squeaked out, trying to wipe at my face without messing up my makeup. "Thank you."

Cash wrapped an arm around my shoulders, jostling me. "I call dibs as maid of honor."

I laughed and shoved at him playfully. "You can't be my maid of honor."

"Well, then what about flower boy? I can toss beer cans or something to the crowd as I walk down the aisle," he replied with a grin.

Another laugh escaped me. "I actually think that sounds kinda cool."

"See!" Cash whirled to face Charlie. "I told you it was a good idea. You're just bein' no fun, Charlie girl."

Charlie rolled her eyes even as a grin lit up her face. "Why are you even complainin', dummy? You're already in the wedding!"

I grinned at their exchange and silently soaked up all of the happiness around me in that moment.

Who would have thought that planning my dad's wedding in Texas would lead to new friends, a new home, a new career, a soulmate, and the promise of happily ever after?

The lights overhead flickered, and a commentator's voice reverberated through the indoor arena, announcing the start of events. Excitement thrummed to life as the opening ceremony full of music and strobing lights and pyrotechnics commenced. They introduced all the teams competing, each of their men walking into the arena to stand and wave to the crowd.

"And folks, you're in for a special treat tonight as we have two time World Champion bull rider, Huxson Lane with us, who came outta retirement for this last ride."

There had been no point fussing over my tears before, because they just started anew as an archway of fire blazed to life in the middle of the arena and Hux walked through it, waving a hand in the air as he made his way forward. If he was nervous, he didn't show it. I could see the bright grin on his face from the huge screen hanging in the middle of the arena.

He was so handsome, and full of life and confidence. He'd argue that when we met, he was washed up and broken. But I'd never seen him that way. He was like a diamond in the rough. Beautiful, magnificent, he just needed something to help him shine again.

"Go get em', cowboy," I whispered under my breath as I clutched my hands to my chest, sending up a silent prayer that he came back to me.

Chapter Forty-Five
Open The Gate

Hux

*E*IGHT SECONDS.

All I needed was eight. Damn. Seconds.

I'd forgotten how loud it was down in the thick of all the action. The other contestants shouting orders and cheers and words of encouragement to those listening. The roar of the crowd and the thumping beat of the music. The bulls thrashing against the pipe-stall. The smack of the gate as it slammed open.

I could see everything in my mind. I'd been to this arena before. Ridden here. The setup was always the same.

Rolling out my neck, I gripped the collar of my Kevlar vest like my life depended on it while I tried to focus.

You got this. Breathe. You got this.

A wave of déjà vu overwhelmed me so thoroughly I struggled to suck down enough air in my lungs to keep from passing out. Doubt clawed for purchase in my chest. Was I really going to do this? Was I really going to risk my life, my relationship, my dream with my future wife for just eight damn seconds?

But this was so much more than eight seconds.

It was a defining moment. A final ride. A death of an era.

It was my one shot to face my fear, sit on its back, and ride it one last time.

I'd demanded they let me ride Lights Out—who only had three scored rides on him since I last rode him. In some weird, cosmic way, him and I were connected in all this. He'd been what I thought was the end of my career once before. It felt fitting to end it all on his back.

A hard smack to my shoulder startled me from my thoughts. I fought back a cringe and gritted my teeth, hating that I would likely never get used to some things now that I couldn't see.

"You ready?" Reid asked.

I chewed on my bottom lip a moment, sucked in a deep breath through my nose, and blew out slowly, letting all of my worries and fears out with it. "Yeah," I nodded.

I could sense the pride in his tone, in the way he gripped my shoulder. "I just gotta say, I've been waitin' for the day to do this again. Us here, together. I'm glad I get to be here for this. You're makin' history, Hux."

I swallowed past the lump in my throat and nodded, gripping his shoulder right back. "Thanks, man."

We shared a moment of quiet, and then he said, "Whenever you're ready."

My nerves sloshed through me like an angry sea as he helped guide me to the chute. My legs felt wobbly, my hands trembled as I climbed over the pipe-stall and slid onto the bull's back. I tried to force air into my lungs as I settled myself, noting the twitch of Lights Out's muscles as he tensed and shifted beneath me.

I fumbled with the bull rope, but Reid and a few others were there to help me. All of them offering words of support and encouragement.

"You got this."

"Come on, man. Ride that sonofabitch."

"You're a fuckin' legend, dude."

Forcing air into my lungs in slow, deep breaths, I let the world wash away. For once, I was grateful for the darkness. I focused on it, urging the sounds of the arena to fade. One by one, it all left me, until all that was left was the feel of the bull beneath me and the sound of his fast labored breath. My heartbeat danced to the same pace as it.

I'd never been too religious, that was Mama's thing, but I'd be a fool not to send up a silent prayer to the big man upstairs.

Please let me get back to her.

A rush of warmth that reminded me of her light, loving presence trickled through my veins and determination replaced the fear. Her words echoed through my mind. *"Go ride that bull. Face your fears, Huxson Lane. Then come back to me. We got a wedding to plan."*

With a final exhale, I nodded.

I was ready.

The gate slamming open sounded like the boom of a cannon. Lights Out lurched beneath me, and I squeezed my hand tighter around the bull rope. Each buck and twist held the power of a fucking hurricane in it, ripping the air from my lungs while I clung to the bull's back. My arm screamed in protest with the movements, but I wasn't about to let up or let go. I knew that any second now, he'd pull out that move I was all too familiar with, and I'd be damned if I fell for that shit again. Holding the rope tighter, spurring him onward, I rode Lights Out like my life depended on it.

It only spanned seconds, but it might as well have been a lifetime. A lifetime of just me and him. Our movements, our breaths becoming one.

The buzzer cut through the heavy silence in my mind, just as he lurched himself forward like a tsunami crashing against the shore. But I rode the wave, disentangling myself from the bull rope, and all but jumped from his back, hoping, praying I didn't land on my head or break my damn neck.

I had a girl to marry after all.

Despite the tons and tons of dirt they used to fill the arena, it still hurt like hell when I landed on my side, my arm caught beneath me. Pain erupted in my wrist, and even amidst the chaos, I didn't miss the pop it made. Well, at least I wasn't dead.

I hopped up, hoping like hell that the rodeo clowns kept Lights Out away from me. I had no fucking clue where I was in the arena. Was the bull chute behind me? Ahead of me? Left or right? Where the hell was the bull?

"Here! Here, Hux!" Reid's voice was nearly drowned out by the roar of the crowd and the music. But clutching my broken wrist, I hurried toward the voice.

A moment later, a rough hand grasped me by the shoulder, Reid's familiar voice in my ear. "You're good, man. He ain't gonna getcha."

I stopped in the middle of the arena, all of the adrenaline washing away like a receding tide. In its place was a sense of accomplishment, pride. With a huff, I struggled to pull the helmet I'd worn off—a difficult feat with my wrist screaming in pain. I dropped the helmet, and with a deep, shaking breath I turned my unseeing gaze skyward.

I'd done it.

Moisture slid down my cheeks and a laugh escaped me.

"Thank you," I whispered to the sky.

I'd never know why life happened the way it did. But I was thankful for this moment. For this opportunity. For this chance to end things on my own.

I was more than a two time World Champion bull rider. I was more than a cowboy. I was a survivor. I was a son and a brother. I was the owner of a ranch and a project that gave me a purpose. And I was the lucky guy who got to love and marry the most amazing woman in the fucking world.

I was Huxson Lane, and I was lucky as hell to be alive.

Want To

Epilogue- Quinn

"**W**HY THE HELL ARE we out in one of the pastures?" Hux asked.

Seriously, nothing got by him. I bit back a laugh and pulled my jacket a little tighter against me. I swear, The day before it had been warm enough to wear shorts, but apparently ten days into November, Texas finally got the memo it was autumn. And as much as I loved the fact that I could wear leggings and cute sweaters now, I wasn't ready for the, like, forty degree temperature drop in a night.

"You didn't get another damn horse did you? I already got a barn full of 'em now. I don't need another," he grumbled.

I couldn't help but smile. He was such a grump, and also *so* full of shit. We didn't even have a full barn yet, and even if we did, he loved every second of being out there with those horses. Most nights I had to go out and drag him back to the house.

"Don't worry, it's not a horse," I said, glancing at Reid—who tried to keep a white bull entertained until I was ready for his big reveal. The surprisingly gentle giant kept trying to knock Reid's hat off as if it were some funny game.

I spoke before Hux had the opportunity to say anything else. "I just figured you'd want to meet your new retirement buddy."

Hux's brows furrowed together, his mouth dipping into a frown. "What are you talkin' about, Quinn?"

Oh, he was seriously nervous. One thing I'd quickly come to realize about him was he almost never used my real name unless he was upset or scared. It was always darlin', which I don't think I'd ever get tired of.

I wondered what was going through his mind. Grabbing his hand, I led him toward the bull before placing his palm on the behemoth's forehead. "I think you'll like him, he's, like, super sweet. I was kinda scared of him at first, but he's basically just an oversized puppy dog."

Hux trailed a tentative, trembling hand back along the bull's forehead before coming into contact with his horns. "You got me a bull?"

"Not just any bull. Lights Out, to be exact."

I watched as a myriad of emotions rippled across his features—disbelief, shock, appreciation, and a bit of wonder. He chewed his lip a moment, his sunglasses stare fixed on the bull we stood before as he huffed out a small breath through his nose. Clearing his throat, he croaked out, "You got me Lights Out?"

Pursing my lips, I glanced at Reid once more. Had I made the right decision? Was this too much? "Well, technically Reid paid for him, so I owe him a massive favor at some point in the future, but it was my idea. Also, say hi, Reid—"

"Hi," he called out awkwardly. Reid was probably the kindest, most helpful guy I'd ever met. When I'd come to him with the idea, he'd been ecstatic and made it his personal goal to help me make this happen.

Hux cleared his throat once more. "How? Why?" It's like he couldn't talk.

Worry ate at me. I could have sworn he'd like this idea, but each moment left me feeling more and more unsure.

"The other night, you fell asleep with one of your podcasts playing," I sputtered out. "I was about to turn it off, when I heard them mention something about Lights Out being retired." When he made no attempt to interrupt, I continued on. "Apparently, he tore a muscle in his shoulder during your last ride. After further examination from the vet, they determined that if he keeps competing on it, it'll continue tearing and they'd eventually have to put him down. So, he's retired now. And, you'd mentioned to me before how you felt you and him were connected in a way... This is, like, basically proof that you're right. I figured it would be kinda cool for you two to live out retirement together."

"And, ya'll can breed him still. He'd bring in a heft stud fee," Reid added in when Hux remained deathly quiet. "Money from that can help with the ranch. Seemed like a good idea."

For a long moment, he did nothing. Didn't move, didn't speak. My heart jack-hammered in my chest with each passing second. Hux's hand dropped from the bull as he turned in my general direction.

He opened his mouth. Closed it. Pulled off his sunglasses to wipe at his eyes, then opened his mouth to speak once more. "I can't believe y'all fuckin' got me Lights Out." The words themselves could come across as harsh, but the warmth in his tone, the smile toying on his lips, spoke volumes.

He took a step toward me, and I pressed a gentle hand to his chest. "Is this okay? Are you mad?"

But when he drew me into his arms, when he kissed me so fiercely it stole the very breath from my lungs, there was no anger there. Only love. Lots and lots of love.

"Thank you," he whispered against my lips.

I pulled back enough to look up at him, reveling in his rugged beauty. He'd laugh if I said that aloud, but he truly was beautiful.

And strong. And brave. And resilient.

And I was the lucky girl who'd get to marry him in a week from now.

Yep...it was official. Our love story was, and always would be, my favorite.

Acknowledgements

This book would not have been possible without so many different people, but first and foremost:

Thank you, Ella! Thank you for constantly hyping, encouraging, commiserating, and cheering me on. Thank you for your friendship. Getting to critique partner with you through this book has been one of the best experiences ever! Love you, girlie! You're up next!

To my love, Cody—thank you for putting up with me. I know I'm a pain in the ass, but your guidance, words of encouragement, and late night critiques have helped shape me into the writer I am. Thank you for constantly reminding me to stay true to myself and my voice. You're the most amazing collaborator and husband. Love you!

To Clare and Amy S.—I'm so incredibly grateful for you both. You are my rocks and I wouldn't be able to function without you two in my life. Your words of encouragement and confidence in my books mean the world to me.

Landyn, Megan, Rachel, and Kayla—Y'all have been the best betas ever! Thank you for every comment, every suggestion, and each and every text you have sent me throughout this journey in regards to this book. I am so incredibly grateful for you all and this book wouldn't be what it is today without your help!

To my friends and family who support and believe in me—thank you! I see you, I know you, and I love you!

About the author

Shelby Storme is just a girl who loves tattoos, animals, crystals, and writing steamy romance. For as long as she can remember, storytelling has consumed her soul. She's a California transplant living in small town Texas with her amazing real-life cowboy husband, a sweet-as-pie son, and a sassy little daughter. When she isn't writing, she is working as a competitive gymnastics coach and a freelance editor. She loves rodeos, Country music, and Texas sunrises—all of which inspired her s eries.